ENVY

Novels by Sandra Brown

Outfox

Tailspin

Seeing Red

Sting

Friction

Mean Streak

Deadline

Low Pressure

Lethal

Mirror Image

Where There's Smoke

Charade

Exclusive

Envy

The Switch

The Crush

Fat Tuesday

Unspeakable

The Witness

The Alibi

Standoff

Best Kept Secrets

Breath of Scandal

French Silk

Slow Heat in Heaven

PRAISE FOR #1 *NEW YORK TIMES* BESTSELLING AUTHOR SANDRA BROWN

"Brown deserves her own genre."

—*Dallas Morning News*

"[Brown] is a masterful storyteller, carefully crafting tales that keep readers on the edge of their seats."

—*USA Today*

"Sandra Brown just might have penned her best and most ambitious book ever, a tale that evokes the work of the likes of Don DeLillo, Greg Iles and Robert Stone . . . . SEEING RED is an exceptional thriller in every sense of the word, a classic treatment of the costs of heroism and the nature of truth itself. Not to be missed."

—*Providence Journal*

"Brown's novels define the term 'page-turner.'"

—*Booklist*

"Author Sandra Brown proves herself top-notch."

—Associated Press

"A novelist who can't write them fast enough."

—*San Antonio Express-News*

"Brown's storytelling gift is surprisingly rare."

—*Toronto Sun*

ENVY

SANDRA BROWN

GRAND CENTRAL
PUBLISHING
NEW YORK BOSTON

Copyright © 2001 by Sandra Brown Management, Ltd.
Excerpt from *Outfox* copyright © 2019 by Sandra Brown Management, Ltd.

Grand Central Publishing
Hachette Book Group
1290 Avenue of the Americas, New York, NY 10104
grandcentralpublishing.com
twitter.com/grandcentralpub

Originally published in hardcover in August 2001
First trade paperback edition: July 2017
Reissued: October 2019

Grand Central Publishing is a division of Hachette Book Group, Inc. The Grand Central Publishing name and logo is a trademark of Hachette Book Group, Inc.

The publisher is not responsible for websites (or their content) that are not owned by the publisher.

The Hachette Speakers Bureau provides a wide range of authors for speaking events. To find out more, go to www.hachettespeakersbureau.com or call (866) 376-6591.

Library of Congress Control Number: 2001026316

ISBNs: 978-1-5387-3409-4 (trade paperback reissue), 978-1-4555-4647-3 (ebook)

Printed in the United States of America

LSC-C

10 9 8 7 6 5 4 3 2 1

ENVY

"Envy" Prologue
Key West, Florida, 1988

Saltines and sardines. Staples of his diet. Add a chunk of rat cheese and a Kosher dill spear and you had yourself the four basic food groups. There simply wasn't any finer fare.

That was the unshakable opinion of Hatch Walker, who had a sun-baked, wind-scoured visage that only a mother gargoyle could love. As he munched his supper, eyes that had blinked against the sting of countless squalls squinted narrowly on the horizon.

He was on the lookout for the lightning flashes that would signal an approaching storm. There was still no sign of it here onshore, but it was out there somewhere, gathering energy, sucking moisture up from the sea that it would send back to earth in the form of wind-driven rain.

But later. Above the harbor, a quarter moon hung in a clear sky. Stars defied the neon glare on the ground. But Hatch wasn't fooled. He could feel impending meteorological change in his bones before the barometer dropped. He could smell a storm even before clouds appeared or a sail caught the first strong gust of wind. His weather forecasts were rarely wrong. There'd be rain before dawn.

His nicotine-stained teeth crunched into his pickle, and he savored the garlicky brine, which he chased with a bite of cheese. It just didn't get any better. He couldn't figure out folks who were willing to pay a week's wages on a meal that wouldn't fill a thimble, when they could eat just as good—and to his mind a hell of a lot better—on a buck and a half. Tops.

Of course, they were paying for more than the groceries. They were financing the parking valets, and the starched white tablecloths, and the waiters with rings in their ears and cobs up their butts, who acted like you were putting them out if you asked them to fetch you an extra helping of bread. They were paying for the fancy French name slapped on a filet of fish that used to be called the catch-of-the-day. He'd seen pretentious outfits like that in ports all over the world. A few had even cropped up here in Key West, and those he scorned most of all.

This being a weeknight, the streets were relatively quiet. Tourist season was on the wane. *Thank the good Lord for small favors,* Hatch thought as he swigged at his can of Pepsi and belched around a har-rumph of scorn for tourists in general and those who flocked to Key West in particular.

They descended by the thousands each year, slathered in sunscreen that smelled like monkey barf, toting camera equipment, and dragging along whining kids who'd rather be up in Orlando being dazzled by Disney's man-made marvels than watching one of the most spectacular sunsets on the planet.

Hatch had nothing but contempt for these fools who worked themselves into early coronaries for fifty weeks a year so that for the remaining two they could work doubly hard at having a good time. Even more bewildering to him was that they were willing to pay out their soft, pale asses for the privilege.

Unfortunately, his livelihood depended on them. And for Hatch that represented a moral dilemma. He despised the tourists' invasion, but he couldn't have made a living without it.

Walker's Marine Charters and Rentals got a share of the money the vacationers spent during their noisy occupation of his town. He equipped them with scuba and snorkeling gear, leased them boats, and took them on deep-sea fishing expeditions so they could return to shore and have their grinning, sunburned mugs photographed with a noble fish, who was probably more affronted by the asinine picture-taking than by being caught.

Business wasn't exactly thriving tonight, but the trade-out was that it was quiet. Peaceful, you might say. And that wasn't a bad thing. Not by a long shot. Not compared to life aboard merchant ships, where quarters were noisy and cramped and privacy was nonexistent. He'd had a bellyful of that, thank you. Give Hatch Walker solitude and quiet anytime.

The water in the marina was as still as a lake. Shore lights were mirrored on the surface with hardly a waver. Occasionally a mast would creak aboard a sailboat or he'd hear a telephone ringing on one of the yachts. Sometimes a note or two of music or several beats of percussion would waft from one of the waterfront nightclubs. Traffic created an incessant swish. Otherwise it was quiet, and, even though it meant a lean week financially speaking, Hatch preferred it this way.

Tonight he might have closed up shop and gone home early, except for that one boat he had out. He'd leased the twenty-five-footer to some kids, if you could rightly call twenty-somethings kids. Compared to him they were. Two men, one woman, which in Hatch's estimation was a volatile combination under any circumstances.

The kids were tan and lean, attractive and self-assured to the point of cockiness. Hatch figured that between the three of them they probably hadn't done an honest day's work in their lives. They were locals, or at least permanent transplants. He'd seen them around.

They were already half lit when they boarded the craft just before sunset, and they'd carried a couple of ice chests on board with them. Heavy as anchors, by the way they were lugging them. Odds were good that those chests contained bottles of booze. They had no fishing gear. They were going offshore strictly for a few hours of drinking and debauchery or his name wasn't Hatch Walker. He had debated whether or not to lease a craft to them, but his near-empty till served to persuade him that they were not flat-out drunk.

He'd sternly ordered them not to drink while operating his boat. They flashed him smiles as insincere as a diamond dealer's and assured him that such wasn't their intention. One bowed at the waist and could barely contain his laughter over what he must have considered a lecture from a grizzled old fart. The other saluted him crisply and said, "Aye, aye, sir!"

As Hatch helped the young woman into the boat, he hoped to hell she knew what she was in for. But he figured she did. He'd seen her around, too. Lots of times. With lots of men. An eye patch would have covered more skin than her bikini bottom, and Hatch would have no right to call himself a man if he hadn't noticed that she might just as well not have bothered wearing the top.

And she didn't for long.

Before they were even out of the marina, one of the men snatched off her top and waved it above his head like a victory banner. Her attempts to get it back turned into a game of slap-and-tickle.

Watching this as the boat had chugged out of the marina, Hatch had shaken his head and counted himself lucky that he'd never had a daughter with a virtue to protect.

* * *

Finally one last sardine remained in the tin. Hatch pinched it out of the oil, laid it diagonally across a saltine, added the last bite of pickle and sliver of cheese, doused it real good with Tabasco, stacked another cracker on top, and put the whole thing in his mouth, then dusted the crumbs off his beard.

Chewing with contentment, he happened to glance toward the entrance of the harbor. What he saw caused the sandwich to stick in his throat. The corner of a cracker scratched his esophagus as he forced it down, muttering, "Hell does he think he's doin'?"

No sooner had Hatch spoken his thought aloud than a long blast from the approaching boat's horn nearly knocked him off his stool.

He would have come off it anyway. Because by the time the intact sardine sandwich hit his stomach,

Hatch was out the door of the weather-beaten shack that housed his charter service and angrily lumbering down the quay, waving his arms and shouting at the boat's pilot—probably a tourist from one of those square, landlocked states who'd never seen a body of water bigger than a watering trough—that he was coming into the marina way too fast, that he was violating the "no wake" rule, and that his recklessness would cost him a whopping fine if not a couple nights in jail.

Then Hatch recognized the boat as his. His! The damn fool was abusing his boat, the finest and biggest in his fleet!

Hatch fired a volley of expletives, wicked holdovers from his years as a merchant marine. When he got his hands on those kids, they'd regret the day their daddies spawned them. He might be old and ugly and bent, he might have gray whiskers and a slight limp from an unfortunate run-in with a knife-wielding Cuban, but he could hold his own with a couple of pretty beach boys—"And make no mistake about that, you arrogant little fuckers!"

Even after the boat cleared the buoys it didn't slow down. It kept coming. It missed a forty-two-foot sailboat by inches and set it to rocking. A dinghy slammed into the side of a multimillion-dollar yacht, and the folks sipping nightcaps on the yacht's polished deck rushed to the rail and shouted down at the careless mariner.

Hatch shook his fist at the young man at the wheel. The drunken fool was steering straight for the pier, kamikazelike, when he suddenly cut the engine and spun the wheel sharply to port. The outboard sent up a rooster tail of spume.

Hatch had barely a second to leap out of the way before the boat crashed into the quay. The young man clambered down the steps of the cockpit and across the slippery deck, leaped onto the aggregate pier, tripped over a cleat, then crawled a few feet forward on all fours.

Hatch bore down on him, grabbed him by the shoulders, and flipped him over as he would a fish he was about to gut. In fact, if he'd had his filleting knife in hand, he might have slit the guy from gonads to gullet before he could stop himself. Luckily he was armed only with a litany of curses, threats, and accusations.

But they sputtered and died before they were spoken.

Up till then Hatch's focus had been on his boat, on the recklessness and speed with which it had been steered into the marina. He hadn't paid much attention to the young man piloting her.

Now he saw that the boy's face was bloody. His left eye was swollen practically shut. His T-shirt was in shreds, clinging to his lean torso like a wet rag.

"Help me. God, oh, God." He threw Hatch's hand off his shoulder and scrambled to his feet. "They're out there," he said, frantically motioning toward the open sea. "They're in the ocean. I couldn't find them. They...they..."

Hatch had witnessed a man get shark-bit once. He had managed to pull him from the water before the shark could get more than his left leg. He was alive but in bad shape, in shock, scared shitless, blubbering and making no sense as he bled buckets into the sand.

Hatch recognized the same level of wild panic in this young man's eyes. This was no prank, no showing off, no drunken escapade, as he'd originally thought.

The kid—the one who'd smartly saluted him earlier—was in distress to the point of hysteria.

"Calm down, sonny." Hatch took him by the shoulders and shook him slightly. "What happened out yonder? Where are your friends at?"

The young man covered his face with hands that, Hatch noticed, were also bloody and bruised. He sobbed uncontrollably. "In the water."

"Overboard?"

"Yeah. Oh, God. Oh, Jesus."

"That asshole nearly wrecked my yacht! What the fuck was he doing?"

A man wearing flip-flops came slapping up, hands on hips, reeking of a cologne that any self-respecting whore would think was too strong. He was wearing only a Speedo swimsuit beneath an overhanging belly covered with black curly hair. He had a thick gold bracelet on his right wrist and spoke with a nasally northeastern accent—just the kind that never failed to get on Hatch's fighting side.

"The boy's hurt. There's been an accident."

"Accident my ass. He put a big dent in the *Dinky Doo*." They'd been joined by the man's female companion, who was dressed in a bikini and a pair of high heels. Her tan and tits were store-bought. Under each arm she was holding a toy poodle. The pets had pink ribbons tied to their ears and were yapping in angry synchronization.

"Call 911," Hatch said.

"I want to know what this son of a bitch intends to do—"

"Call 911!"

* * *

The interior of Hatch's "office" smelled of sardines, damp hemp, dead fish, and motor oil. It was uncomfortably warm and stuffy inside, as though the shack couldn't provide enough oxygen for three men because it was usually occupied only by one.

The limited floor space was crowded with trunks of fishing and diving gear, coils of rope, maps and charts, maintenance supplies and equipment, a vintage metal file cabinet in which Hatch rarely filed anything, and his desk, which had been salvaged from a shipwreck and bought at auction for thirty dollars.

The kid who'd crashed his boat had heaved twice into his toilet, but Hatch figured the nausea was more from nerves and fear than from the shot of brandy he'd sneaked him when no one was looking.

Of course, the kid had had a lot to drink prior to the brandy, and that wasn't just an assumption. He'd admitted as much to the Coast Guard officer who was currently questioning him. Key West police had had their turn at interrogating him about crashing the boat into the marina. He was then turned over to the Coast Guard officer, who wanted to know what had happened onboard that had caused his two companions to wind up in the Atlantic.

He'd provided their names and ages, their local addresses. Hatch had checked the information against the rental agreement the two young men had filled out before embarking. He confirmed the data to the officer.

Hatch resented having to share his private space with strangers, but he was glad he hadn't been asked to wait outside while the laws interrogated the kid. The marina was now swarming with onlookers who'd been drawn to the scene of the drama like flies to a pile of manure. And you couldn't swing a dead cat without hitting some breed of uniformed personnel.

Having intimate knowledge of jails in numerous ports on several continents, Hatch had an aversion to uniforms and badges. He would just as soon avoid authority of any kind. If a man couldn't live by his own set of rules, his own sense of right and wrong, what was the good of living? That attitude had landed him in paddy wagons all over the globe, but that was his philosophy and he was sticking to it.

But, in all fairness, Hatch had to hand it to the Coast Guard officials and local policemen who'd questioned the young man and organized a search-and-rescue party: They hadn't been assholes about it.

It was clear that the kid was on the brink of total breakdown. The badges had been savvy enough to realize he might crack if they applied too much additional pressure, and then where would they be? In order to calm him down and get answers, they'd gone pretty soft on him.

He was still wearing wet swim trunks and sneakers that leaked seawater onto the rough plank flooring whenever he moved his feet. In addition to giving him the brandy, Hatch had thrown a blanket over him, but he'd since discarded it, along with his tattered T-shirt.

Outside, running footsteps and an excited voice brought the kid's head up. He looked hopefully toward the door.

But the footsteps ran past without stopping. The officer, who'd had his back turned while helping himself to Hatch's coffeepot, came around and correctly read the kid's expression. "You'll know something as soon as we do, son."

"They've got to be alive." His voice sounded like someone who'd been outyelling a storm for a long time. Every now and then it would crack over a word. "I think I just couldn't find them in the dark. It was so damned dark out there." His eyes bounced back and forth between Hatch and the officer. "But I didn't hear them. I called and called, but... Why weren't they answering me? Or calling out for help? Unless they..." He was unable to say out loud what they all feared.

The officer returned to Hatch's stool, which he'd placed near the chair in which the boy sat with his shoulders hunched forward. For several weighty minutes, the officer did nothing but sip his hot coffee. *Schwoop. Schwoop.*

It was irritating as hell, but Hatch remained quiet. This was the law's business now, not his. His boat was insured. There'd be paperwork out the wazoo, and a suspicious, seersucker-suited adjuster to haggle with, but in the long run, he would come out okay. Maybe even a little better off than he'd been.

He was less optimistic about how this kid would fare. No amount of insurance was going to make his life easier after this. As for the two who'd gone into the water, Hatch didn't hold out much hope. The percentages were stacked against them.

He had known a few men who had foundered and lived to tell about it, but not many. If you went into the water, drowning was probably the most merciful way to die. Exposure took longer. And to predators you were just another source of food.

The Coast Guard officer cradled the chipped coffee mug between his palms and swirled the contents. "How come you didn't use the radio to call for help?"

"I did. I mean, I tried. I couldn't get it to work."

The officer stared into his swirling coffee. "Coupla other boats heard your SOS. Tried to tell you to stay right where you were. You didn't."

"I didn't hear them. I guess..." Here he glanced

across at Hatch. "I guess I didn't pay much attention when he was showing us how to operate the radio."

"Costly mistake."

"Yes, sir."

"Fair to say you're not a seasoned sailor?"

"Seasoned? No, sir. But this is the first time I've had any trouble."

"Uh-huh. Tell me about the fight."

"Fight?"

This drew a frown from the officer. "Don't bullshit me now, son. Your eye's all but swollen shut. You've got a bloody nose and busted lip. Your knuckles are scraped and bruised. I know what a fistfight looks like, okay? So don't play games with me."

The young man's shoulders began to shake. His eyes streamed, but he didn't even bother trying to stem the tears or to wipe his dripping nose.

"Was it over the girl?" the officer asked in a gentler voice. "Mr. Walker here says she was a looker. A party girl, best he could tell. She belong to one of you?"

"Like a girlfriend, you mean? No, sir. She's just a casual friend."

"You and your buddy fight over her favors?"

"No, sir. Not...not exactly. What I mean is, she wasn't the reason it started."

"Then what was?"

The boy sniffed but remained mute.

"Just as well tell me now," the officer said, "because when we find whatever we're going to find out there, we'll keep hounding you until we get the truth of it."

"We were drunk."

"Uh-huh."

"And...and..." The kid raised his head, looked

over at Hatch, then back at the officer, and said earnestly, "He's my best friend."

"All right. So what happened?"

He licked mucus off his upper lip. "He got mad. Mad as hell. I've never seen him like that."

"Like what?"

"Crazy. Violent. Like he snapped or something."

"Snapped."

"Yes, sir."

"What'd you do to piss him off, cause him to snap?"

"Nothing! One minute he's down below with her. I gave them some privacy, you know?"

"For sex? They were having sex?"

"Yeah. I mean, really going at it, having fun. Next minute, he's back up on deck, coming at me."

"For no reason? Just like that?"

The kid's head wobbled up and down. "It was supposed to be a party. A celebration. I don't understand how it went to hell so quick. I swear to God I don't." He lowered his battered face into his hands and began to sob again.

The officer looked over at Hatch as though for consultation. Hatch stared back at him, wanting to ask what he was looking at him for. He wasn't a counselor. He wasn't a parent. He for damn sure wasn't an officer in the Coast Guard or a cop. This was no longer his problem.

When he failed to volunteer anything, the officer asked if he had anything to add to the boy's story.

"No."

"Did you see or hear them fighting?"

"The only thing I saw them doing was enjoying themselves."

The officer turned back to the young man. "Best friends don't fight for no reason. Not even when they've had too much to drink. They might swap some harsh words, maybe throw a punch or two. But once it blows over, it's over, right?"

"I guess," he replied sullenly.

"So I want you to come clean with me now. Okay? You listening? What brought on the fight?"

The kid struggled to swallow. "He just attacked me."

"How come?"

"All I did was defend myself. I swear," he blubbered. "I didn't want to fight him. It was a party."

"Why'd he attack you?"

He shook his head.

"Now, that's not true, is it, son? You know why he attacked you. So tell me. What caused your best friend to get mad enough to start beating up on you?"

Silence stretched out for about twenty seconds, then the kid mumbled a single word.

Hatch wasn't sure he'd heard correctly, mainly because the first clap of thunder from the predicted storm rattled the small square window in his shack just as the boy spoke, and also because what he thought he heard the boy say was a strange answer to the question.

The officer must have thought so, too. He shook his head with misapprehension and leaned forward to hear better. "Come again? Speak up, son."

The young man raised his head and took a swipe at his nose with the back of his hand. He cleared his throat. He blinked the officer into focus with his one functioning eye.

"Envy," he said gruffly. "That's what this is all about. Envy."

P.M.E.
St. Anne Island, Georgia
February 2002

Chapter 1

B ut there's got to be." Maris Matherly-Reed impatiently tapped her pencil against the notepad upon which she had doodled a series of triangles and a chain of loops. Below those she'd rough-sketched an idea for a book jacket.

"P.M.E., correct?"

"Correct."

"I'm sorry, ma'am, there's no such listing. I double-checked."

The idea for the book jacket—an autobiographical account of the author's murky relationship with her stepsibling—had come to Maris while she was waiting for the directory assistance operator to locate the telephone number. A call that should have taken no more than a few seconds had stretched into several minutes.

"You don't have a listing for P.M.E. in this area code?"

"In any area code," the operator replied. "I've accessed the entire U.S."

"Maybe it's a business listing, not a residential."

"I checked both."

"Could it be an unlisted number?"

"It would appear with that designation. I don't have anything under those initials, period. If you had a last name—"

"But I don't."

"Then I'm sorry."

"Thank you for trying."

Frustrated, Maris reconsidered her sketch, then scribbled over it. She wasn't going to like that book no matter what the jacket looked like. The incestuous overtones made her uncomfortable, and she was afraid a large number of readers would share her uneasiness.

But the editor to whom the manuscript had been submitted felt strongly about buying it. The subject matter guaranteed author appearances on TV and radio talk shows, write-ups in magazines, probably a movie-of-the-week option. Even if the reviews were poor, the book's subject matter was titillating enough to generate sales in large numbers. The other decision makers in the hardcover division of Matherly Press had agreed with the editor when she pled her case, so Maris had deferred to the majority. They owed her one.

Which brought her back to the prologue of *Envy* she had read that afternoon. She had discovered it among a stack of unsolicited manuscripts. They had been occupying a shelf in her office for months, collecting dust until that unspecified day when her schedule permitted her to scan them before sending the anxious authors the standard rejection letter. Imagining their crushing disappointment when they read that impersonal and transparent kiss-off, she felt that each writer deserved at least a few minutes of her time.

And there was always that outside, one-in-a-million, once-in-a-blue-moon chance that the next Steinbeck or Faulkner or Hemingway would be mined from the slush pile. That, of course, was every book editor's pipe dream.

Maris would settle for finding a bestseller. These twelve pages of prologue had definite promise. They had excited Maris more than anything she had read recently, even material from her portfolio of published authors, and certainly more than anything she'd read from fledgling novelists.

It had piqued her curiosity, as a prologue or first chapter should. She was hooked, eager to know more, anxious to read the rest of the story. Had the rest of the story been written? she wondered. Or at least outlined? Was this the author's first attempt at fiction writing? Had he or she written in another genre? What were his/her credentials? Did he/she have any credentials?

There was nothing to indicate the writer's gender, although her gut feeling said male. Hatch Walker's internal dialogue rang true to his salty character and read like the language in which a man would think. The narrative was in keeping with the old sailor's poetic, though warped, soul.

But the pages had been sent by someone totally inexperienced and untutored on how to submit a manuscript to a prospective publisher. All the standard rules had been broken. An SASE for return mailing hadn't been enclosed. It lacked a cover letter of introduction. There was no phone number, street address, post office box, or e-mail address. Only those three initials and the name of an island that Maris had never heard of. How did the writer hope to sell his manuscript if he couldn't be contacted?

She noticed that the postmark on the mailing envelope was four months old. If the author had submitted the prologue to several publishers simultaneously, it might have already been bought. All the more reason to locate the writer as soon as possible. She was either wasting her time or she was on to something with potential. Whichever, she needed to know sooner rather than later.

"You're not ready?"

Noah appeared in her open office door wearing his Armani tuxedo. Maris said, "My, don't you look handsome." Glancing at her desk clock, she realized she had lost all track of time and that she was, indeed, running late. Raking her fingers through her hair, she gave a short, self-deprecating laugh. "I, on the other hand, am going to require some major renovation."

Her husband of twenty-two months closed the door behind him and advanced into her corner office. He tossed a trade magazine onto her desk, then moved behind her chair and began massaging her neck and shoulders, which he knew were the gathering spots for her tension and fatigue. "Tough day?"

"Not all that bad, actually. Only one meeting this afternoon. Mostly I've used today to clear some space in here." She gestured toward the pile of rejected manuscripts awaiting removal.

"You've been reading the stuff in your slush pile? Maris, really," he chided lightly. "Why bother? It's a Matherly Press policy not to buy anything that isn't submitted by an agent."

"That's the official company line, but since I'm a Matherly, I can bend the rules if I wish."

"I'm married to an anarchist," he teased, bending down to kiss the side of her neck. "But if you're planning an insurrection, couldn't your cause be something that streamlines our operation, instead of one that consumes the valuable time of our publisher and senior vice president?"

"What an off-putting title," she remarked with a slight shudder. "Makes me sound like a frump who smells of throat lozenges and wears sensible shoes."

Noah laughed. "It makes you sound powerful, which you are. And awfully busy, which you are."

"You failed to mention smart and sexy."

"Those are givens. Stop trying to change the subject. Why bother with the slush pile when even our most junior editors don't?"

"Because my father taught me to honor anyone who attempted to write. Even if the individual's talent is limited, his effort alone deserves some consideration."

"Far be it from me to dispute the venerable Daniel Matherly."

Despite Noah's mild reproof, Maris intended to continue the practice of going through the slush pile. Even if it was a time-consuming and unproductive task, it was one of the principles upon which a Matherly had founded the publishing house over a century ago. Noah could mock their archaic traditions because he hadn't been born a Matherly. He was a member of the family by marriage, not blood, and that was a significant difference that explained his more relaxed attitude toward tradition.

A Matherly's blood was tinted with ink. An appreciation for it seemed to flow through the family's veins. Maris firmly believed that her family's admiration and respect for the written word and for writers had been fundamental to their success and longevity as publishers.

"I got an advance copy of the article," Noah said.

She picked up the magazine he'd carried in with him. A Post-It marked a specific page. Turning to it, she said, "Ah, great photo."

"Good photographer."

"Good subject."

"Thank you."

" 'Noah Reed is forty, but could pass for much younger,' " she read aloud from the article. Angling her head back, she gave him a critical look. "I agree. You don't look a day over thirty-nine."

"Ha-ha."

" 'Daily workouts in the Matherly Press gym on the sixth floor—one of Reed's innovations when he joined the firm three years ago—keeps all six feet of him lean and supple.' Well, this writer is certainly enamored. Did you ever have a thing with her?"

He chuckled. "Absolutely not."

"She's one of the few."

On their wedding day, Maris had teasingly remarked to him that so many single women were mourning the loss of one of the city's most eligible bachelors, she was surprised that the doors of

St. Patrick's Cathedral weren't draped in black crepe. "Does she get around to mentioning your business acumen and the contributions you've made to Matherly Press?"

"Farther down."

"Let's see...'graying at the temples, which adds to his distinguished good looks'...So on and so forth about your commanding demeanor and charm. Are you sure—Oh, here's something. 'He shares the helm at Matherly Press with his father-in-law, publishing legend Daniel Matherly, who serves as chairman and CEO, and Reed's wife, Maris Matherly-Reed, whom he claims has perfect selection and editorial skills. He modestly credits her with the company's reputation for publishing bestsellers.'" Pleased, she smiled up at him. "Did you say that?"

"And more that she didn't include."

"Then thank you very much."

"I only said what I know to be true."

Maris read the remainder of the flattering article, then set the magazine aside. "Very nice. But for all her ga-ga-ness she overlooked two major biographical points."

"And they are?"

"That you're also an excellent writer."

"*The Vanquished* is old news."

"But it should be mentioned anytime your name appears in print."

"What's the second thing?" he asked in the brusque tone he used whenever she brought up his one and only published novel.

"She said nothing about your marvelous massage techniques."

"Happy to oblige."

Closing her eyes, Maris tilted her head to one side. "A little lower on your...Ahh. There." He dug his strong thumb into a spot between her scapulas, and the tension began to dissolve.

"You're in knots," he said. "Serves you right for scavenging through that heap of garbage all day."

"As it turns out, it might not have been time wasted. I actually found something that sparked my interest."

"You're joking."

"No."

"Fiction or non?"

"Fiction. Only a prologue, but it's intriguing. It starts—"

"I want to hear all about it, darling. But you really should shake a leg if we're going to get there in time."

He dropped a kiss on the top of her head, then tried to withdraw. But Maris reached for his hands and pulled them over her shoulders, holding them flattened against her chest. "Is tonight mandatory?"

"More or less."

"We could miss one function, couldn't we? Dad begged off tonight."

"That's why we should be there. Matherly Press bought a table. Two empty seats would be noticeable. One of our authors is receiving an award."

"His agent and editor are attending with him. He won't be without a cheering section." She pulled his hands down onto her breasts. "Let's call in sick. Go home and shut out the world. Open a bottle of wine, the cheaper the better. Get in the Jacuzzi and feed each other a pizza. Make love in some room other than the bedroom. Maybe even two rooms."

Laughing, he squeezed her breasts affectionately. "What did you say this prologue was about?" He pulled his hands from beneath hers and headed for the door.

Maris groaned with disappointment. "I thought I was making you an offer you couldn't refuse."

"Tempting. Very. But if we're not at this dinner, it'll arouse suspicion."

"You're right. I'd hate for people to think that we're still acting like newlyweds who crave evenings alone."

"Which is true."

"But...?"

"But we also have professional responsibilities, Maris. As you are well aware. It's important for industry insiders to know that when they refer to Matherly Press, it damn well better be in either the present or future tense, not the past tense."

"And that's why we attend nearly every publishing event held in New York," she said as though it were part of a memorized catechism.

"Precisely."

Their calendars were filled with breakfasts, luncheons, dinners, receptions, and cocktail parties. Noah believed it was extremely important, virtually compulsory, that they be seen as active participants within literary circles, especially since her father could no longer be involved to the extent he once had been.

Recently Daniel Matherly had slowed down. He didn't attend as many insider gatherings. He was no longer accepting speaking engagements, although the requests still poured in. The Four Seasons was calling daily now to inquire if Daniel would be using his reserved table for lunch or if they were free to seat another party there.

For almost five decades, Daniel had been a force to be reckoned with. Under his leadership, Matherly Press had set the industry standards, dictated trends, dominated the bestseller lists. His name had become synonymous with book publishing both domestically and in foreign markets. He had been a juggernaut who, over a period of months, had voluntarily been decreasing his momentum.

However, his semi-retirement did not spell the end, or even a weakening, of the publishing house's viability. Noah thought it was vitally important that the book publishing community understand that. If that meant going to award dinners several times a month, that's what they would do.

He checked his wristwatch. "How much time do you need? I should let the driver know when we'll be downstairs."

Maris sighed with resignation. "Give me twenty minutes."

"I'll be generous. Take thirty." He blew her a kiss before leaving.

But Maris didn't plunge into her overhaul right away. Instead, she asked her assistant to place a call. She'd had another idea on how she might track down the author of *Envy*.

While waiting for the requested call to be placed, she gazed out her office windows. Extending nearly from floor to ceiling, they formed a corner of the room, providing her a southeastern exposure. Midtown Manhattan was experiencing a mild summer evening. The sun had slipped behind the skyscrapers, casting a premature twilight on the streets below. Already lights were coming on inside buildings, making the brick and granite structures appear to twinkle. Through the windows of neighboring buildings, Maris could see other professionals wrapping up for the day.

The avenues were jammed with competing after-work and pretheater traffic. Taxies vied for inches of space, nosing themselves into impossibly small channels between buses and delivery trucks. Couriers on bicycles, seemingly with death wishes, perilously played chicken with motor traffic. Revolving doors disgorged pedestrians onto the crowded sidewalks, where they jostled for space and wielded briefcases and shopping bags like weapons.

Across Avenue of the Americas, a queue was forming outside Radio City Music Hall, where Tony Bennett was performing this evening. She, Noah, and her father had been offered complimentary VIP tickets, but they'd had to decline them because of the literary award banquet.

Which she should be dressing for, she reminded herself, just as her telephone beeped. "He's on line one," her assistant informed her.

"Thanks. You don't need to wait. See you tomorrow." Maris depressed the blinking button. "Hello?"

"Yeah. Deputy Dwight Harris here."

"Hello, Deputy Harris. Thank you for taking my call. My name is Maris Matherly-Reed."

"Say again?"

She did.

"Uh-huh."

Maris paused, giving him time to comment or ask a question, but he didn't, so she went straight to the reason for the call. "I'm trying to reach someone, an individual who I believe lives on St. Anne Island."

"That's in our county."

"Georgia, correct?"

"Yes, ma'am," he proudly replied.

"Is St. Anne actually an island?"

"Not much o' one. What I mean is, it's small. But it's an island, awright. Little less than two miles out from the mainland. Who're you looking for?"

"Someone with the initials P.M.E."

"Did you say P.M.E.?"

"Have you ever heard of anyone who goes by those initials?"

"Can't say that I have, ma'am. We talking about a man or woman?"

"Unfortunately, I don't know."

"You don't know. Huh." After a beat or two, the deputy asked, "If you don't even know if it's a man or woman, what do you want with 'em?"

"It's business."

"Business."

"That's right."

"Huh."

Dead end. Maris tried again. "I thought you might know, or might have heard of someone who—"

"Nope."

This was going nowhere and her allotted time was running

out. "Well, thank you for your time, Deputy Harris. I'm sorry to have bothered you."

"No bother."

"Would you mind taking down my name and numbers? Then if you think of something or hear of someone with these initials, I would appreciate being notified."

After she gave him her telephone numbers, he said, "Say, ma'am? If it's back child support or an outstanding arrest warrant or something like 'at, I'd be happy to see if—"

"No, no. It's not a legal matter in any sense."

"Business."

"That's right."

"Well, okay, then," he said with noticeable disappointment. "Sorry I couldn't he'p you."

She thanked him again, then closed her office and hurried down the hallway to the ladies' room, where her cocktail dress had been hanging since she'd arrived for work early that morning. Because she frequently changed from business to evening attire before leaving the building, she kept a full complement of toiletries and cosmetics in a locker. She put them to use now.

When she joined Noah at the elevator fifteen minutes later, he gave a long wolf whistle, then kissed her cheek. "Nice turnaround. A miracle, actually. You look fantastic."

As they descended to street level, she assessed her reflection in the metal elevator door and realized that her efforts hadn't been in vain. "Fantastic," was a slight exaggeration, but considering the dishevelment she'd started with, she looked better than she had any right to expect.

She'd chosen to wear a cranberry-colored silk sheath with narrow straps and a scooped neckline. Her nod toward evening glitter came in the form of diamond studs in her ears and a crystal-encrusted Judith Leiber handbag in the shape of a butterfly, a Christmas gift from her father. She was carrying a pashmina shawl purchased in Paris during a side trip there following the international book fair in Frankfurt.

She had gathered her shoulder-length hair into a sleek, low ponytail. The hairdo looked chic and sophisticated rather than desperate, which had been the case. She had retouched her eye makeup, outlined her lips with a pencil, and filled them in with gloss. To give color to her fluorescent-light pallor, she had applied powdered bronzer to her cheeks, chin, forehead, and décolletage. Her push-up bra, an engineering marvel, had created a flattering cleavage that filled up the neckline of her dress.

" 'Her tan and tits were store-bought.' "

The elevator doors opened onto the ground floor. Noah looked at her curiously as he stepped aside to let her exit ahead of him. "I beg your pardon?"

She laughed softly. "Nothing. Just quoting something I read today."

Chapter 2

———◦●◦———

Although it had stopped raining a half hour earlier, the air was already so moisture-laden the rainwater couldn't evaporate. It collected in puddles. It beaded on flowers' petals and the fuzz of ripe peaches ready to be picked. The limbs of evergreens were bowed under the additional weight. Fat drops rolled off hardwood leaves recently washed clean and splashed onto the spongy, saturated ground.

The slightest breeze would have shaken water from the trees, creating miniature rain showers, but there was scarcely any movement of air. The atmosphere was inert and had a texture almost as compacted as the silence.

Deputy Dwight Harris alighted from the golf cart he had borrowed at the St. Anne landing. Before starting up the pathway to the house, he removed his hat and paused, telling himself that he needed a moment to get his bearings, when what he was actually doing was second-guessing his decision to come here alone after sundown. He didn't quite know what to expect.

He'd never been here before, although he knew about this house, awright. Anybody who was ever on St. Anne Island had heard stories about the plantation house at the easternmost tip of the island, situated on a little finger of land that pointed out toward Africa. Some of the tales he'd heard about the place stretched credibility. But the descriptions of the house were, by God, damn near accurate.

Typical of colonial Low Country architecture, the two-story white frame house was sitting on top of an aged brick basement. Six broad steps led up to the deep veranda that extended all the way across the front of the house and wrapped around both sides. The front door had been painted a glossy black, as had all the hurricane shutters that flanked the windows on both stories. Six smooth columns supported the second-floor balcony. Twin chimneys acted like bookends against the steeply pitched roof. It looked pretty much like Deputy Harris had imagined it would.

He hadn't counted on it looking so spooky, is all.

He jumped and uttered a soft exclamation of fright when a raindrop landed on the back of his neck with a hard splat. It had dripped from a low-hanging branch of the tree under which he was standing. Wiping the wetness away, he replaced his hat and glanced around to make sure no one had seen his nervous reaction. It was the gathering dusk and the inclement weather that was giving the place an eerie feel. Cursing himself for behaving like a coward, he forced his feet into motion.

Dodging puddles, he made his way up the crushed-shell path, which was lined by twin rows of live oaks, four to a side. Spanish moss hung from the branches in trailing bunches. The roots of the ancient trees snaked along the ground, some of them as thick as a fat man's thigh.

Altogether, it was an impressive front entry. Majestic, you might say. The back of the house, Harris knew, overlooked the Atlantic.

The house hadn't started out this grand. The four original rooms had been built more than two centuries ago by the planter who'd bought the island from a colonist who decided he preferred dying of old age in England to succumbing to yellow fever in the newly founded American nation. The house had expanded with the plantation's success, first with indigo and sugar cane, then with cotton.

Several generations into the dynasty, those first four rooms were converted into slave quarters, and construction of the big house was begun. In its day, it was a marvel, at least for St. Anne Island. Building materials and all the furnishings had been shipped in, then dragged on sleds pulled by mules through dense forests and fertile fields to the home site. It had taken years to complete, but it had been sturdily constructed, withstanding Union army occupation and the lashings of a couple dozen hurricanes.

Then it succumbed to a bug.

Around the beginning of the twentieth century, the boll weevil ruined more than the cotton crop. More damaging than weather and war, the boll weevil crushed the local economy and destroyed life as it had been lived on St. Anne.

A descendant of the plantation's original owner had correctly forecast his imminent doom and hanged himself on the dining room chandelier. The rest of the family stole off the island in the middle of the night, never to be heard of again, leaving debts and unpaid taxes.

Decades passed. The forest eventually reclaimed the property surrounding the house, just as it did the fields once white with cotton. Varmints occupied rooms once inhabited by aristocracy and visited by one United States president. The only people to ever venture inside the dilapidated mansion were crazy kids accepting a dare or an occasional drunk looking for a place to sleep it off.

It remained in ruin until a little over a year ago when an outsider, not an islander, bought it and commenced a massive renovation. Harris figured he was probably a northerner who'd seen *Gone With the Wind* several times and wanted himself an antebellum mansion on southern soil, a Yankee with more money than good sense.

Word around the island, though, was positive about the new owner. He'd made noticeable improvements on the place, folks said. But in Harris's opinion there was still a lot to be done if it was going to shine as it had in its heyday. The deputy didn't envy the new owner the monumental task or the expense involved in such an undertaking. Nor was he envious of the bad luck that seemed to go hand in glove with this place.

Legend had it that the hanged man's ghost still resided in the old house and that the dining room chandelier swung from the ceiling for no reason that anybody could detect.

Harris didn't put much stock in ghost stories. He'd seen flesh-and-blood people do much scarier stuff than any mischief a ghost could drum up. Even so, he would have welcomed a little more illumination as he mounted the steps, crossed the veranda, and approached the front door.

He tapped the brass knocker tentatively, then harder. Seconds ticked by as ponderously as rain dripped from the eaves. It wasn't that late, but maybe the resident was already in bed. Country folk tended to turn in earlier than city dwellers, didn't they?

Harris considered leaving and coming back some other time—preferably before the sun went down. But then he heard approaching footsteps. Seconds later the front door was pulled open from the inside—but not by much.

"Yes?"

Harris peered into the crack formed by the open door. He had psyched himself up to expect anything from the hanging ghost to the twin barrels of a sawed-off shotgun aimed at his belly by a disgruntled homeowner that he'd unnecessarily dragged out of bed.

Thankfully he was greeted by neither, and the man seemed reasonably friendly. Harris couldn't see him well and the features of his face blended into the shadows behind him, but his voice sounded pleasant enough. At least he hadn't cussed him. Yet.

"Evenin', sir. I'm Deputy Dwight Harris. From the sheriff's office over in Savannah."

The man leaned forward slightly and glanced past him toward the golf cart parked at the end of the path. To discourage tourism and unwelcome visitors to the island, there wasn't a ferry to St. Anne from the mainland. Anyone coming here came by a boat they either owned or chartered. When they arrived, they either walked or rented a golf cart to get around the island's nine thousand acres, give or take a few hundred. Only permanent residents drove cars on the narrow roads, many of which had been left unpaved on purpose.

The golf cart wasn't as official-looking as a squad car, and Harris figured it diminished his authority a bit. To stoke his self-confidence, he hiked up his slipping gun belt.

The man behind the door asked, "How can I help you, Deputy Harris?"

"First off, I apologize for disturbing you. But I got a call earlier this evening. From a gal up in New York." The man waited him out, saying nothing. "Said she was trying to track down somebody who goes by the initials P.M.E."

"Really?"

"That's what she said. I didn't let on like the name registered with me."

"Did it?"

"Register, you mean? No, sir. Can't rightly say it did."

"Nevertheless, you're here."

"I'll admit she got my curiosity up. Never knew anybody to go only by his initials, you see. Don't worry, though. 'Round here, we respect a person's privacy."

"An admirable practice."

"St. Anne has a history of folks hiding out on her for one reason or another."

The moment it was out, Harris wished he hadn't said it. It smacked of an accusation of some sort. A long silence ensued. He cleared his throat nervously before continuing. "So anyhow, I thought I should oblige this lady. Came over in the department's motor launch. Asked around at the landing and was directed here."

"What did this lady from New York want?"

"Well, sir, I don't rightly know. She said it wasn't a legal matter or nothing like 'at. Just that she had business with P.M.E. I thought you might be a big winner in one of those sweepstakes, thought Ed McMahon and Dick Clark might be looking for you."

"I've never entered a sweepstakes."

"Right, right. Well, then..."

Harris tipped his hat forward so he could scratch the back of his head. He wondered why in hell the man hadn't invited him in or, short of that, why he hadn't turned on any lights. Pussyfooting hadn't gotten him anywhere, by God, so he bluntly asked, "You P.M.E. or what?"

"Did she leave her name?"

"Huh? Oh, the lady? Yeah." Harris fished a piece of notepaper from the breast pocket of his uniform shirt, which he was embarrassed to discover was damp with sweat. However, the man seemed not to notice or care about the dampness as he took the sheet and read what Harris had written down.

"Those're her phone numbers," Harris explained. "All of 'em. So I figured this business of hers must be pretty important. That's why I came on out tonight."

"Thank you very much for your trouble, Sheriff Harris."

"Deputy."

"Deputy Harris."

Then, before Harris could blink, the man closed the door in his face. "Good evenin' to you, too," he mouthed as he turned away.

His boots crunched the shells of the path. The evening had deepened into full-blown darkness, and it was even darker beneath the canopy of live oak branches. He wasn't afraid, exactly. The man behind the door had been civil enough. He hadn't been what you'd call hostile. Inhospitable, maybe, but not hostile.

All the same, Harris was glad to have this errand over and done with. If he had it to do over again, he might not assign himself this duty. What was it to him if some lady from up north was successful or not with her unspecified business?

When he sat down on the seat of the golf cart, he discovered it had been dripped on from the tree overhead. His britches were soaked through by the time he reached the landing where he'd tied up the boat.

The man from whom he had borrowed the golf cart—no charge for lawmen—eyed him distrustfully as Harris returned the key. "Find him?"

"Yeah, thanks for the directions," Harris replied. "You ever see this guy?"

"Now and again," the man drawled.

"Is he a weird sort?"

"Not so's you'd notice."

"He ever make any trouble around here?"

"Naw, he stays pretty much to hisself."

"Island folks like him okay?"

"You need any gas before headin' back?"

Which was as good as an invitation to leave and take his nosy questions with him. Harris had hoped to get a clearer picture of the man who occupied the haunted mansion and hid behind doors when folks came calling, but apparently he wasn't going to get one. He had no cause to investigate further—beyond his natural curiosity as to why a man went only by his initials and what a woman in New York City was wanting with him.

He thanked the islander for the use of the golf cart.

The man spat tobacco juice into the mud. "No problem."

Chapter 3

$$\text{━━━◆◉◆━━━}$$

J ust one more picture, please, Mr. and Mrs. Reed?"

Maris and Noah smiled for the photographer who was covering the literary banquet for *Publishers Weekly*. During the cocktail hour, they'd been photographed with other publishers, with their award-winning author, and with the celebrity emcee. The former women's tennis champion fancied herself an author now that she'd had a ghostwriter pen a roman à clef about her days on the professional circuit.

The Reeds had been allowed to eat their dinner in relative peace, but now that the event had concluded, they were once again being asked to pose for various shots. But, as promised, the photographer snapped one last picture of them alone, then scuttled off to catch the exercise guru whose latest fitness book topped the nonfiction bestseller list.

As Maris and Noah crossed the elegant lobby of the Palace Hotel, she sighed, "At last. I can't wait to get into my jammies."

"One drink and we'll say our good nights."

"Drink?"

"At Le Cirque."

"Now?"

"I told you."

"No, you didn't."

"I'm sure I did, Maris. Between the main course and dessert, I whispered to you that Nadia had invited us to join her and one of the award recipients for a drink."

"I didn't know you meant tonight."

Maris groaned with dread. She disliked Nadia Schuller intensely and for this very reason. The book critic was meddlesome and pushy, always roping Noah and her into a commitment from which there was no graceful way out.

Nadia Schuller's "Book Chat" column was syndicated in major newspapers and carried a lot of weight—in Maris's opinion simply because Nadia had ramrodded herself into being the country's only book critic whose name was recognized by the general public. Maris held her in low regard both professionally and personally.

She was adroit at making it seem as though this sort of arranged meeting were for the benefit of the parties she was bringing together, but Maris suspected that Nadia's matchmaking was strictly self-serving. She was a self-promoter without equal and refused to take no for an answer. Whatever her request, she extended it assuming that it would be granted without a quibble. Noncompliance to her wishes was met with a veiled threat of consequences. Maris was wise to her manipulations, but Noah seemed blind to them.

"Please, Noah, can't we decline? Just this once?"

"We're already here."

"Not tonight," she implored.

"Tell you what. Let's compromise." He pulled her around to face him and smiled affectionately. "I think this might be an important meeting."

"Nadia always makes it sound not just important but imperative."

"Granted. But this time I don't think she's exaggerating."

"What's the compromise?"

"I'll make your excuses. I'll tell Nadia that you have a headache or an early breakfast appointment tomorrow morning. Have the driver take you home. After one drink, I'll follow you. Half an hour, max. I promise."

She slid her hand inside his tuxedo jacket and stroked his chest through the stiffly starched shirt. "I have a better compromise, Mr. Reed. I'll tell Nadia to take a flying leap into the East River. Then let's go home together. Those jammies I mentioned? They can be dispensed with."

"You ended your sentence with a preposition," he noted.

"You're the writer. I'm a mere editor."

"I'm a *former* writer."

"There's no such thing." She took a step closer and aligned her thighs with his. "What do you say? About the jammies."

"Noah? We're waiting."

Nadia Schuller approached with the bearing of a military general about to address the troops, except that she was better dressed and had her phony smile in place. She was skilled at turning on the charm at will—to intrude, disarm, and promote herself. Many fell for it. She was a frequent and popular guest on talk shows. Letterman loved her, and he was just one of her celebrity friends. She made it her business to be photographed with actors, musicians, supermodels, and politicians whenever possible.

She had elevated herself to heights that Maris felt were undeserved. She was a self-appointed, self-ordained authority with no meaningful credentials to support her opinions on either writing or the business of publishing. But authors and publishers couldn't afford to offend her or they risked their next book being slammed in her column.

Tonight her arm was linked with that of a bestselling novelist who looked a little dazed. Or stoned, if the gossip about him was true. Or maybe he was only dizzy from being propelled through the evening by the turbo engines of Nadia's personality.

"They won't hold our table forever, Noah. Coming?"

"Well..." He hesitated and glanced down at Maris.

"What's the matter?" Nadia asked in a voice as piercing as a dentist's drill. She addressed the question to Maris, automatically assuming that she was the source of the problem.

"Nothing's the matter, Nadia. Noah and I were having a private conversation."

"Oh, my. Have I interrupted one of those husband/wife things?"

The critic could have been pretty if not for her edge, which manifested itself in the brittleness of her smile and the calculation in her eyes, which seemed to miss nothing. She was always impeccably dressed, groomed, and accessorized in the best of taste, but even arrayed in fine silk and finer jewelry there was nothing feminine about her.

It was rumored that she went through men like a box of Godivas, chewing up and spitting out the ones who didn't challenge her or who could do nothing to further her career—in other words, the ones with soft centers. Maris had no problem believing the gossip about Nadia's promiscuity. What surprised her was the number of men who found her sexually appealing.

"Yes, we were having a husband and wife *thing*. I was telling Noah that the last thing I want to do is join you for a round of drinks," Maris said, smiling sweetly.

"You do look awfully tired," Nadia returned, her smile just as sweet.

Noah intervened. "I'm sorry, Nadia. We must decline tonight. I'm going to take my wife home and tuck her in."

"No, darling," Maris said. She wouldn't play the wounded wife in front of Nadia Schuller. "I wouldn't dream of keeping you from this obligation."

"It's hardly that," Nadia snapped. "More like a rare opportunity to talk shop with one of publishing's most exciting novelists."

The exciting novelist had yet to utter a peep. He was bleary-eyed and seemed oblivious to their conversation. Maris gave Nadia a knowing look. "Of course it is. That's what I meant." Back to Noah, she said, "You stay. I'll see myself home."

He regarded her doubtfully. "You're sure?"

"I insist."

"Then it's settled." Nadia gave the writer's arm a sharp tug. Like a sleepwalker, he fell into step beside her. "You two say your good-byes while we go claim the table. Shall I order your usual, Noah?"

"Please."

Then to Maris she called back airily, "Get some rest, dear."

* * *

Parker Evans stared out the window into nothingness.

He couldn't see the shoreline from this vantage point, but if he concentrated, he could hear the surf. Rain clouds obscured the moon. There was no other source of light, natural or man-made, to relieve the darkness.

From this first-floor window overlooking the rear of his property, Parker could see across a breast of lawn to the point where it sharply dropped off several degrees before sloping more gradually toward the beach. That edge of the lawn appeared to be the threshold of a black void that melded with the ocean farther out. No wonder ancient sailors had feared the unknown terrors that lay beyond the brink.

The room behind him was also dark, which wasn't an oversight. He had deliberately left the lights off. Had they been on, his reflection would have appeared in the window glass. He preferred looking at nothing to looking at himself.

Anyway, he didn't need a light in order to read the list of telephone numbers he held in his hand. In fact, he no longer needed to read them at all. He had committed them to memory.

His six months of waiting had finally paid off. Maris Matherly-Reed was trying to contact him.

As recently as yesterday, Parker had come close to scratching his plan and devising another. After months of not hearing from her, he figured that she had read the prologue of *Envy*, hated it, tossed it, and hadn't even had the courtesy of sending him a rejection notice.

It had also occurred to him that the partial manuscript had never reached her desk, that mailroom staff had misdirected it or hurled it into a Dumpster within minutes of its delivery. Few of the major publishing houses even had slush piles anymore. Manuscripts either got in through literary agents or they didn't get in at all.

If his pages had survived that first selection process, a junior editor who was paid to cull material from slush piles could have deep-sixed the *Envy* prologue before it ever got to her office. In any case, he'd almost convinced himself that this plan was a bust and that it would be necessary to plot another.

That was yesterday. Just went to show what a difference a day could make. Apparently the pages *had* made it to her desk, and she *had* read them, because today she *had* tried to contact him.

Marris Madderly Reade. The deputy had misspelled all three of her names. Parker hoped he was more adept at taking down telephone numbers.

Business, she had told Deputy Dwight Harris when he had asked why she was looking for P.M.E. She had business to discuss. Which could mean good news for Parker. Or bad. Or something in between.

She could be calling to say that his writing stunk and how dare he presume to send her prestigious publishing house such unsolicited shit. Or maybe she would take a softer approach and say that he had talent but that his material didn't fit their present publishing needs, and wish him luck at placing his book with another house.

But those responses usually came in the form of rejection letters, written in language firm enough to discourage another submission but with enough encouragement to keep the rejected writer from jumping off the nearest bridge.

Ms. Matherly-Reed didn't know where to address such a letter to him, however. He'd made certain that she couldn't reach him by mail. So if her intention had been to reject *Envy*, he probably would never have heard from her at all. Instead, she had tried to track him down. From that, he deduced her response must be favorable.

But it wasn't yet time to ice down the champagne. It was a little early to award himself a gold star for being such a clever boy. Before he got too carried away, he forced himself to keep his heartbeat regular, his breathing normal, and his head clear. Success or failure hinged not on what he'd done up to this point but on what he did next.

So instead of celebrating this milestone, he had stared for hours out this window into the rainy, moonless night. While the calm surf swept the shoreline, he weighed his options. While his distant neighbors on St. Anne slept, or watched late-night TV, or made love under their summer-weight bedcovers, Parker Evans plotted.

It helped that he already knew the ending to this story. Not once did he consider changing the outcome from his original plot. He never considered letting Maris Matherly-Reed's attempt to reach him go unacknowledged, never thought about dropping this thing here and now.

No, he'd come this far, he was committed to seeing it all the way through the denouement. But between here and there, he couldn't make a single misstep. Each chapter had to be carefully thought out, with no mistakes allowed. It had to be the perfect plot.

And if his resolve to finish it ever faltered, he had only to remember how fucking long it had taken him to reach this point in the saga. Six months.

Well...six months and fourteen years.

* * *

Maris groped for the ringing telephone. She squinted the lighted clock on her nightstand into focus. Five-twenty-three. In the morning. Who—

Then panic brought her wide awake. Was this that dreaded, inevitable phone call notifying her that her father had suffered a coronary, stroke, fall, or worse?

Anxiously she clutched the receiver. "Hello?"

"Maris Matherly-Reed?"

"Speaking."

"Where do you get off screwing around with my life?"

She was taken completely off guard and it took a moment for the rude question to sink in. "I beg your pardon? Who is this?"

She sat up, switched on the lamp, and reached out to rouse Noah. But his side of the bed was empty. She gaped at the undisturbed linens, at the pillow that was still fluffed.

"I don't appreciate you calling the sheriff," the caller said hotly.

Where is Noah? "I'm sorry...I was...you caught me asleep....Did you say sheriff?"

"Sheriff, *sheriff.* Ring any bells?"

She sucked in a quick breath. "P.M.E.?"

"A deputy came to my house, snooping around. Who the—"

"I—"

"—hell do you think you are?"

"I—"

"To mess with people's—"

"You—"

"—lives. Thanks for nothing, lady."

"Will you please be quiet for one second?"

Her raised voice brought him to an abrupt silence, but Maris sensed waves of resentment pulsing through the line. After taking a couple of calming breaths, she assumed a more reasonable tone. "I read your prologue and liked it. I wanted to talk to you about it, but I had no way of contacting you. You *left* me no way to contact you. So I called the sheriff's office in the hope that—"

"Send it back."

"Excuse me?"

"The prologue. Send it back."

"Why?"

"It's crap."

"Far from it, Mr.—"

"I shouldn't have sent it."

"I'm glad you did. These pages intrigue me. They're compelling and well written. If the rest of your book is as good as the prologue, I'll consider buying it for publication."

"It's not for sale."

"What do you mean?"

"Look, I've got a southern accent, but I'm still speaking English. Which part didn't you understand?"

His voice was geographically distinctive. Usually she found the soft *r*'s and slow drawl of southern regions engaging. But his manner was abrasive and disagreeable. If she hadn't seen real potential in his writing, recognized an untapped talent, she would have ended the conversation long before now.

Patiently she asked, "If you didn't want your book published, why did you submit the prologue to a book publisher?"

"Because I suffered a mental lapse," he answered, imitating her precise enunciation. "I've since changed my mind."

Maris took another tack. "Do you have a representative?"

"Representative?"

"An agent."

"I'm not an actor."

"Have you ever submitted material before?"

"Just send it back, okay?"

"Did you multiple-submit?"

"Send it to other publishers, you mean? No."

"Why did you send it to me?"

"You know what, forget sending it back. Toss it in the nearest trash can, use it for kindling, or line your birdcage with it, I don't care."

Sensing he was about to hang up, she said quickly, "Just one more moment, please."

"We're on my nickel."

"Before you decide against selling your book, a decision I think you'll regret, I'd welcome the chance to give you my professional opinion of it. I promise to be brutally honest. If I don't see any merit in it, I'll tell you. Let me decide if it's good or not. Please send me the entire manuscript."

"You have it."

"I have it?"

"Did I stutter?"

"You mean the prologue is all you've got?"

"It's not all I've *got*. It's all I've *written*. The rest of the story is in my head."

"Oh." That was disappointing. She had assumed that the remainder of the book was completed or nearly so. It hadn't occurred to her that the manuscript consisted of only those first twelve pages. "I urge you to finish it. In the meantime—"

"In the meantime, you're running up my long-distance bill. If you don't want to spend any money on return postage, then shred the damn thing. Good-bye. Oh, and don't send any more deputy sheriffs to my door."

Maris held the dead phone to her ear for several seconds before thoughtfully hanging up. The conversation had been almost surreal. She even thought that perhaps she had dreamed it.

But she wasn't dreaming. She was wide awake. By Manhattan standards, it was practically the middle of the night—and her husband wasn't in bed with her. If the strange telephone call weren't enough to wake her up, then Noah's unexplained absence certainly was.

She was concerned enough to call the hospital emergency rooms. But when she'd last seen Noah, he'd been in the company of Nadia Schuller. Which made her angry enough to throw something against the wall.

In either case, her night had ended and she was up for good. Throwing off the covers, she got out of bed and was reaching for her robe when Noah strolled into the bedroom, politely covering a wide yawn with his fist. He was still dressed in his tuxedo trousers and shirt, although he had removed the studs and his shirttail was hanging out. His jacket was slung over his shoulder. He was carrying his shoes.

He said, "Did I hear the telephone ring?"

"Yes."

"Was it Daniel? There's nothing wrong, I hope."

She was greatly relieved to see him, but dumbfounded by his nonchalance. "Noah, where in God's name have you been all night?"

Her tone stopped him in his tracks. He looked at her with puzzlement. "Downstairs on the sofa in the den."

"Why?"

"You were already asleep when I came in. I hated to disturb you."

"What time did you get home?"

He arched an eyebrow in silent disapproval of the third-degree tone of her questions. "About one, I think."

His calm manner only fueled her irritation. "You said—you promised—you'd be half an hour behind me."

"We had two rounds of drinks instead of one. What's the big deal?"

"The big deal is that I was awakened at five-twenty-something in the morning, and I was alone in bed," she exclaimed. "Call me irrational, but unless I know the reason why not, I expect my husband to be sleeping beside me."

"Obviously I wasn't missed until you were awakened."

"And whose fault is that?"

Her voice had gone shrill. It was the voice of a ranting wife. It called to mind the caricature dressed in a shapeless flannel robe and fuzzy scuffs, curlers in her hair, holding a rolling pin above her head as she caught her cheating husband sneaking in the back door.

She took a moment to get her temper under control, although she was still bristling with anger. "If you'll recall, Noah, I tried to seduce you into coming home with me straight from the office. But you elected for us to go to that interminably long banquet instead. Following that, I tried to talk you into salvaging at least part of the evening just for us, but you chose to have drinks with Vampira and that dopehead."

He dropped his shoes to the floor, removed his shirt, then unzipped his trousers and stepped out of them. "Each book that 'dopehead' writes sells over a half million copies in hardcover. His paperback sales are triple that. But he thinks he can get even higher numbers. He's unhappy with his present publisher and is considering moving to another.

" 'Vampira' set up the date for drinks, thinking that it would be a beneficial meeting for both parties. Indeed it was. The author agreed to let us work up a publishing proposal. We'll be hearing from his agent to discuss terms. I had hoped to surprise you and Daniel with this good news tomorrow, but . . . " He shrugged eloquently, then moved to the bed and sat down on the edge of it.

"And just to come completely clean with you," he continued, "I confess that the dopehead got so drunk we couldn't conscientiously put him into a taxi by himself. Nadia and I accompanied him to his apartment and put him to bed. Not a pleasant chore, I assure you. Then she and I shared a taxi back uptown. I dropped her off at Trump Tower, then after arriving home I came up-stairs, saw you sleeping soundly, and decided not to disturb you.

"Throughout the evening, I was acting in what I thought was your—our—best interest." He placed his hand over his heart and bowed his head slightly. "Forgive me my thoughtlessness."

Despite his logical explanation, Maris still believed she had a right to be angry. "You could have called, Noah."

"I could have. But knowing how exhausted you were, I didn't want to disturb you."

"I don't like being obligated to Nadia."

"I don't like being obligated to anyone. On the other hand, it's not very smart to intentionally alienate Nadia. If she likes you, she bestows favors. If she dislikes you, she can inflict serious dam-age."

"And either way—if you're a man—you get screwed."

That caused him to smile. "Why is it that a woman, and espe-cially you, is never more beautiful than when she's angry?"

"I was."

"I know."

"I *am*."

"Don't be. I'm sorry I worried you. I didn't mean to." He looked at her and smiled gently. "You have no reason to be jeal-ous, you know."

"Oh, really?" she asked, deadpan. "I think I have every right to be paranoid, considering the number of affairs you had before we were married."

"You had affairs, too, Maris."

"Two. You had that many a week, and you had a ten-year head start."

He grinned at her exaggeration. "I'm not even going to honor that with a comment. The point is that I married you."

"Sacrificing all that fun."

Laughing, he patted the spot beside him on the bed. "Why don't you stop this nonsense, retract the talons, and simply forgive me? You know you want to."

Her eyes narrowed with feigned malevolence. "Don't push it."

"Maris?"

Reluctantly she moved toward him. When she was still a distance away, he reached out far enough to take her hand and draw her down beside him on the bed. He tucked a strand of her hair behind her ear and kissed her cheek. She put up token resistance, but not for long.

When their first long kiss ended, she whispered, "I hankered for this all day yesterday."

"All you had to do was ask."

"I did."

"So you did," he said with a regretful sigh. "Let me make it up to you."

"Better late than never."

"Didn't you say something earlier about dispensing with these jammies?"

Moments later they were both down to their skin. Nibbling her neck, he asked, "Who called?"

"Hmm?"

"The telephone call that woke us up. Who was it?"

"That can wait." Seizing the initiative, she guided his hand down her belly to the notch of her thighs. "If you want to talk now, Noah, talk dirty."

Chapter 4

Daniel Matherly laid aside the manuscript pages and thought-fully pinched his lower lip between his thumb and fingers.

"What do you think?" Maris asked. "Is it my imagination or is it good?"

Taking advantage of the mild morning, they were having breakfast on the patio of Daniel's Upper East Side townhouse. Terra-cotta pots of blooming flowers provided patches of color within the brick enclosure. A sycamore tree shaded the area.

While Daniel was reading the *Envy* prologue, Maris had helped Maxine put together their meal. Maxine, the Matherlys' housekeeper, had been practically a member of the family a full decade before Maris was born.

This morning she was her cantankerous self, protesting Maris's presence in her kitchen and criticizing the way she squeezed the fresh orange juice. In truth, the woman loved her like a daughter and had acted as a surrogate since the death of Maris's mother when she was still in grade school. Maris took the housekeeper's bossiness for what it was—an expression of her af-fection.

Maris and Daniel had eaten their egg-white omelets, grilled tomatoes, and whole-wheat toast in silence while he finished reading the prologue. "Thank you, Maxine," he said now when she came out to clear away their dishes and pour refills of coffee. "And yes, dear," he said to Maris, "it's good."

"I'm glad you think so."

She was pleased with his validation of her opinion, but she also valued his. Her father was perhaps the only person in the world who had read and reread more books than she. If they disagreed on a book, allowances were made for their individual tastes, but both could distinguish good writing from bad.

"New writer?"

"I don't know."

He reacted with surprise. "You don't know?"

"This wasn't a typical submission by any stretch." She explained how she had come to read the prologue and what little she had learned about the elusive author. She ended by recounting her predawn telephone conversation with him.

When she finished, she asked crossly, "Who goes strictly by initials? It's juvenile and just plain weird. Like The Artist Formerly Known as Prince."

Daniel chuckled as he stirred cream substitute into his last permitted cup of coffee for the day. "I think it adds a dash of mystery and romance."

She scoffed at that. "He's a pain in the butt."

"No doubt. Contrariness falls under the character description of a good writer. Or a bad one, for that matter."

As he contemplated the enigmatic author, Maris studied her father. *When did he get so old?* she thought with alarm. His hair had been white almost for as long as she could remember, but it had only begun to thin. Her mother, Rosemary, had been the widowed Daniel's second wife and fifteen years his junior. By the time Maris was born, he was well into middle age.

But he'd remained physically active. He watched his diet,

grudgingly but conscientiously. He'd quit smoking cigarettes years ago, although he refused to surrender his pipe. Because he had borne the responsibility of rearing her as a single parent, he had wisely slowed down the aging process as much as it was possible to do.

Only recently had the years seemed to catch up with him. To avoid aggravating an arthritic hip, he sometimes used a cane for additional support. He complained that it made him look decrepit. That was too strong a word, but secretly Maris agreed that the cane detracted from the robust bearing always associated with him. The liver spots on his hands had increased in number and grown darker. His reflexes seemed not to be as quick as even a few months ago.

But his eyes were as bright and cogent as ever when he turned to her and asked, "I wonder what all that was about?"

"All what, Dad?"

"Failing to provide a return address or telephone number. Then the telephone call this morning. His claims that the prologue was crap. Et cetera."

She left her chair and moved to a potted geranium to pluck off a dead leaf that Maxine had overlooked. Maris had urged the housekeeper to get eyeglasses, but she claimed that her eyesight was the same now as it had been thirty years ago. To which Maris had said, "Exactly. You've always been as blind as a bat and too vain to do anything about it."

Absently twirling the brown leaf by its stem, she considered her father's question. "He wanted to be sought and found, didn't he?"

She knew she'd given the correct response when Daniel beamed a smile on her. This was the method by which he had helped her with her lessons all through school. He never gave her the answers but guided her to think the question through until she arrived at the correct answer through her own deductive reasoning.

"He didn't have to call," she continued. "If he hadn't wanted to be found, he could have thrown away my telephone numbers. Instead he calls at a time of day when he's practically guaranteed to have the advantage."

"And protests too loudly and too much."

Frowning, she returned to her wrought-iron chair. "I don't know, Dad. He seemed genuinely angry. Especially about the deputy sheriff."

"He probably was, and I can't say that I blame him. But he couldn't resist the temptation to establish contact with you and hear what you had to say about his work."

"Which I think is compelling. That prologue has me wondering about the young man in the boat. Who is he? What's his story? What caused the fight between him and his friend?"

"Envy," Daniel supplied.

"Which is provocative, don't you think? Envy of what? Who envied whom?"

"I can see that the prologue served its purpose. The writer has got you thinking about it and asking questions."

"Yes, he does, damn him."

"So what are you going to do?"

"Try and establish some kind of professional dialogue. If that's possible to do with such a jerk. I don't fool myself into thinking it will be easy to work with this character."

"Do you even know his telephone number?"

"I do now. Thanks to caller ID. I checked it this morning and recognized the area code I called yesterday."

"Ah, the miracles of advanced technology. In my day—"

"In your day?" she repeated with a laugh. "It's still your day."

Reaching for his speckled hand, she patted it fondly. One day he would be gone, and she didn't know how she was going to survive that loss. She'd grown up in this house, and it hadn't been easy to leave it, even when she went away to college. Her bedroom had been on the third floor—still was if she ever wanted to use it. Daniel's bedroom was on the second floor, and he was determined to keep it there despite the pain involved in getting up and down the stairs.

Maris recalled Christmas mornings, waking up before daylight, racing down to his room and begging him to get up and go downstairs with her to see what Santa Claus had left beneath the tree.

She had thousands of happy and vivid recollections of her childhood—the two of them ice-skating in Central Park, strolling through street fairs eating hot dogs or falafel while rummaging in the secondhand book stalls, having high tea at the Plaza following a matinee, reading in front of the fireplace in his study, hosting formal dinner parties in the dining room, and sharing midnight snacks with Maxine in the kitchen. All her memories were good.

Because she had been a late-in-life only child, he had doted on her. Her mother's death could have been a heartache that wedged them apart. Instead, it had forged the bond between father and daughter. His discipline had been firm and consistent, but only rarely necessary. Generally, she had been obedient, never wanting to incur his disfavor.

The most rebellious offense she'd ever committed was to sneak out one night to meet a group of friends at a club that Daniel had placed off-limits. When she returned home in the wee hours she discovered just how vigilant a parent her father was—the kitchen window through which she had sneaked out had been locked behind her.

Forced to ring the front doorbell, she'd had to wait on the stoop for what seemed an excruciating eternity until Daniel came to let her in. He didn't yell at her. He didn't lecture. He simply told her that she must pay the consequences of making a bad choice. She'd been grounded for a month. The worst of the punishment, however, had been his disappointment in her. She never sneaked out again.

She'd been indulged but not spoiled. In exchange for spending money, she was required to do chores. Her grades were closely monitored. She was praised for doing well more frequently than she was punished for mistakes. Mostly she had been loved, and Daniel had made certain every day of her life that she knew it.

"So you think I should pursue *Envy*?" she asked him now.

"Absolutely. The author has challenged you, although he might not have done it intentionally and doesn't even realize that he has. You, Maris Matherly-Reed, can't resist a challenge." He'd practically quoted from an article recently written about her in a trade journal.

"Didn't I read that somewhere?" she teased.

"And you certainly can't resist a good book."

"I think that's why I'm so excited about this, Dad," she said, growing serious. "In my present capacity, most of my duties revolve around publishing. I work on the book once all the writing and editing have been done. And I love doing what I do.

"But I didn't realize until yesterday when I read this prologue how much I'd missed the editing process. These days I read the final, polished version of a manuscript just before I send it to production. I can't dwell on it because there are a million decisions about another dozen books that are demanding my attention. I've missed working one-on-one with an author. Helping with character development. Pointing out weaknesses in the plot. God, I love that."

"It's the reason you chose to enter publishing," Daniel remarked. "You wanted to be an editor. You were good at it. So good that you've worked your way up through the ranks until now your responsibilities have evolved away from that first love. I think it would be stimulating and fun for you to return to it."

"I think so too, but let's not jump the gun," she said wryly. "I don't know if *Envy* is worth my attention or not. The book hasn't even been written yet. My gut instinct—"

"Which I trust implicitly."

"—tells me that it's going to be good. It's got texture, which could be fleshed out even more. It's heavy on the southern overtones, which you know I love."

"Like *The Vanquished*."

Suddenly her balloon of enthusiasm burst. "Yes."

After a beat or two, Daniel asked, "How is Noah?"

As a reader, as well as his wife, she'd been massively disappointed that Noah hadn't followed his first novel with a second. Daniel knew that, so mentioning the title of Noah's single book was a natural segue into an inquiry about him.

"You know how he is, Dad. You talk to him several times a day."

"I was asking as a father-in-law, not as a colleague."

To avoid her father's incisive gaze, her eyes strayed to the building directly behind them. The ivy-covered brick wall enclosing Daniel's patio blocked her view of the neighboring building's ground floor, but she watched a tabby cat in a second-story window stretch and rub himself against the safety bars.

Maxine poked her head outside. "Can I get either of you anything?"

Daniel answered for both of them. "No, thank you. We're fine."

"Let me know."

She disappeared back inside. Maris remained quiet for a time, tracing the pattern of her linen place mat with the pad of her index finger. When she raised her head, her father had assumed the listening posture he always did when he knew there was something on her mind. His chin was cupped in his hand, his index finger lay along his cheek, pointing toward his wiry white eyebrow.

He never pried, never pressured her into talking, but always patiently waited her out. When she was ready to open up, she would, and not a moment before. It was a trait she had inherited from him.

"Noah came home very late last night," she began. Without going into detail, she gave him the gist of their argument. "We ended up lovers and friends, but I'm still upset about it."

Hesitantly Daniel asked, "Did you overreact?"

"Do you think I did?"

"I wasn't there. But it sounds to me as though Noah had a logical explanation."

"I suppose."

He frowned thoughtfully. "Are you thinking that Noah has reverted to the habits he had while living a bachelor's life?"

Knowing the admiration and respect her father had for Noah, she was reluctant to recite a litany of complaints against him, which, when spoken aloud, would probably sound like whining at best and paranoia at worst. She could also appreciate that using her father as a sounding board placed him in an awkward position. He wasn't only Noah's father-in-law, he was his employer.

Daniel had brought Noah into their publishing house three years ago because he had proved himself to be the smartest, shrewdest publisher in New York, save Daniel himself. When Maris and Noah's relationship became more social than professional, Daniel had expressed some reservations and cautioned her against an office romance. But he had given his approval when Noah, after being with Matherly Press for one year, confided in Daniel his plans to marry his daughter. He had even offered to resign in exchange for Maris's hand. Daniel wouldn't hear of it and had embraced Noah as his son-in-law with the same level of enthusiasm as he had hired him as vice president and business manager of his publishing house.

For almost two years, they had successfully managed to keep their professional and personal roles separate. Airing her wifely grievances could jeopardize the balance. Daniel wouldn't want to say too much or too little, wouldn't want to choose one side over the other or trespass into marital territory where a father-in-law didn't belong.

On the other hand, Maris needed to vent, and her father had always been her most trusted confidant. "In answer to your question, Dad, I'm not thinking anything that specific. I don't believe that Noah's having an affair. Not really."

"Something's bothering you. What?"

"Over the last few months, I don't feel like I've had Noah's full attention. I've had very little of his attention," she corrected with a rueful little laugh.

"The champagne fizz of a honeymoon doesn't last forever, Maris."

"I know that. It's just..." She trailed off, then sighed. "Maybe I'm too much a romantic."

"Don't blame yourself for this stall. It doesn't have to be anyone's fault. Marriages go through periods like this. Even good marriages. Dry spells, if you will."

"I know. I just hope he isn't getting tired of me. We're coming up on our two-year anniversary. That's got to be some kind of record for him."

"You knew his record when you married him," he reminded her gently. "He had a solid reputation as a ladies' man."

"Which I accepted because I loved him. Because I had been in love with him since I read *The Vanquished*."

"And out of all those women, Noah returned your love and chose to marry you."

She smiled wistfully, then shook her head with self-deprecation. "You're right, Dad. He did. Chalk this up to hormones. I'm feeling neglected. That's all."

"And I must assume some of the blame for that."

"What are you talking about?"

"I've vested Noah with an enormous amount of responsibility. He's doing not only his job, which, God knows, is demanding enough, but he's begun taking up the slack for me as well. I've slowed down, forcing him to accelerate. I've suggested that he hire someone to shoulder some of his duties."

"He has difficulty delegating."

"Which is why I should have *insisted* that he bring someone else on board. I'll make a point to see that he does. In the meantime, I think it would be a good idea for the two of you to go away together for a few days. Bermuda, perhaps. Get some sun. Drink too many tropical drinks. Spend a lot of time in bed."

She smiled at his candor, but it was a sad smile. He'd said practically those same words last year when he'd packed them off to Aruba for a long weekend. They'd gone in the hope of returning pregnant. Although they'd made every effort to conceive and had enjoyed trying, they hadn't been successful. Maris had been greatly disappointed. Maybe that's when she and Noah had started drifting apart, though the rift had only recently become noticeable.

Daniel sensed that he'd touched on a topic best forgotten, or at least left closed for the present. "Take some time away together, Maris," he urged. "Away from the pressures of the office, the zaniness of the city. Give yourselves a chance to get back on track."

Although she wouldn't say this to Daniel, she didn't share his confidence that spending time in bed would solve their problem and set things right. Their disagreement this morning had ended with sex, but she wouldn't call it intimacy. To her it had felt that they were doing what was most expedient to end the quarrel, that they had taken the easy way out. Their bodies had gone through the familiar motions, but their hearts weren't in it.

Noah had defused her with flattery, which, in hindsight, seemed ingratiating and patronizing. She'd been genuinely angry, which wasn't an ideal time to be told how beautiful she was.

Falling into bed together had been a graceful way to end an argument that neither had wanted to have. She hadn't wanted to accuse him further, and he hadn't wanted to address her accusations, so they'd made love instead. The implications of all that were deeply troubling.

For Daniel's benefit, she pretended to think over his suggestion of a tropical vacation, then said, "Actually, Dad, I was thinking of going away by myself for a while."

"Another good option. To the country?"

Frequently, when the city became too claustrophobic, she went to their house in rural western Massachusetts and spent long weekends catching up on paperwork and reading manuscripts. In the Berkshires, without the constant interruptions imposed on her in the office, she could concentrate and accomplish much in a relatively short period of time. It was natural for Daniel to assume that she would choose their country house for her retreat.

But she shook her head. "I think I'll go to Georgia."

* * *

Noah took it with equanimity. "I'm all for your getting away for a few days," he told her when she announced her intention to take a trip south. "A change of scenery will do you good. But what in heaven's name is in Georgia? A new spa?"

"An author."

"You'll be working? The whole point of taking a few days off is to relax, isn't it?"

"Remember the prologue I told you about yesterday?"

"The one from the slush pile?"

She ignored the skeptical slant of his grin. "I had difficulty locating the author but finally did."

"Difficulty?"

"Long story, and we've got that meeting in ten minutes.

Suffice it to say he's not your routine writer trying to get published."

"In what way is he different?"

"Recalcitrant. Rude. And unenlightened. He doesn't realize how good his writing is. He's going to need some stroking, possibly some coaching, and a great deal of coaxing. I think a face-to-face meeting will yield more than telephone calls and faxes."

Noah was listening with only one ear. He was shuffling through a stack of telephone messages that his assistant had discreetly carried in and laid in front of him before slipping out. Then, checking his wristwatch, he stood up and began gathering materials off his desk for the upcoming meeting. "I'm sorry, darling, but a continuation of this conversation will have to wait. This meeting won't keep. When do you plan to leave?"

"I thought I'd go tomorrow."

"So soon?"

"I need to know if I should get excited about this book or drop it. The only way to find out is to talk to the author."

He rounded his desk and gave her a perfunctory kiss on the cheek. "Then let's go out tonight, just the two of us. I'll have Cindy make reservations. Where would you like to go?"

"My choice?"

"Your choice."

"How about having Thai brought in? We'll eat at home for a change."

"Excellent. I'll pick the wine."

They were almost through his office door when he drew up short. "Damn! I just remembered, I have a meeting tonight."

She groaned. "With whom?"

He named an agent who represented several notable authors. "Join us. He'd be delighted. Then we can go somewhere alone for a nightcap."

"I can't be out all evening, Noah. I have things to do before I can leave town, packing included."

"I've postponed this engagement twice," he said with regret. "If I ask for another rain check, he'll think I'm avoiding him."

"No, you can't do that. How late will you be?"

He winced. "As you know, this guy likes to talk, so it might be late. Certainly later than I'd like." Sensing her disappointment, he stepped closer and lowered his voice. "I'm sorry, Maris. Do you want me to cancel?"

"No. He's an important agent."

"Had I known you planned to go away, I—"

"Excuse me, Mr. Reed," his assistant said from just beyond the doorway. "They're waiting for you and Mrs. Matherly-Reed in the conference room."

"We're coming." Once his assistant had withdrawn, he turned back to Maris. "Duty calls."

"Always."

"Forgive me?"

"Always."

He gave her a hard, quick hug. "You're the most understanding wife in the history of marriage. Is it any wonder I'm crazy about you?" He kissed her briskly, then nudged her toward the door. "After you, darling."

"Envy" Ch. 1
Eastern State University, Tennessee, 1985

Members of the fraternity thought it brilliant of their chapter founders to have designed and built their residence house to correlate with the diamond shape of the fraternity crest.

But what they attributed to genius had actually come about by happenstance.

When shopping for a lot on which to build their fraternity house, those thrifty young men in the class of 1910 had purchased the least expensive property available, a deep corner lot a few blocks from campus whose owner was eager to sell. Its appeal was not its shape or location but its price. They acquired it cheaply.

So the lot came first, not the architectural renderings. They designed a structure that would fit on their lot; they didn't choose a lot that would accommodate their design. After the fact, some members might have noticed that the house was indeed diamond-shaped like their crest, but the similarity was coincidental.

Then, in 1928, a university planning and expansion committee fortuitously decided that the main avenue bisecting the campus should be converted into a landscaped mall open only to pedestrian traffic. They rerouted motor traffic onto the street that passed in front of the unusually shaped chapter house.

Consequently, through no genius of the founders, this location at a key intersection gave the fraternity a commanding presence on campus that was coveted by every other.

The front of the three-story house faced the corner, with wings extending at forty-five-degree angles from either side of it. Between the wings in the rear of the building were a limited and insufficient number of parking spaces, basketball hoops sans baskets, overflowing trash cans, two rusty charcoal grills, and a chain-link-fence dog run that was occupied by Brew, the fraternity's chocolate Lab mascot.

The building's facade was much more imposing. The stone path leading up to the entry was lined with Bradford pear trees that blossomed snowy white each year, providing natural decoration for the fraternity's annual Spring Swing formal.

Photographs of these trees in full bloom frequently appeared on the covers of university catalogues and brochures. This bred resentment in rival fraternities. Whenever threats of chain saws circulated, pledges were ordered to post twenty-four-hour guard. Not only would the fraternity lose face on campus if their trees were cut down, their residence hall would look naked without them.

In autumn the leaves of the Bradford pears turned the vibrant ruby red they were on this particular Saturday afternoon. The campus was uncharacteristically quiet. The football team was playing an away game. Had the team been at home, the front door of the fraternity house would have been open. Music would have been blaring from it. It would be a raucous gathering place for the members, their dates, their parents, and their alums.

Game-day traffic would be backed up for miles, and because every vehicle had to pass through this crossroads to reach the stadium, the members would enjoy a front-row seat for this bumper-to-bumper parade. They'd jeer at the rival team's fans and flirt with the coeds, who flirted back and sometimes, upon a spontaneous invitation, would leave the vehicles they were in to join the party inside the house. It was documented that several romances, and a few marriages, had originated this way.

On game days, the campus was drenched in crimson. If the school color wasn't worn, it was waved. Brass and drums from the marching band echoed across campus for hours prior to kickoff. The campus was energized, hopping, festive.

But today it was practically deserted. The weather was rainy and dreary, incompatible with any sort of outdoor activity. Students were using the day to catch up on sleep, study, or laundry—things they didn't have time to do during the week.

The halls of the fraternity house, smelling dankly of beer and boys, were dim and hushed. A few members were gathered around the large-screen TV that a prosperous alum had donated to the house the year before. It was tuned to an NCAA football game on which money was riding. Occasionally either a cheer or a groan filtered up the staircases to the resident rooms on the second and third floors, but these sounds did little to compromise the sleepy quiet of the corridors.

A quiet that was punctured by, "Roark! You asshole!" followed immediately by a slamming door.

Roark dodged the wet towel hurled at his head and started laughing. "You found it?"

"Whose is it?" Todd Grayson brandished a Styrofoam cup that contained his toothbrush. Which wouldn't have been remarkable except that the cup had been used as a spittoon. The bristles of Todd's toothbrush were steeping in the viscous brown fluid in the bottom of the cup.

Roark was reclined on the three-legged sofa beneath their sleeping lofts, which were suspended from the ceiling by short chains. To maximize the small room's floor space, the lofts had been designed and constructed by the two young men in direct violation and defiance of fraternity house rules against any alteration to the structure of the building.

A couple of stacked bricks served as the sofa's fourth leg, but the eyesore was the focal point of their habitat, the "nucleus of our cell," Todd had intoned one night when he was particularly drunk. When furnishing their room, they'd found the atrocity in a junk store and bought it for ten bucks apiece. The upholstery was ripped and ratty and stained by substances that remained unidentified. The sofa had become so integral to the overall ugliness of their room, they had decided to leave it there upon their graduation as a legacy for the room's next occupants.

But Todd, who had once waxed poetic about the sofa, was so angry now that every muscle in his body was quivering. "Tell me. Whose spit cup is this?"

Roark was clutching his middle, laughing. "You don't want to know."

"Brady? If it's Brady's, swear to God I'll kill you." Brady lived down the hall. He was a terrific guy, an ideal fraternity brother, the type who, on a moment's notice and without any complaint, would come out and get you if your car broke down on a snowy night. Brady had a heart of gold. Personal hygiene, however, wasn't one of his strong suits.

"Not Brady."

"Castro? Jesus, please tell me it's not Castro's," Todd groaned. "That fucker's diseased!" The second man under consideration wasn't Cuban. His real name was Ernie Campello. He'd been dubbed Castro because of his talent for growing curly black hair, not only on his head and the lower half of his face, but all over his body. "God only knows what's crawling around in that pelt of his."

Roark laughed at that, then said, "Lisa somebody called."

The casual statement instantly doused Todd's anger. "Lisa Knowles?"

"Sounds right."

"When?"

"Five minutes ago."

"Did she leave a message?"

"Do I look like a secretary?"

"You look like an asshole with teeth. What'd she say?"

"She said you had a pencil-dick. Or did she say needle-dick? Gee, Todd, I can't remember. Sorry. But I did write down her number. It's on your desk."

"I'll call her later."

"Who is she? Is she hot?"

"Yeah, but she's seeing some Delt. She's in my North American history class and she needs notes."

"Too bad."

Todd shot his grinning roommate a dirty look, then tossed the offensive cup into their trash can. He'd been showering in the communal bathroom down the hall when Roark sneaked in and put his toothbrush in tobacco-laced sputum.

"Don't be pissed," Roark said as Todd rummaged in a bureau drawer for a pair of boxers. "It was a damn good joke and worth the expense of a new toothbrush. It was worth twice the expense."

"Are you going to tell me whose it was?"

"Don't know. Found it on a windowsill on the third floor."

"Jesus. It could be anybody's."

"That was the general idea."

"I'll get you back," Todd threatened as he pulled on a T-shirt. "I mean it. You've just screwed yourself but good, buddy."

Roark merely laughed.

"Didn't you have anything better to do? You've been lying on your ass all day."

"Gotta finish this over the weekend." Roark held up a paperback copy of *The Great Gatsby.*

Todd snorted scornfully. "The most pussy-whipped character in the history of American fiction. Want to go get something to eat?"

"Sure." Roark rolled off the sofa and shoved his feet into a pair of sneakers. As they went through the door, he and Todd ritualistically kissed their fingers and slapped them against the Playmate of the Month on their calendar. "Later, sweetheart."

* * *

It was their place. They were regulars. The moment they cleared the door of T.R.'s, T.R. himself drew them a pitcher of beer and delivered it to their booth.

"Thanks, T.R."

"Thanks, T.R."

There were no menus, but it wasn't even necessary for them to order. Knowing what they liked, T.R. waddled back behind the counter and started building their pie. It and their beer would go on their joint account, which they would pay when they got around to it. T.R. had been providing his customers with this kind of personalized service for thirty-something years.

The story was that he'd enrolled in the university as a freshman, but ended his first term by skipping finals. He used his second-semester tuition money to make a down payment on this building, which was then on the verge of being condemned. T.R. hadn't bothered to make renovations and it stood today as it had when he assumed occupancy. Engineering and architectural instructors continued to use the building as a case study for load-bearing beams.

The light fixtures were layered with generations of greasy dust. The linoleum floor was slick in some spots, gritty in others. No one dared look beneath the tables for fear of what he would find, and only in emergency situations did beer-bloated bladders seek relief in the restroom.

It wasn't much of a place, but it was an institution. Every guy on campus knew T.R.'s because it provided two basic needs of the male collegiate—cold beer and hot pizza.

By midterm, T.R. could call every customer by name, and even if the name escaped him, he knew how he liked his pizza. Todd's and Roark's never varied— thick crust, pepperoni, extra mozzarella, with a little crushed red pepper sprinkled on top.

Roark ruminatively chewed his first wonderfully cheesy bite. "You really think so?"

"Think what?"

"That Gatsby was a puss."

Todd wiped his mouth with a paper napkin from the table dispenser, took a gulp of beer. "The guy's rich. Lives like a frigging prince or something. He has everything a man could want."

"Except the woman he loves."

"Who's a selfish, self-centered airhead, borderline if not full-fledged neurotic, who continually craps on him."

"But Daisy represents to Gatsby what his money couldn't buy. The unattainable."

"Respectability?" Todd lifted another slice of pizza from the bent metal platter and took a bite. "With his money, why should he give a shit whether or not he's accepted? He paid the ultimate price for an ideal." Shaking his head, he added, "Not worth it."

"Hmm." More or less agreeing, Roark drank from his frosted mug. They discussed the merits of Gatsby, then of Fitzgerald's work in general, which brought them around to their own literary aspirations.

Roark asked, "How're you coming on your manuscript?"

A novel of seventy thousand words, minimum, was their senior project, their capstone prior to receiving a bachelor of arts degree. The one obstacle standing between them and graduation was the scourge of every creative writing student, Professor Hadley.

Todd frowned. "Hadley's up my ass about characterization."

"Specifically?"

"They're cardboard cutouts, he says. No originality, spontaneity, depth, blah, blah, blah."

"He says that about everybody's characters."

"Yours included?"

"I haven't had my critique yet," Roark replied. "Next Tuesday, bright and early, eight o'clock. I'll be lucky to escape with my life."

The two young men had met in a required composition class their first semester as freshmen. The instructor was a grad student, who they later decided didn't know his dick from a dangling participle. The first week of class, he assigned a five-page essay based on John Donne's *Devotions.*

Taking himself far too seriously, the instructor had assumed a professorial stance and tone. "You may not be entirely familiar with the text, but surely you'll recognize the phrase 'for whom the bells toll.' "

"Excuse me, sir." Todd raised his hand and innocently corrected him. "Is that the same as 'for whom the bell tolls'?"

Recognizing a kindred spirit, Roark introduced himself to Todd after class. Their friendship was established that afternoon. A week later, they negotiated a swap with the roommates the university had randomly assigned them. "Suits me," Roark's grumbled when they proposed the idea to him. He gave Todd a word of warning. "He pecks on that goddamn typewriter twenty-four hours a day."

They received the two highest grades in the class

on that first writing assignment. "The jerk wouldn't dare award an A," Roark sourly observed. Scrawled on the cover of his blue book was a large B+.

"At least you got the plus sign after yours," Todd remarked of his B.

"You would have if you hadn't been a smart-ass that first day. That really pissed him off."

"Fuck him. When I write the Great American Novel, he'll still be grading freshmen writing assignments."

"Ain't gonna happen," Roark deadpanned. Then he flashed a wide white smile. "Because *I'm* going to write the Great American Novel."

Love of books and the desire to write them was the foundation on which their friendship was built. It was a few years before cracks were discovered in that foundation. And by the time those fissures were discovered, massive damage had already been done and it was too late to prevent the structure's total collapse.

They were well-rounded students, maintaining good grades in the required subjects, but excelling in the language arts. Their second semester, they pledged the same fraternity. They were avid sports enthusiasts and good athletes. They played on their fraternity football and basketball teams, sometimes competing with each other as avidly as with rival teams.

They were active and well-known on campus. Todd was elected to the Student Congress. Roark organized a campus-wide food drive to benefit a homeless shelter. Both wrote occasional editorials, articles, and human interest stories for the student newspaper.

After one of his stories was published, Roark was approached by the dean of the journalism school. He was highly complimentary of Roark's work and asked him to consider switching the focus of his endeavors from creative writing to journalism. Roark declined. Fiction was his first love.

Roark never told Todd about that conversation, but he celebrated when Todd won first place in a national collegiate fiction-writing competition. Roark's submission hadn't even earned an honorable mention. He tried to conceal his jealousy.

They caroused and partied with their fraternity brothers. They drank enough beer to float a fleet. Occasionally they shared a joint, but they didn't make a habit of it and never tried hard drugs. They nursed one another's hangovers, loaned each other money during temporary financial crises, and when Roark contracted strep throat and his temperature shot up to one hundred and three, it was Todd who rushed him to the campus infirmary.

When Todd was notified of his father's sudden death, Roark drove him home across two state lines, and then stayed on through the funeral to lend the emotional support his friend needed.

Disagreements arose now and then. Once, when Roark borrowed Todd's car, he backed into a fireplug and dented the rear fender. Todd asked several times when he planned to have it repaired. He asked so frequently that it became a touchy subject.

"Will you get off my goddamn back about that?" Roark snapped.

"Will you fix my goddamn car?"

That heated exchange was the extent of the disagreement. Roark took the car to be repaired the following day, and Todd never mentioned it again.

And then there was the case of the missing Pat Conroy.

Roark drove to a bookstore in Nashville and stood in line for over two hours to meet the author and obtain a signed copy of *The Great Santini.* He admired Conroy more than any other contemporary novelist and nearly embarrassed himself when Conroy wished him good luck with his own writing pursuits. The autographed book was his most prized possession.

Todd asked to borrow it. He claimed that when he finished reading it, he replaced it in Roark's bookshelf. It never turned up, not even when Roark practically tore their room apart searching for it.

What happened to the book remained a mystery. They eventually stopped arguing about it, but Roark never loaned Todd a book again, and Todd never asked to borrow one.

They were good-looking, each in his own way, so there was never a shortage of girls. When they weren't talking about books, chances were very good that the subject was women. If one of them got lucky and a young lady stayed over, the other bunked down in a neighboring room.

One morning after a young lady had taken the "walk of shame" down the hallway of the fraternity house on her way out, Todd looked over at Roark and said morosely, "She wasn't all that hot, was she?"

Roark shook his head. "Last night you were looking at her through beer goggles."

"Yeah," Todd sighed. Then with a sly smile he added, "But it all feels good in the dark, doesn't it?"

They talked about women tirelessly and shamelessly, unabashedly adhering to the double standard. Only Roark came close to having a serious relationship, and only once.

He met her during his food drive. She had volunteered to help. She had a beautiful smile and a slender, athletic body. She was a smart and conscientious student and could converse intelligently on any number of subjects. But she also had a good sense of humor and laughed at his jokes. She was an excellent listener who focused on the topic when it turned to something serious. She taught him how to play "Chopsticks" on the piano, and he persuaded her to read *The Grapes of Wrath*.

She was a passionate kisser, but that's as far as she would go. She clung to a strict moral code, founded on her religion, and she didn't intend to break it. She hadn't in high school with her longtime sweetheart, and she wasn't going to until she knew she was with the man she would marry and grow old with.

Roark admired her for it, but it was damned frustrating.

Then she called him one night and said she had just finished reading the Steinbeck classic, and if he wasn't busy, she would like to see him. He picked her up, they went for a drive, then parked.

She had loved the classic novel and thanked him for sharing it with her. Her kisses that night were more passionate than ever. She raised her sweater and pressed his hand against her bare breast. And if caressing her and feeling her response wasn't the most physically gratifying sexual experience Roark had ever had, it was certainly the most meaningful. She was sacrificing something of herself to him, and he was sensitive enough to realize it.

He wondered if he was falling in love.

A week later, she dumped him. He was tearfully informed that she was resuming the relationship with her high school sweetheart. He was dumbfounded and not a little angry. "Do I at least get to ask why?"

"You're going to be somebody great, Roark. Famous. I know it. But I'm just a simple girl from small-town Tennessee. I'll teach elementary school for a couple of years, maybe, then become a mother and the president of the PTA."

"There's nothing wrong with that."

"Oh, I'm not apologizing for it. It's the life I choose, the life I want. But it's not the life for you."

"Why do we have to plan the rest of our lives now?" he argued. "Why can't we hold off making major decisions and just continue to spend time together, enjoy each other, wait and see what happens?"

"Because if I continue seeing you, I'll sleep with you."

"Would that be so terrible?"

"Not at all terrible. It would be..." She kissed him deeply, her sweet mouth tugging on his with the restrained passion he had come to expect. "I want to," she whispered against his lips. "I want to so bad. But I made a pledge of abstinence. I can't break it. So I can't see you anymore."

To his mind, that was totally irrational, but she would not be dissuaded. He was depressed and testy for weeks. Todd, sensing that the budding romance had suddenly withered and died, walked on eggshells around him.

Finally, however, he'd had all the moodiness he could stand. "Christ, get over it already." He insisted that the only cure for one woman was another woman. He practically dragged Roark from their room. They got drunk and got laid that night.

Roark wasn't "cured," but eventually he came

around because he had no choice. And, in retrospect, everything she had said was right. Maybe not the part about his guaranteed greatness. That remained to be seen. But regarding everything else, she had been inordinately insightful.

At the end of the semester, she transferred to a college nearer her hometown, where the boyfriend was attending. Roark wished her well and told her that her sweetheart was the luckiest bastard on the planet. She blushed, thanked him for the compliment, and said she would be watching for his name in print.

"I'll buy a dozen copies of your books and distribute them to all my friends, and boast that I once dated the great Roark Slade."

That was as close as either he or Todd came to having a serious romantic entanglement. But women consumed their thoughts and fueled their lusts, and on that rainy Saturday evening, it was a girl that brought to a close their conversation about Professor Hadley's grueling, demoralizing critiques.

A pair of coeds were actually brave—or brazen—enough to enter the testosterone-charged sanctum of T.R.'s just as Roark was advising Todd to deflect Hadley's comments. "After all, they're just his opinion."

Todd, who was facing the door, changed the subject by saying, "Well, it's my opinion that that is one hot chick."

Roark glanced over his shoulder at the two girls. "Which one?"

"Blue sweater. Packing Tic Tacs." That was their coded reference to evident nipple projection.

"She's hot, all right," Roark agreed.

Todd grinned at her and she grinned back.

Roark said, "Hey, Christie."

"Oh, Roark, hi." Her drawl stretched the single-syllable words into roughly three apiece. "How are you?"

"Great. You?"

"Couldn't be better."

When Roark came back around, Todd was swearing into his beer mug. "You son of a bitch. I might've known."

Roark merely smiled and sipped his beer.

Todd continued to ogle. "She's a fox. I don't remember you ever going out with her."

"We didn't go out."

"Casual acquaintance?"

"Something like that."

"My ass," Todd scoffed. "You got on her."

"I—"

"Didn't you?"

"Maybe. Once. I think. We might've just mugged during a party."

The girls were now receiving instruction from several other customers on how to line up a pool shot. The lesson required bending over the billiard table, which provided Todd an anatomical perspective of Christie that actually caused him to moan. "Damn."

"Try not to drool, okay?" Roark admonished. "It's embarrassing."

He slid from the booth and approached the laughing group. The other men eyed him resentfully when he took Christie's elbow and steered her toward the booth. "Christie, Todd, my roommate. Todd, this is Christie."

Roark ushered her into his side of the booth, so that they were seated across from Todd. "Hi, Christie."

"Hi."

"Would you like a beer?"

"Love one."

Todd signaled T.R. to bring another pitcher and a third mug. "Pizza?"

"No, thanks."

Roark waited through the pouring of the beer before saying to Christie, "Listen, this is a bitch, but I gotta split. Are you okay with me leaving you in Todd's company? He's fairly harmless."

Her pout could have sold a million tubes of L'Oréal lipstick—to men. "It's Saturday night, Roark," she whined. "Where do you hafta go?"

"I left Gatsby, Daisy, and the gang waiting on me. I need to get back to them." He tilted his head toward Todd. "If he gets out of line, let me know. I'll knock him around for you."

She glanced flirtatiously at Todd. "I can handle him just fine."

"I bet you can," Todd said, bobbing his eyebrows. "Anytime, sweetheart."

Roark left her giggling over the innuendo. It was hours later before he returned to his and Todd's room. After listening at the door for several moments, he knocked tentatively.

"Huh?"

"Okay if I come in?"

"Yeah."

Todd was alone in his loft, lying on his back, one bare leg and foot dangling over the side. He looked completely done-in but managed to mumble, "Thanks for keeping your distance. Where've you been all this time?"

"The library."

"How's Gatsby?"

"No more pussy-whipped than you, ol'boy. When did Christie leave?"

"About ten minutes ago. Your timing was perfect."

"Happy to oblige."

"You know, she actually asked if they were friends of yours."

"Who?"

"That's what I asked. And she said, 'Those people waiting for him.' "

"You're kidding."

"Nope. Never heard of Gatsby. But who the hell cares? She fucks like she invented it."

Roark crossed to the window and opened it. "Smells like sex in here."

"Oh, before I forget, our favorite professor called and left you a message."

"Hadley?"

"Said he has a conflict at eight, so he bumped your appointment up to nine o'clock Tuesday morning."

"Fine by me. I won't have to get up so early."

Todd yawned and turned toward the wall. "Thanks again for Christie. She was something else. G'night."

Chapter 5

F ollowing the meeting that she and Noah had been required to attend, Maris went home from the office alone.

There was a moment, while she was getting mail from their box, that she was tempted to ask the night-duty doorman if he had noticed what time Noah had come in that morning, but she couldn't think of a way to ask without embarrassing both of them, especially herself.

She had a Thai dinner delivered. As she ate, she reviewed the revisions an author had made to her manuscript, signed off on them, and marked the manuscript ready to go to a copy editor.

She checked her calendar one final time to make certain that she and her assistant hadn't overlooked an appointment that needed to be rescheduled. She had blocked out the remainder of the week for her trip to Georgia, which might be a tad optimistic considering that the author hadn't been notified of her pending visit.

But in this instance, begging forgiveness was preferable to asking permission. She had to be assertive. With him, her approach must be proactive and aggressive. Timidity wouldn't make a dent. Rearranging her busy schedule and making travel arrangements had cemented her determination to go and see him whether or not he was agreeable.

Having put off for as long as possible the unpleasant chore of alerting him to her arrival, she dialed the number that had appeared on her caller ID machine that morning. The telephone rang four times before it was answered.

"Yeah?"

"This is Maris Matherly-Reed."

"Jesus."

"No, Maris Matherly-Reed."

He said nothing to that, not even a cranky *What do you want?* although his hostile silence spoke volumes.

"I was thinking..." She halted. Wrong tack. *Give him no outs, Maris, not even wiggle room.* "I'm coming to St. Anne Island to see you," she declared.

"I beg your pardon?"

"I was speaking English, wasn't I? Which part didn't you understand?"

After a moment, he made a gruff sound that could have passed for a laugh. "That's two. You're on a roll tonight."

"Well, I try."

"So you're coming to St. Anne."

"Yes, I am."

"I gotta warn you, it's different from what you're used to. Folks like you—"

"Folks like me?"

"—usually vacation on the more developed islands. Hilton Head. St. Simons. Amelia."

"This isn't a vacation trip."

"No?"

"I'm coming to talk to you."

"We've talked."

"Not face-to-face."

"What've we got to talk about? The flora and fauna of Georgia's sea islands?"

"Your book."

"I've already told you that my book isn't for sale."

"You also told me that there is no book. Which is it?" She had trapped him. His stony silence indicated that he knew it. "I'll be arriving tomorrow evening."

"It's your money."

"Could you recommend a—" She was talking to a dead line. He'd hung up on her. Stubbornly she dialed him back.

"Yeah?"

"I was asking if you could recommend a hotel in Savannah?"

When he hung up on her again, Maris laughed. As her father had said, he was protesting too loudly and too much. Little did Mr. P.M.E. know that the more he balked, the more determined she became.

She had just slid her suitcase from beneath the bed to begin packing when the telephone rang. She expected it to be the author. He'd probably invented some very good reasons why it was inconvenient or impossible for him to see her when she arrived tomorrow.

Bracing herself for a barrage of excuses, she answered with a cheerful, "Hello." To her surprise, a man with a broad Brooklyn accent asked to speak with Noah. "I'm sorry, he isn't here."

"Well, I gotta know what to do with this key."

"Key?"

"We don't make house calls after hours, ya know. Only, see, Mr. Reed give me twenty extra bucks to get it here tonight. You his ol' lady?"

"Are you sure you have the right Noah Reed?"

"Deals with books or something?"

"Yes, that's my husband."

"Well, he give me this address in Chelsea, said—"

"What address?"

He recited an address on West Twenty-second. "Apartment three B. He axed me to change out the lock yesterday, on account of he'd already moved some stuff in there and didn't want old keys floating 'round, ya know? Only I didn't bring an extra key yesterday, and he said he needed at least one extra. So I tole him he'd have it tonight.

"I'm here with the key, but the super's out for the evening. There's a note on his door, says call, but a call ain't gonna help me, is it? I don't trust leaving a key to Mr. Reed's apartment with the neighbors. You never know about people, am I right?"

"What kind of stuff?"

"Huh?"

"You said some stuff had already been moved into the apartment."

"Stuff. Furniture. You know, the kinda stuff rich folks have in their places. Rugs and pictures and shit. Could I afford nice stuff like that? Forget about it. All I know is, I'm ready to get my butt home and in my lounger on account of the Mets game. Only I don' wanna offend Mr. Reed. He give me twenty extra—"

"Bucks. So you said. I'll give you twenty more if you'll wait for me. I'll be there in fifteen minutes."

Maris left her building and practically ran the two blocks to the subway station at Seventy-second and Broadway. A taxi would take too long to get downtown. She wanted to see sooner rather than later the nice stuff that Noah had moved into an apartment in Chelsea that she knew nothing about. She wanted to learn sooner rather than later why he needed an extra apartment. And she wanted to know for whom he was having an extra key made.

* * *

Ivy clung to the old brick, contributing warmth and charm to the building's exterior. Flowers bloomed in window boxes on either side of the narrow stoop, which was separated from street level by eight steps. The block was lined with similar buildings that had been quaintly refurbished by urbanites trying to create a neighborhood feel and recapture the spirit of a kinder, gentler, bygone New York.

The leaded glass entrance door was unlocked. The locksmith was waiting for Maris in the foyer. Somehow he had managed to zip a khaki jumpsuit over a belly that extended a good two feet beyond his chest. "Who buzzed you in?" she asked him after introducing herself.

"I ain't a locksmith for nothin'," he said with a snort. "Only, truth be told, it wasn't locked. Too hot to wait outside. I was sweating like a pig."

The air-conditioning was cooling her own damp skin, a dampness she attributed to being in close confines with other sticky passengers on the subway train. The stations were notorious for being drafty and frigid in the winter and completely airless in the summer. But she was also sweating anxiously over what she would find on the third floor in Apartment B.

"You wanna settle up with me?"

She looked at him quizzically, then remembered the promised twenty dollars. After paying him, she asked for the key.

"I gotta check it out first," he told her. "It ain't as easy as people think, making keys. I never leave one with a customer before seeing if it works okay."

"All right."

"There ain't no elevator. We gotta climb."

She nodded for him to precede her up the staircase. "Why didn't you just go up, test the key, and then leave it in the apartment? Wouldn't the door have locked behind you when you left?"

"Not the deadbolt. Besides, that's all I need," he said, speaking to her over his shoulder as they rounded the second-floor landing. "Something turns up missing, I'm the first one accused of stealing."

"I doubt that."

"I ain't taking no chances goin' into a man's apartment when he ain't there. Forget about it."

He was huffing and puffing by the time they reached the third level. As he approached the door, he withdrew the spare key from the pocket of his jumpsuit and slipped it into the lock. "Pouyfect," he said as he swung open the door. Then he stood aside and motioned for Maris to go in. "The light switch is there on your right."

She felt for the switch and flipped it on.

"Surprise!"

The shout went up from fifty or so people, all of whom she recognized. Her mouth dropped open like a trapdoor. She pressed a hand to her lurching heart. Everyone was laughing over her dumbfounded expression.

Noah separated himself from the others and came toward her, grinning from ear to ear. He embraced her tightly, then soundly kissed her mouth. "Happy anniversary, darling."

"B-but our anniversary isn't until—"

"I know when it is. But you always catch on to my attempted surprises. This year I thought I'd get the jump on you. Judging by your reaction, I'd say I was successful." He looked beyond her shoulder and addressed the locksmith. "You were terrific."

As it turned out, he was an actor hired to play the role. "You had me convinced that I was about to catch my cheating husband," Maris told him.

"Happy anniversary, Mrs. Reed," he said in a voice that resonated with the Queen's English. It was explained to her later that his most notable role was Falstaff. Now he reached for her hand and kissed the back of it. "Enjoy your special evening."

"Don't go. Stay and enjoy the party." She prevailed upon him, and he accepted her invitation.

"It's okay, isn't it?" she asked Noah when the actor joined the other guests in line at the buffet.

"Whatever makes you happy, darling."

"Whose apartment is this?"

"That part of his dialogue was true. It's mine."

"It really is?"

"Whose did you think it was?"

"I—"

"You need some champagne."

"But Noah—"

"You'll get a full explanation later. I promise."

After seeing to it that she had a brimming flute of bubbly, he maneuvered her through the crowd to greet their guests, which included most of the editorial staff of Matherly Press. Many remarked on how difficult it had been to keep the secret. One confessed to almost asking her what she was going to wear. "Noah would have killed me if I'd spoiled the surprise."

"And look what I turned out in," Maris groaned. "A wrinkled business suit and a shiny face. I didn't know I was coming to a party."

"I would kill to look like you on your worst day," the woman said.

Among the guests were also a handful of local authors with whom Maris worked, and friends whose careers were in other areas entirely, including an anesthesiologist and her husband who taught chemistry at NYU, a stockbroker, and a movie producer who had turned one of the books Maris had edited into a gripping feature film.

Then the crowd parted to reveal Daniel. He was seated with one hand resting on the engraved silver head of his cane while the other was saluting her with a glass of champagne.

"Dad!"

"Anniversary wishes a few weeks early, sweetheart."

"I can't believe you were in on this!" She bent down to kiss his cheek, which glowed with a champagne flush. "You gave nothing away this morning."

"Which was hard, considering the topic of our conversation." His meaningful look reminded her of the marital concerns she had shared with him.

Feeling her own cheeks grow warm with embarrassment, she said softly, "This explains why Noah has been distracted lately. I feel like a fool now."

"Don't," Daniel ordered, his brows lowering sternly. "A fool is someone who ignores warning signs."

She kissed him again quickly before being pulled away to mingle. Noah had done an outstanding job, not only of putting over the surprise, but of planning a wonderful party. The chef of her favorite restaurant had prepared the food and was on hand to see that it was properly served. Champagne was poured liberally. The music got louder as the evening progressed, and, although it was a weeknight, guests stayed late. Eventually, however, they said their good nights.

Daniel was the last to leave. "Age has its benefits," he told Maris and Noah at the door. "Not many, mind you, but a few. One is that you can get tipsy on a weeknight and sleep late in the morning because there's nowhere you absolutely must be."

Maris hugged him exuberantly. "I love you, Dad. And I learn something new about you every day."

"For instance?"

"That you're damn good at keeping secrets."

"Watch your language, young lady, or I'll have Maxine wash your mouth out with soap."

"It wouldn't be for the first time," she said with a laugh. After another hug, she asked Daniel if he could manage the stairs all right.

"I got up here, didn't I?" he growled querulously.

"Sorry I asked." Even so, she motioned for Noah to accompany Daniel down. "Is a car waiting to take him home?"

"It's at the curb," Noah assured her. "I've already checked."

"Good. Dad, remember I'll have my cell phone with me in Georgia. I told Maxine to call—"

"And she will, the old busybody. Get me out of here, Noah. Please. Before Maris decides I'm ready for adult diapers."

Noah guided him down the hallway toward the staircase. "I'll be right back, darling," he called to Maris. "I haven't given you your present yet."

"There's more?"

"Just wait. And no snooping!"

Now that the apartment was empty of guests, she could see it well for the first time. Tall windows on the far wall of the living room overlooked the rooftop garden on the next building. The "stuff" was nice, but not as pricy as the "locksmith" had implied. There were pictures on the walls, and an area rug beneath the seating arrangement of chairs and sofas, but the emphasis was on functionality and comfort.

The galley kitchen was narrow, even by New York standards. Off the living room, a closed door led to what she assumed was a bedroom. She was making her way toward that door when hands seized her around the waist.

"I thought I told you not to snoop," Noah said, nuzzling her ear.

"I didn't know that I was. When are you going to tell me why you leased this apartment?"

"In good time. Be patient."

"Is my present behind door number one?"

"Let's take a look." He walked her toward the door. "You may open it now."

The room was a small cubicle, but a generous window made it appear larger. It was furnished with a desk, a leather swivel chair, and shelves only partially filled with books. It was further equipped with a telephone, a computer and printer, and a fax machine. A yellow legal tablet lay on the desk beside a metal pencil holder filled with sharpened pencils.

Maris took in every detail, then turned and looked at Noah.

He laid his hands on her shoulders and massaged them gently. "I know you've wondered about the late hours I've been keeping, as well as the unaccounted-for time I've spent away from home and office."

"I confess."

"I apologize for causing you to worry. I wanted this place to be completely set up before you saw it. It's taken me weeks to get it ready. Months, if you factor in the time I spent searching for a suitable space."

"A suitable space for what?"

"Well, not for conducting the illicit affair you thought I was having."

She lowered her eyes. "Again, I confess."

"With Nadia?"

"She topped the list of suspects."

"Maris," he said reproachfully.

She tossed her head back and shook out her hair, as though freeing herself of a burden. "God, I'm glad it's not that."

"Feel better?"

"Immeasurably. But, if this apartment wasn't designated as a love nest, what did you lease it for?"

He ducked his head in what could only be described as shyness. "Writing."

"Writing?" she repeated on a thin breath.

"That's your anniversary present. I've begun writing again."

For several moments she was too stunned to speak, then she threw herself against him. "Noah! That's wonderful. When? What made you... You always get so defensive whenever I mention it. Oh, I'm thrilled. Thrilled!"

She rained kisses over his face. He laughed and indulged her enthusiasm. Finally he set her away, keeping her at arm's length. "Don't get carried away. I'll probably fail miserably."

"You won't," she said adamantly. "I don't believe for a moment that you're the one-book wonder you fear you are. The author of *The Vanquished*—"

"Which I wrote years ago, Maris, when I was full of passion, a young man with stars in his eyes."

"And *talent*," she stressed. "Talent like yours isn't depleted by one book, Noah. It doesn't simply disappear. On the contrary, I think it ripens with age and experience."

"We'll see." He glanced at the computer dubiously. "In any case, I'm willing to test your theory. I'm going to give it a shot."

"You're not just doing it for me, are you?"

"I couldn't do it just for you. Writing is damn hard work. It's borderline masochistic. If your heart's not in it, you're doomed before you start." He rubbed his knuckles against her jaw. "This is something I want to do. Very much. And if it pleases you, that's a bonus."

"It pleases me very much. I couldn't be more pleased." She hugged him tightly, then kissed him with more heat than she could remember feeling for a long time.

As their lips clung, Noah slipped off his jacket. Her heart quickened. The surroundings were unfamiliar and untried. It would feel a shade illicit if they made love in this new apartment, on the sofa, on the rug. Hell, on the desk. Why not? They were grown-ups.

She slid her hands up his chest and began working on the knot of his necktie. But he moved her aside, sat down at the keyboard, and booted up the computer.

"I'm so anxious to get started."

"*Now?*"

He swiveled his chair around and looked up at her, grinning sheepishly. "Do you mind? It's taken me weeks to set up my new playground, but I haven't had time to play in it. I barely got the finishing touches put on this afternoon before the chef and waiters arrived. I'd like to install my software and maybe jot down a few notes. I've been toying with an idea. I'm afraid if I don't commit it to paper, it'll vanish. Do you mind if I work awhile?"

She forced herself to smile. "No. Of course not. Not at all."

There wasn't to be a romantic conclusion to the evening, and that was disappointing. But, fairly, she couldn't complain. This was what she had wanted. This was what she had been encouraging him to do for years.

"I'll say good-bye and leave you to your work."

"You don't have to go, Maris. You can hang around if you like."

She shook her head. "I don't want to be a distraction. Besides, I need to go home and pack for my trip."

He took her hand and kissed the palm. "Will you be all right hailing a cab?"

"Don't be silly. Of course." She leaned on the arms of his desk chair, bringing her face down to the level of his. "It was a lovely surprise party, Noah. Thank you for everything, but especially for this. I can't wait to read your next novel. Look what happened after I read the first one."

As they kissed, his hand followed the curve of her hip down to the back of her thigh. When she withdrew, he continued to stroke her leg. "On second thought, maybe I'll postpone starting until tomorrow."

She aimed her finger at the computer keyboard. "Plot!"

* * *

Fifteen minutes later, Noah let himself into another apartment. It was half a block away—seventy-seven steps, to be exact—from the one where he had set up an office he planned never to use. He dropped his key onto the console table in the short entry hall and moved into the living area, where he drew up short.

"I started without you," Nadia said.

"So I see."

She was lying on the sofa, one foot on the floor, naked except for a royal blue silk robe that lay open. Her eyes were half closed. Her hand was rhythmically moving between her thighs. "I'm close. You'd better hurry if you want to get in on this one."

He sauntered over to the sofa, reached down, and fingered her stiff nipple. It was enough to make her come. Smiling as he watched, Noah continued tweaking her until her arching body had squeezed every bit of pleasure it could from the orgasm, then relaxed and resettled into the sofa cushions.

"You're shameless, Nadia."

"I know." She raised her arms above her head and stretched. "Isn't it delicious?"

He began undressing. "The surprise party was a stroke of genius. Maris is now completely defused."

"Ooh, tell me."

"She admitted to harboring a suspicion that I was having an extramarital affair."

"And who, pray tell, was the suspected correspondent?"

He gave her a look that caused her to purr with wicked satisfaction.

Continuing his account, he said, "Now that my wife has seen my writer's retreat, which made her positively misty, I can use it as an excuse to get away at any time of day or night."

"For this."

"Definitely for this. Along with the other business in which we're involved."

"Maris is only half the problem, though. What about Daniel?"

"He's an old man, Nadia. In his dotage."

"He'll never sell Matherly Press. He's gone on record a thousand times."

Nonchalantly Noah pulled his belt through the loops of his trousers and lightly spanked her thigh with it. "Not to worry, my dear. I'll have Matherly Press sold before either of them knows what's what. Maris is hot for a new author she's discovered in her slush pile. That'll keep her distracted. Daniel has virtually retired, entrusting the company's business dealings almost entirely to me. The first they hear of the pending sale will probably be when they read about it in *Publishers Weekly,* and then it'll be too late to stop it. I'll have Daniel's position and all the benefits that go with it, along with ten thousand shares of WorldView stock in my portfolio, and a cool ten million in my bank account."

"And the Matherlys will be left with only each other."

"I suppose. I really couldn't care less."

He stepped out of his trousers and underwear. Nadia's eyes widened with appreciation for his jutting penis. "Is Maris responsible for that? Remind me to thank her."

"Nothing to thank her for."

"You didn't get any tonight?"

"This morning."

"I thought tonight's party was an anniversary celebration."

"Maris has her way of celebrating, and I have mine."

Laughing, she encircled his penis with her hand and stroked it. "Sometime you must tell me all about it."

"Nothing much to tell."

She rolled her thumb over the smooth bulb. "Miss Maris doesn't fuck dirty?"

"Miss Maris doesn't fuck." He knelt between Nadia's thighs and pushed them wider apart. "She makes love."

"How sweet."

"That's what I like about you, Nadia."

"There's a lot you like about me. You'll have to be more specific."

He jammed himself inside her. "You're never sweet."

Chapter 6

The roads on St. Anne Island were banked on either side by woods that were deeper and darker than any Maris had seen in the Berkshires near their country house, deeper and darker than any she had seen anywhere. They were as deep and dark as the menacing forests described in a story written by the Brothers Grimm.

The undergrowth was dense and the trees were towering, making the shadows beneath them impenetrable. Occasionally the rustling of leaves in the thick brush alerted her to the presence of animals, the species and level of danger to human beings unknown. Afraid of what she might see if she looked too closely, she felt safer keeping her eyes fixed on the road.

She had arrived later than anticipated. Stormy weather in Atlanta had delayed her connecting flight to Savannah for three hours. By the time she checked into a hotel and made arrangements for transportation to the island, the sun was setting. The sea island would have been alien territory to her in broad daylight, but the gloaming exaggerated its strangeness and lent it a sinister quality that filled her with misgivings.

As she chugged along in her rented golf cart, she felt extremely vulnerable. The menacing woods intimidated her. They were as unfriendly as the man at the landing from whom she had rented the golf cart.

When she asked him for directions to the home of the local writer, he had responded with a question of his own. "Whada ya want with 'im?"

"Do you know him?"

"Yeah."

"Do you know where he lives?"

"Sure do."

"Can you give me directions, please? He's expecting me."

He looked her up and down. "Is that right?"

She'd unfolded the crude map of the island, given to her by the pilot of the small boat she had hired to bring her over from the mainland. "I'm here, right?" She indicated on the map the landing where the boatman had docked only long enough for her to disembark. "Which way do I go from here?"

"Well, there's only one road leading outta here, ain't there?"

"I can see that," she said with strained patience. "But according to the map the main road branches off in three directions. Here." She pointed out the marking to him.

"You ain't from around here, are you? You from up north someplace?"

"What difference does it make?"

He had snorted a derisive sound and spat tobacco juice into the dirt, then a stained, chipped fingernail traced the fork she should take. "You go along, hmm, 'bout three-quarters of a mile beyond the split. A turnoff to the left takes you straight to the house. If you wind up in the 'lantic, you've done went too far." His grin revealed large gaps where teeth should have been.

She had thanked him curtly and set out on the final leg of her trip. The landing's "commercial district" was limited to two places of business—the cart rental, and Terry's Bar and Grill. So read a hand-painted sign nailed above a screened door.

Terry's was a circular structure with a corrugated tin roof. The top two-thirds of the exterior walls were screened, but the interior lighting was so dim that all Maris could see was the glow of neon beer signs on the far wall and light fixtures hanging from the ceiling, the kind usually suspended above pool tables. Several vehicles, mostly pickup trucks, were parked at one side of the building. Recorded music emanated through the screened walls.

Out front, a man, presumably Terry, was cooking meat on a large grill while sipping from his longneck bottle of beer. Even after she drove past, she could feel his eyes boring holes in her back until she rounded a bend in the road and was no longer in sight.

She had the road all to herself. No cars or trucks had passed. It seemed the dock was the last outpost of civilization. Having endured this harrowing—and she felt that was a fair adjective— journey, she wished she could look forward to being graciously received when she arrived at the author's home. Unfortunately, her expectations of how she would be greeted were very low.

Eventually she detected salt air over the dominant scent of evergreens. Realizing that the beach couldn't be much farther, she began looking for the turnoff, but when she reached it, she overshot it. There was no sign to mark it. It was so narrow and so well camouflaged by foliage that had she not been specifically looking for it, she would have missed it altogether.

Executing a tight U-turn, she steered the cart into the lane. The roadbed was rougher than the main road. The cart jounced over potholes. Tree branches formed an opaque canopy overhead. The forest here was even thicker, more silent, more foreboding.

She was beginning to think that this venture was foolhardy, that she should be sensible and retreat to the safety of her hotel room in gracious and hospitable Savannah. She could have a room-service meal, a bubble bath, a glass of wine from the mini bar. Thus restored, she could call and try to persuade the author to meet her on neutral turf.

But then she caught her first glimpse of the house and was instantly enchanted.

It was beautiful. Poignantly so. Beautiful in the way that evokes sadness. An aging film star whose once-gorgeous face now evinced the passage of decades. An antique wedding dress, its lace now yellowed and tattered. A gardenia whose creamy petals had turned brown. The house showed visible signs of former grandeur now lost.

But with its obvious flaws softened by the waning light, it was as lovely as a watercolor painted from a faded but fond memory.

Maris stepped out of the cart and followed a pathway marked by twin rows of spectacular, moss-shrouded live oaks. She climbed the steps as soundlessly as possible. When she reached the veranda, she had a silly urge to tiptoe across it as Jem Finch had done in *To Kill a Mockingbird,* so as not to alert the spooky Boo Radley to his presence in a place where he was a trespasser, where he didn't belong, and where he wasn't welcome.

Instead she bolstered herself with a deep breath and walked boldly to the front door and reached for the brass knocker.

"Maris Matherly-Reed?"

Startled, she jumped. The knocker dropped against the metal plate on the door with a loud clatter. Following the direction from which the unexpected voice had come, she stepped back and looked down the long veranda. A face was peering at her through one of the tall front windows.

"So," he said, "you really came."

"Hello."

He continued to stare at her through the screen, putting her at a distinct disadvantage. She was aware that he could see her much more clearly than she could see him, but she stood her ground. She had come this far.

Finally he said, "Come on in."

She pushed open the glossy black front door and stepped into a wide foyer. He emerged from one of the rooms opening off it, wiping his hands on a stained rag. He was dressed in khaki shorts and an ordinary chambray work shirt, the sleeves rolled up to his elbows. Both articles of clothing were rather baggy and as stained as the rag. On his feet he wore a pair of sneakers that had seen better days.

He glanced beyond her. "You came alone?"

"Yes."

"Mosquitoes are getting in."

"Oh. Sorry." She turned and closed the front door.

"No deputy sheriff along for the ride?"

His voice contained a trace of admonishment. She felt an explanation was called for. "I resorted to calling the sheriff's office out of desperation. I asked Deputy Harris if he knew anyone living in his county who went by the initials P.M.E. I had no idea he would conduct a search, and I apologize for any embarrassment that caused."

He harrumphed, but whether to accept her apology or dismiss it, she couldn't tell. She was just relieved that he hadn't cursed her and ordered her out. He wasn't as intimidating as she had anticipated. He was older and less physically imposing than his telephone voice had suggested. The drawl was there, but not the brusqueness.

However, he wasn't being overly friendly. His blue eyes were regarding her warily.

"I wasn't sure what to expect when I arrived," she said, hoping to disarm him with her honesty. "I was afraid I wouldn't even be invited inside."

He gave her a once-over that made her rethink her decision not to take the time to freshen up in Savannah. Now she wished she had at least changed clothes. Her traveling suit had been seasonally lightweight for New York, but was too heavy for this climate. It looked citified and grossly out of place. It was also wrinkled from rides in taxis, planes, and a boat.

"You're a long way from Manhattan, Mrs. Matherly-Reed."

His remark more or less summed up everything she'd been thinking. "More than just geographically. Except for the golf carts, St. Anne could be in another century."

"The island is primitive in many ways. The people who live here want to keep it that way."

From that she inferred that she was an outsider whom they would have rather remained outside. Feeling self-conscious and wanting to divert attention away from herself, she took a quick look around.

A commanding, unsupported staircase swept upward from the floor of the foyer, but the second story was dark. A dozen questions about the history of the house sprang to mind, but, not wanting to press her luck at having gotten this far, she merely said, "The house is extraordinary. How long have you lived here?"

"A little over a year. It was in total disrepair."

"Then you've already done a lot to it."

"There's still a lot to be done. In fact, I've been working on a project in the dining room. Would you like to see it?"

"Very much."

He smiled at her, and she smiled back, then he turned and made his way back into the room from which he'd come. The crystal chandelier in the center of the ceiling was swinging slightly. He caught her looking at it.

"One of the first renovations was to install central air-conditioning. The vent blows directly on the chandelier and causes it to sway. At least that's what I choose to believe." He gave an enigmatic laugh, then motioned toward the fireplace.

The ornately carved mantel had been stripped down to the naked wood and was being prepared for refinishing. "It's become more of a project than I had counted on," he admitted. "Had I known how many layers of varnish and paint former owners had applied, how painstaking and time-consuming it was going to be to strip it all off, I would have hired a professional to do it."

She moved to the mantel and reached out to touch it, then hesitated and looked back at him. "May I?" He motioned for her to go ahead, and she ran her fingertips over the intricate carving of a flowering vine.

"The owner who built the house kept a detailed diary of its construction," he explained. "A slave carved that mantelpiece as well as the balustrade of the staircase. His name was Phineas."

"It's lovely. I'm sure it will be even lovelier when you're finished."

"Parker's expecting it to be. He's a perfectionist."

"Parker?"

"The owner."

She dropped her hand and turned back to him. "Oh. I assumed you owned the house."

He shook his head in amusement. "I only work here."

"That's awfully generous of him."

"Generous of who?"

"Of Mr. Parker. That he opens his home to you and lets you write here."

He stared at her with perplexity for a moment, then began to laugh. "Mrs. Matherly-Reed, I'm afraid that you're operating under a misconception here, and it's entirely my fault. Obviously you've mistaken me for Parker, the man you've come to see. Parker Evans."

It took a second for her to process, then she smiled with chagrin. "Parker Evans. Middle initial *M*."

"You didn't know his name?"

"He didn't tell me."

"You've never heard his name before?"

"Not that I recall. Should I have?"

He studied her for a long moment, then smiled and extended his hand. "I'm Mike Strother. Forgive me for not making that clear to you when you arrived. I thought you would know immediately that I wasn't Parker."

"I'm pleased to meet you, Mr. Strother."

"Mike."

She smiled at him, liking the older gentleman and wondering how she could have mistaken him for the abrasive individual she had spoken to on the telephone. His eyes were kind, although she sensed that he was still taking her measure, sizing her up, appraising her. His wariness of her had diminished somewhat, but it was still there. Of course, there was no telling what his boss had said about her. It couldn't have been flattering.

"Are you the contractor in charge of the house's restoration?"

"Lord, no. I'm just trying my hand at this refinishing. I've worked for Parker since long before he bought this place."

"In what capacity?"

"I do a little bit of everything," he explained. "I'm the chief cook and bottle washer, housekeeper, gardener, valet."

"Is he a demanding taskmaster?"

He chuckled. "You have no idea."

Apparently she didn't. Her preconceptions of Parker M. Evans were being dispelled one by one. He certainly hadn't sounded like a man who would have a manservant at his beck and call. "I'm looking very forward to meeting him."

Mike's eyes shifted away to avoid looking directly at her. "He's not here."

Although she had already gathered that, having it confirmed was not only a crushing disappointment, it was perturbing. "He knew I was coming."

"Oh, he knew, he knew," Mike said, nodding. "He said you sounded just stubborn enough to travel all this way even after he'd told you it would be a waste of your time. But nobody on earth can outstubborn Parker. He didn't want to be sitting around here when you arrived as though he were waiting on you. So he went out."

"Out? Where?"

* * *

Maris angrily marched up to the man who'd rented her the golf cart. "Why did you send me all the way out to Mr. Evans's house?"

He smirked. "Knew you's lying 'bout him expecting you."

"Why didn't you tell me he was here?"

"Don't recollect you askin'."

She was seething, but he was too coarse and stupid to waste her anger on. She would save it for Mr. Parker Evans. She had a lot to say to him. He had probably known about the wild goose chase she'd been sent on. Terry, the cook, surely had. His charcoal grill had gone cold, but he was tending bar when she pulled open the squeaky screen door to his establishment and went inside.

She crossed a bare concrete floor, splashed through a puddle of what she hoped was beer, and strode past the pool tables straight to the bar at the back of the room. The man who had rented her the cart followed her inside.

Billiard balls stopped clacking. Conversations died. Someone turned off the boom box. The floor show was about to begin, and the angry New Yorker was the featured act.

Terry was grinning at her sardonically.

"Give me a beer."

His grin slipped a notch. He hadn't expected that. But he reached into an ice chest and pulled out a longneck bottle of beer. He uncapped it and passed it to her. Foam oozed from the neck. Maris shook it off her hand, took a long drink, then set the bottle on the bar with a hard thump.

"I'm here to see Parker Evans," she announced.

Terry planted his hairy forearms on the bar and leaned across it toward her. "Who should I say is calling?"

His customers guffawed. Terry basked in the success of his clever comeback. He laughed louder than anyone. Maris spun around and confronted the room at large. The interior was thick with tobacco smoke despite the screened walls and the over-head fans. Their desultory rotations didn't eliminate the smog but only stirred it into the warm, humid air.

A dozen pairs of eyes were focused on her. There was only one other woman in the place. She was wearing crotch-hugging shorts and a clinging tank top that barely contained her pendulous breasts and the tattooed cobra whose flared head and wicked tongue rose out of her cleavage. One hand was insolently propped on her hip, the other held a smoldering black cigarette.

The tavern smelled of beer and grilled meat, tobacco smoke and male sweat. Maris drew a deep breath and tasted those essences in the back of her throat.

"Isn't this rather juvenile, Mr. Evans?"

No one said a word. There was little movement beyond one man glancing at another, jabbing him in the ribs and winking. Another gave her a mocking salute with his beer bottle. One sitting near a pool table idly chalked the tip of his cue.

"To say nothing of rude," she continued.

Forcing herself to move away from the false security of the bar, she approached a group of three men sitting around a table. She looked at each of them carefully. Judging from their moronic leers, she doubted any of them could read without moving his lips, much less write fiction.

"I've come an awfully long way to see you."

"You can go back the same way." The voice issued from a shadowed corner and elicited more chuckles.

She gazed into the face of a man sitting alone. He was about Mike Strother's age, with a neglected white beard and the weather-beaten face of a seaman. He seemed not to be aware of her or anyone else. His rheumy eyes were fixed on the glass of dark liquor cradled between his callused hands.

"Mr. Evans, the least you could do is give me ten minutes of your time."

"Come on over here and bend over, honey," a nasally voice invited. "I'll give you the best ten minutes you've ever had."

"In your dreams, Dwayne," the tattooed woman drawled. "You can't keep it up more'n two."

Laughter erupted, louder than before. The woman was high-fived by the man standing nearest her, but he said, "Ol' Dwayne's got the right idea, though."

"Yeah, Yankee lady. You don't know what you're missin' till you've been rid hard by a horny southern boy."

Maris had experienced catcalls from construction workers made anonymous by distance and hard hats. She had received obscene propositions by crank callers and men lurking in recessed doorways on the sidewalks of the city. When she was seventeen, she had been groped in the subway, and to this day the memory of it made her skin crawl.

But having been the victim of crude behavior hadn't made her immune to it. Their vulgarity got to her, but not in the way they expected. It didn't frighten her; it made her angry. In fact, it made her mad as hell.

Not even attempting to disguise her contempt, she said, "Whoever you are, Mr. Evans, you're a damn coward."

The snickering ceased abruptly. Silence fell like a lead curtain. Any other insult was pardonable, but apparently cowardice wasn't. Name-calling couldn't get more serious than that.

Using it as her exit line, she made a beeline for the door. As she passed a billiards table, a pool cue arced down in front of her like the arm of a toll gate. She ran into it, connecting with her pelvic bones hard enough to make a smacking sound.

She pitched forward, but broke her fall against the stick. She took hold of it in a tight grip and tried to shove it out of her way, but it was unyielding. Turning her head toward the man holding it, she realized he was the one she'd noticed earlier chalking the pool cue.

"I'm Parker Evans."

Maris was astonished. Not by his audacity or the hostile eyes that reflected the red glow of a neon sign as they glared up at her.

What astonished her was the wheelchair in which he sat.

Chapter 7

The contraption was green, a cross between a golf cart and a pickup truck. Maris learned later that it was called a Gator, but she had never seen one before Parker Evans nodded her toward the one parked outside Terry's Bar and Grill. He invited her to get in.

Still reeling from the shock of finding him in a wheelchair, she did as he requested and climbed into the passenger seat. She kept her head averted as he used his arms to lift himself onto the driver's seat. Then he leaned down, folded his chair, and swung it up into the shallow trailer.

The Gator had been reconfigured for him. The brake and accelerator were hand-controlled. He handled the vehicle with an ease that comes from practice as he steered it away from Terry's and headed it toward the dock.

"I can take you only as far as the ramp," he said. "It's too steep for my chair. I'd make it down okay, but I might have trouble stopping and would wind up in the drink. Which you probably think I deserve."

She said nothing.

"But even if I didn't go hurtling into the sound, I couldn't get back up the ramp on my own."

Maris was at a complete loss. "Ramp?"

"Down to the dock. Where you left your boat."

"I don't have a boat. I paid someone to bring me over."

"He didn't wait to ferry you back?"

"I didn't know how long I'd be here. I told him I'd call."

He brought the Gator to a stop, looking displeased that he wasn't going to shake her as soon as he thought. His shirt was chambray like Mike's, except that the sleeves had been cut out of Parker Evans's, revealing muscled arms that compensated for the limitations his legs imposed. Those muscles went to work as he pulled the steering wheel into a sharp turn.

"Shouldn't take a boat long to get over here. Terry will call for one. You got the number?"

"Couldn't we talk for a while, Mr. Evans?"

He braked the Gator again. "About what?"

"Look, be obtuse on somebody else's time. I've come a very long way—"

"Without an invitation."

"You invited me when you sent me that prologue."

He registered mild surprise over her snappishness and raised his hands in mock surrender.

She took a moment to collect herself, then continued in a more conciliatory tone. "It's been a very long day for me. I'm tired. A hot bath and cool sheets sound wonderful. But I'm here, so I'd like to make this trip worth my time, trouble, and expense by having a civil conversation with you before I leave."

He folded his arms across his chest in what she supposed could be viewed as a civil gesture. But it also looked smart-alecky, and that, she thought, was probably closer to his intention.

Doggedly she continued. "You sent me your work. You meant for me to read it or you wouldn't have sent it. Despite your claims to the contrary, you want this book to be published. I publish books. We could work together. You don't even have to meet me halfway. I'll go three-quarters of the way. In fact, I believe I already have by coming here. So could we please have that conversation?"

Despite his arrogance, he had a disconcerting way of staring. His expression was inscrutable, giving no indication of what he was thinking. He could have been seriously weighing her arguments or planning to toss her out of the Gator and letting her swim back to the mainland. One was as viable a guess as the other. Or he might have been thinking neither.

Taking his silence as permission for her to continue, she did. "I know it's rather late in the day to be talking shop, but I promise not to take up too much of your time. Mike said he would—"

"I know what Mike said. He called me at Terry's after you left the house. He's acting like a complete fool."

"He didn't strike me as a fool. Anything but."

"Ordinarily, no. Ordinarily he's levelheaded, calm, cool, and collected, the voice of reason, a goddamn pillar of sensibility. But you've got him in a dither. He's tearing around straightening up the house, fixing supper, acting like an old maid about to receive her first gentleman caller." His eyes were shadowed, but she could tell they were moving over her. "You must've laid on the charm double thick."

"I did nothing of the sort. Mike is just a nice man."

He barked a harsh laugh. "Unlike me."

"I didn't say that."

"Well," he drawled, "you just as well have, because it's true. I'm not at all nice."

"I'm sure you could be if you wanted to."

"See, that's the kicker. I don't want to."

Then, before she could prepare herself, he reached across the space separating them, hooked his hand around the back of her neck, and yanked her forward, bringing her mouth up to his. It was more an assault than a kiss. Hard, grinding, insistent. His tongue stabbed at the seam between her lips until it forced them apart.

Making angry sounds of protest, she pushed against his chest, but he didn't stop. Instead he continued to plumb her mouth forcefully as his lips twisted upon hers. Imperceptibly the thrusts became slower and gentler, more exploratory than invasive. His thumb stroked the underside of her chin, her cheek, and very near the corner of her lips. Her anger shifted into distress.

When he ended the deep kiss, he rubbed his lips against hers lightly before breaking contact with them, and even then they remained close, merely a breath apart. Only after he let his hands fall away did he pull back.

Maris turned her head away. She stared out across the water of the sound. It was relatively calm compared to the choppy currents circulating through her bloodstream. The lights on the shore of the mainland seemed very distant. Much farther than before. Now a world away. She felt strangely disconnected, as though that narrow body of water had widened into a gulf that couldn't be spanned.

Somewhere out on the sound a boat's horn bleated a warning. Inside Terry's, the boom box had been restarted and was playing a wailing song about a love gone wrong. Closer, she could hear the gentle slap of the water against the rocky beach at the bottom of the steep ramp that Parker Evans was unable to navigate in his wheelchair.

"It won't work, Mr. Evans," she said quietly. "I'm not going to flee in terror of you."

She turned then to look at him and was surprised by the absence of smugness in his expression. He didn't look contrite or apologetic, either, but he wasn't wearing the triumphant sneer she had expected. He was staring at her in the same disconcerting, inscrutable way as before.

"I ignored the vulgarities inside Terry's, just like I'm going to ignore that kiss. Because I know why you subjected me to that," she said, hitching her head in the direction of the bar, "and I know why you kissed me."

"You do."

"I'm calling your bluff."

"Bluff."

"You kissed me to scare me off."

"All right."

" 'All right'?"

"You can think that if you want to." He held her gaze for several seconds, then put the Gator into forward motion. "Did Mike happen to mention what's for supper?"

* * *

It turned out to be smoked ham sandwiches served in a casual room on the back of the house. Mike referred to it as the solarium.

"Fancy name for a glassed-in porch," Parker commented wryly.

"It was a porch," Mike explained to Maris as he spooned potato salad onto her plate. "You can't tell, now that it's dark, but this room overlooks the beach. Parker decided to enclose it with sliding glass panels that give us the option of closing it completely or opening it up. Now he can write in here during any kind of weather."

Maris had pretended not to notice the computer setup in one corner of the room, which was otherwise furnished with rattan pieces. Nods toward decoration were limited. A few throw pillows. One struggling potted plant that looked doomed to lose the struggle. That was all. It was a bachelor's room. A writer's retreat.

Stacked around the computer terminal, on the stone tile floor, in shelves, on every conceivable surface, were books. Reference books, literary novels and classics, mysteries, romances, science fiction, horror, westerns, autobiographies, biographies, poetry, childrens' books, histories, self-help, and inspirational. Every kind of book imaginable, some in hardcover, some in paperback, some of which, she was pleased to see, bore the Matherly Press imprint on the spine. Gauging by the worn appearance of the books, his library wasn't just for show. Parker Evans was well read.

"Whatever you call this room, I like it," she told them. "It's a wonderful place to read. And write." She gave Parker a sly glance, which he chose not to see as he spread mustard onto his sandwich.

After serving them, Mike sat down across the table from her, confirming what she had guessed, that he was as much a friend and companion as he was a valet—the need for which was now sadly apparent. "You went to far too much trouble, Mike."

"No trouble. We planned to have a late supper anyway, and I'm awfully glad to have a guest in the house. Parker isn't always the best company. In fact, when he's writing, he sometimes doesn't speak for hours, and when he does, he can be a real grouch."

Parker shot him a sour glance. "And you're a perpetual pain in the ass."

Maris laughed. Despite the swapped insults, the affection between them was obvious. "I've experienced Mr. Evans's grouchiness firsthand, Mike, but I don't take it personally. I'm used to it. I work with writers every day. A gloomy bunch, for the most part. I probably don't catch the verbal abuse their agents do, but I get my share."

Mike nodded sagely. "Artistic temperament."

"Precisely. I'm not complaining. Based on my experience— and confirmed only yesterday by my father—bad temperament is often an indicator of good writing."

She blotted her lips with her napkin and was shocked to realize that they were still tender. She'd checked her reflection in the framed mirror above the basin when Mike kindly directed her into the powder room shortly after she and Parker arrived. The only visible trace of the kiss was a slight abrasion above her upper lip. She'd applied powder to the whisker burn and then quickly switched off the light, afraid she would see in her eyes even more telling evidence of the kiss, which she had resolved to deny—a resolve jeopardized by whisker burns and such.

She and the author had spoken little on the drive to his home. She had kept her eyes trained on the twin beams the Gator's headlights cast onto the road. The darkness within the forest made it easier to ignore, although at one point she couldn't resist taking one furtive glance into the trees.

"Oh!" she exclaimed.

"What?"

"Fireflies. There in the woods."

"Lightning bugs," he said. "Down here, we call them lightning bugs."

"I haven't seen any in years."

"Insecticides."

"Unfortunately. When I was little, I used to see them around our house in the country. I'd catch them and put them in a glass and keep it on my nightstand overnight."

"I did that, too."

She turned to him in surprise. "You did?"

"Yeah. The kids in my neighborhood used to hold contests to see who could catch the most."

So he had been able to chase fireflies. He hadn't always been confined to a wheelchair. Naturally she was curious about the nature of his disability, but she was too polite to ask.

He wasn't the first person she had known who was similarly incapacitated. She had enormous respect for those individuals who had made the best of their misfortune. Some were the most optimistic, upbeat people she had ever had the pleasure of knowing. What they lacked in physical stamina and strength, they made up for with courage and spiritual fortitude.

Parker Evans seemed to have the raw power of physically challenged triathletes who competed in the Ironman competitions, men and women who achieved Herculean feats with the strength of their arms—and willpower—alone. Frequently they were athletes or otherwise active young people whose pursuits had been ended in one fateful second, victims of tragic accidents. She wondered what had happened to Parker to change his life so dramatically.

She glanced across the table at him now. He was picking at the bread crust on his plate but, as though feeling her eyes, raised his and caught her looking at him. He gave her a frank return stare.

He was undeniably attractive, although years of pain or unhappiness or disillusionment or a combination thereof had etched lines into his face, making him appear older than he probably was. His rare smiles were tainted by bitterness. His brown hair was thick and threaded with gray. Grooming it would probably be an afterthought. He was wearing two days' worth of stubble.

His eyes weren't a definitive color like blue or green or brown. They were best described as hazel and would have been unremarkable except for the occasional amber spots that flecked the irises. That unique feature, coupled with his amazing ability to remain focused on something for an incredible length of time, made his eyes compelling.

Staring at her now, he seemed to know exactly what she was thinking. His eyes were issuing a challenge. *Go ahead,* they seemed to say. *You're dying to know why I'm in this chair, so why don't you just ask?*

She wasn't going to take up that dare. Not now. Not until she knew him better, or not until she got at least a verbal commitment from him that he would finish his book.

"Have you written any more, Mr. Evans?"

"Want a refill of iced tea?"

"No, thank you."

"Another sandwich?"

"I'm full, thank you. Have you got more for me to read?"

He looked pointedly at Mike, who took the hint. "Excuse me. I need to put some things away." The older man got up and left the room through a connecting door.

As soon as Mike was out of earshot, he said, "You're a very determined woman."

"Thank you."

"I didn't mean it as a compliment."

"I know."

He backed away from the table, turned his chair, and stared through the glass as though he could penetrate the darkness and see the surf. Maris gave him this time. If he was balancing the pros and cons of a decision, she wanted to say nothing that might tip the scales against her.

After a time, he turned back. "Do you really think it's that good?"

"Do you think I would travel to a remote spot on the map if I'd had a lukewarm response to your writing?"

"In plain English, please."

"Yes, Mr. Evans, it's good."

He looked at her with exasperation. "My tongue has been inside your mouth, which makes the 'Mr. Evans' a bit ridiculous, don't you think? My name is Parker. Call me that, okay?"

She swallowed but refused to look away from him. "Okay. And you can call me Maris."

"I planned to."

He seemed determined to provoke her one way or the other, but she was equally determined not to let him. "Where are you from, Parker? Originally. The South, I know that."

"Shoot! What gave me away?" He spoke in an exaggeration of his natural drawl.

She laughed softly. "Well, there is the accent, but Yankees have a hard time distinguishing regional nuances. For instance, Texans don't sound like South Carolinians, do they?"

"Texans don't sound like anybody."

Again she laughed. "Where did your particular accent originate?"

"Why is that relevant?"

"Some of the words you use..."

"Like?"

"Like 'fixing' instead of preparing or cooking supper. And the word 'supper' itself, instead of dinner. 'Dither,' 'gentleman caller,' things like that."

"I guess those colloquialisms crop up now and then in my speech. I try and keep them out of my writing."

"Don't. They season it."

"A little seasoning goes a long way."

She acknowledged his point with a nod. "I see you've thought about it. You're conscientious about using idioms in your prose." Propping her arms on the table, she leaned forward. "You put a lot of thought and hard work into your writing, Parker. Why are you reluctant to have it read?"

He had the answer ready. "Fear of failure."

"Understood. Creative people are cursed with self-doubt. It's the nature of the beast." She gestured toward his bookcase. "But aren't we glad that most don't submit to it?"

"Many do, though, don't they?" he argued. "They couldn't stand the ridicule of critics, or the fickle whims of the buying public, or the pressure of living up to expectations, or the darkest goddamn doubt of all, which is that they had no talent to begin with and that exposure of that reality is just around the corner. How many writers can you name who drank themselves to death? Or made it quick and blew their brains out?"

She thought the question over, then said, "Tell me, Parker,

does that require more courage, or less, than becoming a recluse on an out-of-the-way island?"

The shot struck home. For several long moments he seemed to wage a battle with himself, then he whipped his chair about and rolled it to the worktable. He booted up the computer, saying to her over his shoulder, "This means nothing, understand?"

She nodded agreement, although she was certain that they were both lying. Whatever *this* was, it meant *something*.

"I've written a first chapter."

"In addition to the prologue, you mean?"

"Correct. If you want to read it, I'll let you. With the understanding that I'm under no obligation to you. Whether you like the material or not, I'm making you no promises."

Maris moved beside his chair and together they watched the pages as they rolled out of the printer. "Does the first chapter start where the prologue left off?"

"No. The scene in the prologue comes toward the end of the story."

"So you go back and bring the reader forward?"

"Right."

"How far back?"

"Three years. Chapter one takes place when Roark and Todd are college roommates."

"Roark and Todd," she repeated, trying out the character names and deciding she liked them. "Which is which?"

"What do you mean?"

"Which one do we see in Hatch Walker's office in the prologue? Who crashes the boat and who has gone overboard?"

This time his grin was free of bitterness.

"You're not going to tell me, are you?" she asked.

"If I did, what would be the point of your reading the rest of the book?"

"The rest? So you *are* planning to finish it?"

His grin slipped a fraction. "Let's see what you think first."

"I can't wait."

"Don't get too excited, Maris. It's only one chapter."

He removed the pages from the tray on the printer, then tapped the edges on the table to even them up before passing them to her. She grasped them, but he continued to hold them. She looked at him expectantly.

"When I kissed you? It didn't have a damn thing to do with trying to scare you off."

Before she could respond, he released the pages and shouted for Mike. "Bring her a phone so she can call for a boat," he told the older man when he appeared in the doorway. "It'll take about as long for it to get to the island as it takes for you to get her back to the landing. Should time out just right."

"But it's after eleven o'clock," Mike exclaimed. "You can't send her back at this time of night."

Maris, flustered, said a little too quickly and loudly, "It's fine, Mike. I'll be fine."

"I won't hear of it." Ignoring Parker's warning look, Mike declared, "You'll stay here tonight. In the guest house."

Chapter 8

To avoid the parties being seen together in a public restaurant, the luncheon meeting was held in a private dining room on the thirty-first floor of WorldView Center. The paneled room was discreetly and expensively furnished. The hand-woven carpet was thick and sound-absorbing, the floral arrangements were elaborate and still dewy, the lighting was indirect and subdued. To add to the dignified ambience, heavy draperies had been drawn across the expansive windows, which ordinarily would have provided a magnificent view of the Midtown skyline.

The host, seated at the head of the dining table, asked politely, "More coffee, Nadia? Mr. Reed?"

Nadia Schuller indicated to the white-gloved waiter that she would like her cup refilled. Noah declined. They had dined on vichyssoise, lobster salad, and marinated asparagus. Strawberries Romanoff and selected chocolates had been served for dessert.

Noah thanked their host for the sumptuous meal. "It was excellent."

"I'm glad you enjoyed it." Morris Blume thanked and then dismissed the servers.

As Nadia idly stirred cream into her coffee, Noah exchanged a look with her that said social hour was over and business was about to commence.

In addition to Morris Blume, five other representatives from WorldView were seated around the table. Six months earlier, Nadia had arranged an introductory meeting between Blume and Noah. Blume hadn't been coy at that initial meeting. Rather, he had stated plainly that he wished to acquire Matherly Press for WorldView.

Immediately upon adjournment of that meeting, his corporate lawyers had begun working feverishly on an acquisition proposal. After months of researching and analyzing, drafting flow charts, drawing market-share graphs, and making projections, the final rendition had been delivered to Noah in an enormous three-ring binder. This meeting was for the purpose of hearing his response to it.

"You've had a month to study our syllabus, Mr. Reed," Blume said. "I'm eager to hear your impressions."

Morris Blume was whipcord thin and strikingly pale, a feature emphasized by his prematurely bald head. A rim of sparse hair continued to grow from his scalp, but he shaved it every morning, which left a gray shadow beneath his shiny dome. He wore eyeglasses with silver wire frames and always dressed in conservative gray. The man seemed to have an innate aversion to color.

He had been at the helm of the international media conglomerate since his hostile takeover four years ago. Only thirty-six at the time, he had ruthlessly ousted his predecessor along with anyone on the board of directors who adhered to what Blume termed "archaic and unenlightened mind-sets."

Under his leadership, WV, as it was affectionately known on the stock exchange, had expanded from its base entertainment and broadcast entities into Internet commerce, satellite communications, and fiber-optics technology. Blume had catapulted WorldView into the twenty-first century, increasing its worth from a mere billion dollars to nearly sixty billion in only forty-eight months. Stockholders easily forgave his brash methods of doing business.

So what did a mammoth like WorldView want with a gnat like Matherly Press?

That was the question Noah now posed to Blume.

"Because it's there?" the pale CEO glibly replied. Everyone at the table laughed, including Noah. He could appreciate the son of a bitch's arrogance because he was an arrogant son of a bitch himself.

"You've already acquired a publishing house in the U.K.," Noah pointed out. "The ink is barely dry on that contract."

"True." Blume nodded solemnly. "Platt/Powers will be a good investment for us. Their magazine division is the strongest in the British Isles. They distribute everything from a well-respected world news weekly to the sleaziest of sleazy porno." He gave Nadia a smile that was disturbingly reptilian. "I assure you, Nadia, that I'm far more familiar with the former than the latter."

She looked at Blume over the rim of the china cup as she took a sip of coffee. "How disappointing."

Blume let the resultant laughter wane before he resumed. "Platt/Powers had twelve bestsellers in hardcover last year."

"Thirteen," one of the bean counters at the table supplied.

"More than that in paperback," Blume continued. "As part of WorldView, it will dominate the bestseller lists this year. We've got the know-how and the budget to make that happen."

"I've already interviewed two writers whom you pirated from their former publishers," Nadia remarked. "They're very excited about your marketing strategies, particularly the ones that will give them greater exposure here in the States."

"We utilize our media resources," Blume explained. "All of them. They are vast and unmatchable."

He folded his bloodless hands together on the table and assumed an earnest demeanor. Focusing on Noah, he said, "By buying Platt/Powers, WorldView acquired a healthy publishing house. But the U.K. market is smaller than the American market. Significantly so. We want one on this side of the pond. We want Matherly Press.

"You publish books with mass appeal. Moneymakers, if you will. But you also publish literary works. Without question yours is a profitable house. It's also a venerable publishing institution. It has a cachet of respectability. We'd like that for our little company."

The fatuous understatement elicited a twitter from the WV group, but Noah let it pass without even a smile. Blume seemed to take that as a sign that he should stop and let the other side talk for a while.

"I've studied the proposal thoroughly," Noah began. "You did your homework. The research was impressive. The projections are exciting but within the realm of achievability."

"This is sounding very good," Blume said, throwing grins all around.

Noah held up a cautionary hand. "However, before we move forward, there are a couple of points that must be addressed."

"That's the purpose of this meeting."

"First, what about antitrust laws? Are you going to be in violation? I don't want to become embroiled in a protracted legal dispute with the federal government."

"I assure you that we don't, either, and we've taken every precaution to avoid it."

One of the lawyers was given the floor to explain why the probability of that happening was slim. Noah asked several questions, which he didn't allow to be dismissed with legal doubletalk. He kept at the counsel until his concerns were addressed and given the attention they deserved.

"Good," Blume said when explanations had been provided to Noah's satisfaction. "What's your second point?"

Noah plucked an invisible piece of lint off the sleeve of his suit jacket, then looked over at Blume and said blandly, "Matherly Press isn't for sale."

* * *

"To which he said?" Daniel Matherly asked.

"Nothing that bears repeating," his son-in-law replied.

"Something about stubborn old men who refuse to see the light, I'd bet."

"Nothing that blatant, but definitely along those lines."

They were having drinks together in Daniel's home study. Maxine had poured them the first round. "One is his limit. He can't have another," she told Noah before leaving them.

"I'll see that he doesn't," he called after her as she left the room. But a conspiratorial wink at Daniel nullified his promise to the housekeeper.

Now, a half hour later, they were enjoying their second round. "Fetch me my pipe, will you, please?"

Noah retrieved Daniel's pipe from where he'd left it on the desk. He delivered it and a tobacco pouch to the large leather wing chair where Daniel sat with his feet propped on an ottoman. Methodically he packed his pipe and put a match to it.

"If Maxine smells that smoke—"

"I'll claim it was you who was smoking." He exhaled a plume of smoke toward the ceiling. Thoughtfully, his eyes remained fixed on the crown molding. "The mongrels are closing in on us, Noah. They're mean and they have sharp teeth."

Noah sipped his scotch. "WorldView?" He made a negligent gesture. "I don't know how I could have stated it any more plainly. Matherly Press isn't for sale."

"They'll persist. Particularly that Blume bastard."

"It's said he pisses ice cubes."

Daniel chuckled. "I don't doubt it." He puffed on his pipe for a moment. "Even if Morris Blume falls by the wayside or gives up and goes away, another mongrel, even meaner than he, won't be far behind."

"Let them come. We can stave them off."

Daniel smiled at his son-in-law's confidence. Everyone in the industry had become acquainted with Noah Reed a decade ago following the publication of *The Vanquished*. The novel, set during the Reconstruction, had taken the nation by storm. There wasn't a publisher in New York who hadn't wished he'd been lucky enough to nab it, Daniel Matherly included.

But to everyone's surprise, and his new fans' dismay, Noah's ambitions lay not in writing, but in publishing. He had followed every step of the publishing process on *The Vanquished* and had derived more enjoyment out of that than he had from writing the novel.

He was an engaging young man with superior intelligence and razor-sharp instincts. Some of his ideas on how best to market his book had been implemented by his publisher, and they had worked. The house reasoned that Noah would be equally successful publishing other books and had hired him.

The junior editor had quickly proved his mettle. During his first year, he acquired an obscure manuscript from an unknown author, who became a bestseller with that first novel and remained one to this day.

Noah had been a quick study editorially, but the business side of the industry was where he truly distinguished himself. His inventive marketing strategies were so successful that they were blatantly copied by other publishers.

He was a fearless negotiator, whom literary agents admired but dreaded facing across the bargaining table. He was a born leader. Once, on the eve of a labor strike, he had traveled to a printing company in Pennsylvania to personally appeal to the disgruntled workers. Acting as a mediator between them and plant management, he helped settle the dispute, quelled the strike, and prevented an industry crisis.

Noah Reed was bright, ambitious, even shrewd. Daniel had been rightly accused of being shrewd himself, so he didn't regard it a derogatory term. So when, to Daniel's surprise, Noah had come to him three years ago, covertly expressing his unhappiness with the limits placed upon him by his present employer and boldly stating his desire to make a move, Daniel had listened with interest. Noah's ideas were innovative but didn't conflict with the ideals on which Daniel's ancestors had founded Matherly Press. Indeed, Noah shared them.

Additionally, Noah had appealed to Daniel's vanity, though he would never admit it. The younger man had reminded him of himself when he'd been that age—aggressive, determined, confident to the point of conceit, which Daniel also regarded more a virtue than a vice.

Daniel told Noah he would need a few days to think it over. He was reluctant to bring in someone who wasn't family and install him in a position of authority. On the other hand, the business had expanded to the point where he and Maris needed another pair of hands at the helm.

For Maris's part, she was positively giddy over the possibility of working daily with the author of her favorite book. Though she'd met Noah only once, at a literary function, she held him in high esteem and had harbored a secret romantic crush on him for years.

With her urging, Daniel created the job of vice president of business affairs for Noah. He'd never regretted that decision.

"You still agree with it, don't you?" Daniel asked him now.

"With what?"

"The company philosophy."

He gave his father-in-law a retiring look. "From the beginning of our association, I've known how you felt about mergers, Daniel. Unquestionably there would be benefits. We would have more funds at our disposal, more venues for marketing and promotion."

"But we'd no longer be autonomous."

"Which was the point I was about to make," Noah said. "Autonomy was the basis on which Matherly Press was founded. I knew the family mantra even before I married into it."

When Maris began seeing Noah outside the office, Daniel had nursed some reservations. He had been concerned on several levels. First, their ten-year age difference bothered him, but not overly so. Second, Noah's business acumen wasn't the only thing on which he'd built a solid reputation. It was rumored that he was a notorious womanizer. With so many rumors circulating for that many years, Daniel had to believe there was some basis for them. His greatest concern, however, was Noah's personal agenda. By marrying the last eligible Matherly, his career would receive a distinct boost.

Of course, when it came right down to it, it wasn't Daniel's decision to make. It was his daughter's, and Maris wanted Noah for her husband. Because of her mother's untimely death, she had always been mature beyond her years. Necessity had forced her to grow up quickly. She had begun forming her own opinions and making her own decisions at an early age. He had reared her to think for herself and to trust her instincts. It would have been wrong of him to second-guess her choice of a life partner.

To his credit, Noah had, without Maris's knowledge, approached his future father-in-law and told him that if he entertained any doubts regarding the marriage, it would never take place. He loved Maris to distraction, he had said, but he would walk away, forsake his position at Matherly Press, and disappear from her life unless Daniel could give his wholehearted approval of the union.

Daniel had given the couple his blessing, but, where Maris's happiness was concerned, he remained a vigilant watchdog. Yesterday, she had been a bit downcast, although the surprise party was a logical explanation for Noah's recent inattention.

Maris didn't talk about it, but Daniel also sensed that she was ready for children and was slightly disappointed that she hadn't become pregnant. It was too early to worry unnecessarily about that. Maris was still young. Noah had expressed a desire for children on numerous occasions. There was plenty of time for them to have a family.

Selfishly, Daniel wished for grandchildren soon. He would enjoy bouncing the next generation on his knee before he checked out.

Thinking of his daughter now, he asked, "Have you heard from Maris?"

"Not since she left this morning." Noah checked his wristwatch. "She should be there by now. It was a long way to travel and I'm afraid it will turn out to be a bust."

"Hopefully not. She seems very excited about this writer. Speaking of which, she told me about her present."

"Present?"

"Last night."

"Oh." Noah smiled with chagrin. "She's awfully easy to please, isn't she?"

"Your writer's cell is no small thing to her, Noah. She called from the airport this morning just prior to boarding her flight. If you'd given her a diamond ring, she couldn't have been happier. She's always wanted you to resume writing."

Noah frowned. "I hope she doesn't expect too much from me. I'll probably disappoint her."

"Your effort alone will make her happy."

"I'd like to get in a few hours of effort tonight." Noah set his empty tumbler on the end table and stood up.

"Stay and have dinner with me. We'll play chess afterward."

"Tempting, Daniel. But I should use this time that Maris is away to crank out a few pages. There's only one way to write, and that's to write," he said with a smile. "Can I refresh your drink before I go?"

"Thanks, no. Maxine will be measuring the amount left in the decanter as it is."

"Then I for sure want to clear out before the fireworks start." Noah pulled on his suit jacket and retrieved his briefcase. "Anything else I can do for you?"

"As a matter of fact, there is," Daniel said. "The next time someone approaches you with an offer to buy my publishing house, tell him to fuck off."

Noah laughed. "Shall I quote you?"

"Absolutely. In fact, I would prefer it."

* * *

Two vodka martinis hadn't dulled the edges of Nadia's nerves. They seemed to be on red alert and had been since Noah had recounted for her his conversation with Daniel.

For half an hour she'd been pacing the hardwood floor of her Chelsea apartment, which was used strictly for romantic trysts. The apartment she owned in Trump Tower was her official address. Not even her accountant knew about this apartment.

"No matter how blasé he seems, I don't trust the old codger," she said. "How do you know he can't see through your act?"

"Because he isn't looking." Noah's voice conveyed his impatience.

"I don't mean to question your perception, Noah."

"Don't you?"

"No. I'm just afraid that something might go wrong. I want this deal so badly for you."

"I want it for *us*."

Her anxiety dissolving, she stopped pacing and moved to where he stood. Coming close, she rested her hands on his shoulders. "Damn you," she said softly. "By saying that, you've completely disarmed me."

Their kiss was passionate and deep. She unbuttoned his shirt and slipped her hand inside. When they pulled apart, she continued to tweak his chest hairs. "It's just that Daniel Matherly has been overseeing that publishing house for...how long?"

"He's seventy-eight. His father died when he was twenty-nine. Daniel's been in control since then."

"So almost fifty years."

"I can subtract, Nadia."

"All I'm saying is this: He hasn't made himself into a living legend by being a dimwit. He didn't become successful by misreading people. He's smart. He's savvy. He's—"

"Not as sharp as he used to be."

"Maybe. Or maybe he just wants you to think so."

Noah disliked being second-guessed and resented even a hint of criticism. Pushing her away, he moved into the kitchen, where he refilled his highball glass with ice cubes and splashed scotch over them. "I think I know my father-in-law at least as well as you do, Nadia."

"I'm sure—"

"If you were sure of me, you wouldn't be nagging me about this." He treated his drink like a shot, then set his glass on the countertop and took a moment to contain his temper before turning back to her. "Your job is to keep Blume and company pacified and reassured."

"I'm having dinner with Morris tomorrow night. The Rainbow Room."

"Good. Be a knockout. Eat, drink, and dance. Blow in his ear. Keep him happy. Let me handle the Matherlys. I've been handling them quite well for three years. I know how they think. I know how they react to given situations. This must be carried out with extreme delicacy. It can't be rushed or the whole thing could blow up in our faces."

His timetable had been in place for years. Now that the finish line was in sight, he wasn't going to sacrifice all his careful planning and strategizing to recklessness. By doing it his way, on his schedule, everything had gone according to plan.

The first step had been accomplished when Daniel Matherly hired him. By toeing the company line, he had earned the old man's trust. A major hurdle had been cleared when he married Maris, further solidifying his position. Then, when the time was right, he had subtly, through Nadia, telegraphed to Blume his interest in a merger. Blume was still working under the misconception that the idea had originally been his. Not at all. WorldView had been in Noah's game plan from the start.

Up to this point everything had been done Noah Reed's way, the only way that Noah Reed would have it. He wasn't going to screw himself now by rushing toward a quick finish.

"I don't know why you're being testy with me," Nadia said. "Morris issued the deadline today, not I."

That had been the one crimp in Noah's plan that he hadn't seen coming, and the reason for his querulousness tonight. Throughout his cocktail hour with Daniel, he'd been only half listening to the old man's rambling speech. Instead he'd been remembering Blume, with his lizardlike smile, imposing on him a two-week deadline to either fish or cut bait.

Blume had reminded Noah that he had been extended ample time in which to review the proposal, that either he was interested enough to move forward and make this deal happen or he wasn't. Noah had reminded him that his father-in-law wasn't a minor stumbling block but a major obstacle. "Daniel has stated unequivocally that his company is not for sale."

"Then you must take bold steps to see that he changes his mind, mustn't you?"

Blume concluded the meeting by reminding Noah that there were other publishing companies, almost as prestigious as Matherly Press, that would leap at the chance of becoming part of WorldView.

The hell of it was, Noah knew that Blume's threat was viable.

Many smaller publishing houses were hanging on by a thread. They couldn't compete with the distribution capabilities and robust publicity budgets of media giants. They would welcome the financial relief and stability that WorldView would bring to them. Unlike Daniel, their primary concern was survival by any means possible, and to hell with sentiment.

There wasn't a sentimental bone in Noah's body, but he was well acquainted with Daniel's fanatical adherence to tradition and his family's history. The old man wasn't going to let go easily. It was an intricate complication that seemed beyond Blume's understanding.

"I'm well aware of Blume's deadline," Noah told Nadia now. "I'll see that it's met."

"What about Maris?"

"She's busy in Florida."

"Georgia."

"What?"

"You told me she went to Georgia."

"Whatever. I'm going to chip away at Daniel while she's gone. I began tonight by pointing out the advantages of Blume's offer."

"What happens when Maris gets back?"

"She'll go the way Daniel goes."

"That wasn't what I was talking about."

I should be so lucky. Sighing wearily, Noah closed his eyes and pinched the bridge of his nose. Jesus, he didn't need a discussion of this right now. He had enough to deal with.

"I know what you were talking about, Nadia." Lowering his hand and opening his eyes, he looked at her. "Think about it. Does it make sense for me to ask Maris for a divorce now? No. I can't do that until I have that WorldView contract signed, sealed, and delivered."

He expelled a breath of exasperation. "Do you think I've enjoyed being married to her? Do you think I've liked kissing Daniel's ass all these years?"

"That's a revolting thought."

"Isn't it? So imagine it from my perspective." He hoped the remark might cause her to smile; it didn't.

"And Maris?" she asked. "Will you miss kissing her ass?"

He gave a dry laugh. "I won't miss my wife, but I'll regret losing a good editor. However, with the operating budget Blume has promised me, I'll be able to hire three of her. Five of her. And even if none prove to be as good as she, I'll have my ten million to console me."

She held his gaze for a moment, her expression turning sulky. "You really don't mind my blowing in Morris Blume's ear?"

"Figure of speech."

"So what you said earlier…"

"About?"

"About your wanting this deal for *us*. Did you mean it?"

By way of answer, he pulled her against him and kissed her.

She finished unbuttoning his shirt, then spread it open and put tongue to nipple, flicking it lightly. "You did?"

"Right now I'd swear to anything."

Laughing huskily, she stroked him through his trousers. "I don't like sharing you with Maris. I'm impatient to have this all to myself."

"I'm rather impatient myself." He unzipped his trousers and pushed down his shorts. Nadia dropped to her knees and nuzzled him. She traced the length of his erection with her tongue before taking him into her mouth. Noah grunted with satisfaction.

"You stick to doing what you do best, Nadia, and leave the problem of the Matherlys to me."

Chapter 9

Parker was at his computer. He'd been up for hours. His mind was skipping like a stone over water.

Mike delivered a third cup of coffee to him. "Your guest just left the cottage. She's dawdling along the way, taking in the seascape, but she'll soon be making an entrance."

He had asked Mike to be on the lookout for her and acknowledged the report with a nod.

Mike was uncharacteristically careless as he replaced Parker's empty coffee mug with the full one. Hot coffee sloshed out. The spill spread across the table and stained several sheets of handwritten notes. Parker stared at the mess, then raised his head and gave the older man a look.

"Sorry," Mike said.

"I'll bet."

Mike snorted.

"Look, if you've got something to say, why not act like a grown-up and just say it?"

"I think you know what I have to say, Parker."

"How about 'congratulations'?"

"How about 'get real'? Do you really expect me to congratu-
late you?"

"She's here, isn't she?"

"Yes. She's here." Mike looked none too happy about it,
though.

Parker raised his shoulders in a shrug, asking impatiently,
"What? The reverse psychology worked. She took the bait.
Which is what we hoped she would do. If you had qualms, you
should have thrown away her phone numbers when that deputy
gave them to you. But you didn't. You passed them on to me. I
called her and she came. So what's eating you?"

Mike turned away and stamped back into the kitchen. "My
biscuits are burning."

Parker returned to his computer screen, but the interruption
had log-jammed his creative flow. He couldn't focus on the last
few sentences he'd written. They now seemed a jumble of words
and phrases beyond translation. In an effort to assign them
meaning, he forced his eyes to stop on each word separately. But
no matter how hard he concentrated, he couldn't make sense of
them. They could have been written in Sanskrit.

And then he realized why reading and understanding his
own words had suddenly become a challenge: He was nervous.
Which is odd, considering that everything had fallen into place
more or less as he had planned. He'd made a few spontaneous
adjustments to accommodate Maris Matherly-Reed's personality, but she was responding to him and his situation even better
than he had dared hope she would.

Now that he thought about it, getting her here had been almost too easy. He had pulled the strings, and, like a puppet, she
had made the correct moves. He figured that's what had Mike's
shorts in a wad this morning. Her innocent cooperation had lent
her a certain vulnerability and made her seem almost a victim.

But she isn't, he told himself stubbornly.

Yeah, he had tugged some strings to guide her in the direction he wanted her to go, but ultimately she was in control. Everything depended on how well she liked *Envy*, or if she liked it at all.

And that's what had *his* shorts in a wad. Not only from the standpoint of the overall plan, but as a writer, he was nervous to hear what she thought of the pages she had curled up with last night. What if she thought they stunk? What if she thanked him for the opportunity to review more of his work but declined it and said her good-byes?

His plot would be screwed, and he would feel like shit.

Agitated, he turned his wheelchair on a dime and saw her picking her way along the path between the main house and the cottage. Originally it had been the detached kitchen of the plantation house. Parker had converted it into a guest house. Not that he entertained a lot of guests. Not that he planned to in the future. Nevertheless, the interior of the structure had been gutted and he had spared no expense to have it completely and comfortably renovated.

Accomplished with only one guest in mind—the one presently occupying it.

Maris glanced up and saw him watching her from behind the glass panels of the solarium. She smiled and waved. Waved? He couldn't remember the last time someone had waved at him. Feeling rather goofy, he raised his hand and waved back.

She let herself in through the sliding door. "Good morning."

"Hi."

Her skin looked dewy. She smelled like floral-scented soap. Magnolia, maybe. She had his manuscript pages with her.

"It's gorgeous here, Parker," she exclaimed a bit breathlessly. "Last night it was too dark for me to fully appreciate the property. But seeing it in daylight, I understand why you fell in love with this place." She looked out across the expanse of green lawn, the sugary beach, and the sparkling Atlantic. "It's wonderful. So peaceful."

"I forgot a hair dryer."

Self-consciously she tucked a strand of damp hair behind her ear. "I searched but couldn't find one. Actually, it's such a warm morning, it felt good to leave it wet. A hair dryer is all the cottage lacked, however. You did an excellent job on it."

"Thanks."

He continued to scrutinize her, and, as he intended, his scrutiny increased her self-consciousness. "The furnishings are charming. I especially like the iron headboard and the claw-footed bathtub."

"Mike's ideas."

"Good ones."

"Yeah, he's into all that. Iron beds. Bathtubs. Mantels."

"He has an eye for detail."

"I guess."

The conversation lagged for several moments, then they spoke at the same time.

He said, "Your blouse is wet."

She said, "I read the new pages."

"What'd you think?" he asked.

"My blouse?"

"It's damp."

She looked down and saw what had held Parker's attention from the moment she stepped inside. She was dressed in the same skirt and blouse she had arrived in. Following supper last night, Mike had wheedled and pleaded, then insisted that she stay in their guest house. She had finally accepted the invitation, but because of the hour, it had been impractical to try and retrieve her luggage from the hotel in Savannah.

Consequently she had dressed in the same clothes this morning, except for her suit jacket, which she'd left off in deference to the climate. A damp pattern had appeared on the front of her blouse in the exact shape of her bra.

She rolled the sheets of manuscript into a tube, probably to stop herself from using them to shield her chest. "I washed out some things last night."

Things, plural. If she'd washed out *things*, what had been left for her to sleep in? Surmising made Parker go a little dewy himself.

"I guess they didn't get quite dry," she explained lamely.

"The humidity."

"I suppose."

Their eyes connected but only for a millisecond before she looked away. She was embarrassed, and that was good. In fact, that was excellent. He wanted to keep her rattled and off balance. Too fucking bad if Mike disapproved of the strategy.

Leaning forward from the wheelchair, he reached out and took the rolled pages from her. "You read them?"

"Three times."

He raised his eyebrows inquiringly.

"I have some comments."

His chin went up defensively.

"Who's ready for breakfast?" Mike asked.

He appeared in the doorway pushing a wheeled cart on which were platters of scrambled eggs, bacon, and wedges of pastel melons. Fresh from the oven, the biscuits had been wrapped inside a towel and placed in a wire basket. A gravy boat was filled to the rim, and a dish of steamy grits had an island of melting butter in its center.

Parker's stomach growled and his mouth began to water, but Mike's timing couldn't be worse, which Parker was sure had been deliberate. Mike avoided making eye contact with him until Parker said, "I'm on to you, old man."

"What?" Mike asked innocently.

Parker shot him a wry look, which Mike ignored and instead motioned Maris toward a small table on which Parker sometimes took his meals when he was writing.

"Good Lord." She watched in dismay as Mike filled her plate. "A bagel and coffee usually do it for me."

Scoffing, Mike reminded her that breakfast was the most important meal of the day. "Do you like grits?"

"I'm not sure. What exactly is a grit?" Parker laughed along with Mike as she took her first tentative bite, which she gamely swallowed. Politely she said, "Maybe it's an acquired taste."

"Break open your biscuit and let me ladle gravy over it," Mike told her.

Bacon gravy was also new to her, but she declared it delicious. "Do you eat like this every morning?"

"This is a special occasion," Mike said.

"He's trying to impress you," Parker told her.

"It worked."

She flashed a smile at Mike that should have caused his heart to melt and made Parker irrationally jealous. He grumbled into his plate, "You could've impressed her by remembering to put a hair dryer in the guest cottage."

She and Mike took their time, chatting about this and that as they ate, but he cleaned his plate in record time. Feeling fidgety, he wheeled himself into the kitchen—"No, don't bother," he told Mike when he was about to get up. "I'll get it."—and returned with the carafe of coffee riding on a tray on his lap.

He refilled their cups, then impatiently sipped from his while they exhausted the topic of cultivating rhododendrons, as if flower bushes mattered a shit. He lasted through a discussion on the merits of *Cats* over *Sunset Boulevard* and a heated debate over whether women should be allowed to play in the NBA before he rudely interrupted.

"Can we talk about my book now?"

"What's your rush?" Mike asked.

"We're not running a bed and breakfast here."

"I wish we were." Mike began collecting their used dishes and loading them onto the service cart. "At least I'd have someone pleasant to talk to now and then."

"I'm pleasant."

"As a skin rash."

Laughing, Parker balled up his napkin and tossed it onto the cart as though shooting a free throw. "Hurry up with those dishes and get back in here. You've been a good and gracious host, but I know you're itching to hear what Maris has to say about *Envy.*"

Mike went out, muttering under his breath.

"Bet I came out none too well in that monologue," Parker said when Mike was out of earshot.

"Are you two related?"

"Not by blood."

"He loves you."

Parker looked at her sharply. When he saw that she wasn't being caustic, he bit back a snide retort. He pondered her simple statement, then said slowly, "Yes, I suppose he does."

"You never considered it?"

"Not in words."

"Has he always taken care of you?"

"Not always."

"I meant since your accident."

"Accident?"

She gestured toward his wheelchair. "I assumed..."

"What made you assume it was an accident?"

"Wasn't it?"

Mike reappeared but, sensing that he'd walked in on a serious conversation, hesitated on the threshold. Parker waved him forward, this time grateful for the man's timing. Again, he figured it was intentional. Not much escaped Mike Strother.

Parker took a deep breath, blew it out, and, turning to Maris where she had sat down on the rattan sofa, said, "Okay, let's get this over with."

She laughed lightly. "It's not an execution, Parker."

"It's not?"

"Not at all. What you've written is good. Very good." She paused, glancing from him to Mike and back to him.

"Why do I feel that there's a 'however' in my near future?"

She smiled, then said quietly, "You've written a terrific outline."

Mike coughed softly and stared down at his shoes.

"Outline?"

"What you have is excellent." She wet her lips. "But it's...It skims the surface. You haven't delved deeply enough."

"I see."

"This isn't bad news, Parker."

"It's pretty bad."

Turning his chair around, he rolled it closer to the wall of windows and watched the shallow waves break against the sand. St. Anne Island didn't have much of a surf at any time, but especially not on a day like today, when the wind would barely qualify as such and there wasn't an offshore low pressure system churning up the elements.

"I'm not in the least bit discouraged by what I've read so far," Maris said. "Quite the contrary."

Her voice was even quieter now than before and sounded timid in the uncomfortable silence. From the kitchen came the swishing gurgles of the dishwasher, but otherwise the house was hushed.

Parker's shoulders began to shake. He covered his mouth to trap in the sound that issued up out of his chest.

Maris was instantly alarmed. "Oh, Parker, please don't."

Suddenly he spun his wheelchair around and looked at Mike, who joined in his laughter. "You win, you old son of a bitch. Fifty fucking bucks."

"I told you," Mike said, chuckling. "I've got great gut instincts."

"Along with a knack for alliteration."

Mike executed a neat, quick bow.

Maris, who had come to her feet, divided an angry look between them. She planted her hands on her hips—which she really shouldn't have done since the stance drew the damp cloth tighter across her chest, detailing lace beneath it.

"Obviously I'm the butt of an inside joke. Would you kindly let me in on it?"

"Not exactly a joke, Maris." Mike curbed his laughter and even looked a little sheepish. "It was more like an experiment. A test."

"Test?"

"A few months back we read the article about you in the publishing magazine. To me you came across as a knowledgeable editor and publisher. But Parker said that your daddy probably paid for the article—"

"I said bribed."

"—then commissioned your publicity department to write the piece."

"Which explained why it was so flattering."

"He said that you were no doubt riding on the coattails of your daddy's reputation, that you looked too young and...uh...inexperienced—"

"Actually, the word I used was 'shallow.' "

"—to know good writing from bad. That your reading was probably limited to magazine articles."

"On how to multiply your orgasms."

"And that you probably wouldn't know a good book from a good...uh..."

"Fill in the blank," Parker concluded with a beatific smile.

She had listened without interrupting or altering her expression. Now she came around slowly to face Parker, and he could fully appreciate all the metaphors he'd read about sparks shooting from someone's eyes.

Maris's eyes were bluish gray, like the rain clouds that rolled in from the west on summer afternoons and benevolently blocked the hot sun. They were basically benign, their turbulence only temporary. But even if short-lived, the turbulence was occasionally fierce. Her eyes had darkened to the hue of a storm cloud about to spawn a lightning bolt.

"I'm sure you're pissed." He shrugged, an unrepentant gesture. "I did everything I could, said everything I could think of to say, to discourage you from coming down here. But you came anyway. Last night when I..." He glanced at Mike and immediately decided not to mention kissing her. "When I tried convincing you to leave, you chose to stay."

His explanation fell short of earning her forgiveness. "You are an unmitigated son of a bitch, aren't you?"

"Pretty much, yeah," he said agreeably.

"You tried to trap me."

"Guilty."

"If I had gushed over how good your writing was, you would have known I was insincere."

"Or a lousy editor."

"But I knew better," Mike interjected. "I've read books that you edited, Maris. I told Parker, made a fifty-dollar bet with him, that his low opinion of you was unfounded and just plain wrong."

Maris heard all this, of course, but she hadn't even glanced in Mike's direction. Her anger was fixed on Parker. He smiled the sly grin of a gator that had just devoured a nest of ducklings, a grin that he knew would only make her more angry. "Sorry you came? Want to call the boat to take you back now?"

She tossed back her damp hair. "What caused Todd's father's death?"

Parker's heart gave a little flutter of gladness and relief. His wicked grin had been a lying indicator of the anxiety he'd been harboring.

"Was his death sudden or did it follow a lingering illness?" she asked.

"Does this mean you're still interested?"

"Did Todd take his death hard or was he glad to see the end of him? Was his father his idol? Or did the death release him from years of emotional abuse?"

She pushed an armchair close to him and snatched the pages from his hands as she sat down. "Do you understand what I'm getting at?"

"The characters need to be fleshed out."

"Precisely. Where do they come from? What were their families like? Rich, poor, middle class? Did they have similar upbringings or were their childhoods vastly different? We know they want to be writers, but you haven't told us why. Simply for the love of books? Or is writing a catharsis for Roark, a way for him to vent his anger? Is it a panacea for Todd's unhappiness?"

"Panacea?"

"Are you listening?"

"I'll look it up later."

"You know what it means," she snapped.

He smiled again. "Yes. I do." From the corner of his eye, he noticed Mike leaving the room and pulling the door closed behind him.

Maris was still in high gear. "Life in the fraternity house—"

"There's more of that in the next chapter."

"There's a next chapter?"

"I worked on it this morning."

"Great. I liked that part. Very much. It's vivid. As I read, I could smell the gym socks." She shuddered delicately. "And the bit with the toothbrush..."

"Yeah?"

"It's almost too outrageous to be fiction. Personal experience?"

"What else needs work?" he asked.

"Ah. I get it. Personal questions are disallowed."

"If you washed out your undies last night, what did you sleep in?"

She sucked in a quick breath, opened her mouth to speak, then thought better of it. Her teeth clicked softly when she closed her mouth.

Tilting his head, he squinted his eyes as though to bring her into sharper focus. "Nothing, right?"

She lowered her eyes to her lap. Or maybe to his lap. He was tempted to say, *Yeah, it works, but if you're curious, why not touch it and find out?* But he didn't because she just might summon that boat to the mainland after all.

"You've made your point," she said gruffly. "No personal questions."

Picking up the manuscript pages again, she thumbed through them to refresh her memory on the notes she had jotted in the margins. "I'd like to see you expand, well, just about all of it." She glanced up at him to gauge his reaction, and when he declined to respond, she sat back with a sigh. "You expected this, didn't you? You knew what I was going to say."

He nodded. "I skimmed the surface, just as you said."

"To test my competence."

"Hmm."

"You auditioned me."

"Something like that."

Her smile was self-deprecating. She was being a good sport and letting him off more lightly than he deserved. Actually he would prefer that she rant and rave, lambast him with foul language, haul off and let him have it right in the kisser. What he had to do would be easier to do if she were as much of a bitch as he was a bastard. They were unequally matched opponents. She was out of her league and didn't even know it.

He said, "You had every right to tell Mike and me to go fuck ourselves."

"My father would never have tolerated that kind of language from me."

"So you *are* a daddy's girl?"

"Big time. Because he's such a good daddy. He's a gentleman and a scholar. He would like you."

He laughed harshly. "Not if he's a gentleman, he wouldn't."

"You're wrong. He would admire your audacity. He'd probably even call it 'balls.' "

Parker smiled. "A man after my own heart."

"He read your prologue and liked it. He encouraged me to pursue this project."

He gestured toward the manuscript pages. "So pursue it."

Consulting her notes again, she resumed. "Take your time, Parker. There's no page limit. Leave the trimming and editing to me. That's my job. You don't need to reveal all the background information in the first few chapters. It can be scattered throughout, but learn what the lives of these characters were like prior to the time they met."

"I already know." He tapped his temple. "Up here."

"Excellent. But the reader can't read your mind."

"I understand."

"That's it, for now."

She evened up the edges of the sheets, then laid them in her lap. "I'm glad I passed that silly test of yours," she said candidly. "I've missed being involved in this stage of the process. I didn't realize how much I'd missed it until I began making these notes last night. I love molding the story, brainstorming with the writer, especially a talented writer."

He pointed to himself. "And that would be me?"

"That would be you. Definitely."

Her gaze, so candid and earnest, made him uncomfortable. He looked out toward the ocean so he wouldn't have to see her sincerity, wouldn't have to feel . . . so he wouldn't have to feel, period.

Maybe he was the one playing out of his league.

Leaning toward him, she nudged his knee and lowered her voice to a near whisper. "I don't suppose you've changed your mind about letting me know which character—"

"Beat it, will ya?" He spun his chair away from her and pushed it toward his worktable. "I've got a bitch of an editor and she's piled a shitload of work on me."

"Envy" Ch. 4
1985

T hat Tuesday morning two days before Thanksgiving dawned cloudy and cold. As though on cue, as though roasted turkey and pumpkin pie would be incompatible with mild weather, a cold front lowered the temperature just in time for the holiday.

Roark's alarm clock was set for seven-thirty. By seven-forty-five, he was shaved, showered, and dressed. By ten minutes to eight, he was downstairs in the residence dining hall, drinking coffee, glancing through his manuscript, and wondering how much abuse Professor Hadley was going to inflict on this creative effort into which he had poured his heart and soul.

The quality of his Thanksgiving holiday depended upon the outcome of the conference. He would either spend the long weekend relaxed and comfortable in the knowledge that his work had met with his professor's approval or foundering in the lake of misery called self-doubt.

Either way, he didn't have much longer to wait. The verdict would be read soon. Whether Hadley's remarks were good, bad, or ugly, hearing them would be a relief. This anticipation was hell.

"Sweet roll, Roark?"

He glanced up to see the house mom standing beside his chair. "Sure, Mom, thanks."

Soon after pledging, Roark had ordained the fraternity house mother the most long-suffering woman alive. Mrs. Brenda Thompson had given up a peaceful widowhood to voluntarily move into a three-story house with eighty-two men who behaved like miscreants sent away to a nine-month summer camp.

They respected nothing, neither persons nor property. Nothing was sacred—not God or country, one's hometown, one's pet, one's sister, or one's mother. It was open season on anything an individual held near and dear. Everything was subject to ribald ridicule.

They had the decorum of swine. As male *Homo sapiens* tend to do when gathered in groups of two or more, these eighty-two had regressed to the level of cavemen not nearly as refined as Neanderthals. Everything their mothers had forbidden them to do at home, they did in the fraternity house. Zealously and with relish, they celebrated rude behavior.

Mrs. Thompson, a soft-spoken and dignified lady, tolerated their language, which was foul, and their personal habits, which were fouler. Her maternal nature invited their confidences and earned their affection. But, unlike a parent, she exercised no discipline over them.

She turned a blind eye to the drinking, cussing, and fornicating, in which they participated with wild abandon. Without a complaint from her they could play their sound systems as loudly as they wished. They could sleep on their sheets for a semester or longer before laundering them. When they shaved the fraternity letters into the fur of a cat belonging to a girl who had jilted one of their members, Mom's only comment was on how nicely they had lined up the letters.

In her presence, particularly on Wednesday evenings during their one formal meal of the week, where jackets and ties and some semblance of civilization was required, they apologized for their expletives, belches, and farts with an obligatory and questionably sincere, "Excuse me, Mom." With a patient little smile, she always pardoned the offender, even though a similar offense would be forthcoming seconds later.

In her they had the Dream Mom.

Roark suspected that she favored him over some of the others, although he couldn't imagine why she did. He'd been as crude and badly behaved as any. After a toga party his sophomore year, he had passed out under the baby grand piano in the downstairs parlor and woke himself up choking on Jack Daniel's-flavored vomit.

Mrs. Thompson appeared in a long flannel robe and slippers, patting his shoulder and asking him if he was all right. "I'm fine," he mumbled, although clearly he wasn't.

Without censure and with the dignity of a nun, she removed the blanket that someone had tossed over an inflatable doll, the anatomically obscene, unofficial house mascot, and carried it back to Roark. She covered him with it where he lay, miserably cold, sick as a dog, and stinking to high heaven.

From that night forward, Mom seemed to have a special fondness for him. Maybe because when he had sobered up, he thanked her for the kindness and apologized for disturbing her sleep. Maybe because he'd had the rug beneath the piano cleaned at his own expense. No one else in the house had noticed—either that he had soiled the rug or that he'd had it cleaned. But Mrs. Thompson had noticed. He supposed these nods toward common decency demonstrated to her that he was redeemable, that he had at least some breeding.

"You're up earlier than usual, aren't you?" she asked now as she placed a jelly doughnut on a paper plate beside his coffee mug.

Ordinarily she didn't serve the boys food. They served themselves from a cafeteria-style line, taking what they wanted from the fare a surly cook put out for them in the manner of a farmer filling the feed trough for his herd.

"I'm meeting with my senior advisor this morning," he explained. In deference to her, he remembered to use a napkin instead of licking the doughnut's sugar glaze off his fingers.

She motioned to his manuscript. "Is that the book you're writing for your capstone?"

"Yes, ma'am. What I've got so far."

"I'm sure it'll be very good."

"Thanks, Mom. I hope so."

She wished him good luck with his meeting, then went over to say good morning to another boy who had just straggled in. He was the most handsome member in the house and attracted girls like moths to flame. His brothers wanted to hate him for his unearned good fortune, but he was too nice a guy to hate. Rather than exploit his movie-star looks, he downplayed them, seemed almost embarrassed by them. He glanced over at Roark and raised his cleft chin in greeting. "What's up, Shakespeare?"

"What's up, RB?"

Everyone had a nickname, and the accepted house greeting was, "What's up?" To which no one ever replied. That's just what they said.

Roark's nickname—to everyone except Todd—was Shakespeare. His fraternity brothers knew he liked to write, and William Shakespeare was the one writer that most of them could possibly call to mind if a gun were held to their heads. He had never tried to explain that Shakespeare wrote plays in blank verse, while he wrote stories in prose. Some concepts were just too complex to grasp, especially for individuals like the fraternity brother who, upon being asked by his English lit teacher to identify the bard by his portrait, had responded, "How the fuck you expect me to know all the presidents?"

Roark was flattered by the nickname, but this morning it seemed particularly presumptuous. Checking his wristwatch, he saw that he had fifteen minutes to reach Hadley's office. More than enough time. Nevertheless, he drained his coffee, stuffed his manuscript back into its worn folder, put the folder into his backpack, and left the dining hall.

Not until he got outside did he realize the drastic change in the weather that had occurred overnight. The wind chill put the temperature down around the freezing point, not cold enough to freeze the pond in the center of campus, but enough to make him wish he had grabbed a heavier coat before setting out.

The Language Arts Building, like most on campus, was basically Georgian in design. Older and statelier than the newer halls, it had a wide portico with six

white columns. The aged red brick on the north wall
was completely covered in Boston ivy that had turned
from green to orange in a matter of days.

As soon as Roark was in sight of the building, he
picked up his pace, more for warmth than for fear
of being late. Despite his conservative upbringing,
which had included church on Sundays, he was ambiguous about the existence, nature, and disposition
of a Supreme Being. He wasn't certain that an entity with the omniscience attributed to God would
give a flip about Roark Slade's daily trials. But today
wasn't the day to reject any possible advantage, so
he offered up an obscure little prayer as he crossed
the portico and entered the building.

He was assailed by the burning-dust smell of old
furnaces. Apparently they'd been cranked up to full
capacity this morning, because the building was uncomfortably warm. He shrugged off his backpack and
jacket as he jogged up the stairs to the second floor.

He was greeted by several students with whom
he shared his major. One, a rail-thin hippy with pink-
tinted John Lennon glasses and stringy hair, loped up
to him. "Yo, Slade."

Only girls called him Roark. Except for Todd, he
wasn't sure there was a male on campus who even
knew his first name.

"Coffee later? We're getting together a study group
for finals. Ten o'clock in the Union."

"I don't know if I'll be free. I'm on my way to see
Hadley."

"You mean like now?"

"As we speak."

"Fuck, man, that sucks. Good luck."

"Thanks. Later."

"Later."

Roark continued down the hallway. The jelly doughnut hadn't been such a good idea. It felt like a bowling ball in his stomach. The coffee had left a sour taste in his mouth, and he admonished himself for not having a breath mint. When he arrived at office number 207 he paused to draw a deep breath. The door was standing slightly ajar. He wiped his damp palm on the leg of his jeans and knocked softly.

"Come in."

Professor Hadley was seated behind his desk. His feet, laced into a pair of brown suede Hush Puppies, were propped on the open top drawer. A stack of reading matter was in his lap, which was only one of myriad surfaces in the room that was stacked with reading matter. An inestimable number of trees had sacrificed their lives to provide the paper that filled Hadley's office. Per square inch, it was probably the largest consumer of paper globally.

"Good morning, Professor."

"Mr. Slade."

Was it just his imagination, or did Hadley's greeting sound peremptory?

The advisor's manner could never be described as friendly. Unlike some instructors, he didn't get chummy with his students. In fact, it was customary for him to treat them with barely concealed contempt. Even a respectable grade on a writing assignment didn't inoculate one against his scorn.

His teaching style was to make a student feel like an ignoramus. Only after the student had been knocked off the pedestal of his self-esteem, and the pedestal itself reduced to rubble, did Hadley drive home his point and teach him something. He seemed to believe that abject humility sharpened one's ability to learn.

As he stepped into the cramped office, Roark reassured himself that the curtness was a habit with Hadley and that he shouldn't take it personally.

"No, don't close the door," Hadley told him.

"Oh. Sorry." Roark reached back to catch the door, which he had been about to close.

"You should be."

"Sir?"

"Is there something wrong with your hearing, Mr. Slade?"

"My hearing? No, sir."

"Then you heard me correctly when I said that you should be sorry. You are now..." He glanced at something beyond Roark's left shoulder. "Fifty-six and one-half minutes late."

Roark turned. On the wall behind him was a clock. White face. Stark black numerals. A dash marking each of the sixty minutes. The short hand was already on the nine. The minute hand was three dashes away from the twelve.

The old man's lost it, Roark thought. *Something's pickled his brain. Paper fumes, maybe. Is there such a thing?*

He cleared his throat. "Excuse me, sir, but I'm right on time. Our meeting was scheduled for nine."

"Eight."

"Originally, yes. But don't you remember calling and changing it to nine? You left a message with my roommate."

"I assure you that my memory is in perfect working order, Mr. Slade. I made no such call." Hadley glared up at him from beneath dense eyebrows. "Our meeting was at eight."

Chapter 10

———◆———

He was an old man.

Not until recently had Daniel Matherly thought of himself as aged. He had refused to acknowledge his elderly status far past the reasonable time to do so. Unsolicited literature mailed to him by the AARP was discarded unopened, and he declined to take advantage of senior citizen discounts.

Lately, however, the reflection in his mirror was tough to dispute, and his joints made an even better argument that he was definitely a...graduating senior.

Today, as he sat behind his desk in his home study, Daniel was amused by his own thoughts. If reflecting on one's life wasn't proof of advancing age, what was? His preoccupation with his degenerating body was a firm indication that it was degenerating. Who else but the very old dwelled on such things?

Young people didn't have the time. They didn't ponder death because they were too busy living. Getting an education. Pursuing their chosen profession. Entering or exiting marriages. Rearing children. They couldn't be bothered with thoughts of death. "Mortality" was just a word that they kept shelved to think about in the distant future. Occasionally they might glance at it and grow uneasy, but their attention was hastily diverted to matters related to living, not dying.

But the distant future inexorably drew closer until the day arrived when one could no longer save the topic of his own mortality for later contemplation, when one must take it from the shelf and examine it closely. Daniel wasn't morbidly fixated on the inevitable, but he knew that the time had come for him to address it and consider all its implications.

The faithful Maxine thought that he slumbered peacefully every night, but he didn't. When he told Maris that he slept like a baby, she had no reason to doubt him. As a young man, he had never required more than four or five hours of sleep per night. Those required hours had decreased in proportion to his aging. Now, if he was lucky, on any given night he would sleep for two or three hours.

The others he spent lying in bed reading his beloved books— classics he had devoured as a boy, bestsellers that other houses had been lucky enough to publish and profit from, books he himself had edited and published.

When he wasn't reading, he reflected on his life—his proud moments and, in fairness, those he wasn't proud of. He thought frequently about the prep school friend who had died of leukemia. If he'd been born several decades later, he probably would have been treated and cured to live a long and fulfilling life. To this day, Daniel missed him and longed for the years of friendship they had been denied.

He remembered the pain of losing his first love to another man. Looking back, he acknowledged that the young lady's choice had been right for both of them, but at the time, he had believed he would die of a broken heart. He never saw her after her wedding day. He heard that she and her husband had moved to California. He wondered if her life there had been happy. He wondered if she was still living.

His first wife had been a lovely woman, and he'd been dev-astated when she died. But then he'd met Rosemary, Maris's mother, and she had been, without question, the love of his life. Beautiful, charming, gracious, artistic, intelligent, a perfect com-panion and ardent lover. She had been supportive of a husband who put in long hours at the office and was too often distracted by the pressures of managing a business. He had appreciated her patience and devotion to him and their marriage but was certain he had failed to let her know the extent of his appreciation.

In hindsight, he regretted all the times his responsibilities at Matherly Press had kept him from Rosemary. He wished he had those days back. His choices would be different. He would re-arrange his priorities, appropriate more time and energy to his family.

Or, in all honesty, he would probably make the same bad choices, commit the same mistakes all over again.

Thankfully, his regrets were few and minor, although there were a couple of major ones. Once he had fired an editor out of pique, over a silly difference of opinion. Slyly, he had leaked the secret that the man was homosexual, this at a time when it wasn't accepted or even tolerated. He hinted that the man's per-sonal life had begun affecting his work—which was an outright lie. The man was an excellent editor and his work ethic was im-peccable.

Despite his qualifications, no one would hire him because of Daniel's rumor. He became a pariah in the industry he loved and ultimately moved away from the city. Daniel's spite had ruined the man's promising career and had cost publishing a talented con-tributor. He would carry the guilt over that to his grave.

Several years following Rosemary's death, he had engaged in an affair he wasn't proud of. It had been difficult for a middle-age bachelor to conduct a romance while living with a teenage daughter. It required finesse and a constant juggling of sched-ules. The woman had been jealous of his relationship with

Maris. She became demanding, continually forcing him to choose between her and Maris. Daniel finally let his head overrule his desire. He realized that he could never love anyone who didn't love and accept his daughter wholly, completely, and without reservation. He ended the affair.

Through decades he had managed to maintain his reputation as an excellent publisher. He seemed to have been blessed with a sixth sense for which manuscripts to grab and which to decline. During his tenure, he had increased the company's worth a hundredfold. He had earned more money than he could possibly spend, more than Maris could spend in her lifetime, and probably more than her children could spend.

Money was a nice by-product of his success, but it wasn't what motivated him. His drive came from wanting to preserve what his ancestors had worked so painstakingly to create. Before he turned thirty, he had inherited the stewardship of the family business. It had fallen to him to protect and improve it for the next generation.

Which was Maris, his crowning achievement. She was a thousand times more precious to him than Matherly Press, and he was more dedicated to protecting her than he was to protecting his publishing house from the wolves that got bigger and hungrier each year.

He couldn't shelter her completely, of course. No parent could spare his child life's knocks, and even if he could, it would be unfair. Maris had to live her own life, and integral to living were mishaps and mistakes.

He only hoped that her disappointments wouldn't be too severe, that her triumphs and joys would outnumber them, and that when she reached his age, if she was fortunate to live that long, she would look back on her life with at least the same degree of satisfaction as he had been graced to do.

He wasn't afraid of death. To no one's knowledge, save Maxine's, he'd had several recent discussions with a priest. Rosemary had been a devout and practicing Catholic. He'd never converted, but he had absorbed some of her faith through osmosis. He firmly believed that they would enjoy the afterlife together.

He didn't fear dying.

He did fear dying a fool.

That was the worry that had robbed him of sleep last night. Deeply troubled, he'd been unable to read the nighttime hours away. Morning had brought no relief from this pervasive uneasiness.

He couldn't shake the feeling that he was missing something, that a revealing word or deed or demeanor that he would have detected when he was younger and sharper—five years ago, even one year ago—was escaping him.

Was this paranoia valid? Or a symptom of encroaching dementia?

Before his grandfather's death, Daniel remembered him ranting about his nurse's thievery. One day he accused her of being a German spy on a mission to assassinate U.S. war veterans. With the conviction of the mentally unhinged, he had claimed that the housekeeper was pregnant with his child. Nothing could convince him that the sixty-seven-year-old Englishwoman couldn't possibly be with child.

Was that where he was headed? Was this obscure and unnamed disquiet the harbinger of full-blown senility?

Or—and this is what he chose to believe—was it an indication that he had lost none of his faculties, that he was as astute as ever, and that the intuitiveness that had successfully guided him through fifty years of publishing was still reliable?

Until they proved to be untrustworthy, he chose to trust his instincts. They were telling him that something wasn't right. He sensed it as a stag senses the presence of a stalking hunter from a mile away.

Perhaps he was just overly troubled by Maris's unhappiness. She wasn't as good as she believed at concealing her feelings from him. He'd picked up signals of marital disharmony. The cause and severity of that disharmony he didn't yet know. But if it was disharmonious enough to visibly disturb Maris, it disturbed him.

And then there was Noah. He wanted to trust the man both as a protégé and as a son-in-law, but only if Noah deserved his trust.

Grunting with the effort, Daniel brought his leather desk chair upright and opened a desk drawer. He withdrew his day planner and unzipped it, then removed a business card from one of the smaller compartments.

"William Sutherland," the card read. No company name or address. Only that name and a telephone number engraved in crisp navy blue block letters.

Daniel thoughtfully fingered the card, as he often had since obtaining it several weeks ago. He hadn't called the number. He hadn't yet spoken to Mr. Sutherland personally, but after this morning's ruminations, he felt that the time was right to do so.

It was a sneaky and underhanded thing to do. Merely thinking about it made him feel deceitful. No one ever need know, of course. Unless—God forbid—something came of it. Probably nothing would. Probably he was overreacting. But it wasn't within his makeup to be careless. There was too much at stake to let twinges of guilt overshadow prudence. Given a choice between conscience and caution, there was no choice. The adage applied: Better to be safe than sorry.

As he reached for the telephone, he resolved to be more watchful, alert to nuances in speech and expressions, more attuned to what was going on around him. He didn't want to be the last to know...anything.

He didn't fear dying. But he did fear dying a fool.

* * *

"You should stay away from it. It's ready to fall down," Mike told Maris as he took a swipe at the mantel with a piece of fine sandpaper.

"If it's that dilapidated, is it safe for Parker to go there alone?"

"Of course not. But try telling him that."

"Mike..."

Sensing her hesitation, he turned toward her.

"Never mind," she said. "It wouldn't be fair to either you or Parker for me to ask."

"About...?"

"His disability."

"No, it wouldn't be fair."

She nodded, shook off the solemn mood, and asked, "How do I get there?"

"It could be dangerous."

"I promise to run if it starts to fall down."

"I wasn't talking about the building. I meant you could be in danger from Parker. He doesn't like to be disturbed."

"I'll take my chances. Is it close enough to walk?"

"Do you walk a lot in New York?"

"Every day, if the weather's good."

"Then it's close enough to walk."

After giving directions, he cautioned her once again. "He won't like it when you show up."

"Probably not," she replied, laughing lightly.

She had spent all day indoors, reading until her eyes felt strained. It was good to get outside, although by no stretch of the imagination could this be referred to as "fresh air." The heat was impossible, the humidity worse. The sunlight was glaring and relentless, but even shade offered little relief from the sweltering heat.

Still, the island was exotically beautiful, and the climate was essential to it. The live oak trees had an ancient, almost mystical dignity that was enhanced by the curly Spanish moss draping their limbs. The dense air smelled of salt water and fish, not altogether unpleasant when mingled with the intoxicating perfumes of the flowering plants that bloomed in profusion.

Maris passed a house that was set well back from the road. Children were playing in the yard. The boy and girl were young enough to dance around the lawn sprinkler without self-consciousness. They squealed in glee as they took turns leaping over the oscillating spray.

At another house, she spotted a large dog lying in the shade of a pickup truck. She crossed the road and watched him warily as she moved past, but she needn't have worried. He raised his head, looked at her with disinterest, stood, stretched, made three tight circles in the dirt, then resumed his original spot and closed his eyes.

She met no cars on the road. Her only company were the cicadas that buzzed loudly but lazily under cover of the thick foliage.

The abandoned cotton gin was located right where Mike had said it would be, although if his directions hadn't been so precise she might have missed it. The forest had reclaimed the structure. From some angles, it would have been totally camouflaged by the greenery that enfolded it.

To reach it from the road, one had to take a crushed-shell path. It wasn't much of a path, however. Maris regarded it dubiously. It was no more than a yard wide, at most. Tall weeds grew on either side of it. Looking down at her bare ankles, she seriously considered passing up the gin in favor of the island's other points of interest that Mike had recommended.

" 'Fraidy-cat," she muttered.

She looked around for a stick, and when she found one that was suitable, she started up the path, reaching far out in front of her to beat at the tall weeds. She wanted to alert any varmints, reptilian or otherwise, to her presence and give them an opportunity to relocate before she saw them.

Thankfully, she made it up the path without encountering any local fauna. She dropped her stick, dusted off her hands, and took a good look at the hulking building. It was, as Mike had described, a structure on the brink of collapse.

The wood was gray and weathered. The tin roof had been corroded by rust. Large patches of the exterior and part of the roof were covered by an impenetrable carpet of vines. One species bloomed bright purple flowers that seemed incompatible with the overall feeling of dilapidation and abandonment.

With misgiving, Maris approached the wide door that was standing open. The interior was even larger than indicated by the exterior. It was cavernous and dark inside, with only an occasional stripe of sunlight shining through a separation in the vertical wooden slats that formed the walls or a miniature spotlight cast on the dirt floor by a hole in the roof.

The rear half of the lower story was covered by a loft. The ceiling of the overhang was built of massive wood beams. A large wheel about ten feet in diameter was situated just beneath this ceiling and was connected to the dirt floor by a wood column as big around as a barrel. Maris had never seen anything like it.

She blinked to adjust her eyes to the gloom. "Hello?" Receiving no answer, she stepped inside and took a few hesitant steps forward. "Parker?" After a moment, she repeated, "Hello?"

"Here."

She jumped and flattened her hand against her heart, coming about quickly. He was in a corner behind her, invisible except for one ray of sunlight coming through the roof and reflecting off the chrome of his chair.

Recovering, she asked crossly, "Didn't you hear me?"

"Are you serious? All that thrashing? You'd never make it as an Indian brave."

"Then why didn't you say something?"

"How'd you get here?"

"Walked. How'd you get here?"

"How do I get everywhere?"

"You can roll your chair along that path?"

"I manage."

He remained where he was, but she could feel him looking at her and realized that she must appear only a silhouette against the square of light behind her. She advanced farther inside but only a few steps.

"Where'd you get the clothes?"

She glanced down at her casual skirt, shirt, and sandals as though she'd never seen them before. It was an outfit she usually took to their country house for a summer weekend of cookouts and antique shopping. She'd packed it herself in New York just two days ago, but it seemed much longer ago than that and much farther away.

"Mike arranged for my suitcase to be picked up at the hotel and sent over. He went to the dock and met the boat."

"He's gone dotty."

"Pardon?"

"He's got a crush on you."

"He's just being nice."

"We've had this conversation already."

They had. She didn't want to repeat it. The last time, it had ended...She didn't want to think about how it had ended.

A silence ensued. Her eyes had adjusted to the dimness, but she could still barely see him where he remained in the deep shadows of the corner. To fill the awkward silence, she said, "This is a picturesque building."

"Which you accidentally happened upon?"

"Mike gave me directions."

"Mike talks too much."

"Not that much. He gives away none of your secrets."

"Until a few minutes ago this building was my secret. I come here to be alone."

She ignored the implication that he didn't welcome her company and took a look around. The dirt floor was littered with animal droppings and trash. At one time, someone had built a fire. Traces of ash and charred wood were still scattered about. A staircase attached to one wall led up to the second level, but many of the steps were missing, and those that remained appeared incapable of supporting anything heavier than a beetle. All in all, it was a spooky old place, especially the rear portion with its low overhang and antiquated industrial apparatus that looked to her like something an evil giant might use to physically torture an enemy giant. She couldn't imagine why Parker chose to spend time here.

"What's its history?"

"Do you know anything about cotton?"

Cheekily she quoted a popular TV commercial. " 'It's the fabric of our lives.' "

To her surprise, Parker laughed. A real laugh, not that scornful sound that usually served as his laugh. Taking advantage of this rarity, she added, "It's also useful when it comes to removing nail polish."

His laughter subsided, making the resulting silence even more noticeable. Then he said gruffly, "Come here."

Chapter 11

Parker waited out her hesitation. He didn't repeat the request, figuring she would call his implied dare, and she did. After a moment or two of consideration, she carefully picked her way across the distance separating them.

Her hair had been gathered into a makeshift ponytail that subtracted at least five years from her appearance. Her white shirt was tied in a knot at her waist. Her khaki skirt was short enough to show a couple inches of thigh. Smooth, shapely thighs that invited libidinous speculation.

"When this gin was first built," he said, "three sides of it were left open. The machinery was animal-powered."

"Animal-powered?"

"Follow me."

He wheeled toward the back of the building. As she followed him beneath the overhang, she reflexively ducked her head, causing him to smile. She had cleared the low, spider-infested ceiling, but not by much.

"I've never had that problem myself," he said. He then pointed to the faint ring in the hard-packed earth. "If you look closely, you can see a circular depression there in the dirt. That's the path worn by the mules that turned the drive wheel that powered the gin stand."

"Up there?"

"Right. When cotton was king, it was brought here by the wagonload. Long-strand sea island cotton. High grade. Silky in texture and more easily separated from its seeds than other varieties."

"Therefore very desirable."

He nodded. "And the island's sandy soil was ideal for growing it. It was unloaded onto a platform outside and carried up to the second floor, where the gin separated the fiber from the seeds.

"The lint was then blown out, collected, and carried to an outdoor screw press, which was also mule-powered. Once it was pressed into bales, they were bagged and hauled cross-island to the dock for transport to the cotton exchanges on the mainland."

"It sounds very labor-intensive."

"You're right. From the time a cotton seed was planted in early spring until the last bale of the crop was shipped out, the process took a year."

"Was this the only gin on the island?"

"Right again. One planter, one gin, one family. The family that built my house. They had a monopoly that made them rich until the whole market collapsed. They tried to switch to oyster canning, which was being done on other sea islands, but they didn't know anything about it, went completely broke within a year, and cleared out."

"So this structure more or less chronicles the island's history."

"Nineteenth century history for sure," he said. "It's documented that in 1878 a little girl, a child of a worker, walked behind one of the mules turning the screw press outside. The ornery animal kicked her in the head. She died two days later. Her father put down the mule, execution-style. The details of what he did to the carcass are gruesome. A duel between feuding brothers is also recorded. They shot and killed each other in 1855.

"Then there's a romantic myth about the love affair between a white overseer and a beautiful slave woman. It's told that their affair was looked upon with such vicious disfavor that they were cast off the island in a small boat. It's said they were bound for Charleston, but folks watching their departure through spy-glasses reported that they saw them capsize and perish, which many thought was a befitting punishment.

"However, years later, a colony of mulattos was discovered living peacefully on another sea island previously thought to be uninhabited. These people were believed to be the descendants of the mixed couple and the survivors of a shipwrecked slave ship. They were an incredibly handsome clan. Some had skin the color of café au lait and eyes as green as jade.

"A visiting French nobleman, who was deep-sea fishing in the area, sought refuge from a storm on their island. While he was there, one of the nubile young ladies caught his eye and captured his heart. They married and he took all her family back to France with him. Where they lived happ'ly ever after."

Maris drew in a long, slow breath. "You tell good stories, Parker."

"It's a fable. Probably untrue."

"It's still a good story."

"So you're a romantic?"

"Unabashed." She smiled, then said, "You know a lot about the gin. Was your family in the cotton business?"

"I think my great-granddaddy picked it by hand during the Depression. But so did just about every able-bodied person in the South. Women, children, blacks, whites, all struggling to survive. Hunger doesn't discriminate."

"What did your father do?"

"Physician. Family practice. The gamut. From delivering babies to lancing boils."

"Is he retired?"

He shook his head. "He couldn't break a forty-year habit, and he couldn't heal himself when lung cancer caught up with him. He died long before he should have."

"And your mother?"

"Outlived him twelve years. She died several years ago. And before you ask, I'm an only child."

"So am I."

"I know."

After registering momentary surprise that he knew that, she said, "Oh. The article."

"Yeah."

Several strands of hair had come loose from her ponytail and were lying against her nape. The wheat-colored strands appeared slightly damp and curled from the humidity. He caught himself staring at them.

He looked away to clear his vision. "Yeah, that article was chock-full of information about you, your father, and your husband. What's he like?"

"Very robust. Especially for a man of seventy-eight."

"I meant your husband. Is he also very robust?"

"We agreed not to ask any personal questions."

"That's personal? What don't you want me to know about your husband?"

"Nothing. It's not that."

"Then what?"

"I followed you here to talk about *Envy.*"

"Want to sit down?"

Apparently confused by his sudden shift of topic, she shook her head. "There's nowhere to sit." She glanced at the beams overhead. "Besides, it's creepy under here."

He swept his arm toward the front part of the building and she preceded him from beneath the overhang. Her attention was drawn to a circle of bricks in the dirt floor. They were stacked two deep, forming an enclosure roughly five feet in diameter. "What's that?"

"Careful," Parker warned as he quickly rolled his chair to her side. "That's an abandoned well."

"Why in here?"

"One of the more innovative patriarchs of the cotton dynasty decided to convert the gin to steam power. He began digging this well for the water supply, but died of diphtheria before the project was completed. His heir abandoned the idea as impractical. Rightly, I believe. It wasn't economically feasible for the amount of their production."

She peered over the rim of bricks into the darkness of the hole. "How deep is it?"

"Deep enough."

"For what?"

After holding her gaze for a moment, he backed up, then wheeled past her. He hitched his chin toward an upended crate. "That'll do for a perch if you're not too particular."

After testing the crate's sturdiness, she gingerly sat down on the rough wood.

"Be careful of splinters," he warned. "Although my picking them out of the backs of your thighs is a bewitching thought."

She shot him a withering look. "I'll take care not to fidget."

"I'm sure I would enjoy extracting the splinters, but I'm equally sure your very robust husband wouldn't approve."

"Was that thunder?"

"Changing the subject, Maris?"

"Yes."

Grinning, he glanced over his shoulder toward the open door. It had grown noticeably darker outside as well as in. "Afternoon thunderstorms frequently boil up during the summer. Sometimes they pass over in an hour or less, sometimes they linger through the night. You never can tell." Overhead the first raindrops struck the roof with fat-sounding slaps.

She inhaled deeply. "You can smell the rain."

"Smells good, doesn't it?"

"Sounds wonderful, too."

"Um-huh."

The rain didn't cool the air much, but it had a definite effect on the atmosphere. It became closer, denser. He was aware of it. And so was Maris. She probably couldn't characterize this sudden change any better than he could, but it was distinctly felt.

Her eyes moved away from watching the rain through the open door and found his. They stared at each other through the deepening gloom. Oddly, it wasn't an uncomfortable exchange. If he'd been forced to use an applicable adverb to describe the way in which they were looking at one another, he would choose "expectantly," a modifier that combined curiosity with caution, wonderment with undertones of wariness.

He felt her gaze like a tug on his chest drawing him closer, and he was looking at her with the same level of intensity. Given the electricity arcing between them, he was curious to know what she would say.

She played it safe by commenting on *Envy*. "That was a rotten trick that Todd played on Roark."

"Rigging it so he missed his appointment with Hadley."

"You set me up perfectly. I didn't see it coming."

"That's good."

"Now what is Roark going to do about it?"

"What do you think he should do?"

"Beat the hell out of Todd."

He whistled at her vehemence.

"Well, isn't that what a guy would do?"

"Probably," he replied. "Fury would be his initial reaction, and he would seek a physical outlet. But let's talk about it. Remember, Todd was only paying Roark back for the toothbrush stunt."

"But that was a prank," she exclaimed. "Gross and disgusting, granted. But college boys do stuff like that to each other, don't they?"

"Did you know college boys who did stuff like that?"

"I attended a girls' school."

"Right, right, I read that," he said, as though just reminded of that part of her bio, which he knew as well as if he'd written it himself. "So it's safe to assume that you have no experience of college boys and how they act."

"No, it's safe to assume that my experience is limited to how they act on dates with girls, which is different from how they interact with each other."

"Is that how you met your husband? On a date during college?"

"Much later than that."

"How much later?"

"When he came to work at Matherly Press."

"Smart move on his part. He married the boss's daughter."

That irked her. So much so that Parker knew he wasn't the first to connect those two dots. It had crossed her mind, too. Perhaps too often for comfort. Her expression turned professional and peeved.

"Can we get back to your book, please?"

"Sure. Sorry for the digression."

While taking a moment to collect her thoughts, she pulled her lower lip through her teeth a couple of times and absently fiddled with a button on her blouse. Parker wondered when those two insignificant, subconsciously feminine gestures had become so goddamn sexy.

"A prank is one thing," she said. "But Todd's joke had a meanness about it that was unmistakable. It wasn't harmless. It couldn't be undone as easily as buying a new toothbrush. He was tinkering with Roark's future. This practical joke could damage Roark's grade, compromise his capstone, affect his writing ambitions, and possibly even crush them. He can't let it pass and do nothing."

"True. Roark won't fold. He won't easily forgive the experience, but it'll sure as hell motivate him."

"Yes, yes," she said excitedly. "This will fuel his determination to succeed."

"To reach a level of success that Todd will—"

"Envy," she said, finishing the thought for him.

He grinned. "Per your suggestion, I'll let him blow off steam, land a few punches, which Todd will concede he deserved."

"So they remain friends?"

"It wouldn't be a book if they didn't. If their friendship fell apart here, the story would be over."

"Not necessarily. It could be just as powerful if they became bitter enemies at this point."

"Wait and see, Maris."

"What?"

"Give me time."

Her eyes widened marginally. "You've got it plotted already, don't you?"

"For the most part," he confessed with a negligent shrug. "There are some details still to hammer out."

She tried, but failed, to looked piqued. "You've been stringing me along."

"To get you excited."

"I'm excited." Her animation proved it. "May I make another suggestion?"

"I don't promise to take it."

"Agreed."

"Then fire away."

"Could we see Roark falling in love?"

"With the girl who went back to her boyfriend?"

"Yes. You told the reader that he fell in love, but we didn't get to see it. We didn't experience it along with him. You don't even give this girl a name. I think it could be very poignant, as well as useful toward developing his character. How he handles the disappointment. That kind of thing. And what if..."

"Go on," he said when she hesitated.

"What if Todd were somehow involved in their breakup?"

Frowning, he thoughtfully scratched his cheek, reminding him that he hadn't shaved that morning. "Wouldn't that be too much antagonism too soon? In those first few chapters, I'm trying to establish that these two guys are truly friends. Eventually the friendship is overtaken and then ultimately destroyed by their competitiveness. But if Todd interferes with Roark's love life, then screws him over with Hadley, that immediately makes him out the villain and Roark the hero."

"Isn't that the way it's supposed to be? I think of them that way."

"You do?"

"You're surprised?"

"The story isn't over yet. By the time you get to the ending, you might change your mind."

Her eyes probed his, as though trying to see the denouement behind them. "I really don't have a choice, do I?"

"No."

"Okay. In the meantime, what do you think of my suggestion about Roark's love life?"

"I repeat, Maris, give me time."

She leaned forward eagerly. "You've already changed it, haven't you? There's more, isn't there? Same girl?"

"Why don't you have your navel pierced?"

"I beg your pardon?"

"If you're going to wear hip-riding skirts and shirts that tie at the waist, why don't you have—"

"I heard you."

"Then why?"

"Because I don't want to."

"Too bad."

"The thought of it gives me the willies."

"A small loop. A tiny diamond stud. It'd be sexy. Er. *Sexier.*" His eyes moved up from her midsection to her face. "Those glimpses of your belly button are already a major turn-on."

She squared her shoulders. "Parker, if we're going to have a professional relationship, you cannot talk to me like that."

"I can talk to you any damn way I please."

She gave a stubborn shake of her head. "Not if you want to work with me, you can't."

"You're free to go."

But she stayed seated on the crate, as he'd known she would. As he'd hoped she would.

Thunder rumbled and rain pelted the roof, but the racket only emphasized the strained silence between them. Parker rolled his chair closer to her until his knees were only inches from hers. "What did you tell your husband?"

"About what?"

"Being here. I assume you called him."

"I did. I left word that things were going well."

"Left word?"

"With his secretary."

"He doesn't have a cell phone? See, he strikes me as the kind of guy who would have one of those damn things practically glued to his ear."

"He was having lunch with the editor of our electronic publishing division. I didn't want to interrupt them. I'll call him later."

"As you're going to bed?"

"Possibly. What difference does it make?"

"I was just wondering if you'll be wearing a nightie tonight. Or do you always sleep sans raiment like you did last night?"

"Parker—"

"What'll you talk about?"

"None of your damn business."

"That good, huh? Or that bad?"

She drew a deep breath and said tightly, "I'll tell him that I've discovered an extremely talented writer who—"

"Please, I'm blushing."

"Who is also the crudest, rudest, most obnoxious man I've ever met."

He grinned. "Well, that would be the truth." Then his smile gradually faded. Giving the wheels of his chair a small push, he rolled another inch or two nearer to her. "I bet you won't tell him I kissed you," he said in low voice. "I bet you omit that part."

She stood up hastily, knocking the crate over backward. She tried going around him, but he moved equally fast and used his chair to block her path. "Get out of my way, Parker. I'm going back to the house now."

"It's raining."

"I won't melt."

"Melt down, maybe. You're angry. Or afraid."

"I'm not afraid of you."

"Then sit back down." When she failed to move, he motioned toward the door. "Fine. Go. Get drenched. Which will mean making explanations to Mike. It'll get messy, but if that's what you want..."

She glanced outside at the downpour, then reluctantly upturned the crate and resumed her seat on it, primly and looking pissed.

"Tell me how you met your husband, Maris."

"Why?"

"I want to know."

"What for?"

"Call it creative curiosity."

"Call it nosiness."

"You're right. Euphemisms are a crutch. I'm nosy."

Gauging her expression, he expected her to clam up and

refuse to continue their conversation, but she folded her arms across her middle—no doubt to hide her navel—and said, "Noah came to work at Matherly Press. But long before that, I knew him by reputation as the brains behind a rival publishing house. When he joined us, I was thrilled at the opportunity to be working with him. Over time, however, I realized that my feelings ran much deeper than admiration for a colleague. I was in love with him.

"At first my father was concerned about my entering into an office romance. He was also worried that Noah is ten years older than I. He encouraged me to date other men and even dabbled in some blatant matchmaking with sons and nephews of his friends and associates. But Noah was the one I wanted. Luckily he felt the same. We married." She bobbed her head for punctuation. "There. Satisfied?"

"How long have you been married?"

"Almost two years."

"Children?"

"No."

"How come?"

She glared at him and he held up a hand in conciliation. "You're right, that's too personal. If you're sterile—"

"I'm not."

"So it's him?"

She was about to come off the crate again, but he patted the air between them. "Okay, okay, the topic of children is taboo. I won't go there." He paused as though realigning his thoughts. "So you were seeing Noah every day at work and fell head over heels in no time."

"Actually I had had a mad crush on him even before I met him."

"How's that?"

"I had read his book."

The Vanquished.

"You know it? Oh, of course, the article again. It referenced Noah's novel."

"Yes, but I was already familiar with it," he said. "I'd read it when it came out."

"So did I. About fifty times."

"Are you kidding?"

"No. I love it. The main character, Sawyer Bennington, became the man in my romantic fantasies."

"You have fantasies?"

"Doesn't everyone? It's nothing to be ashamed of."

"Maybe not for you. But I've had some fantasies that were pretty shameful. Want to hear them?"

"You're irrepressible."

"That's exactly how my preschool teacher described me to my mom."

"When...?"

"When for three days straight she caught me in the boys' restroom test-driving my new favorite toy."

"I won't even ask."

"You'd be better off not to. Anyway, what were we talking about?"

"Sawyer Bennington."

"Right. Your hero and the object of your romantic fantasies. Which strikes me as strange."

"Why?"

"Wasn't he a criminal of some sort?"

"A thief and a murderer."

"Generally considered criminal."

"But his crimes were justified because of what was done to his wife and child. When he discovered their bodies, I cried buckets. I still cry every time I read it." Her expression turned dreamy and wistful.

"Sawyer is such a hard man. With everybody except Charlotte. They loved so passionately, and it was the kind of love that even death couldn't destroy. When they hanged him for his crimes, he was thinking about…"

Her voice trailed off. Embarrassed, she gave a slight shrug. "Forgive me, Parker. I guess you can tell how much I love that novel."

"You talk about the characters as though they're real."

"Noah did such a fantastic job of drawing them that sometimes I forget they're fiction. I actually start missing them. When I do, I open my copy to any page and read a few paragraphs, and it's like I've visited them."

"Didn't they make a movie?"

"It was junk that didn't do the book justice. But to be fair to the moviemakers, I don't think any movie could have. Some critics touted *The Vanquished* as the best historical novel since *Gone with the Wind*."

"Strong praise."

"But, in my opinion, warranted."

"So what'd he follow it with?"

"He didn't." Her exuberance waned considerably. "Noah got very involved with publishing *The Vanquished* and decided that his calling was in that arena, not writing. And, I suppose, when your debut novel receives such critical and popular acclaim, the thought of following it with something equally good is daunting. Even terrifying. He never wrote again. Not until recently."

Parker's gaze sharpened. "He's writing again?"

"He's set up an office specifically for that purpose. I'm very pleased."

But she didn't look very pleased, or even moderately pleased. A shallow but distinct vertical line had formed between her eyebrows. Parker doubted she realized how revealing her facial expressions were or she would school them better.

After a quiet moment, he asked, "What other fictional characters have played key roles in your fantasies?"

"Several," she admitted with a light laugh. "But none to the extent of Sawyer Bennington."

Parker leaned forward in his chair and spoke only loud enough to be heard above the pounding rain. "Maris? Is it remotely possible that you fell in love with the character and not the author?"

Her expression turned angry, but the anger came and went with the speed of a lightning flash. She smiled with chagrin. "Considering the way I've carried on about Sawyer, I suppose that's a fair question. I've had authors tell me that readers frequently superimpose them onto a character they've created, and that when readers meet them at book signings, they're disappointed to find that they're ordinary people. They don't live up to the larger-than-life image the reader had formed of them."

"Good discourse, but it didn't answer any question."

Her irritation returned. "Don't be ridiculous. I fell in love with my husband. His talent first and then the man himself. I'm still in love with him."

He stared at her for a long moment. "What was he thinking?"

"Who, Noah?"

He shook his head. "The hero of the book. Sawyer. You said when they hanged him he was thinking..."

"Oh. He was thinking about the first time he saw Charlotte."

She hesitated, but Parker motioned for her to continue.

"Noah wrote that passage so vividly, with such detail, that I could see the orchard, smell the ripening fruit, feel the heat. Sawyer had been traveling for days, remember? He comes upon Charlotte's family's farm, where he hopes to get water for himself and his horse.

"No one is around, the place seems deserted. But as he makes his way toward the water trough, he spots Charlotte sleeping on a pallet of quilts in the shade of a peach tree. A baby is sleeping beside her. Sawyer assumes the child is hers." Maris smiled and added softly, "He's glad to learn later that the child is her baby brother."

Parker was entranced by the cadence of her voice. He felt himself being pulled into the scene.

"Charlotte is the most beautiful woman Sawyer has ever seen. Her long hair was unbound. Descriptions of it, her complexion, her lips, go on for paragraphs. Because of the heat, she had raised her dress as high as her knees, and she's barefoot. Sawyer is a lusty young man. Seeing her bare calf and foot inflames him. She might just as well have been naked. He's fascinated by the breathing motion of her bosom. And yet, there's a reverent aspect to his admiration of her, as though she were as untouchable as the Madonna.

"He should have been a gentleman and politely withdrawn the moment he saw her. Instead, he stays and gazes at her until he hears a wagon approaching, announcing the return of her family, who had gone into town for supplies.

"Charlotte never knew that Sawyer had watched her sleeping that day. He never told her, which I think was particularly dear of him. It was too special a memory to share even with her. It was so special that he called it forward on the day of his execution. He was reliving it when the trapdoor of the gallows dropped open beneath him. Because it was the most pivotal day of his life, he died reliving his first sight of Charlotte."

Parker had listened. Motionless. Intent on every word. For several moments after she stopped speaking, they just looked at one another. Neither was capable of dispelling the mood, or willing to.

When he finally spoke, his voice was abnormally husky. "You should have been the writer, Maris."

"Me? No," she said, shaking her head and laughing softly. "I envy the gift. I can recognize it in those who've been blessed with it, but I'm a facilitator, not a creator."

He pondered that for a time, then said, "Do you know what made that scene so erotic?"

She tilted her head inquisitively.

"It was his having that much access to a woman, his having cerebral intimacy with her, without her knowledge."

"Yes."

"His eyes and mind had touched what his hands and lips wanted to. He hadn't seen much, but he felt guilty for looking at all."

"The forbidden."

He nodded and said in an even lower voice, "The strongest sexual stimulant of all. What isn't good for us. What we can't have. What we want so badly we can taste but can't touch."

Maris drew in a shaky little breath and exhaled it slowly. For the first time becoming aware of the loose strands of hair on her neck, she raised her hand to them, but repair seemed beyond her. She lowered her hand back to her lap, but not before it made a brief stop at that button she had fiddled with before. This time, she merely brushed it with her fingertips as though to reassure herself that it was still there. But Parker's gaze fastened on it and remained.

Suddenly she stood up in the narrow space separating them. "I'm going back now. The rain has stopped."

That wasn't altogether true. It had stopped coming down so hard, but it was still raining lightly. Parker didn't argue, however. He let her pass.

Almost.

Before she could take a full step, he reached out and stopped her with his hands. They clasped her just below her waist, the heels of them pressing her hip bones, his fingers curved back toward her hips. He was eye level with that alluring strip of bare skin between blouse and skirt. Slowly, his eyes moved up.

She was looking down at him, startled and apprehensive. Her

arms were raised, her hands in front of her shoulders as though she were unsure where to place them, what to do with them.

"We know why I kissed you last night, Maris."

"To frighten me off."

He frowned. "That doesn't even merit an argument. I kissed you because you braved Terry's and showed up everybody in the place, including me. I kissed you because just looking at you made me ache. I kissed you because I'm a rotten son of a bitch and your mouth looked so goddamn kissable. Simply put, I kissed you because I wanted to. It's something I admit and you damn well know. But there is one question that's driving me fucking crazy."

His eyes focused harder on hers and, by doing so, penetrated. "Why did you kiss me back?"

Chapter 12

—◈—

Maris's call came at an inopportune time, but Noah figured he had better take it to avoid her becoming suspicious. Even though he had a meeting scheduled in ten minutes, he asked his assistant to put her call through. "Darling! I'm so glad to hear from you."

"It's nice to finally talk to you, too," she said. "It's been so long, your voice sounds strange."

"Strange?"

"My ears have become attuned to a southern drawl."

"God help you."

"Even worse, I've actually slipped and said 'y'all' a few times, and I've acquired a taste for grits. The secret is lots of salt and pepper and drenching them in butter."

"Keep packing down a diet like that and you'll return to me fat."

"Don't be surprised if I do. What the southerners don't cook in butter, they cook in bacon grease, and it's all delicious. Have you ever had fried green tomatoes?"

"Like the movie title?"

"And the book. Both named after the real thing. Dredged in cornmeal, fried in bacon grease, they're scrumptious. Mike taught me how to make them."

"The author extraordinaire also cooks?"

"Mike's not the author. He's...well, Mike does just about everything around here except the writing."

Noah checked the sterling Tiffany clock on his desk and wondered when he could gracefully break this off. "Is the book coming along? How's it working out with the author?"

"He's talented, Noah. He's also opinionated, difficult at times, and impossible at others. But he's a challenge I can't resist."

"So the trip has been productive?"

"Yes. And unless there's something that requires me to come home, I'm going to stay here through the weekend and spoon-feed him constructive criticism and encouragement. There's no reason for me to rush back, is there?"

"Besides my missing you, no."

"Your missing me is no small thing."

"I wouldn't selfishly have you return strictly on my account. I can tell by the enthusiasm in your voice that you're enjoying being a hands-on editor again."

"Very much. Are you writing?"

"When I can. I've been busy going over second-quarter reports, but I've managed to put in a couple hours writing each evening." After a short pause, he asked, "You aren't going to start nagging me about my output, are you?"

"I wouldn't call it nagging."

"Just remember it's a part-time job, Maris. It can't take precedence over my responsibilities here."

"I understand. It's just that I'm eager to read something new by my favorite author."

"Don't hold your breath. It might take a while and the process can't be rushed."

"Has your idea gelled?"

"It's getting there," he replied evasively.

"Whatever you write will be well worth the wait."

"If you've got that much time for leisure reading, we're not keeping you busy enough."

"No worry there," she said with a laugh. "I've got my hands full with this project, in addition to the other manuscripts coming due in the next few months. I'll be editing in my sleep."

He liked the sound of that. If she was distracted by work, he'd be freer to devote more time to finalizing his deal with WorldView. He was feeling the pressure of the deadline unexpectedly set by Morris Blume. While it was uncomfortably compressing, he welcomed having a definite goal, a finish line toward which to make a final push.

He wasn't panicked, but he definitely experienced an adrenaline rush every time he thought about it. He was confident he would meet the deadline. If for any reason he didn't, he was equally confident that he could persuade Blume to extend it. The CEO coveted Matherly Press too much to relinquish it over a matter of days.

Meanwhile, this was a perfect time for Maris to be out of town. Her absence made it more convenient for him to manipulate Daniel. The old man had to be carefully finessed. Subtlety was key. Hit Daniel over the head with something, and he would fight it to his dying breath. Stroke him lightly, and his mind could be changed. Perhaps not as easily as most, but Noah didn't doubt his ability to eventually whittle down all of his father-in-law's objections to a merger.

Maris's absence also allowed him more time with Nadia. She could be a harpy if she was unhappy, and she was unhappiest when deprived of the time and attention she felt she deserved.

"I can't wait for you to read this book, Noah," Maris said, drawing him back into their conversation.

What had she been talking about for the last few minutes?

Lost in his own thoughts, he hadn't retained a word of what she'd said. He couldn't see that his inattention mattered much.

"The author hasn't shared with me the whole plot," she went on, "but I think it's going to be good."

"If you think it's going to be good, then it will be. Listen, darling, I hate to cut short our conversation, but I'm due down the hall in two minutes."

"So what else is new?" She posed the question tongue-in-cheek and without rancor. Their exchanges during work hours were typically brief.

"I have a meeting with Howard, and you know what a stickler he is about punctuality." Howard Bancroft was Matherly Press's chief counsel and head of the legal department. "If I'm a nanosecond late, he'll stay miffed for days."

"What's the meeting about?"

"I can't recall off the top of my head. Something to do with one of our foreign licensees, I believe."

"I hate to get you on Howard's bad side," she said, "but there is something else I wanted to talk about."

He had to work at keeping the impatience out of his voice. "Then I'll take the time. What's on your mind?"

"Is Dad all right?"

"Seems to be. I saw him last evening and talked to him again this morning."

"He came into the office?"

"No, he called to ask if I could muddle through without him today. I urged him to take off not only today but the remainder of the week. You're not here, so we haven't any scheduled meetings that I can't handle alone. It's an ideal time for him to take it easy."

"He'll get bored."

"Actually he's got a fairly heavy schedule. He said he planned to spend the morning at his desk at home to handle some personal chores, then he was having a late lunch with an old crony. They were meeting at the Four Seasons."

"Lunch with an old crony," she repeated absently. "I hope he doesn't drink too much wine."

"He's certainly earned the right to have a few glasses of wine at lunch if he wants them, Maris."

"I know, but I worry about him negotiating the stairs at home. With that weakness in his joints—"

"He needs full command of his equilibrium. I see your point."

"When someone his age falls and breaks a hip, they sometimes never completely recover. He couldn't abide being bedridden."

"I'll ask Maxine to keep a closer eye on him."

"No! That would start World War Three," she exclaimed. "He'll get mad at her for babying him, and then he'll get mad at me for asking her to."

"Another good point," he said. "How about..."

"What?"

"Well, I was going to suggest that I talk to him about it. Caution him confidentially. Man to man."

"Yes," she said, sounding relieved. "I like that plan much better."

"Then I'll go over this evening and have a chat with him."

"Thank you, Noah."

"You're welcome. Anything else?"

"Why?"

"Howard's waiting on me."

"Oh, I'm sorry, I forgot. I shouldn't have kept you."

"Nonsense. This was important." He wanted to end the call quickly, but he didn't want to leave her worrying over Daniel. Concern might bring her rushing back. "Maris, don't worry about Daniel," he said tenderly. "He's a tough old bird, stronger than we give him credit for. There's really no cause for alarm. If anything, over the past few days he's seemed more like his old self. Full of piss and vinegar."

"I'm sure you're right. It's just that when I'm not with him, my imagination gets away from me and I start worrying."

"Unnecessarily, I assure you. Now, forgive me, but I really must run."

"Apologize to Howard for me. Tell him it's all my fault that you're late."

"Don't worry. I will." He chuckled. " 'Bye, now."

"Noah," she added just before he disconnected, "I love you."

For a moment, he was taken aback. Then, in the absent-minded way of a devoted but preoccupied husband, he replied, "I love you, too, darling."

Professions of love meant nothing to him. They were sequences of words without any relevance. He'd told many a woman that he loved her, but only when trying to woo her into bed. He'd vocally expressed his love for Maris when they were courting because it was expected. He'd vowed his love for her in order to win her father's blessing on their marriage, and he'd played the expressive newlywed husband to the hilt. But in the last several months his avowals had become increasingly infrequent.

By contrast, Maris had an affectionate nature. She was touchy-feely to an irritating degree. She declared her love at least once a day, and while he'd become accustomed to hearing it, he still felt no connection to the sentiment.

But this most recent profession of love gave him pause. It wasn't the words themselves that had been curious, but the manner in which she'd spoken them. It had sounded to him almost as though she were trying to reestablish, either in his mind or her own, that she loved him. Had the surprise anniversary party failed to reassure her of his devotion? Did she still suspect him of infidelity?

As he breezed past Bancroft's assistant with barely a nod and entered the counsel's private office, the exchange with Maris lingered on his mind. It had raised questions that required further thought. Her "I love you" had been declared with an undercurrent of desperation. He must determine what, if anything, that signified.

One thing was certain: She would not be proclaiming her love for him if she knew the contents of the folder he carried into the lawyer's office with him.

"Hello, Howard. Sorry I'm late." He banged ahead to prevent Bancroft from remarking on his tardiness. "I was on the telephone with Maris, informing her that she would be receiving this document either tomorrow or the day after at the latest. She's in the boonies, on the outskirts of nowhere, but she assured me that the parcel carriers deliver."

Without invitation he sat down on an upholstered love seat and spread his arms along the back of it, a study in nonchalance. Looking through the windows behind the attorney's desk, he remarked, "You know, Howard, I don't know what you did to rate this office. It's got an incredible view."

His cavalier attitude was calculated to distract Bancroft from the business at hand. But he knew from experience that the little Jew was no pushover. His wizened appearance added a decade to his age. He stood five feet five inches tall in elevated shoes. He had a bald, pointed head with a distinct knob on the crown. He favored wide suspenders and wore them with tweed trousers regardless of the season. On his nose were perched small round reading glasses. Howard Bancroft looked like a gnome. Or exactly what he was—a shrewd legal mind.

"Is the document ready?" Noah asked, even though the referenced document was lying in plain view on the lawyer's desk.

"It's ready," Bancroft replied.

"Thank you for preparing it so expediently."

Noah leaned forward and reached for the document, but Bancroft laid his heavily veined and spotted hand on it. "Not so fast, Noah. I'm unwilling to let you have this today."

"Why's that?"

"I followed your directives and drew up the document as you requested, but...May I be candid?"

"That would save time."

"I was reluctant to write the document as you specified. Its content is troubling."

The lawyer removed his glasses and began polishing them with a large white handkerchief he'd taken from his pants pocket. Shaking it out, it looked to Noah as though he were waving a flag of surrender, which he might just as well do. Howard Bancroft could not win this fight.

"Oh? How is it troubling?" Noah gave his voice just enough edge to caution the attorney that Noah's reasons for requesting the document were not open for discussion. They weren't even to be questioned. Bancroft, however, did not take the hint.

"You're certain that Maris approves of this?"

"I made the request on her behalf, Howard."

"Why does she feel that such a document is necessary?"

"You know as I do, as Maris does, that publishing isn't the gentleman's cottage industry it was a century ago. It's gone cutthroat like everything else. If you stand still in this marketplace, you'd just as well be backing up. If you're merely maintaining the status quo, your competitors will pass you by, and before you can blink, you're in last place. We don't want Matherly Press to be choking on the heel dust of the others, do we?"

"That's a stirring speech, Noah. I suggest you deliver it at the next sales conference to rally the troops. However, I fail to see how the valid points you made relate to either my question or this document."

"That document," Noah said, pointing to it where it still lay on the desk, "is our safety net. Publishing is changing constantly and swiftly. Matherly Press must be prepared for any contingency. We must be able to operate with fluidity, so that if an opportunity arises, it can be immediately seized."

"Without Daniel's consent."

Noah assumed a sad expression. "Ah, Howard, that's the hitch. It breaks Maris's heart, as it does mine, that Daniel is getting on in years. That's a sad fact we've been forced to accept. If

he should take a sudden downward turn, say a stroke that ren-
ders him incapable of making business decisions, this power of
attorney guarantees a smooth transition and protects the company from being pitched into chaos."

"I wrote the provisos, Noah. I know their purpose. I also know
that similar documents are already in place and have been for
years. Daniel's personal lawyer, Mr. Stern, drew them up when
Maris turned twenty-one. I've got copies in my files, so I know
that these documents include a living will and, as you say, cover
every contingency. Should the unforeseen happen, Maris has
been granted full power of attorney to make all Daniel's decisions for him, personally and professionally."

"I'm aware of the previous documents. This one's different."

"Indeed it is. It supersedes the others. It also grants *you* power
of attorney to make Daniel's decisions for him."

Noah took umbrage. "Are you suggesting that I'm insinuating
myself—"

"No." Bancroft raised his hands, palms out. "Both Daniel and
Maris have mentioned to me the need to amend their power
of attorney documents to include you. But that responsibility
should fall to Mr. Stern, not to me."

"You're more convenient."

"To whom?"

Noah glared at him. "What else do you find so *troubling*,
Howard?"

The lawyer hesitated, as though knowing it was ill-advised to
continue, but apparently his convictions won out over caution.
"It feels sleight of hand. I get the impression that this is being
done behind Daniel's back."

"He's authorized it. You said so yourself not thirty seconds
ago."

Obviously frustrated, Bancroft ran a hand over his knobby
head. "It also bothers me to release such an important document
when it hasn't been signed and witnessed in my presence."

"I told Maris that I refuse to sign it until she has," Noah said. "I was adamant about that. She'll have her signature notarized in Georgia. When the document is returned, I'll sign it. As soon as she gets back, we'll meet with Daniel. Frankly, I think he'll be relieved that it's a fait accompli. No one likes to think of himself as vulnerable to incapacity or death. He'll be glad that we relieved him of this responsibility."

"I've never known Daniel Matherly to shrink from life's realities no matter how grim," Bancroft argued. "But, that aside, why not wait until Maris's return and do it all at one time? Explain to me the urgency."

Noah sighed as though getting a grip on his diminishing patience. "Her being away is one reason Maris wanted this done with dispatch. She's working with a reclusive fledgling author. Until his manuscript is finished, she'll be pulled away frequently, and she'll be out of town for extended and unspecified periods of time. Shit happens, Howard. Plane crashes. Car accidents. Sudden illness. In a worst-case scenario, she wants Matherly Press protected."

"Is that why the document becomes valid with your signature alone?"

Noah said tightly, "I told Maris, and I'm telling you, I will not sign it until her signature is in place."

Bancroft exchanged a long stare with him, then shook his head. "I'm sorry, Noah. I need Maris's verification that this is the document she wants, and even then I will advise her to rethink its provisos. They're unorthodox and inconsistent with prudence. I've worked for the Matherlys for a long time. They rely on me always to act in their best interest. Therefore, I'm sure you understand my precaution."

"Which is completely unnecessary, besides being a flagrant insult to me."

"Even so."

"All right. Call Maris." He gestured toward the telephone. It was a bluff, but he was gambling that Bancroft wouldn't call it. "Or better yet, Daniel's at home today. Ask him to come in and review this."

"I'd like to reacquaint myself with their original documents prior to a meeting with either of them. Until I've had an opportunity to do that, I don't wish to waste their time." Bancroft folded his hands on top of the document, a gesture that was a statement in itself. "Unless Daniel or Maris calls me and gives me authorization, I cannot release this document to you today."

Noah leveled a hard look on him. Then he grinned. And grinned wider. He had actually hoped the meeting would result in a standoff between him and Bancroft. He had hoped that the dwarf wouldn't capitulate too soon and spoil his fun. Everything till now had been a warm-up for this, the big finish. He was going to enjoy it to the fullest.

"Well, Howard," he said with soft menace, "it seems as though you suspect me of corporate subterfuge."

"I suspect you of no such thing," the lawyer returned blandly.

"That's good. I'm relieved to hear that. Because I would hate for you to suspect me of duplicity. I find that despicable, don't you? Duplicity. Betrayal. Disloyalty to one's family. One's race."

Noah held the lawyer's gaze as he picked up the folder that he'd brought in with him. Gently he set it on the desk and slid it toward Bancroft, who stared at it with the misgivings of one who must remove the lid from a basket, knowing that a cobra was coiled inside. After a full minute of palpable silence and dread, the attorney opened the cover and began to scan the printed material inside.

"Who would have thought it, Howard?" Noah said. "Your mother fucked Nazis."

Bancroft's narrow shoulders sagged forward.

"See, Howard, knowledge equates to power. I make it a point to learn all I can about the people around me, especially those who could be a hindrance. Investigating your background cost me a lot of money and took up valuable time, but I must say it yielded more than I bargained for.

"I paid your mother a visit in the nursing home where you had sequestered her. After a little arm-twisting, she confessed her shameful secret to me, and, for a nominal fee, an attendant wrote it all down word for word. Your mother signed it. Recognize her signature there on the last page? At that point she was so weak, she could barely hold the pen. Frankly, I wasn't surprised that she died just a few days later.

"You know the story well, Howard, but I was fascinated. She was twenty-three when she was dragged from her home in Poland. The rest of her family, her brothers, sister, parents, were backed against a wall and shot. She was lucky enough to be transported to a concentration camp.

"At that time, in the Old World, twenty-three was borderline spinsterhood. Your mother had prevented her younger sister from marrying an ardent suitor because she hadn't married first. Her inability to attract a man had created quite a rift in the family.

"But at the camp, she received a lot of attention from men. From the guards. See, Howard, your mother bartered her pussy for her life. Routinely. Over the next five years. She came to like the favors she was granted and flaunted them. She could have toiled alongside the other women prisoners, had her head shaved, subsisted on bread and water, lived in daily fear of her life. But no, she fucked her way into comfortable quarters. Ate well. Drank wine. Made merry with Nazis. She was the camp whore. And for that, she was despised.

"Now, is it any wonder she changed her name and created a fictitious history for herself when she emigrated to America?

"That story she told about the Jewish freedom fighter who had sacrificed his life for her and his unborn child was sweet, but it was completely untrue, as you yourself discovered when you were...what? Seven? Eight? Old enough to get the gist of the accusations hurled at her. You came home from school one day and asked your mother why everyone called you ugly names and spat on you. That's when she decided to relocate."

Howard Bancroft's hands were trembling so badly that when he removed his eyeglasses this time, he dropped them onto his desk. He covered his eyes and uttered a low moan.

"She couldn't be sure which of the camp guards was your father. She had spread her legs for so many, you see. But she suspected it was an officer who shot himself in the head hours before the Allied troops liberated the camp. You were born four months later. She was too far gone to abort you, I guess. Or maybe she had a soft spot for this particular officer. I've heard that even whores have feelings.

"Howard, Howard, what a nasty secret you've kept. I don't think the Jewish community would look too kindly on you if they knew that your mother happily serviced the men that marched them into the gas chambers, and that your father had ordered thousands of their people to be tortured and exterminated, do you?

"Considering the advocate you've been for Holocaust survivors, they might regard your crusade as hypocritical. Your friends in Israel—which are many, I understand—would revile you. Your blood is tainted with that of a traitorous whore and an Aryan murderer.

"Now, you might say to me, *You can't prove this.* But your reaction is proof enough, isn't it? Besides, I don't need to prove it. The rumor alone would effectively destroy your reputation as a good Jew. Even a hint of something this shameful would do irreparable damage.

"Your family would be shattered. Because even your wife and children believe the fabrication that you and your mother concocted. I shudder to think of the impact this would have on them. Imagine them having to explain to your grandchildren that Grandpa started as Nazi ejaculate. You would never be esteemed or trusted by anyone, ever again. Indeed, you would live in infamy as a liar and a traitor to your religion and your race, just as your mother was."

Howard Bancroft was weeping into his hands, his whole body shaking as uncontrollably as if he'd been inflicted with a palsy.

"No one need ever know, of course," Noah said, switching to an upbeat tone. He stood up and retrieved both his folder and the power of attorney document. "I can keep a secret. Cross my heart." He drew an invisible X on his chest.

"However, I'm sure you understand my precaution," he said, making a mockery of the lawyer's earlier statement. "A copy of your mother's confession is in my safe-deposit box. Another is with an attorney I retained solely for this purpose. He's an oily, unscrupulous, litigious individual with strong anti-Semitic leanings.

"Should anything untoward happen to me, he's under strict instructions to distribute your mother's signed statement to all the synagogues in and around the five boroughs. It would make for very interesting reading, don't you think? Especially the accounts of her sucking off the SS officers. Some were too fastidious to have intercourse with a Jewess, but apparently fellatio didn't count."

Noah crossed to the door. Although the lawyer had made no effort to move but continued to cry into his hands, Noah said, "No, no, Howard, don't bother seeing me out. Have a nice day."

Chapter 13

———◦◦◦———

Y ou're leaving tomorrow?"

"In the morning," Maris replied. Nervously her gaze moved around the solarium, never stopping directly on Parker. "Mike arranged for a boat to pick me up. I have a nine-thirty flight out of Savannah, connecting in Atlanta to La Guardia."

"Have a nice trip." His surly expression suggested he hoped she would have the trip from hell.

This was the first time she'd seen Parker today. This morning she had slipped into the kitchen for a quick breakfast of cold cereal, she'd skipped lunch altogether, and then had asked Mike to bring her a sandwich to the cottage for dinner. She used work as her excuse for the solitude. She wanted to reread the manuscript with total concentration and without distraction. Mike had accepted the explanation. At least he'd pretended to.

If Parker's scowl was any indication, she'd been smart to keep her distance all day. He looked ill-tempered, spoiling for a fight. The sooner she said what she had to say and left, the better.

"Before I leave," she began, "I thought we should have one

last discussion about the manuscript. I spent most of the day reevaluating it."

"Reevaluation. That's what we're calling it?"

"Calling what?"

"Your avoidance of me."

Okay. He wanted a fight. Why disappoint him? "Yes, I was avoiding you, Parker. Can you blame me? After—"

She broke off when Mike appeared with a service tray. "Fresh peach cobbler," he announced.

Parker's scowl deepened. "How come there's no ice cream?"

"Did you want it to melt before I could get it served? Jeez." Mike deposited the tray on the table, then stamped back into the kitchen, muttering about how grouchy everybody had been today. He returned with a carton of vanilla ice cream, which he scooped over the steaming portions of cobbler.

"I'm having mine in my room," he said, taking one of the bowls for himself. "There's a Bette Davis film festival on TV tonight. If *you* need anything, you can fetch it yourself," he said to Parker. "Maris, if you need something, just knock on my door. Upstairs. First door on your right."

"Thank you, Mike. I can't imagine that I'll need to disturb you. The cobbler looks delicious."

"Enjoy."

After Mike left them, Parker attacked his helping of cobbler and ice cream as though he were angry at it. When he finished, he dropped the spoon into the empty bowl with a loud clatter, returned it to the tray, then rolled his chair over to the computer desk. "Do you want to read what I've been working on, or what?"

"Of course I want to read it."

While the new pages were printing out, Maris ate her cobbler. Carrying the crockery bowl with her, she moved slowly along the crammed bookcase, surveying the titles in Parker's extensive collection. "You like mysteries."

His head came around. "If they're well written."

"You must think Mackensie Roone writes well."

"He's okay."

"Just okay? You have the entire Deck Cayton series."

"Ever read one?"

"A few, not all." She pulled one of the books from the shelf and thumbed through it. "I wish we were publishing them. They sell like hotcakes."

"Why do you think that is?"

"Why do you like them?"

He thought about it a moment. "They're fluff, but they're fun."

She nodded. "Millions of readers worldwide think so, too. The character of Deck Cayton appeals to both men and women, and why not? He's independently wealthy. Detective work is just his hobby. He lives on a fabulous houseboat, drives fast cars, flies his own jet. He's as comfortable in a tuxedo as he is in blue jeans."

"And even more comfortable out of them."

"You must've read the one about the murder in the nudist colony."

He grinned devilishly. "My personal favorite."

"Why am I not surprised?"

"Getting back to the character..."

Absently, she licked some dripping ice cream off her spoon. "Deck Cayton is well drawn. He's charming, witty, good-looking. He's—"

"A jerk."

"Sometimes he is. With a capital *J*. But he's been so engagingly written that a reader forgives his flaws. The author allows him to be human, and the readers appreciate and identify with that. And even though he's armed and dangerous and tough-talking, Deck has an underlying vulnerability."

"Because of his wife's death."

"Right. It's referred to, but I haven't read that particular book."

"First of the series," he explained. "Skiing accident. He challenged her to a downhill race, and she crashed into a tree. Autopsy revealed she was several weeks pregnant. They hadn't known. You should read it."

"I definitely will." She tapped the spoon against her front teeth. "Do you see how the author built in a reason for Deck's vulnerability? Readers can empathize with him because of that tragic and fatal accident."

"You're sounding like an editor."

She laughed. "Habit, I guess."

"You've given it a lot of thought."

"I analyze every bestseller. Especially the competition's. I need to know why Deck Cayton strikes such a positive chord. Part of my job is trying to predict what the buying public wants to read."

She polished off her cobbler. "But that doesn't make me any less a fan. Character motivation notwithstanding, Deck is your basic larger-than-life action hero who never fails to solve the mystery, nab the bad guy, bed the babe."

"And make her come."

Maris closed the book with a decisive snap and replaced it on the shelf among the others. He'd only said that to provoke her, and it had worked. But damned if she would let it show. "As I said, he appeals to men and women alike."

Her understatement made him grin, but he let it pass without comment. "Which was your favorite of the series?"

"*Loose Change.*"

He grimaced. "Seriously? In that book Deck came dangerously close to being a wimp."

"Because he showed more sensitivity toward the female character?"

Scornfully, Parker placed his hands over his heart. "He got in touch with his feminine side."

"But he soon reasserted himself as a real cad. By the end of the book, he was back to being the smooth operator that every man fantasizes being."

"Did he live up to your fantasy?"

"Deck Cayton?"

"Your husband. His book acted like a spark plug to your fantasy life. Did his performance in bed—*does* it—live up to your expectations?"

She faced him squarely. "Parker, that is an inappropriate question."

"That means it doesn't."

"That means it's none of your business. Your curiosity over my personal life is out of line. Which is precisely why I avoided being alone with you last night and all day today. What happened in the gin made me uncomfortable. I'm married."

"What happened in the gin? I don't remember anything happening in the gin that would compromise you as a married woman."

His feigned innocence infuriated her, but she wouldn't give him the satisfaction of showing it. She changed tactics and assumed an air of indifference as she returned her empty bowl to the tray on the table.

"You attached far too much significance to that kiss, Parker. You asked why I allowed it, and since you seem confused on that point, let me clarify. I allowed it because fighting you off would have been undignified and embarrassing for both of us. A glorified golf cart is no place to conduct a wrestling match to protect my virtue. And don't for a moment delude yourself into thinking I was afraid of you." She shot him an arch look. "I could've outrun you."

"Ouch! That one hurt, Maris. Now you're fighting dirty."

"Which is the only kind of fighting I think you understand."

"It's the only kind of fighting, period."

"In other words, what's the point of fighting if you don't fight to win?"

"Damn straight," he said tightly. "Win at all costs. No matter what it takes, no matter what you have to do. I learned—or rather was taught—that lesson. If you want to come out on top, you must be willing to go the distance."

Although his intensity on the topic intrigued her, there was a dangerous glint in his eyes that warned her against probing any further.

"I wanted to work with you on *Envy*. If one meaningless kiss bought me that opportunity, it was a small enough price to pay. Can't we put that childish episode behind us and concentrate on what brought me here in the first place? Your book and my desire to buy it."

"For how much?"

The subject of money had never been broached, and she was caught off guard by the introduction of it now. "I haven't thought about it."

"Well, do."

"It's premature."

"Maybe for you, not for me."

"I haven't seen a complete manuscript, Parker. I won't go to contract until I have."

"And I won't bust my balls finishing a book that you might ultimately reject."

"I'm sorry, that's the way the system works."

"Not my system."

The recently printed sheets were neatly stacked in his lap. She was itching to read them. But his jaw was squared, and he was just ornery enough to stick to his guns. "We could compromise."

"I'm listening," he said.

"I would be willing to offer you a moderate advance once I see a detailed outline."

"No sale. I don't want to do an outline."

"Why?"

"Because I enjoy the spontaneity of writing without one."

"You wouldn't have to adhere to it. If along the way a better idea occurs to you, I won't hold you to the outline. All I require is a general idea of where you're taking the story, a synopsis of the plot."

"That would spoil the surprises."

"I'm your editor. I don't need to be surprised."

"Of course you do. You're a reader first, an editor second. You're the first barometer of whether the book is good or it's crap. Plot twists are essential to its being good. Besides, I'd rather channel my energy into the story than to writing a stupid outline."

"I urge you to take the time, Parker. For your benefit as well as mine."

"I ain't doing it."

"You sound like Todd."

"Todd?"

She moved to the table where she had left her copy of the *Envy* manuscript. "Let's see...I think it's in chapter six. No, seven. It's a scene between him and Roark. He's telling Roark that Professor Hadley had suggested changes in his character's attitude toward his father, and Roark thinks the suggestion is a valid one."

She scanned the pages of text. "Here. Page ninety-two. Todd says, 'When our esteemed professor writes a book, he can do with his characters whatever he likes. You can do with yours what you want. But these are *my* characters. I created them. I know what makes them tick. I won't change them to suit Hadley. No. No, sir. I ain't doing it.' "

She looked over at him. He shrugged. "Okay. So I'll let Todd speak for me."

"God, you're stubborn."

They stared at one another until he finally asked, "Do you want to hear what I wrote today while you were busy avoiding me?"

Ignoring his sarcasm, she said, "Of course I want to—did you say *hear* it?"

"I thought I would read it to you because it's very sloppy. I was writing fast. Didn't bother with capital letters, punctuation, stuff like that. Have a seat."

She sank into the deep cushions in one of the wicker armchairs, slipped off her sandals, and tucked her legs beneath her. He rolled his chair near hers, engaged the brake, and adjusted the shade of a floor lamp so that the light was directed down onto the pages. Except for that small pool of light, the room was dark.

"I took your advice, Maris, and enhanced the girl's role. She's interwoven into other scenes, but this one between her and Roark takes place on the night following his snafu with Hadley.

"The professor rescheduled their appointment for after the Thanksgiving holiday. Roark returns to the frat house, pulls Todd off his sleeping loft, and, as you suggested, commences to beat the hell out of him. Some frat brothers break up the fight. Roark inflicts no more damage than a busted lip and a bloody nose. Todd apologizes."

"He does?"

"He does. He says he thought it would be a good practical joke, but didn't think through the ramifications of screwing Roark with Hadley. Says he hadn't counted on Hadley being so severe when Roark turned up late. He had figured Roark would get the equivalent of a slap on his hand, and then Hadley would proceed with his consultation."

"Is Todd sincere?"

"We have no reason to believe otherwise, do we?"

"No. I suppose not."

"Okay, so Roark has accepted Todd's explanation and apology, but he's still mad as hell. Forlorn. In a crap mood. He calls up the girl and makes a date with her for that evening. He tells her that he really wants to see her, that he's had a shitty day, stuff like that."

"He's in need of some TLC."

"Exactly." Scanning as he went, Parker flipped through the top several pages, letting them drift one by one to the floor at the side of his chair. "You can read this transition on your own. Oh, I've named the girl Leslie."

"I like it."

"To paraphrase, Roark takes her to a Sonic Drive-in. They have chili Tater Tots and cherry limeades."

"Big spender."

"Hey, give him a break, okay? He's a kid on a budget. Besides, he happens to like chili Tater Tots and cherry limeades."

"Sorry. Go on."

"After they eat, Roark drives them out to the lake. He parks. He leaves the radio off. Somehow the silence seems appropriate. Let's see...yeah, here. 'The silence that enfolded him was as calming and comforting as a mother's breast. His day had been a chain of chaotic events, a jarring series of starts and stops. Between outbursts of anger, he'd suffered bone-crushing disappointment in his friend, in himself.' "

"Good."

"Thanks," he returned absently as he continued to scan the pages. "Throughout the evening Leslie has been unusually subdued, not her effervescent self. Roark figures that his dour mood must've been contagious, that it had rubbed off on her. Over the Tater Tots they'd carried on a desultory conversation about blah, blah, blah. You can read this for yourself."

He ran his finger down the page until he located the passage he sought. "Okay, listen."

"I'm listening."

" 'A full moon hovered just above the horizon and was reflected in the water at such a severe angle that its wavering spotlight spanned the entire breadth of the lake. But it shed a chill light. On the far shore, towering pines and denuded hardwoods were unmoving in the windless night, stark and still, like India ink etchings against the sky that had turned wintry just that day.' "

"I like it."

"To encapsulate, their conversation has been forced, stilted. Leslie hadn't asked Roark where they were going when they left the Sonic. On the drive to the lake, she hadn't uttered a peep. . . . Jesus, did I write that?" He took a red pencil from his shirt pocket and made a slash through that line. "But by now her silence is beginning to wear on Roark's nerves. He wants to know what she's thinking."

He began to read again from the text. " 'Roark withheld asking until his chest felt tight enough to crack. "What are you so quiet for?" His tone of voice should have pissed her off. It would have pissed him off if somebody who had been as glum as an undertaker all evening had implicitly accused him of being the source of some unacknowledged complication.

" 'But when Leslie turned toward him, he saw only kindness in her expression. Instead of rebuke, understanding. And Roark was suddenly struck by how beautiful she was.

" 'Oh, the first time he saw her he'd thought she was pretty. Eye candy. He and the guys he'd been carousing with that night had picked her out of a crowd of coeds. Among themselves they had appraised her, lewdly remarking on the physical attributes that men lewdly remark upon. She had scored high.

" 'But tonight she was beautiful to him in a way that had nothing to do with the pleasant arrangement of her features or the proportions of her figure. She exuded a beauty that was deeper than her flawless complexion and rarer even than her extraordinarily blue eyes.

" 'She radiated a beauty that wasn't particularly appreciated. By contemporary society's standards, it didn't have much value. It wasn't sophisticated and cool, but homespun and warm. It made you feel loved and accepted despite your shortcomings, despite everything. Tonight Leslie was beautiful like you hoped your life partner would be.' "

When Parker stopped reading and glanced up at her, Maris

managed only a slight nod and a motion for him to continue.

"Leslie asks him what had happened that day to put him in such a funk. Words to that effect." Parker sent that page sailing over the armrest of the wheelchair and found the spot on the following page where he wanted to resume reading.

" 'Roark talked for ten solid minutes. The words gushed out in an uninterrupted stream, as though all day his subconscious had been choosing them and arranging them into an order that would give them the most impact and would most eloquently express the level of his despair.

" 'But eventually his dejection turned to outrage. He articulated the fiery internal argument he'd been having with himself, the argument that justified his anger toward Todd. "Fuck his apology!" He closed his hand into a tight fist. "He can't undo the damage he's done that easily."

" 'When he finished venting about Todd, he cursed the pompous professor for being such an unrelenting bastard, at the same time admitting to his fear of never reestablishing a rapport with Hadley and thereby guaranteeing a dismal grade on his capstone.

" 'The words finally ebbed, then stopped altogether. Roark fell silent again and hunkered down into his jacket, not for the warmth it provided but from shame for sounding like such a goddamn crybaby.' "

Again, Parker raised his head and looked at Maris. "Well? Should I trash it or continue?"

"Continue. Please."

"I'll pick up with Leslie's response."

Returning to the manuscript, he read, " 'She waited until the smoke of his wrath had cleared, when it became noticeable that the cold from outside was seeping into the car. Her breath formed plumes of vapor between them. She spoke quietly, as one would to a temperamental animal who was momentarily docile. "What happened today is a good thing, Roark."

" 'He snorted, looked over at her. "Good? How in God's

name is it good? Not that I believe in God."

" 'He knew she wouldn't like the atheistic remark. She was a devout believer who took offense at jokes made over anything religious. Ordinarily she admonished him for making them and asked him to kindly keep his irreverent comments to himself. This time, she elected to overlook it.

" ' "The reason you're taking this so hard is because your writing means so much to you."

" 'It was a good point. He wanted to hear more. "And because it means so much to you, you'll succeed. If you were able to shrug off the misunderstanding with Professor Hadley or laugh about it, then I would advise you to rethink your choice of career. You could dismiss this incident only if you had no passion for writing.

" ' "What happened illustrates the depth of your passion. Your despondency over this...what really amounts to a hiccup in the grand scheme of things...demonstrates the level of your desire to write and write well. It hit you where it hurts most, which affirms that you're doing what you were born to do." She smiled. "I didn't need it affirmed. But perhaps you did. And if you did, then this experience was worth all the anxiety it's caused."

" 'She reached for his hand and pressed it between hers. "Think about it, Roark, and you'll realize that I'm right." ' "

When Parker paused, Maris said, "She's a very intuitive young woman."

"You think?"

She nodded. Noticing the sheets still lying in his lap, she asked, "How does Parker respond?"

"The way most men respond to any emotionally charged situation."

"Which is?"

"Well, depending on if we're stimulated to feel bad or good, we either want to strike something or fuck something."

Chapter 14

Maris cleared her throat. "I don't suppose Roark feels like striking something."

"Wasn't it you who suggested that I enhance their relationship?"

"It was."

"Okay, then. They kiss, and it gets predictably slippery. Roark opens her coat, cuddles up to her chest. She gives him access to some skin. 'Velvety, warm, fragrant woman skin,' it says here. I'll work on that." He made a notation.

"He caresses her breasts. For the first time since they began dating, he uses his mouth. He kisses her nipples, teaching her something about arousal and the pleasurable possibilities that are available to a man and woman who are willing to explore them."

Maris's heart bumped inside her chest.

"Her scent. Her breath. The texture of her against his tongue. Combined with the day's frustration. The foreplay just isn't hacking it. The guy's dying here. So he guides Leslie's hand inside his jeans and, to put it delicately, she gives him a hand job."

"That's putting it delicately?"

The huskiness of her voice brought his head up and he looked across at her. "Compared to some optional phrases, that's pretty delicate, yeah."

"Okay."

"Roark tells her he loves her."

"Does he mean it?"

"At that moment? With all his heart."

Parker's somber face caused her to laugh. "I'm sure. How does Leslie respond?"

"Ah," he said, frowning. "As it turns out, the hand job is her going-away present. She dumps him."

"Then and there?"

"It's right here in black and white."

"Hmm. Does she break up for the reasons stated in the first draft?"

"Yeah."

"Then she's being kind, isn't she? And smart. As much as it hurts her, she's doing what she realizes is best for both of them, especially Roark. She's thinking first of him and his career."

"Maybe. But I gotta tell you, Maris, fresh after you've climaxed, it's a real bummer if the woman up and walks out on you."

"I suppose."

"Oh, yeah," he said, nodding sagely. "Ask any guy."

"I'll take your word for it."

"In Roark's mind she's being a heartless bitch. He doesn't need her charity, and who the hell does she think she is? He's good and pissed." Maris was about to protest when Parker raised a finger to halt her. "At least initially." He picked up the remaining pages. "Shall I?"

"Please."

" 'The day had started off lousy and then it had gone to pure shit.

" 'He thought about getting drunk, but could see no good purpose in it. Today's disappointments would carry over into tomorrow, and then he would have to confront them with the handicap of a hangover.

" 'Besides, he hadn't earned an excuse to get drunk. That right belonged to a man only if he had a circumstance to celebrate…or to mourn. One was allowed to lament a disaster visited on him by random selection, such as an act of God or a whim of Fate. But regret over his own culpability earned a man no such privilege. Responsibility for one's sorry situation couldn't be that easily removed.

" 'As much as he wanted to lay blame on Leslie, on Hadley, on Todd, for today's miseries, Roark acknowledged that most of the blame, if not all of it, lay squarely with him.

" 'Leslie was wise beyond her years and experience. Moreover, she was honest to a painful degree. Their individual desires were too discordant, their dreams too disparate for them to have a future together. Their goals conflicted now. In the future they would clash resoundingly. When the inevitable separation came, they would be left scarred and embittered.

" 'The wisdom of her choice to return to her small-town aspirations and long-standing sweetheart didn't make it any easier to lose her now, but ending the relationship before it actually started would spare them future heartache. At least they had parted while all the memories were still sweet.

" 'Professor Hadley had been well within his right to be perturbed. He didn't want any stupid students under his tutelage. He had probably been as upset with Roark for being duped by his roommate as he had been by the tardiness. The professor's time was too limited, his instruction too valuable to squander on fools. Taking Todd's word for something as critical as that meeting had been nothing short of stupid.

" 'The challenge facing Roark now was to prove to Hadley that, all evidence pointing to the contrary, he was not an imbecile. He could learn from this experience. He must learn from it. If he didn't, he would be as foolish, as much a waste of time and effort, as Hadley believed him to be.

" 'Today had been the first cold day of the season. It was also the first day of Roark Slade's life as an adult. Without ceremony or sacrament, he had undergone a rite of passage. Whatever remnants of innocence he had awakened with this morning had been stripped from him. After today, trust was only a word, a remote ideal that would never have a practical application in his life. From today forward, any belief he entertained would be contaminated by skepticism.

" 'Roark wasn't aware of this transition until years later, when he leafed back through the pages of his personal history, searching for the defining moment when his life had ceased being charmed and became cursed. His search always ended on this day.

" 'For months following that Tuesday before Thanksgiving, Roark would think about Professor Hadley and what he could learn from that embarrassing experience. He would reflect on all that he had learned from Leslie about himself as a man and a writer. He would think on that quite a lot.

" 'But what he had learned about his best friend Todd, he avoided thinking about altogether.' "

When Parker finished reading the final page, he stared at the last sentence for a time, then let the sheet slip from his fingers and drift down to join the others. By now the floor around the wheelchair was littered with pages of manuscript.

Quietly, and without looking at Maris, he said, "That's it so far."

She slowly unfolded her legs and lowered her feet to the floor. She slid her palms up and down the tops of her thighs, then clasped her hands loosely, raised her shoulders around a deep breath, and released it gradually.

"All right, Parker. It goes against the company's policy as well as my own, but I'll give you a ten-thousand-dollar advance just to finish the manuscript. When it's completed, we'll negotiate the terms of a contract. If you decline our terms and sell the book elsewhere, the ten thousand must be repaid from the first proceeds you receive from the other publisher. If you accept, that initial ten thousand will be applied to the advance we ultimately agree upon. In the meantime, I suggest you get an agent."

"I suggest you get a grip on reality."

"That's a no?"

"Twenty-five thousand. Which barely covers my expenses. I've got to buy cartridges for my printer, paper."

"Mighty expensive paper," she said drolly. "Fifteen. That represents an act of good faith, considering that I don't even have an outline."

He mulled it over for several seconds. "Fifteen, no first-proceeds clause, and the fifteen is not applicable to the advance finally agreed upon. In other words, the fifteen's mine no matter what. If Matherly Press can't afford to gamble fifteen grand, you should padlock the doors tomorrow."

He was right, of course, and, except for saving face, she saw no point in arguing it further. The fierce deal-making could be reserved for the final contract negotiations.

"Deal. As soon as I return to New York, I'll have our legal department draw up a letter of agreement. For now, we have a gentlemen's agreement." She stuck out her hand.

He took her hand and used it to draw her closer to him. "By no stretch of the imagination are you a gentleman."

She leaned even farther forward, bringing her face very close to his and whispering, "Neither are you."

Laughing, he released her hand. "Got that right. Do you want to take the rest of this with you?" He indicated the pages scattered over the floor.

"Please. I'd like my father to read it."

"What about your husband?"

"Noah usually handles the business concerns and leaves the editorial to me, but since I've become so personally involved in this book, I'm sure he'll want to read it, too."

Parker wheeled his chair backward so she could kneel down and gather the manuscript pages. "I'd help, but—"

"No bother."

"—I like it this way. I've actually entertained fantasies of you on your knees in front of me."

"Groveling?"

"That, too."

She looked up at him but wished she hadn't. He wasn't smiling, wasn't teasing. The remark went beyond his typical innuendo.

"*Dirty* fantasies," he added. "In some states I could be arrested."

"Stop it, Parker."

"Okay, I will."

"Thank you."

"When you stop looking like that."

"Like what?"

"Thoroughly fuckable."

"That's not a word."

"Thoroughly? Is, too."

"I should have you charged with sexual harassment."

"I'd deny it."

"That's the only reason I don't." She continued to gather the pages with quick, angry motions. Then she noticed the scar.

He wasn't wearing socks, so his feet were bare inside a pair of docksiders that, sadly, looked new and unscuffed. The scar crossed the vamp of his right foot and crawled up his ankle to disappear inside the leg of his trousers. The flesh was raised and buckled.

"It only gets worse from there. In fact, that one is damn near beautiful compared to some of the others."

She looked up at him. "I'm sorry, Parker."

"No need to apologize. It's human nature to be curious over something that grotesque. I'm accustomed to stares."

"No. I meant I'm sorry for whatever it was that happened to you. It must've been incredibly painful."

"At first." He affected an indifference she knew was false. "But after a few years I learned to live with it. Eventually the pain dwindled to a familiar ache. Except in cold weather. Then it can hurt like a son of a bitch."

"Is that why you moved to St. Anne? To escape harsh winters?"

"One of the reasons." He wheeled his chair around. "I'm going to get more cobbler. Want some?"

With all the sheets now in hand, she came to her feet. "No, thanks. I need to get to bed. I left an early wake-up call with Mike."

"Right."

In a matter of seconds, his attitude had turned frosty. She'd seen his scars, internal ones as well as those on his legs, and he couldn't tolerate that. He equated the scars to weakness, a limitation to his masculinity. Which was ridiculous.

Because, with the exception of those scarred legs, Parker defined maleness. He was broad through his shoulders and chest. As she had noticed the night they met, his arms were heavily muscled. Even his legs, what she could make out of them beneath his trousers, were muscular. In a private conversation with Mike, she had asked why Parker didn't use a motorized chair. He'd said that Parker wanted to stay as fit as possible and wheeling himself around helped keep his muscles toned.

He wasn't as classically handsome as Noah. There was a distinct asymmetry to Parker's features, but the irregularities made his face arresting and interesting. The square jaw, stern visage, and a head of hair over which he exercised limited control, all contributed to an attractiveness that was altogether manly.

A manliness from which the safest distance for a married woman was full retreat.

"I'll be in touch soon, Parker."

"I'm not going anywhere," he said flippantly.

"Write your heart out."

"Yeah. Good-bye, Maris." He wheeled himself into the kitchen, never looking back. He might just as well have sprinted away from her. The door swished shut behind him.

Left standing alone in the empty, dim room, Maris felt awkward and a bit deflated. She didn't know what she had expected, but Parker's desertion seemed anticlimactic. She had what she'd come for—an agreement with him to finish *Envy*. One more handshake to seal that agreement wouldn't have killed him, would it? He hadn't mentioned being around to see her off in the morning. She certainly hadn't expected a protracted and syrupy good-bye; nevertheless, she felt a bit crestfallen.

Honestly? She was sad to be leaving. When she should be eager to return to her turf, where the accents and the cuisine and the night sounds were familiar, she realized she dreaded tomorrow's departure.

The island had captivated her with its lavish landscape and its musical insects whose concert lulled her to sleep every night. At first she'd found the humidity cloying and almost unbearable, but she had actually come to like the feel of it against her skin. With its moss-laden trees that were almost as ancient as the surf, the island was otherworldly, entrancing, and seductive.

And so was Parker Evans. But she shoved that thought aside.

She noticed that the manuscript pages had actually grown damp within her tight grip. Relaxing her fist, she shook her head with chagrin. There was no mystery as to the source of these sensual thoughts. They had taken root in her mind when Parker read that damned passage about slippery kisses and nipples and the pleasurable possibilities available to a man and woman willing to explore them.

She had planned to return to the guest cottage and read these pages for herself, but she changed her mind. They could wait to be read when she was back in New York, under fluorescent lights, in familiar surroundings, behind the safe barricade of her own desk and heavy workload. They could be read when their author wasn't in the next room entertaining fantasies about her that he could be arrested for.

Before she left the solarium, she borrowed a Mackensie Roone novel from Parker's library. She had a feeling that falling asleep was going to be difficult. The mystery would be a pleasant diversion. Deck Cayton could keep her company.

* * *

When Parker entered the gin the following morning, he startled a raccoon. "It's almost daybreak, pal. Better haul ass." The animal scuttled out between broken boards in the wall.

He liked coming to the cotton gin before the sun came up, when it was still reasonably cool and there was a light breeze coming off the ocean. He liked watching the first light find its way through the cracks in the walls. He fancied the building having a soul, awakening at sunrise in the vain hope that the new day would bring life and vitality back to it.

He fancied it because he could identify with it.

He knew what it was like for people to shut you down, lock you up, and go away sadly shaking their heads and saying that you weren't going to be worth much to anybody ever again.

Countless mornings he had awakened like that. Before he had time to remember his circumstances, he would experience a flicker of anticipation for what the day would bring. Then pain would bring him fully awake, and with consciousness came the cruel realization that the day would bring nothing except the same desolation and hopelessness as had the day before, and the one before that.

Thank God he had clawed his way free of that self-defeating miasma.

By an act of will, he had given his days purpose. He had set himself a goal. Although it had cost him excruciating physical pain and many times had beaten his persistence almost into surrender, he had clung to it. Now he was mere weeks away from achieving that goal.

A bird sailed into the building from the open doorway, startling Parker out of his reverie. The brown, spotted thing—Mike was the bird-watcher who could probably identify this one from thirty yards—perched on the edge of the loft and, tilting its feathered head, regarded Parker curiously.

"Bet you're wondering what I'm doing here."

He wondered what the hell he was doing talking to the animals this morning, but it didn't worry him overmuch. He had once screamed invectives at a whole battalion of imaginary rats that were scaling his motionless legs, crawling over his groin and belly and up his chest to attack his neck and face with their long, sharp teeth. So he wasn't too concerned now about rationally addressing something as harmless, and real, as a common bird.

He came here to the emptiness of this ruin to rethink his plot and look for holes in it. He came here to check on his preparedness and to ask himself repeatedly what he could have possibly overlooked. He came to anticipate how sweet it was going to be to have his revenge, to see an end to it, to bring it to closure after fourteen years.

Sometimes he came here simply to escape Mike. Two opinionated bachelors sharing a house had the potential of becoming one opinionated bachelor too many. When tempers sparked, it was always Parker's fault. Compared to him, Mike had the disposition and patience of a saint.

He couldn't do without Mike and couldn't bear to think about the day when he would be forced to. Mike wouldn't 'fess up to his actual age, but Parker knew he must be past seventy. Thank

God he appeared to be in good health and had the energy of a man half his age.

He was really fond of—no, he *loved* that old man.

But there were days when even the long-suffering Mike Strother grated on him, when he needed complete solitude, when one room didn't provide him enough space in which to battle his demons.

This morning he'd come here to think specifically about Maris. Within these weathered walls, he had hatched the plan to get her to St. Anne Island, under his roof, and under his influence.

He hadn't planned on her getting under his skin.

He couldn't go feeling sorry for her, though. If he was to treat Noah Reed to a taste of hell on earth, utilizing Noah's wife was necessary. She would get caught in the crossfire that was sure to come, but that was too damn bad. She would get no better than she deserved for marrying the cocksucker. She looked and talked smart, but she couldn't be very bright.

"I mean, come on, marrying a guy because she fell in love with a character in a book? How stupid can you get?" he asked the sparrow.

No, he couldn't let himself get mushy over Maris Matherly-Reed. So what if she made him laugh? And gave good dialogue? And looked up at him with woeful, watercolor eyes and felt compassion for his scars? He didn't want her pity. He didn't need it. And she damn well wouldn't be pitying him if she knew what was in store for—

"You son of a bitch!"

Parker spun his chair around barely in time to duck the hard-cover book hurled at his head.

Chapter 15

Parker batted the book away a nanosecond before it could connect with his temple. It landed in the dirt beside his chair, sending up a puff of dust. He recognized the cover. It was the first volume of the Deck Cayton series.

Maris was standing just inside the open doorway. The first time she came to the deserted cotton gin, she'd been apprehensive and hesitant to enter. This morning her aura was glowing as red hot as a new star. If the threshold on which she was standing had been the gateway to hell, Parker doubted she would have been intimidated.

Given that he could see the outline of her legs—all the way to the top—through her skirt, her fury was ineffectual. At the very least, it was compromised. His eyes were drawn to that vaguely defined delta, but he concentrated on keeping them in a neutral zone above her waist. God knew he didn't need to provoke her any more than she was already provoked.

Unflappably, he asked, "You didn't like the book?"

"Fuck you."

"I guess not."

With her hands clenched into fists that she held stiffly at her sides, she walked toward him, quoting as she came, " 'At least they had parted while all the memories were still sweet.' " She came to a stop within a yard of his chair and he noted that she was wearing eyeglasses. "You're either a plagiarist or a consummate liar, and either way you're a son of a bitch."

"So you said. I got it the first time."

"Which is it? Just so I'll know. One's as despicable as the other."

"I believe you quoted from chapter seventeen, page two hundred forty-three. Deck is at his late wife's grave." He feigned puzzlement. "I'm not sure if one can plagiarize oneself. Can one?"

She was too angry to speak.

"Deck is grief-stricken but grateful that he'd had her in his life for even a short time," he continued. "It was rather good, I thought."

"Good enough to use again. In *Envy*. After Leslie broke up with Roark."

At what hour of the day had she discovered the telltale passage? he wondered. Had it been late last night as she lay in the guest cottage bed, or had she been reading over her morning coffee? The circumstances really didn't matter. She knew his secret, and she was pissed.

"Why did you lie to me, Parker?"

"I never lied about it," he countered calmly. "You never asked me if I was Mackensie Roone. You never asked me if I wrote a mystery series featuring Deck Cayton. Even when we were talking about him last night, you never once said—"

"Don't be obtuse, Parker! You lied by omission. Otherwise, you would have volunteered that vital piece of information."

"Vital? Hardly. It wasn't even important. It wasn't relevant. If you'd've asked, I would have—"

"Invented some bullshit story. Like this has been from the very beginning."

"If I hadn't wanted to be found out, I wouldn't have deliberately used that sentence in *Envy* and then recommended that you read the first Deck Cayton book."

"Which was another of your games to test how sharp I am," she shouted.

Her hair was tousled and her cheeks were pink, as though she'd run all the way here from the house. Truth be told, she looked adorably disheveled and smelled of the vanilla in freshly baked tea cakes. But she wouldn't welcome the compliments.

"I've never seen you wearing glasses. Do you ordinarily wear contacts?"

Impatiently she raked her hair back. "What I want to know is why."

She had lowered the timbre of her voice, although it appeared to have been an effort. Her chest was rising and falling rapidly as though the volume and vituperation trapped inside were creating inner turbulence.

"Why did you play this ridiculous game with me, Parker? Or Mackensie or whatever the hell your name is."

"Parker Mackensie Evans. Mackensie was my mother's maiden name. When I was deciding on a pseudonym, it seemed a logical choice. Tickled my mom no end for me to use it. It has a nice ring. It's androgynous. It's—"

"Answer me"

"—safe."

"From what?"

"Discovery." He tossed out the word like a gauntlet. For long moments, it seemed to lie there between them on the dirt floor alongside the book. Finally he said, "When I sold the Deck Cayton series, I wished to remain anonymous. I still do."

"The series has been enormously popular. Why hide behind a pseudonym?"

He folded his arms across his chest and gave her a pointed look. "Why do you suppose, Maris?"

Her lips parted as though to speak, but then realization dawned, and her lips closed. She looked away, embarrassed.

"Right. Deck Cayton is every man's fantasy. Every woman's, too, according to you. He's agile and quick, he can chase the bad guys and carry a woman to his bed. Why would I want to dispel his dashing image by showing up at personal appearances in a wheelchair?"

"No author photographs on the book jackets," she mused out loud. "No book signings or personal appearances. I often questioned your publisher's marketing strategy and wondered why it didn't include you. They were protecting you."

"Wrong. I was protecting me. Even my publisher doesn't know who Mackensie Roone is. My editor doesn't know my real name or whether Mackensie Roone is male or female. No one knows anything about Mackensie Roone's true identity. My agent tells me the speculation has run the gamut from—"

"Of course," Maris interrupted on a soft cry. "Mackensie Roone has an agent! I know her. You didn't go through her when you submitted *Envy*. Why?"

"She doesn't know about it."

"Why?"

"Because I haven't told her. She'll get her percentage of anything *Envy* earns because I'll bring her in to negotiate the final contract. But until that time, I chose to go this one alone."

"Why?"

"Is there an echo in here?"

"Before I kill you, I want to understand this, Parker."

Despite the first half of that statement, she appeared more befuddled than angry now, although he sensed he was being granted only a temporary reprieve. If he knew her at all, and he felt he was coming to, once she had time to think about all this at length, she was going to get as mad as hell all over again.

"Explain yourself, Parker. Why the secrecy?"

"I wanted to write a different book. Totally different from

the snappy dialogue and fast-paced action in the Deck Cayton books. Don't get me wrong, they're not easy to write." He grinned ruefully. "Frankly, it surprises the hell out of me how popular they've become.

"But because they're so popular, and Deck is so well-known to the fans—I mean, to some, he's like a member of the family who's merely away from home between books—they expect a lot from me. They want the same, but different. They want each book to take Deck into a new and exciting adventure, but they'd turn vicious if I deviated too far from the formula.

"It's hard to deliver every time out of the chute. Each successive book has outsold the previous one, and I'm glad. But that also raises the stakes and the standard, and makes each book harder to top."

"That's a refrain I've heard from other successful novelists," Maris remarked. "They say it's difficult to top themselves. Noah has said that about *The Vanquished*."

Parker didn't want to talk about Noah and his goddamned success story.

"I've come clean with you, Maris, now be truthful with me. If my agent had called you up one day and said, 'Guess what I've got? Lying on my desk as we speak is a new novel by the author of the Deck Cayton series. Something entirely different from the mysteries. Very hush-hush. And he wants *you* to see it first.' You'd have creamed, right?"

She blinked at the offensive expression, but she didn't shy away from his eyes as they bore into hers.

"I wanted you to cream over *Envy*, Maris. But without knowing anything about me or my past successes."

She looked away, readjusted her eyeglasses, absently brushed a gnat off her arm. When she looked at him again, she said, "All right, yes. I wouldn't have used your crude terminology, but I would've been excited by such a call. Why would that have been such a terrible thing?"

"Because I wanted an unbiased opinion of the writing."

"Which entitled you to make a fool of me."

"No, dammit! That wasn't..." He felt his own ire rising, and he suspected it was because her argument had merit. He began again. "I sent the prologue to you unsolicited because that was the only way to guarantee an impartial reading. I wanted you to approach it without preconceptions. I wanted it to stand on its own, not on my reputation as a bestselling author. I wanted it to be good."

"It would have been just as good without the charade, Parker. My reaction to it would have been the same."

"But I would never have known for sure, would I?" He gave her time to respond, but she didn't. She couldn't. He was right, and she knew it. "I tricked you, yes. But I needed to prove to myself that there was more in me than a scotch-drinking, skirt-chasing hunk with a big gun and a bigger dick."

"Deck Cayton has more substance than that."

"Thanks. I think so. I wasn't sure you did."

She bent down and picked up the book.

"Are you going to bang me over the head with that?"

"Maybe." Her anger hadn't dissipated. It was still there, simmering. She just had it under control. "But even as mad as I am," she said, "I can't abuse a book. It goes against my nature even to dog-ear a page."

"I'm that way, too."

She returned his peacemaking smile with a glare. "Don't you dare try to charm me, Parker." She passed the book down to him and dusted her hands. "What you did was—"

"Terrifying."

"That wasn't the word I was going to use."

"But it's the correct one. When I put that prologue in the mail, I was scared shitless."

"Of what? Rejection?"

"Big time. You could have sent me a curt letter. Said no

thanks. Said I stunk. Said I should give up writing and try string-ing beads or basket weaving instead. I'd have probably bought a package of razor blades and locked myself in the bathroom."

"That isn't funny."

"You're right, it isn't."

"Besides, you're too egotistical for suicide."

How little she knew. There had been times during those dark-est days when his soul had been as twisted as his legs and his emotions were as raw as the flesh that defied healing, when, had he been able to move, he would have taken the path of least re-sistance and ended it there.

But while he was in that pit of despair, he had been imbued with a will to live. Determination had been breathed into him by some omnipotent power or cosmic authority greater than his paltry human spirit.

Not an angel, though. Not an angel as angels are typically portrayed. There was nothing benevolent, God-blessed, or holy about his plans for Noah Reed.

He reached for Maris's hand and squeezed it hard. "Don't un-derestimate how important this is to me."

She didn't squeeze back but searched his eyes. "Why did you send *Envy* to me, Parker? I know your editor for the Mackensie Roone books. He's very capable."

"He is," he agreed solemnly.

"My question stands. There are hundreds of editors in a dozen major publishing houses. What set me apart? Why'd you choose me?"

"The article in the magazine." He hoped she wouldn't detect that he was lying. The answer seemed plausible enough to him, but she was looking at him with an intensity that was unnerving. "The things you were quoted as saying convinced me you were the editor for *Envy.*

"I liked what you said about commerce versus quality, and how the balance in publishing is in danger of shifting in favor of the former. I'm not writing this book for the money. I've got more money than I'll ever need. Deck Cayton has seen to that.

"I'm writing *Envy* for me. If it finds an audience, I'll be pleased. If it doesn't, you still saw something worthwhile in it, and to me that's damn good confirmation of my talent."

"It'll find an audience." She pulled her hand free of his. "I'll see to that. I have too much invested in it not to."

"A measly fifteen grand?"

"I wasn't referring to the advance."

His silly smile collapsed and he matched her gravity. "I know."

"I was referring to..."

He thought he saw the start of tears, but it might have been a tricky reflection off the lenses of her glasses. "I know what you were talking about, Maris."

They exchanged a long and meaningful look. He was consumed with the desire to touch her. "I don't want you to leave."

He hadn't known he was going to say that until he heard his own gruff voice filling the heavy silence. He hadn't made a conscious decision to speak the words, but he meant them. And he meant them for reasons that had absolutely nothing to do with his revenge on Noah Reed.

"Write your book, Parker."

"Stay."

"I'll be in touch." She backed up several steps before turning and walking away from him.

"Maris!"

But she didn't stop or even slow down, and she didn't look back, not even when he called her name again.

Chapter 16

This visit is long overdue. I'm glad you were free." Nadia Schuller sent a smile across the table to her luncheon guest.

As the setting for this intimate get-together, Nadia had chosen a small, cozy restaurant on Park Avenue. Its menu was unaffected; the decor was country French. Nadia thought the lace panels in the windows were a bit precious for Manhattan, but they contributed to the restaurant's friendly ambience.

And that was the note she was trying to strike with this lunch—friendliness.

Which was somewhat of a challenge when you were screwing your guest's husband.

"Thank you for the invitation." Maris offered a strained little smile and opened her menu, a not so subtle hint that she was ready to get lunch under way and over with as quickly as etiquette permitted.

A waiter in a long white apron approached their table. "What would you like to drink, Maris?" Nadia asked.

"Iced tea, please."

"I'm having white wine. Would you rather have that?" She

made it sound as though she were granting Maris permission to have an alcoholic beverage if she preferred.

Addressing the waiter this time, Maris repeated, "Iced tea, please. Lots of ice and a fresh wedge of lemon." Turning back to Nadia, she said, "I formed the habit when I was in the South."

"They drink it year-'round down there, don't they? That and moonshine." Nadia ordered her wine and the waiter withdrew. "I heard all about your trip to Dixie."

"Oh?"

"From your secretary. When I called to invite you to lunch."

"I thought perhaps Noah had told you."

"No, I haven't seen Noah in, hmm... actually, I think it was the night I saw the two of you at the awards banquet."

They made small talk until the waiter returned with their drink order, then listened to his recitation of the chef's specials. Nadia requested a few minutes for them to think over their selections. This delay in the proceedings seemed to perturb Maris, but Nadia wasn't going to be brushed off like a piece of lint.

She didn't like Maris in the least, and she was absolutely certain that her dislike was reciprocated. Both were successful businesswomen, but their approach to their careers, to men, to life in general, couldn't be more dissimilar.

Maris Matherly-Reed had enjoyed all the advantages that Nadia had been denied. Maris had been born into a wealthy and well-respected family and had cut her perfectly straight teeth on a silver spoon.

She had attended exclusive private schools and was a frequent guest at the tony parties held in the tony estates in the Hamptons. Her photograph often appeared in the society columns. She had traveled extensively.

Maris had culture out the ass—an ass that hadn't required painful, expensive liposuction to get it slim and taut. Shapely as it was, however, you couldn't melt an ice cube on it.

Nadia, née Nadine, had been born poor. Her family's poverty was forgivable. It was their ignorance and uncouthness she had found intolerable. As early as preadolescence, she determined not to remain in Brooklyn and marry some boorish loser of a husband with whom she would fight over how they were going to house and feed their ever-increasing brood.

She was destined for far better things.

She lost her virginity at thirteen to her first employer, the manager of a novelty store where she clerked in the afternoons after school. He caught her stealing nail polish and lipstick from the store's stock and had given her a choice between his sweaty coupling or arrest and juvenile court.

Besides the discomfort of being screwed on top of shipping crates in a dank stockroom by someone with clumsy, damp hands and garlic breath, it hadn't been that bad a trade-off.

That was only the first of many times Nadia bartered sex to get something she wanted or to avoid something she didn't. She perceived high school as a sentence she must serve, but amused herself by stealing her classmates' boyfriends.

She didn't give a fig about the broken hearts she caused. It didn't worry her that she didn't have a single girlfriend. As long as there were boys lusting after her, vying for her attention, giving her presents, and taking her places in exchange for doing what she would have enjoyed doing anyway, why should she care?

When her grades fell short of meeting graduation requirements, her rudimentary math teacher agreed to favorably adjust her score in exchange for a blow job. Her world history teacher, a pathetically homely woman, had been tearfully grateful when Nadia professed a secret affection for her. In the span of one rainy evening in the teacher's apartment that smelled of cat-litter boxes, Nadia's grade escalated from a D to a B+.

Once she had her diploma, she eschewed higher education. She had no patience for scholastics. Instead, she plowed straight

into the workforce, moving from job to job at six-month inter-
vals, until she was hired as a copy editor for a local neighborhood
weekly newspaper.

This was the first job that had appealed to her and that she
felt was worthy of her. Within weeks of being hired, she resolved
that this was the field in which she would re-create herself—
beginning with changing her name—and become famous.

Eventually she talked the managing editor into letting her
write an occasional article. The negotiation took place in the
backseat of his car in the shadow of the row house where he lived
with his wife and four children. Nadia had straddled his lap and,
working him into a state of near delirium, got his gasping promise to give her idea a trial run.

The Nadia Schuller pieces were gossipy, chatty, anecdotal
stories about the lives and loves of people who lived in the
neighborhood. It soon became the most popular feature of the
newspaper. Nadia was on her way.

Now, twelve years and countless lovers later, she sat across
from Maris Matherly-Reed, behaving in a civilized manner but
harboring an enormous amount of antipathy for a woman who
bested her without even trying. Were Maris to hate her more,
Nadia would hate Maris less. What she couldn't tolerate was
Maris's seeming indifference toward her. As though she merited
no notice at all.

For instance, when they met at the entrance to the restaurant,
Nadia had remarked on the light tan Maris had acquired while
she was in Georgia and rather cattily reminded her how damaging sun exposure was to the complexion.

Maris's cool comeback had been, "Next time I go, I'll be sure
to take a hat."

They placed their entrée orders with the waiter. As Nadia
passed Maris a basket of bread, she remarked, "Tragic news
about Howard Bancroft."

That elicited a reaction. Maris declined the bread basket with a small shake of her head and her eyes turned sad. "Very tragic. I didn't learn of it until I returned late yesterday afternoon."

"How many years had he been at the helm of your legal department?"

"Since before I was born. We were all shocked."

"Has anyone speculated on why he killed himself?"

"Nadia, I—"

"Oh, this isn't for 'Book Chat.' The facts were in the newspaper account, and it painted a grisly scene. I got the official, sanitized press release from your PR department. It said little about his manner of death and was more about his contribution to Matherly Press."

Howard Bancroft had been discovered in his car, parked half a block from his house on Long Island, with his brains blown to smithereens and a pistol in his hand.

"The people at Matherly Press are a closely knit group. No one picked up warning signals?"

"No," Maris replied. "In fact, Noah had a meeting with him just that afternoon. He said Howard was being typically Howard." She shook her head with remorse. "He was such a well-loved man, especially in the Jewish community. I can't imagine what drove him to commit such a desperate act."

Their main courses arrived. As they ate, they switched to a brighter topic—the books Matherly Press had scheduled for its fall lineup. "I predict that it's going to be a very successful holiday season for us," Maris told her. "Our best ever."

"May I quote that in my column?"

"You may."

Nadia opened her ever-present notebook and asked Maris to enumerate the titles and authors she was especially excited about. After jotting them down, she laid aside her pen and took a dainty bite of grilled sea bass. "Tell me about this project you're working on in Georgia."

"I can't."

Nadia stopped eating. "Why not?"

"It's not open to discussion."

"How positively fabulous. I love projects swathed in mystery."

"This one is and must remain that way. And even my telling you that is off the record. Don't use it."

Nadia took a sip of wine, gazing at Maris over the rim of the glass. "You've just increased my curiosity about a thousand times over."

"You'll have to remain curious."

"The author—"

"Chooses to remain anonymous. That's also off the record. Even my staff doesn't know the writer's identity, so it will do you no good to try and trick or wheedle information from anyone at Matherly Press."

"No one knows who he is?"

"I never said it was a he."

"Right, right, you didn't. Does that mean it's a she?"

"It means I'm not telling."

"Give me something," Nadia cajoled. "Friend to friend."

"You're not my friend."

Nadia was taken aback by Maris's tone. Suddenly, with that terse statement, they were no longer talking about the unnamed writer in Georgia.

She kept her smile in place, saying, "That's true, Maris. We haven't been. We've been too busy with our respective careers to get to know one another and cultivate a friendship, but I'd like to change that. I'd like—"

"We will never be friends, Nadia."

Again, Nadia was taken off guard by Maris's candor. "Why do you say that?"

"Because you want to sleep with my husband."

In spite of herself, Nadia was impressed. Miss Goody-Two-Shoes wasn't so goody after all. She had more grit than the girls' school polish suggested. Dropping all pretense, she met

Maris's level gaze. "You can't wonder why. Noah is an attractive man."

"An attractive *married* man."

"A distinction that has never stopped me."

"That's what I hear."

Rather than being insulted, Nadia laughed. "Good. I love being the topic of scandalous conversation."

She took another sip of wine, then ran her index finger around the rim of the glass as she continued to study Maris with a new appreciation. She admired directness but never would have believed the former debutante capable of it to this degree.

But she wondered how cool Maris would remain if she confessed to her affair with Noah. What if she gave wifey a blow-by-blow—pun intended—account of what they had done in bed last night? She would bet that for all Maris's composure, that would rattle her right down to her Manolo Blahniks.

While that would be fun, it wouldn't be wise. There was too much at stake. Curbing the temptation to flaunt the affair, she asked, "Have you spoken to Noah about this?"

"Yes."

"And what did he say?"

"That his interest in you is strictly business-related. That your column is so influential, he can't risk offending you. That's why he goes along with your obvious machinations."

Nadia shrugged. "There you have it. I've established myself by using people as sources of information. In turn, they use me for free publicity and promotion. Noah understands the way it works."

She had managed to dance around the topic without either lying or telling the whole truth, and she hoped Maris would leave it at that. The WorldView deal needed no further complications.

Taking advantage of Maris's silence, she said, "I'm glad we cleared the air. Would you like a bite of sea bass?"

"No, thank you."

"It's delicious, but I've had my fill."

Actually, she was still hungry, but she pushed her plate away. One area of thigh tissue absorbed fat like a goddamn sponge despite the procedure she had undergone. She fanatically counted every calorie. Exercise was the only religion she believed in or practiced, and she worshiped strenuously every day.

Noah teased her about her rigid fitness regimen, saying she even brought it to bed with her. In fact, she counted sex as an aerobic exercise. She knew precisely how many calories were burned with each act of coitus.

Noah knew her well. He could be the sole man on the planet to whom she might be faithful. She didn't love him, any more than he loved her. Neither of them bought into the myth of romantic love. He had readily admitted that his marriage hadn't been inspired by amorous passion, but rather his burning desire to become part of the Matherly dynasty via the only Matherly available to him.

He had developed a mentor-protégé relationship with Daniel, but even that wasn't enough to satisfy his ambition. Becoming the old man's son-in-law was the next best thing to a blood kinship. Marrying Maris would cement his future, so he had made it happen.

Nadia admired that kind of single-minded scheming and the guts it took to carry out a bold plan. To her, ruthlessness was an aphrodisiac like no other. She spotted it in Noah the first time she met him. Recognizing in him a self-serving ambition that was equal to her own, she had wanted him, and she hadn't played coy.

Their first business lunch date had carried over into an afternoon spent in bed at the Pierre. To her delight, Noah approached sex with the same self-gratifying appetite and animalistic detachment as she. By the time he left her lying tangled up in the damp sheets, she was raw and sore and exhilarated.

They were also compatible out of bed. They understood one

another. Their individual drives to achieve were harmonious but competitive enough to spark arguments and add zest. They were good for each other. They complemented each other. As a team, they would be unconquerable. That was why Nadia wanted to become Mrs. Noah Reed.

Well, that was *one* reason why.

The other was harder for her to acknowledge: There was just enough of Nadine remaining in her to want to be married before she died. She didn't want to grow old alone. Somewhere between power lunches and sundown specials, a single woman became a spinster.

Through her twenties and thirties, she had scorned the very idea of matrimony. To anybody who would listen she claimed no interest whatsoever in monogamy and the marriage bed. What a fucking—literally—bore.

But the truth was that, for all the men who had shared her bed, who had sighed and cried and groaned and crowed between her thighs, not one, not a single one, had ever asked her to be his wife.

And, to be brutally honest, Noah hadn't actually proposed, either. He wasn't the hearts-and-flowers-and-bended-knee type. She had more diamond rings than she had fingers and toes. How their plans for matrimony had come about was that she had told him she wanted to marry him. And Nadia never took no for an answer.

Now her future husband's present wife was finishing a cappuccino that she hadn't wanted. Usually Nadia could sweet-talk or browbeat someone out of a tidbit of information that she could expand into an item for her column, but Maris had remained stubbornly mute about her secret project. She seemed disinclined to talk on any level about the nature of the book or about the writer.

Not that Nadia gave a flip about Maris's silly secret project. The purpose of this lunch had been to keep Maris derailed, unaware, and blissfully ignorant of what Nadia and Noah were doing with WorldView behind her back.

But Maris had tipped her hand. Noah should be warned that

she might not be as malleable and naive as she looked. Nadia hoped her suspicion of an affair had been quelled, because the last thing they needed in these important final weeks was a jealous wife breathing down their necks.

"Anything else, Maris?" she offered graciously. "Another cappuccino?"

"No, thank you. I should get back to the office. I'm playing catch-up after being away, as I knew I would be."

"Then why'd you come?" The question was out before Nadia realized she was going to ask it. But having done so, she owned up to being curious. Why had Maris accepted her invitation?

"For a long time now, we've detested the sight of one another. But we always played polite," Maris said. "I hate phoniness, especially in myself." She looked inward for a second, then added, "Or maybe I'm just disgusted with lies and liars. In any case, I thought it was time to tell you to your face that I'm on to you."

Nadia took it all in, then smiled wryly. "Fair enough." As they made their way to the entrance, she said, "You'll still feed me industry news items, won't you?"

"News. Not gossip."

"When you're ready to reveal this mysterious author and book, will you give me the scoop?"

"The author is very publicity-shy. I doubt—"

"Nadia, what a nice surprise."

Nadia turned at the greeting and found herself looking into the colorless countenance of Morris Blume, the last person on earth she would choose to bump into when Maris Matherly-Reed was standing beside her. She didn't find the surprise nice at all.

"How are you, Morris?" She extended her hand to him but kept her tone aloof and uninviting. "I recommend the sea bass."

"And I recommend the martinis," he said, raising his frosted glass. "In fact, I coached the bartender here on how to make one just right."

"Stirred or shaken?"

"Shaken."

Maris had moved to the coat check to retrieve her raincoat, so Nadia felt free to engage in a mild flirtation. It wouldn't be smart to be too aloof. Her dinner with him at the Rainbow Room had been enjoyable. If she gave him the brush-off now, he would wonder why.

"Gin or vodka?"

"Vodka. Straight up and extra dirty."

One of her artfully waxed eyebrows arched. "I like the sound of that."

"Here." He lifted the pick from his glass and extended it toward her mouth.

Keeping her eyes on his, she touched the tip of her tongue to the olive, then closed her lips around it and sucked it into her mouth. "Hmm. My favorite thing."

"Join me in one?"

"I'm afraid I can't, Morris. Rain check?"

"I'll call."

She flashed him her most promising smile. It had been mastered after years of practice and was now practically habitual. She told him to enjoy his lunch and turned away to rejoin Maris.

To her consternation, the smile worked too well. Blume trailed her, making an introduction to Maris unavoidable. She executed it with as much casualness as she could affect.

As the two shook hands, Blume said, "I've long been an admirer of your publishing house."

"And a suitor," Maris remarked.

He grinned disarmingly. "So you've read the numerous letters I've written to your esteemed father?"

"Along with his replies."

"Do you agree with him?"

"Wholeheartedly. While we're flattered that an entity like WorldView is interested in merging with us, we like ourselves the way we are."

"So your husband told me during our last meeting."

Chapter 17

Noah was reviewing the company's most recent shipping invoices when his wife stormed into his office and slammed the door behind her, stunning his secretary.

She tossed her handbag and damp raincoat into the nearest chair and strode to the edge of his desk. She'd been testy and despondent since her return from Georgia last evening, but she had never looked better. Today she was dressed in a suit tailored for office wear, but it was a form-fitting one he'd always admired. Time spent on the beach had put some color in her cheeks and stripped it from her hair. Sun-bleached strands framed her face, giving her a youthful, healthy appearance.

Her expression, however, wasn't sunny.

"Hello, Maris. How was your lunch?"

"I was just introduced to WorldView's whiz kid, Morris Blume. He told me to give you his regards."

Goddamn Nadia! he thought. Why hadn't she called to warn him of this? Then he remembered: He had given Cindy strict instructions to hold his calls until after he'd had time to review the financial statements stacked on his desk—ironically because of WorldView. He'd been going over the charts and columns entry by entry, becoming intimately familiar with them, seeking potential trouble spots which might cause Blume and company concern. Should they pose any questions, Noah wanted to have an explanation ready.

Remaining as unflappable as possible, he said, "How nice of Mr. Blume to remember me."

"Apparently it wasn't that much of a stretch for him, Noah, given you two had a recent meeting." She braced herself on his desk with stiff arms and leaned toward him, her eyes flashing. "What meeting is he talking about, Noah? And why wasn't I informed of it? *What* meeting?"

He stood up and came around the desk. "Maris, kindly calm down."

"Don't tell me to calm down."

"All right, then, I'm asking you to. Please."

He reached out to take her by the shoulders, but she backed away and slung off his extended hands.

"Would you like a glass of water?"

"I would like an explanation," she said, enunciating each word. "You know how Dad and I feel about conglomerates like WorldView."

"I share your opinion." He hiked his hip over the corner of his desk and placidly folded his hands on his thigh, although he would have liked to wrap them around her slender neck. "That's why I agreed to the meeting with WorldView."

She shook her head in disbelief, as though up until that time she had been clinging to the hope that Blume was lying. "You met with those jackals? You actually did? Behind my back and without my knowledge?"

Noah sighed and gave her a pained look. "Yes, I met with them. But before you go into orbit, can you be reasonable and give me an opportunity to explain?" He took her fuming silence for permission to continue.

"Blume's flunkies had been hounding me for months. They called until I stopped taking or returning their calls. With no regard for that blatant hint, they began faxing me until I got tired of throwing the damn things away.

"They made nuisances of themselves until I determined that the most expedient way to handle the situation was to attend a meeting and tell Blume to his baby's-ass face that we were not interested in anything he had to offer by way of a merger. Period. End of discussion. I don't think I could have made our position any clearer. I didn't tell you about it because you were extremely busy and didn't need any additional stress."

"I'm always busy."

"The meeting was inconsequential."

"I hardly think so."

"And, frankly," he said, "I anticipated that you would react emotionally rather than rationally. I predicted that you would fly off the handle and lose all perspective. I hoped to avoid a scene such as this."

"This isn't a *scene*, Noah. This is a private conversation between husband and wife, between business partners. Two relationships that should come with an implied trust."

"Exactly," he said, raising his voice to match the level of hers. "Which is why I'm amazed, both as your husband and your business partner, by your apparent lack of trust in me."

"Chalk it up to my reacting emotionally, flying off the handle, and going into orbit!"

"Which are fair analogies, Maris. You came barging in here and practically accused me of treason against Matherly Press."

"At the very least you consorted with the enemy!"

A knock on the door brought them around. Daniel was standing on the threshold, leaning heavily on his cane. "I'm exercising one privilege of old age, which is to intrude when uninvited."

Noah shot his cuffs. "Of course you're welcome, Daniel.

Maris has just returned from lunch. We were having a discussion about—"

"I heard. From all the way down the hall." Daniel came in and closed the door. "Maris is upset about the meeting you had with WorldView."

She reacted with a start. "You knew about it?"

"Noah told me of his decision to meet with them. I thought it was a sound idea and was glad he was going instead of me. I don't think I could have stomached it."

"Why wasn't I informed?"

She addressed the question to both of them, but Noah answered. "You were leaving for Georgia. Daniel and I could see how excited you were about this project and were afraid that if you knew about WorldView you'd change your plans. There was no reason to bother you with it."

"I'm not a child." She glowered at him, then at Daniel.

"We made a mistake in judgment," Daniel conceded. "It wasn't our intention to slight you."

"I don't feel slighted, I feel babied. I don't need protection, Dad. Or coddling. Or special favors. When it comes to business, I'm not a daughter or a wife, I'm an officer of this corporation.

"I should have been consulted on something this major, I don't care how busy I was or what my travel plans were. You were remiss and just plain wrong to exclude me from those discussions. I'm also mad as hell at both of you for letting me be made a fool of in front of Morris Blume and Nadia Schuller."

"I apologize," Daniel said.

"So do I," Noah echoed. "I'm terribly sorry that you were embarrassed today at lunch. I take full responsibility for that."

She didn't verbally accept their apologies, but Daniel took her silence as a tacit pardon. "Are we still on for dinner tonight? Maxine's making pot roast."

"We'll see you at seven," Noah confirmed. Daniel split an uneasy glance between them and then left them alone.

Maris went to the window and turned her back to the room. Noah remained where he was, still perched on the corner of his desk. Several minutes passed before she spoke. "I'm sorry I lost my temper."

"It hasn't been that long ago that I told you how beautiful you are when you're angry."

She came around quickly and angrily. "Don't patronize me, Noah."

"Don't be so goddamn sensitive," he snapped.

"I resent belittling, sexist remarks like that."

"That's a sexist remark? Can't I pay you a compliment without your reading something into it?"

"Not when we're fighting."

It was upsetting, and a little alarming, that his charm seemed to have lost some of its effectiveness. "What's with you, Maris? Since you got back yesterday, you've been as prickly as a porcupine. If working on this project," he said, slinging out his hand as though to shake off a contagion, "is going to cause a chronic case of PMS—"

"And that's not sexist?"

"—then I recommend you—"

"This has nothing to do with that!"

"Then what?"

"Nadia."

"Nadia?"

"Did she know about your meeting with Blume?"

He covered his discomfiture with a short laugh. "What? You think I called up our local gossip columnist and leaked the story?"

Folding her arms across her middle, Maris turned back to the window. "You're lying."

He came off the desk. "I beg your pardon?"

"She knew, Noah. Nadia's the most conniving woman I've ever met, and ordinarily she makes no secret of it. In fact, she takes pride in it. But when Blume mentioned his meeting with you, she blanched, looking as though she'd just been exposed. Then she couldn't hustle me away from him and out of there fast enough. As we said good-bye, she oozed goodwill, but nervously." She came around slowly. "She knew."

The look she gave him was so damned superior, it enraged him. He felt blood rushing to his head. He imagined capillaries bursting behind his eyeballs. Fury pulsated through him. Only by an act of will could he keep his voice from revealing it.

"Why would I tell Nadia, Maris? There was nothing to tell. If Nadia knew, she heard it from Blume. I've seen them with their heads together on more than one occasion. They probably stroke each other for inside information."

"Yes, that's how it works," she whispered as though to herself. When she refocused on him, she asked, "If Blume told her, why didn't she write about it in her column?"

"That's simple. WorldView owns a chain of newspapers that carry her column. She couldn't risk inflaming them by blabbing that David had thumbed his nose at Goliath, which is exactly what my meeting with them amounted to. If I'd known it was going to cause this much hullabaloo, I'd have continued avoiding them. I swear to God, I thought that meeting would be the end of their persistence."

"She confessed."

His heart knocked against his chest. It was difficult to keep his features impassive. "What? Who? Confessed what?"

"I told Nadia that I was on to her. That I could see through her and knew that she had designs on you."

"Designs?" he repeated with amusement. "What quaint phraseology."

"I didn't use it to be cute, Noah," she said testily. "Today I had lunch with a woman who told me to my face that she wants to sleep with you."

He rolled his eyes toward the ceiling. "Maris. For God's sake.

Nadia wants to sleep with every man. She's made it her life's quest. She's one giant, raging hormone. She's come on to me, sure. Do you think I'm that easily flattered? She also comes on to waiters and doormen and probably to her garbage collector."

"A lot of men find her attractive."

"She is. But I didn't have an affair with her when I was single, and I sure as hell wouldn't jeopardize my marriage to you by having one with her now." He sighed and shook his head ruefully. "Is that what all this has been about? You let Nadia upset you?"

"No. I was more upset over the WorldView thing than I was about Nadia. If you want Nadia, then you deserve her."

He forced himself to smile. "I'm glad you gave me an opportunity to explain both misunderstandings. These things shouldn't fester. It's bad for our marriage."

He gave her a few moments to ruminate on that, then smiled the tentative smile of a scolded puppy. "If that's the end of the interrogation, I'd like to hug my interrogator."

Since she didn't raise any barriers, either real or suggested, he joined her where she stood and placed his arms around her. He pressed his face into her hair. "I was angry when I made that ludicrous statement about chronic PMS, but it has a basis of truth, doesn't it? You're not yourself." He stroked her back. "Was that little island so horrible?"

"I wondered if you were ever going to express any interest in my trip."

"That's unfair, Maris. Since your return, you haven't exactly invited conversation. You've been sullen and standoffish. In fact, I've considered approaching you with a chair and whip." Undaunted by her failure to laugh, he kissed her temple. "How was your trip? What's the island like?"

"Not horrible at all. Different."

"From what?"

He felt her shrug. "It's hard to explain. Just different."

"And the author, was he as difficult to work with as you expected?"

"More difficult than I expected."

"We've got an impressive slate of books to publish next year from our authors under contract. Why bother with this recluse?"

"Because he writes well. Very well."

"But is he worth the difficulty he puts you through?"

"I won't give up on this book, Noah."

"I'm only thinking of you. If working with him makes you edgy and—"

"It doesn't."

Luckily she couldn't see his expression or she would have realized how close she came to being slapped senseless for interrupting him. He took a moment to tamp down his anger before asking in a deceptively pleasant voice, "What is this literary marvel's name?"

"I'm sworn to secrecy."

"Isn't he carrying the anonymity to a ludicrous degree?"

"There's a reason. He's disabled."

"How so?"

"I really can't talk about it, Noah. I can't betray his trust."

"Are you sure your opinion of the writing hasn't been swayed by his disability?"

"I loved the writing before I knew about his circumstances, which don't affect his talent. He'd be talented in any form. In spite of all the difficulty working with him imposes, I'm enjoying the work. It's going to be good for me. I'm getting to flex some editorial muscle. Over the last few years, I've become fat and lazy."

"A little lazy, maybe, but not fat."

He slid his hands over her butt, a caress he knew she liked and that usually evoked an agreeable response. This time it was less effective. "I was speaking metaphorically, Noah."

"I realize that. Still..." He bent his head and kissed her, first on the cheek, then her mouth. He wanted to be assured that her outburst wasn't an indicator of something more serious, specifically that she doubted his loyalty to Matherly Press.

She returned the kiss. Not with the fervor he sought, perhaps, but when he pulled back she smiled up at him, assuaging his concern.

"If these financials didn't need my attention," he growled, "I'd be tempted to lock the door and take you right here."

"Why don't you say 'damn the financials' and do just that? I could be taken."

He kissed her again, then purposefully set her away from him. "Sorely tempting, darling. But duties call."

"I understand."

"Tonight? After dinner with Daniel?"

"You have a date." She kissed him quickly, then retrieved her raincoat and handbag. "I may stay late and try to clear my desk, so I probably won't change before dinner."

"Then we'll leave straight from here and ride over together. I'll have a car waiting downstairs at six-forty-five."

"See you then."

He blew her a kiss as she went out, then returned to his desk, confident that he had dodged a bullet. As always, Maris had been pacified with a little attention and affection. But her upset over the WorldView meeting was no small matter.

When he considered how close he'd come to being caught today, he wished to watch Morris Blume slowly and agonizingly bleed to death. Telling Maris about that meeting had obviously been Blume's way of reminding him that the deadline was fast approaching. Blume had seized an unplanned opportunity to make a power play, to remind him that WorldView was ultimately in charge of this transaction.

It had been a close call. It had cost him some valuable time. In the long run, however, the incident had caused no permanent damage. Thank God he'd had the foresight to inform Daniel of that meeting with just this contingency in mind. In the event that he or Maris had gotten wind of it—and the industry grapevine was notorious—he had taken the old man into his confidence, thereby throwing him off track.

The Matherlys weren't fools. But they were nowhere close to being as clever as he. He left absolutely nothing to chance. He planned meticulously. His schemes were long-range and therefore took a steely patience and perseverance that lesser individuals lacked.

He relied on his instincts and his intelligence, but also on the best possible resource, the one that was virtually unfailing and always in full supply—human nature. Mind control was easy if you knew a person's likes, dislikes, secrets, weaknesses, fears.

He possessed a gift for getting people to go right where he wanted them to go and to do exactly what he wanted them to do. He was talented that way. He had an uncanny knack for manipulating people, for persuading them to make a decision they mistakenly thought was their own and to act on it. He had done it before. Most recently with Howard Bancroft. But he had honed this particular skill long before he had ever heard of Howard Bancroft.

His desk phone rang. Before he could even speak, Cindy apologized for the interruption. "I'm sorry, Mr. Reed, but Ms. Schuller has called five times and insists on being put through."

"Fine." Noah depressed the blinking button. "Hello, Nadia," he said breezily. "I understand you had quite an exciting lunch."

"Envy" Ch. 12
Key West, Florida, 1986

Todd Grayson's first impression of Key West was a crushing disappointment.

Making the move had been nearly all he'd talked about for months. He'd thought of little else and had practically x-ed off the days of his calendar like a child counting down toward Christmas. He'd resented anything that interfered with his daydreaming and planning, including his final semester's studies. His heart, mind, and soul had been focused singly on getting to his Floridian mecca.

But now, having arrived, having fulfilled a long-held dream, his first sight of it left him less than spiritually enraptured.

He likened the place to an old whore. It looked used, seedy, a little unhealthy, and a lot tired. Continuing the metaphor in his mind as though he were writing it down, Key West appeared to be more a common streetwalker who advertised her wares on a corner, rather than an exotic courtesan who enticed with whispered promises. Once the tacky and rather pathetic attempts at glamour were stripped away, the town had little to offer and nothing to recommend her. She was cheap and common, and the only promise at which she hinted was one of dissipation.

His and Roark's plan had been to depart for Florida the afternoon of their college graduation. They had everything packed and ready, their only chore before hitting the road being to return the caps and gowns in which they'd marched to "Pomp and Circumstance" and received their degrees.

They planned to caravan in their respective automobiles and had agreed to stop just before their arrival and toss a coin to determine which of them got to lead the way to Duval Street.

But fate intervened. Their well-laid plans were changed for them. A family obligation prevented Todd from leaving that day. Roark offered to postpone leaving, too, but after a rushed consultation, they agreed that he should go ahead and start looking for housing.

"I'll be the scout. By the time you get there, I'll have camp set up," Roark had said as they exchanged their dejected good-byes. Roark's Toyota was packed to the gills. Every square inch of interior space had been utilized to transport all that he owned in the world from the fraternity house where he had lived for the past three years to the next phase of his life.

"This sucks," Todd muttered.

"Big time. But hey, it's only a minor setback."

"Easy for you to say. It's not your setback. While I'm languishing, you'll be down there writing your ass off."

"Hardly, man. I'll be busy scoping out things, finding us a place to live. Getting the telephone hooked up. That kinda shit. I won't get any serious writing done."

Todd knew that wasn't true. Roark always wrote—drunk or sober, tired or wired, sick or well. He wrote when he was happy and when he was sad. He wrote just as much when he was in a good mood as he did when he was pissed over something. He wrote when it was flowing easily and when the phrases simply would not come. He wrote no matter what. Any which way you looked at it, despite all his arguments to the contrary, this was giving him a head start, and Todd resented it like hell.

As Roark wedged himself into the driver's seat of his packed Toyota, he tried again to lift Todd's spirits. "I know this seems like a big deal now, but one day we'll barely remember it. You'll see."

As agreed, he had called Todd immediately upon his arrival in Key West. A few days later he phoned again to report that he had rented them an apartment. Todd barraged him with questions about it, but his answers were evasive, his descriptions vague. After hanging up, Todd realized that all he really knew about their new place of residence was that it fit into their budget.

It was six weeks before Todd was able to set out for his relocation to the tip of the continent. The morning of his departure, as he left his childhood home for what would be the last time, he wasted no time on sentiment and never looked back. Instead, he equated it to a release from prison.

He drove almost twenty hours that first day and crossed the state line into Florida before pulling off at a roadside park and napping in the driver's seat of his car. He arrived in Key West at midafternoon the second day. Although not all his expectations were met upon his arrival, some were.

The air, for instance. It was warm and balmy. No more running to an early class on a bitterly cold and windy morning ever again, thank you very much. The sun was hot. Palms and banana trees grew in abundance. Jimmy Buffett music was pervasive, as though it were secreted through the pores of the city.

As he navigated the tourist-clogged streets, following the rudimentary directions Roark had given him, his initial disappointment began to recede and was replaced by flurries of excitement. His mood was buoyed by the sights and sounds and smells.

But this flicker of encouragement didn't last. It was snuffed out when he located his newly leased domicile. Dismayed, he checked the address twice, hoping to God he'd made a wrong turn.

Surely this was one of Roark's practical jokes.

Tall oleander bushes formed a unkempt hedge between the street and the shallow, weedy lawn in front of the building. He expected Roark to leap from between the blooming shrubs, grinning like a jackass and braying, "Man you oughta see your expression. Looks like you've been hit in the face with a sack of buzzard shit."

They would have a good laugh, then Roark would guide him to their actual address. Later they'd go out for a beer and relive the moment, and that would be the first of a thousand times they would retell the story, as they retold all their good stories when they wanted or needed a laugh.

Except the one about the incident with Professor Hadley. That was one story that neither retold. They never talked about it at all.

Todd parked his car at the crumbling curb and got out. He was reluctant even to step between the oleanders—which looked like shrubs on steroids—and follow the cracked sidewalk up to the door of the three-story building. The cinder-block exterior had been painted a flaming flamingo pink, as though the lurid hue would conceal the low-grade building material. Instead, the color accented the lack of quality.

A crack as wide as Todd's index finger ran through the wall of blocks from eaves to foundation. A wild fern was growing out of it at one spot. Hurricane shutters, the color of pea soup, were missing slats and seemed to be clinging to the building only out of fear of falling into the stagnant water that had collected around the foundation. As wide as a moat, it was a flourishing mosquito hatchery.

The frame of the aluminum screen door probably had once been rectangular, but it had been dented and bent so many times that it was grossly misshapen. A large part of the mesh had been peeled away, making it totally ineffectual against flying insects—or chameleons, Todd discovered when he opened the door and stepped into a dank vestibule with a concrete floor. Two of the green lizards were lounging on the interior wall. One scampered away when Todd entered. The other puffed out his red throat as though in protest of the intrusion.

Six mailboxes, which would usually be found on the outside of a building, had been secured to the wall. Once his eyes had adjusted to the dimness, Todd read, to his distress, his and Roark's name on one of the boxes.

There were six apartments in all, two on each floor. Theirs was on the third. Stepping over a puddle of unidentifiable fluid, he started upstairs. When he reached the second-floor landing, he could hear *The Price Is Right* coming from a TV within one of the apartments. Otherwise the building was quiet.

By the time he reached the third floor, he was sweating. He cursed the same balminess he'd been extolling only minutes before as he'd driven through the streets with the car windows rolled down, ogling the bare-shouldered, bare-legged girls strolling the sidewalks.

Surely the individual apartments were air-conditioned, he thought as he tried the door knob on 3A. It was locked. He knocked—three times in all before Roark answered. His suntanned face broke into a wide grin. "Hey, you made it! An hour early."

"No air-conditioning? Are you fucking kidding me?"

The heat inside the apartment was, if anything, more stifling than the unventilated vestibule and staircase. And that was only one of the many amenities the apartment lacked. As Todd surveyed it, his misgivings were realized. And then some.

It was a rat hole, and that was putting it kindly. Actually, it would need to undergo a major renovation to reach the classification of a rat hole. No self-respecting rat would be caught dead here.

An oscillating fan was blowing hot air around the matching beanbag chairs that served as living room furniture. It was also circulating the stench of leftover pizza that had congealed inside its box on the small table that, along with a two-burner hot plate and a sink, comprised the kitchen.

"I was in the shower." Indeed, Roark had answered the door sopping wet. His only nod toward modesty was a hand towel clutched around his hips.

"I thought maybe you'd gone homo," Todd said querulously.

"Come on, you gotta see this." Roark turned and headed toward an open door that led into another room.

Todd was so angry he could barely suck the stifling oxygen into his lungs. His deposit money had been squandered. If Roark had signed a lease on this place, then he could eat it for all Todd cared. He would flatly refuse to be responsible. Obviously his friend had suffered a mental lapse, or had lost their pooled money along the way, or had gotten it stolen, or something.

No rational person, no one who wasn't absolutely destitute and desperate, would voluntarily take shelter in this building. Being homeless had more stability than this, because unless the sky fell, a homeless person wouldn't have to fear being crushed to death by a loose plaster ceiling.

"Roark, damn you!" Todd struck out after him, shouting his name. "Roark! What the fuck?"

The door led into a small cubicle of a room with twin beds. One was groaning under the weight of Roark's belongings, most of which were still packed. Articles of clothing had been pulled from the crates and were spilling out over the tops of them like entrails.

On the other, Roark had been sleeping. And working, apparently. A computer terminal and keyboard were on the bed itself, the tower and printer were on the floor beside it.

"A computer?" Todd exclaimed. "You got a *PC*? When?" They had wanted word processors the way most collegiates covet TransAms. Roark had said nothing to him about buying a computer. "Is that what you spent our money on?"

"My uncle gave it to me for graduation," Roark called in a stage whisper. "Now will you shut up about that and get in here? Hurry."

Todd turned toward the opening where a door should have been. Instead, the detached door had been propped against the adjacent wall. Todd had a fleeting thought that it might have been placed there to provide the wall with additional support.

Through the opening was a bathroom. What differentiated this one from the communal bathroom in the fraternity house was that the one in the frat house had been cleaner and more sanitary—tobacco spit cups, shower fungi, and unattended fixtures notwithstanding.

But even more appalling than the condition of the sink and toilet was the sight of his friend, who had dropped the towel and reentered the shower. He was standing beneath the spray and staring out an open window.

"What uncle? Why didn't you tell me your uncle had given you a PC for graduation?"

Roark glanced over his shoulder. "Are you coming, or what?"

"I'm not getting into that filthy shower with you. I'm waiting for you to tell me what the—"

"Just shut up and come here. Quick. Before they go inside."

Roark's excitement was contagious and compelling. In spite of everything else, Todd was intrigued. He slipped off his sneakers and stepped into the shower fully clothed. Pushing Roark away from the window, he peered through the rusty screen.

On the second-floor roof of the neighboring building, three naked girls were sunbathing. Naked meaning completely nude. Not just topless, but mother nekkid. All they had on was a glistening layer of suntan oil. In fact, while he stood there stupefied, one of the girls was languidly spreading the oil over her torso.

"That one's name is Amber," Roark whispered.

Amber was rubbing her breasts now, smearing the oil over nipples as large and red as strawberries. Todd gulped. "You know them?"

"Hell, yeah. To speak to and call by name. Our buildings share a parking lot. They dance at a strip joint."

Which explained why they were visions of the most carnal variety. This was no trio of ordinary-looking women. They were spectacular. Their tits probably weren't the ones they'd been born with, but who the hell cared?

"The one with the shaved crotch is Starlight," Roark informed him. "For her grand finale it glitters with this sparkly stuff."

"Her pussy glitters?"

"Swear to God. They aim the spotlight right at it."

"Damn."

"The brunette is Mary Catherine."

"Doesn't sound like a stripper's name."

"She strips out of a nun's habit. Then she takes this rosary and—"

"Don't tell me. Let me be surprised." The brunette was lying facedown on her towel. Todd kissed the air. "Look at that ass."

"I have," Roark said with a chuckle. "Like a valentine, isn't it? Frankly I'm partial to her. She's the friendliest, too."

"They do this every day?"

"Except on Sundays. Saturday nights they do three shows, so they usually sleep all day Sunday."

Amber capped the bottle of suntan oil, then lay down on her beach towel, spreading her thighs wide enough to make certain the sun could reach the insides of them.

"Oh, man," Todd groaned.

Laughing, Roark stepped from the shower and retrieved his towel. "I think you need a few minutes of privacy."

"It won't take a few minutes, buddy."

Roark was dressed in a pair of shorts, sitting cross-legged on his bed, his keyboard bridging his knees, when Todd appeared in the doorway and propped himself weakly against the jamb. Roark looked over at him and grinned. "Well, what do you think of the apartment?"

"Fucking fantastic, man. I can't think of anyplace I'd rather live."

Chapter 18

Mike Strother laid the manuscript pages aside. He sipped from his glass of lemonade made with lemons he had squeezed himself. He was taking a day off from working on the mantel. Yesterday he had applied a coat of varnish and was giving it an extra day to dry because of the humidity. That was the explanation he'd given Parker anyway.

Throughout the morning, Mike had worked outdoors. Parker had seen him on his hands and knees turning the soil in the flower beds with a trowel. Later, he'd swept the veranda and washed the front windows. But the afternoon heat had driven him inside in time to prepare Parker's lunch, which he was only now getting around to eating.

He had been writing—actually rewriting—since dawn and was now anxious to hear Mike's reaction to this latest draft.

Parker valued Mike's critiques of his work, even when they were negative. Although he sometimes felt like telling the older man to go to hell and to take his lousy opinion with him, he invariably reread the disputed passages with a different perspective, only to realize that Mike's observations were well founded.

Even if he didn't agree with them, he took Mike's insights into consideration during his rewrites.

Mike was never quick to comment, whether his review was good or bad. But when he was piqued at Parker for one reason or another, he deliberately withheld his remarks until Parker asked for them. Today, he was taking even more time than usual, and Parker knew he was doing so just to be vexing.

But Parker was feeling rather ornery himself. He stubbornly waited as Mike thumbed through the pages a second time, rereading several passages, making noncommittal harrumphing sounds like a physician listening to a hypochondriac's litany of complaints, and tugging thoughtfully on his lower lip.

This continued for at least ten minutes more. Parker was the first to crack. "Could you please translate those grunts into a semblance of verbiage?"

Mike looked across at him as though he had forgotten he was there, which Parker knew to be a ruse. "You use the word 'fuck' and its derivatives a lot."

"That's it? That took ten minutes of contemplation? That's the substance of your critique?"

"I couldn't help but notice."

"Guys their age use that kind of language. Particularly in the company of other guys. In fact, they try and top each other, see who can be the most vulgar, talk the dirtiest."

"I didn't."

"You're an aberration."

Mike scowled but let the insult pass. "You also use the word 'homo.' Very offensive."

"Granted. But in '88, we hadn't yet coined the term 'politically correct.' And, again, I'm staying true to my characters. Randy, heterosexual males having a private conversation aren't going to be sensitive and deferential when referring to gay men."

"Or to the female anatomy, it seems."

"Particularly to the female anatomy," Parker said, ignoring

the implied reproof. "They wouldn't use the polite or clinical word for an act or a body part when there's an off-color alternative. Now that your fussiness over the coarse language has been addressed, what did you think—"

"You didn't go to the cotton gin today, did you?"

"What's that got to do with the manuscript?" Parker asked impatiently.

"*Does* it have something to do with the manuscript?"

"You're being awfully contrary this afternoon. Did you forget to take your stool softener last night?"

"You're changing the subject, Parker."

"Or is that lemonade spiked with Jack Daniel's?"

"More to the point, you're *avoiding* the subject."

"Me? I thought the subject was my manuscript. You brought up—"

"Maris."

"The gin."

"The two are linked," Mike said. "After months of preoccupation with that place, you haven't been back to it since she left."

"So?"

"So the fact that you haven't gone back to the gin has nothing to do with what happened there between you and Maris the morning she left?"

"No. I mean yes. I mean...Shit. Whatever the hell you just said." Parker hunched his shoulders cantankerously. "Besides, nothing happened."

"Going there wouldn't bring back memories either pleasant or disturbing? It wouldn't remind you of her? Wouldn't make you recall something that she said or something that you said that you'd rather forget?"

"You know what?" Parker tilted his head back and eyed Mike down the length of his nose. "You should have been a woman."

"Let's see. During this one conversation you've managed to

accuse me of being a freak, then a closet drunk with bowel problems, and now you're insulting my masculinity."

"You're as nosy as an old woman who has nothing else to do
except butt into other people's business."

"Maris is my business, too, Parker."

His sharp tone changed the character of the conversation and
signaled that the banter was over. Parker turned away and stared
out over the ocean. It was calm this afternoon, a mirror casting
a brassy reflection of the sun off its surface.

As they did each day at about this time, a small flock of
pelicans flew in formation just above the treetops toward their
nighttime roost. Parker wondered if it was constraining or comforting to be part of such a closely knit group. He had been a
loner for so many years, he couldn't remember what it was like
to be a member of a family, or a fraternity, or any community of
individuals.

Mackensie Roone was beloved by readers all over the world.
He resided on their nightstands and in their briefcases. He accompanied them to the beach, to the toilet, and on modes of
mass transit. He was taken into their bathtubs and beds. He
shared a rare intimacy with them.

But Parker Evans was known only by a few and loved by no
one. That had been his choice, of course, and a necessary one.
Recently, however, he had begun to realize the tremendous price
he had paid for his years of reclusion. Over time, he had become accustomed to being alone. But lately he'd begun feeling
lonely. There was a difference. That difference became evident
the moment you realized that you no longer liked being alone as
well as you liked being with someone else. That's when aloneness
turned to loneliness.

Staving off the threatening despair, he quietly apologized to
Mike for involving him in his scheme. "I know you feel responsible to some extent, and I admire you for having a conscience
about it."

"I played along with that ridiculous test we put her through because you asked me to. Was that necessary?"

"Probably not," Parker admitted in a quiet voice.

"I could have told her you were Mackensie Roone. I could have pretended that it slipped out. You would have been angry at me, but you would have gotten over it. Instead, I went along with the whole charade, and I'm ashamed of myself for it."

"Don't be, Mike. You're blameless. This is all my doing. From start to finish, beginning to end—whatever the end may be—I'm the guilty party here, not you."

"That doesn't exactly absolve me for my voluntary participation."

With a rueful shrug, Parker said, "No, but that's the best I can do."

They lapsed into a weighty silence. Eventually Mike picked up his reading glasses, unknowingly reminding Parker of Maris and the eyeglasses she had been wearing the last time he saw her. Which might have been the last time he would ever see her, he reminded himself.

"These young men seem to have reconciled completely," Mike remarked as he thumbed through the pages again. "I don't sense any residual hostility between them."

"Following the incident with Hadley, Roark carried on as though it had never happened," Parker explained. "He made a conscious decision not to let it affect their friendship."

"Noble of him. Nevertheless, it's still—"

"There," Parker interrupted, completing the other man's thought. "Like an unsightly birthmark that mars an otherwise beautiful baby's face. Neither wants to acknowledge the blemish on their friendship. Both look past it, hoping that it will gradually fade and ultimately disappear completely, as some birthmarks do, so that, eventually, no one can remember the baby having had it."

"Good analogy."

"It is, isn't it? I may use it." He jotted himself a note.

"You didn't specify or explain the family obligation that prevented Todd from leaving with Roark."

"It's discussed in the next scene. Roark extends condolences to Todd for his mother's death. She didn't want to worry him during those last few crucial months leading up to his college graduation, so she didn't tell him that she'd been diagnosed with a rampant cancer. She attended the commencement exercise, but it was an effort for her. The therapy she'd been receiving had weakened her, but unfortunately had had no effect on the malignancy. So rather than leaving for Florida, Todd accompanied her home. He stayed with her until she died."

"Quite a sacrifice, especially when you consider what moving to Key West represented to him."

Parker smiled sardonically. "Save the kudos. I have him saying... Wait, let me read it to you." He shuffled through the sheets of handwritten notes scattered across his worktable until he found the one he was looking for.

"Todd thanks Roark for his expression of sympathy, so on and so forth, then he says, ' "Actually, her death was very convenient." ' Roark reacts with appropriate shock. Then Todd adds, ' "I'm only being honest." '

" ' "Cruelly honest," says Roark.

" 'Todd shrugs indifferently. "Maybe, but at least I'm not a hypocrite. Am I sorry she's dead? No. Her dying left me completely untethered and unencumbered. Free. I've got no one to think about except myself now. No one to account to. Nothing to cater to except my writing." ' "

Mike assimilated that. "So the white gloves are coming off in the next segment."

"If by that you mean that Todd's true character will be revealed, no. Not entirely. We do, however, begin to detect chinks in the facade."

"The same way Noah Reed's true character was revealed to you once you moved to Key West. Bit by bit."

Parker felt his facial muscles stiffen as they did whenever Noah was called to the forefront of his mind. "It takes Roark only a few chapters to see his so-called friend for what he really is. It took me a couple of years. And by then it was too late."

He stared hard at his legs for several moments, then, forcing those ugly memories aside, he referred once again to his handwritten notes. "Professor Hadley is also resurrected in the next scene."

Mike poured himself another glass of lemonade, then sat back in his chair and assumed a listening aspect.

"Actually, it's Todd who introduces the subject," Parker explained. "He comments on how wonderful it is that they managed to turn that situation around. He says if he hadn't pulled that trick on Roark, their present relationship with the professor might not be as solid as it is. He says Roark should be thanking him for what he did.

"Roark isn't ready to go so far as to thank him, but he concedes that it worked to their advantage in the long run." Parker took a breath. "This conversation is to inform the reader that Professor Hadley had seen such promise in these talented young men, he's offered to continue critiquing their work even though they're no longer his students."

"Very generous of him."

Parker frowned. "He's not completely selfless. I have a chapter planned, written from his point of view, where the reader learns that he would coach these two young writers simply because he recognizes their talent and wants to see it honed and refined, and then, hopefully, published and shared with an appreciative audience."

"I sense a 'however' coming."

"*However*, wouldn't it be a star in his crown if he discovered the next generation's defining novelists?"

"In other words, he's an opportunistic old bastard."

Parker laughed. "Everyone is opportunistic, Mike. Everyone. Without exception. Only the degree of one's opportunism separates him from others. How far is one willing to go to get what he wants?

"Some fall by the wayside early. They give up, or take another course, or simply decide that what they're after isn't worth the risks or the costs involved in getting it. But others…"

He paused and focused on a spot in near space. "To get what they want, others are willing to go to any lengths. *Any* lengths. They'll go beyond what's lawful, or decent, or moral so long as they come out ahead."

Mike seemed about to remark on that bit of philosophizing, when he changed his mind and asked a question that Parker guessed was less incendiary. "Do you want to assign that much importance to a secondary character?"

"Hadley, you mean? He's important to the plot."

"He is?"

"Integral. I have to set that up."

Mike nodded, seemingly distracted by another thought. Half a minute passed. Finally Parker asked him what was on his mind. "The pacing? The dialogue? Too much narrative about the Key West apartment, or not enough?"

"The brunette stripper on the roof—"

"Mary Catherine."

"Is the girl—"

"In the prologue who accompanies them on the boat. Remember, one of the boys removes her bikini top and waves it above his head before they're even out of the harbor. So it's important that I establish in the reader's mind that she's a friendly, playful sort. There's more about her in an upcoming scene."

"She's a nice girl, Parker."

"The stripper with the heart-shaped ass?"

Mike gave him a sour look.

Parker cursed beneath his breath. Mike was determined to talk about Maris, and when Mike got something into his head to talk about, he would continue dredging it up until it was talked about.

Parker returned his notes to the worktable, knowing that he might just as well get this conversation out of the way so he could get on with the rest of his afternoon. "First of all, Maris is a woman, not a girl. And whoever said she wasn't nice? Not me. Did you ever hear me say she wasn't nice? She says 'please' and 'thank you,' keeps her napkin in her lap, and covers her mouth when she yawns."

Mike fixed an admonishing glare on him. "Admit it. She's not what you expected."

"No. She's taller by a couple inches." He was on the receiving end of another baleful look. He spread his arms wide. "What do you want me to say? That she's not the snob I thought she'd be? Okay, she's not."

"You expected a spoiled rich girl."

"A total bitch."

"An aggressive and abrasive—"

"Ball-buster."

"Who would blow in here, disrupting the peace and trying to intimidate us with her New York sophistication and superiority. Instead, Maris was...well, you know better than I what she was like." As an afterthought, the old man said, "All the same, she did make an impact, didn't she?"

Yes, she had. Just a much softer, more feminine impact than Parker had expected. He glanced at the vase on the coffee table. Maris had gathered sprigs of honeysuckle during a morning stroll and had asked if he would object to her putting them in water. "Just to brighten the room up a bit," she'd said.

Mike, infatuated with her to the point of idiocy, had turned the kitchen upside down until he found a suitable container. For days, the wild bouquet had filled the solarium with a heady fragrance. Now it was an eyesore. The blossoms were shriveled, the water swampy and smelly. But Parker hadn't asked Mike to remove it, and Mike hadn't taken it upon himself to empty the vase. It was a reminder of her they weren't quite ready to relinquish.

The shells she had collected on the beach were still spread out on the end table where she'd proudly displayed them. When she carried them in, her feet had been bare and dusted with sand. They'd left footprints on the tile floor, which she had insisted on sweeping up herself.

His dying houseplant was rallying because she had moved it to a better spot and had watered it just enough, not too much.

Two fashion magazines that she'd browsed through while he worked on his novel were still lying in the chair she'd last occupied.

It was that throw pillow there, the one with the fringe around it, that she had hugged to her breasts while she listened to him reading a passage from his manuscript.

Everywhere he looked, there was evidence of her.

"She's an intelligent woman," Mike said. "She proved that. Smart but sensitive."

Mike was speaking in a hushed voice, as though he felt her spirit in the room and didn't want to frighten it away. Which annoyed Parker more than if he'd scraped his fingernails down a chalkboard. They were acting like saps. He as much as Mike. A pair of sentimental fools.

And anyway, who said his room had needed to be brightened up a bit? He had liked it just fine the way it was before Maris Matherly-Reed had ever darkened the door.

"Don't get misty, Mike," he said, a shade more harshly than he had intended. "She plays sensitive because she wants a book from me."

"A book. Not income. I don't think she cares if *Envy* makes her company a red cent. She loves your writing."

Parker shrugged indifferently, but secretly he agreed. In spite of the haggling, Maris seemed much more interested in the storytelling aspects of his book than in its earning potential.

"She can also laugh at herself. I like that in a person." Then, looking at Parker askance, Mike added, "I guess there's no need mentioning that she's beautiful."

"Then why'd you mention it?"

"So you noticed?"

"What, you think I'm blind as well as lame? Yeah, she's good to look at." He made a gesture that said, *So what?* "Her looks were no surprise. We saw her picture in that magazine article."

"The photo didn't do her justice."

"I expected her to be attractive. Noah never dated an ugly girl," Parker muttered. "Not that I knew about."

When Mike declined to comment one way or another, Parker went on. "You know what? I'm glad she's attractive. Real glad. It'll make what I'm going to do all the more enjoyable."

"What are you going to do?"

"You know I never talk over a plot until I've written at least some of it down. Guess you'll have to use your imagination."

"You're going to use Maris."

"Fuckin'-A. And if you don't approve of my language, cover your ears." He wiped a bead of sweat from his forehead. The air conditioner was working, so why did it feel so damn hot in here? "Now, can we please end this discussion? I've got work to do."

Mike calmly finished his glass of lemonade, then rifled through the manuscript pages again. At last he stood, crossed to Parker, and passed the sheets to him. "It's coming along."

"Don't go overboard with the praise," Parker said drolly. "I might get a swelled head."

On his way out, Mike said, "You may want to rethink your motivation."

"My characters' motivation is perfectly clear."

Mike didn't even deign to turn around and address Parker face-to-face when he said, "I wasn't referring to your characters."

Chapter 19

T his is my favorite room." Maris basked in the familiar comfort of her father's home study, where they were having cocktails.

At the last minute Noah had needed to consult with the contracts manager over a disputed clause, so he had urged her to go to Daniel's house ahead of him. She hadn't minded his being detained. Since her return from Georgia, she hadn't spent any time alone with her father.

"I'm rather partial to this room myself," Daniel said. "I spend a lot of time in here, but I like it even more when you're sharing it with me."

She laughed. "You didn't always feel that way. I remember times when I'd come in here hoping to coax you away from the work that you'd brought home with you. I made a pest of myself." They smiled at the shared recollections, but Daniel's expression turned somber.

"I wish I had those times to relive, Maris. If I did, I'd spend more time skating in the park or playing Monopoly with you. I regret passing up those opportunities."

"I wasn't deprived much, Dad. In fact, I wasn't deprived of anything. Most of all you."

"You're being far too generous, but I thank you for saying that."

Maris sensed a melancholia in him tonight. He'd been very glad to see her, but his jocularity didn't quite ring true. His comic bickering with Maxine seemed forced. His smiles were good counterfeits of the real thing, but they were noticeably strained.

"Dad, aren't you feeling well? Is something wrong?"

He cited Howard Bancroft's funeral. "It's tomorrow morning."

She nodded sympathetically. "Howard wasn't just your corporate lawyer, he was a good and trusted friend."

"I'm going to miss him. He'll be missed all over this city. For the life of me, I can't understand what drove him to do such a terrible thing."

He was grieving his loss, naturally, but Maris wasn't entirely sure that Bancroft's suicide was the only thing weighing heavily on Daniel's mind. She reasoned that his mood might be in response to her own. She wasn't exactly a barrel of laughs tonight, either. She could attribute her moodiness to two things. Well, actually two *people*. Noah and Parker.

Noah's explanation for his meeting with WorldView had been plausible. Daniel had even verified it. Nevertheless, it rankled that they had kept her unaware of something so vitally important to the future of Matherly Press. She had never been *that* busy.

Had she been anyone else, her high ranking in the company would have demanded she be kept apprised. Their personal relationships should not have been a factor. As senior vice president of the corporation, she had deserved to be informed of Blume's poaching. As a wife, she deserved her husband's respect.

That's what had really infuriated her—Noah's nonchalant dismissal of her anger.

He'd treated her like a child who could be easily mollified

with a candy stick, or a pet whose trust could be earned with a pat on the head. His peacemaking platitudes had been textbook standards. Marriage 101, lesson three: How to Fight Constructively.

The way in which he'd placated her had been more belittling than his original offense. Didn't he know her any better than to think she could be so easily defused and dismissed?

"Maris?"

She raised her head and smiled at Daniel with chagrin. "Did I drift?"

"No farther than a million miles."

"I'm sorry. I've got a lot on my mind."

"Would you freshen my drink, please?" When she hesitated, he waved his hand irritably. "I know, I know. You think I'm drinking too much. By the way, I saw through that man-to-man advice Noah gave me. It came straight from you."

"I worry about you navigating the stairs after you've had a few, that's all. You're a little unsteady to start."

"If I get drunk tonight, you can carry me up the stairs piggyback, how's that?" Chastening him with a look, she crossed the room to get his glass and carried it with her to the bar. "While you're at it, why don't you have another?" he suggested. "I think you could use it."

She poured him another scotch and refilled her wineglass with Chardonnay. "Why?"

"Why do I think you need alcoholic reinforcement this evening? Because you look like your puppy has run away from home."

True. She was feeling a huge sense of loss. She'd been reluctant to pinpoint the source of it and assign it a name, but in her heart of hearts, she knew its name: Parker Evans.

She resettled in her chair, and as Daniel methodically refilled the bowl of his pipe, she let her gaze wander around the room. She took in her father's extensive collection of coveted leather-bound first editions. They were meticulously lined up on the shelves of a massive cabinet with gleaming glass doors.

She couldn't help but compare this neat and costly library to Parker's haphazardly crammed bookshelves. She contrasted the expensive furnishings and appointments of this room to the wicker chairs and chintz cushions in Parker's solarium. This room had an imported marble fireplace that had been salvaged from an Italian palace. The wood mantel in Parker's house had been carved by a slave named Phineas.

And she realized that, as much as she loved this house, this room, and the fond memories of childhood they evoked, she was homesick for St. Anne Island, and Parker's house with its creaky hardwood floors, and the cozy guest cottage with its claw-footed bathtub.

She was homesick for Mike's clattering in the kitchen and the click of the keys as Parker typed in his rapid, two-fingered, hunt-and-peck method. She missed the oddly harmonious racket of the cicadas, and the distant swish of the surf break-ing on the beach, and the scent of honeysuckle, and the feel of the salt air, so heavy it was like raiment against her skin, and . . . Parker.

She missed Parker.

"Are you thinking about him?" Daniel asked softly, interrupt-ing her thoughts. "Is he what has made you sad?"

"Made me sad? Hardly," she said, giving her head a firm shake. "Has he made me angry? Yes. Would I like to throttle him? Definitely. He's provoking on every level, starting with how he approaches his profession. Only rarely does he take a sug-gestion or criticism without first putting up an argument, which invariably turns fierce.

"He stays hidden away in that house, on that island. Lovely as the house and island are, he uses them as a refuge. He should be out among people. A writer usually seizes every opportunity to promote his work. But not him. Oh, no. He adopts this lofty attitude and pretends to be above all that, but I know better. The reason he remains a recluse is because of his disability.

"Oh, have I told you that, Dad? He's wheelchair-bound. I didn't learn that until I got there. At first I was shocked because when talking to him over the telephone, I got no indication that he was in any way impaired, except when it came to manners. It took me totally by surprise. But after a while... I don't know, Dad, it's strange. When I look at him now, I don't even see the wheelchair."

She paused to reflect on that, realizing how profoundly true the statement was. She no longer saw Parker's chair or his disability, and she wondered at what point that had happened.

"I suppose it's the potency of his personality that makes his disability seem not just inconsequential, but invisible. He's got an extraordinary command of the language. Even his bawdy— make that crude—vocabulary is impressive.

"He has a sly sense of humor. Wicked, sometimes. He can be awfully grouchy, too, but then I suppose he's entitled to be. Anyone in his circumstances would be resentful. I mean, he's young, in his prime, so his bitterness over being confined to a wheelchair is understandable and forgivable.

"He's self-conscious of his scars, but he shouldn't be. People, especially women, would find him attractive no matter what his legs look like. He's not... not handsome, exactly, but... he's got an... an animal magnetism, I guess you'd call it. You sense an energy radiating from him even when he's sitting still.

"When he speaks to you, you're drawn right into his eyes. The intensity with which he holds your attention makes up for his incapacity. But don't get the impression that he's feeble. He's not. In fact he's quite strong. His hands are..."

His hands. When they had kept her head in place for his kiss. When they had trapped her hips and held her still beside his chair. Those times they had felt incredibly strong and commanding. Yet at other times, like when he had plucked a leaf from her hair, his touch had been light and deft, even playful.

When she'd held a seashell in her palm for him to admire, he had traced the delicate whorls with his fingertip gingerly, as though afraid to apply too much pressure and risk crushing it. A woman would never have to flinch from his touch.

"He's the most complex individual I've ever met," she said huskily. "Extremely talented." She conjured up Parker's face and heard herself saying, "Also angry. Very angry. You can sense it in his writing. But even when he's relaxed and joking with Mike, his anger is detectable.

"His smiles have a disturbing element. There's a cruelty to them, and that's unfortunate because I don't believe he could be cruel at all if not for the anger. It's always there, just beneath the surface.

"There's a passage in his novel where he describes Roark's anger toward Todd. He compares it to a serpent gliding through still, dark water, never surfacing, never revealing itself, but constantly there, silent, sinister, and deadly, waiting to poison them both.

"Probably he's just angry over being trapped in a wheelchair. But I sense there's something...something I don't know, something I've missed, like there's one more secret yet to come to light."

She laughed softly. "I can't imagine what it might be. He's sprung so many surprises on me. Not all of them good." She took a sip of wine and raised her shoulders in a helpless shrug. "That's the best way I know to answer your question."

Daniel studied her thoughtfully for a long moment as he continued to pack tobacco into his pipe. He rarely lighted it. He just liked the ritualistic activity. It gave him something to do while assembling his thoughts.

When he finally spoke, it was to quietly say, "Actually, Maris, my question referred to Noah."

Embarrassed, she flushed hotly. For five solid minutes she had rattled on about Parker. "Oh...oh, well," she stammered, "yes, he...I wouldn't say Noah made me *sad,* but I was upset over his meeting with WorldView. I was even more upset that he chose not to tell me about it."

Daniel set the pipe aside and picked up his tumbler. As he contemplated the amber contents, he asked, "Did Noah tell you that he had a meeting with Howard the afternoon he killed himself?"

The manner in which he had posed the question caused her throat to constrict. This wasn't a casual inquiry. "He mentioned it."

"It took place only a couple of hours before Howard ended his life."

Maris lost all appetite for the wine. Setting the crystal stem on the end table, she wiped condensation, or perspiration, off her palms. "What was the nature of their meeting?"

"According to Noah, Howard needed him to sign off on the final draft of a contract between us and one of our foreign licensees. Noah approved the amended language and that was the extent of it."

That's what Noah had told her, too. "Do you..." She cleared her throat and began again. "Do you doubt that?"

"I have no reason to. Although..." Maris waited in breathless suspension for him to continue. "Howard's secretary told me that his meeting with Noah was his last for the day, and that when he left the office, he wasn't himself."

"Specifically?"

"He seemed distressed. I think her exact words were 'extremely upset.' " Daniel took a sip of whisky. "Of course, one event probably has nothing to do with the other. Howard could have been upset over any number of things, something in his personal life, something that didn't relate to Matherly Press or Noah."

But her father didn't believe that. If he did, they wouldn't be having this conversation. "Dad, do you think—"

"Good. I see you started without me." Noah pushed open the double doors and breezed in. "Darling, I apologize again for making you come over alone." He bent down and kissed Maris, then smacked his lips as though tasting them. "Good wine."

"It is. Very." She got up and moved to the wet bar, trying to hide from the men and herself that her knees were wobbly. "I'll pour you some."

"Thanks, but I'd rather have what Daniel is having. Rocks only. It's been that kind of day."

Noah crossed the room to shake hands with his father-in-law, then rejoined Maris on the love seat and placed his arm around her as she handed him a highball glass. "Cheers." After taking a sip of his drink, he said, "Maxine sent me in with the message that dinner is in ten minutes."

"I hope her pot roast isn't as dry as it was last time," Daniel grumbled.

"Her pot roast is never dry," Maris said, wondering how they could be discussing something as trivial as pot roast when only moments ago the topic had been a man's inexplicable suicide.

"Dry or not, I'm going to wreak havoc on it," Noah said. "I'm starving."

Of course, one event probably has nothing to do with the other.

She clung to her father's statement, desperate to believe it.

This was Noah they were talking about. Her husband. The man she had fallen in love with, and the man she still loved. Noah. The man she slept beside every night. The man with whom she wanted to have children.

She placed her hand on his thigh, and he, without even a pause in his conversation with Daniel, covered her hand with his own and pressed it affectionately. It was an absentminded, husbandly, and reassuring gesture.

* * *

Dinner was delicious and the pot roast lived up to Maxine's standards of excellence. But by the time the lemon tarts were served, Daniel was yawning. As soon as Maxine removed the dessert dishes, he asked to be excused.

"Stay and enjoy another cup of coffee," he told his guests as he stood up. "But I should retire. I'll be up early to attend Howard's funeral. Can't say I'm looking forward to it."

"I need to say good night, too, Dad. Today was long and strenuous."

As they left the dining room, Maris held back and detained Noah. Laying her hands on his lapels, she went up on tiptoe to kissed him tenderly on the lips. "I think I'll go home ahead of you."

He placed his hands at her waist and drew her closer. "I thought you and I had plans for later this evening."

"We do. But I'm about to ask a favor. Would you please stay and help Dad get to bed? I know it's not your place—"

"I don't mind at all."

"He's prickly on the subject of his instability, and it's already come up once tonight. But if you invent an excuse to walk upstairs with him, it won't appear that you're escorting him. I would appreciate it."

"Consider it done, sweetheart. I'll follow your lead."

At the door, she pretended to remember that she wanted to retrieve an old address book from her third-floor bedroom. "I'll have to look for it. I'm not sure where I left it."

Noah offered to get it for her and suggested that she go ahead of him while he searched. She wasn't sure Daniel believed their playacting, but he went along with it.

When they said their good nights, Daniel hugged her tightly. Then he set her away from him and peered closely into her eyes as though trying to decipher the troubling thoughts behind them. "I want to hear more about this new book and the complex man who's writing it."

The reminder of how she'd gone on and on about Parker brought color to her cheeks again. "I always value your input, Dad. I'll have a copy of the manuscript sent over by courier tomorrow. We'll get together later in the week to discuss it."

He squeezed her hand with a confidentiality and caring that made her want to crawl up into his lap as she had when she was little, seeking comfort and assurance that everything was going to be fine, that all her concerns were needless, and that there was no basis for her undefined disquiet.

But, of course, she couldn't. She'd outgrown his lap, and her confidences were a woman's, not a child's. They couldn't be shared with her father.

Daniel moved aside and Noah stepped up to hug her. "Daniel's looking a little down in the mouth tonight," he whispered. "Once he's tucked in, I think I'll offer to have a bedtime brandy with him."

"Do. But make it a short one. I'll be waiting."

* * *

Maris didn't go straight home. She had never intended to. Using her father as a pawn to delay Noah made her feel guilty, but only a little. She would never have deceived them if she weren't desperate to rid herself of nagging doubts that had taken a tenacious hold on her.

She took a taxi downtown to the apartment in Chelsea. By the time she reached the door of the apartment, her heart was beating hard, and not because of the steep staircase. She was anxious about what she might find inside.

She unlocked the door with the key she'd had in her possession since the night of her surprise party and, remembering where the light switch was, flipped it on. The air-conditioning unit was humming softly, but otherwise the apartment was silent. She noted that the cushions on the sofa looked freshly plumped.

Moving into the kitchen, she looked into a spotless dry sink. There were no dishes in the dishwasher, not even a drinking glass. The wastebasket beneath the sink was empty, its plastic liner as pristine as when it had been placed there.

Maid service? Noah hadn't mentioned retaining anyone to clean this apartment, but that didn't mean he hadn't.

Back in the living room she moved toward the room designated as Noah's office. Hand on the doorknob, she paused and said a prayer, although she couldn't specifically say what she was praying for. She pushed open the door.

In a single glance she took it all in, then slumped dejectedly against the doorjamb. The room looked exactly as they'd left it that night. Nothing had been disturbed or changed. There were no paper balls in the trash can, no reference books with pages marked, no notes stuck to the computer screen or scrawled on ruled legal tablets.

She knew what a writer's work area was supposed to look like. Parker's would have cost an obsessive-compulsive years of therapy. It was strewn with coffee-stained notes, and red pencils whose leads were worn down to nubs, and tablets filled with thoughts and diagrams and doodles, and file envelopes with curled, fraying edges, and unstable pyramids of reference material, and paper clips bent out of shape during periods of torturous concentration.

Yet if one thing were touched or moved on Parker's desk, he would bark at the offender. He knew exactly where everything was, and he wanted it left the way he had it. Mike was forbidden to clean in the area, as though the disarray contributed to Parker's creativity.

Noah's writing space was immaculate. Although, upon closer inspection, Maris saw that his computer keyboard sported a fine layer of dust. The keys had never been touched.

Her heart wasn't beating fast now. In fact it felt like a stone inside her chest as she turned off the lights and left the apartment. She conscientiously locked the door behind her, although she didn't know why she bothered. There was absolutely nothing of value to her inside.

She exited the building and descended the front steps, lost in thought, her motions listless. She was weighted down with dread for the inevitable confrontation with Noah. When he returned from her father's house, he would be expecting his docile wife to be waiting for him at home, eager and ready to make love to him.

That's what she had deliberately led him to expect.

She had led him to believe that she was as moldable as warm clay, gullible, blindly accepting, and he had been easily deceived, because up until recently that's exactly what she'd been.

He would arrive home thinking that their argument about WorldView was a forgotten episode, that she didn't question the nature of his meeting with Howard Bancroft, that she had no reason to doubt him when he told her he had resumed writing.

Meek and mild and malleable Maris. Stupid Maris. That's what he thought of her.

But he thought wrong.

As she reached street level, she noticed a passenger alighting from a taxi half a block away. She hadn't expected the good fortune of finding a cab so soon and raised her hand to signal the driver.

As soon as he received his fare, he drove the short distance to where Maris stood at the curb. But she was no longer looking at the taxi. Instead she was watching the man who had alighted from it as he jogged up the steps of another brownstone, entering it with an air of familiarity, as though he belonged.

Gradually Maris lowered her arm, until then not realizing that it was still raised. She motioned the taxi driver to go on.

Walking briskly, she quickly covered the distance to the other apartment building.

It was as quaint as the one she'd just left. There was no doorman or other form of security to prevent her from entering the vestibule. She checked the mailboxes. All except one were labeled with a name. Either the apartment was vacant... or the tenant in 2A received mail at another location.

Again, she climbed stairs. But it was with amazing calm that she approached the door of apartment 2A. She rapped smartly and looked directly into the peephole, knowing that it was probably being looked through from the other side.

Nadia Schuller opened the door, and the two of them stood face-to-face. She was dressed for romance, wearing only a silk wrapper, which appeared to have been hastily tied at her waist as she made her way to answer the door. She didn't even have the decency to look alarmed or shamefaced. Her expression was one of smug amusement as she stepped back and opened the door wider.

Maris's gaze slid past her to Noah, who was coming from a connecting room, presumably a kitchen, with a drink in each hand. He was in shirtsleeves, having wasted no time in removing his jacket and tie.

Upon seeing her, he stopped dead in his tracks. "Maris."

Nadia said, "I hope this doesn't turn into one of those dreadful farces à la a Ronald Reagan movie."

Maris ignored her. Nadia was insignificant. The only thing she signified was Noah's bad taste in mistresses. She didn't waste any contempt on Nadia. Instead she directed it all toward the man she had married less than two years ago.

"Don't bother apologizing or explaining, even if that's what you had in mind to do, Noah. You're a liar and an adulterer, and I want you out of my life. Out. Immediately. I'll have Maxine come over and pack up your things because I can't bear the thought of touching them myself. You can arrange with the doorman a time to pick them up when I'm not there. I don't want to see you again, Noah. Ever."

Then she turned and jogged down the stairs, across the small lobby, down the steps, and onto the sidewalk. She wasn't crying. In fact, her eyes were dry. She didn't feel angry, or sad, or miserable. In fact, she felt surprisingly unshackled and lighthearted. She had no sense of leaving something, but rather of going toward something.

She didn't get far.

Noah gripped her arm from behind and roughly jerked her around. He grinned down at her, but it was a cold and frightening grin. "Well, well, Maris. Clever you."

"Let go of me!" She struggled to pull her arm free from his grasp, but he didn't yield. In fact, his fingers closed more tightly around her biceps. "I said for you to let—"

"Shut up," he hissed, shaking her so hard that she bit her tongue and cried out in pain. "I heard what you had to say, Maris. Every single word. Brave speech. I was impressed.

"But now let *me* tell *you* how it's going to be. Our marriage has been and will remain on my terms. You don't order me out of your life. You don't order me to leave. I leave you only when I'm goddamn good and ready. I hope you understand that, Maris. Your life will be so much easier if you do."

"You're hurting me, Noah."

He laughed at that. "I haven't begun to hurt you yet." To underscore his point, he squeezed her arm tightly, cruelly, his fingers mashing muscle against bone. Although tears of pain sprang to her eyes, she didn't recoil.

"In the meantime, I'll fuck Nadia, I'll fuck whoever I want to, and I don't care if you watch. But you'll stay the obedient little wife, understand? Or I'll make your life, and the lives of everyone dear to you, a living hell, Maris. I can, you know. I will." His eyes glinted with an evil light as he leaned even closer and whispered, "I *will*. I promise you."

Then he released her so suddenly she staggered and fell against the iron fence that enclosed trash receptacles, painfully banging her shoulder.

As he turned away from her and started back toward the brownstone he shared with Nadia, he called cheerfully, "Don't wait up."

Too stunned to move, Maris watched him go and continued to stare at the empty doorway long after he had disappeared inside. She wasn't so afraid as dumbfounded. Incredulity kept her rooted to the concrete. Although her arm was throbbing and she could taste blood in her mouth, she couldn't believe what had just happened. Noah? Threatening her? Physically threatening her with an icy calm that glazed his threats with certainty and made them terrifying?

She shivered then, violently and uncontrollably, her blood running cold with the sudden but unarguable realization that she was married to a total stranger. The man she thought she knew didn't exist. Noah had assumed a role, that's all. He had mimicked a character in a book because he knew she'd been infatuated with that character. He had played the part well, never stepping out of character. Not once. Until tonight.

She was jolted by the fact that just now, for the first time, she had been introduced to the real Noah Reed.

"Envy" Ch. 15
Key West, Florida, 1987

Roark?"

He rubbed sleep from his eyes as he juggled the telephone receiver in the general direction of his ear. "Yeah?"

"Were you sleeping?"

It was four-thirty in the morning. He hadn't gotten to bed until after three. The nightclub where he and Todd worked didn't close until two. One of his responsibilities was to close out the registers, and he couldn't do that until the last customer left. After writing all day, then putting in an eight-hour shift, he hadn't merely been sleeping, he'd been comatose.

"Who is this?"

"Mary Catherine. I hate to bother you."

He swung his legs over the side of the bed. His bare foot knocked over an empty drink can and it noisily rolled across the concrete floor toward Todd's bed. He growled a protest into his pillow.

"What's up?" Roark asked in a whisper.

"Can you come over?"

"Uh...now?"

The strip joint was only a few doors down from the nightclub for which he tended bar and Todd parked cars. Occasionally, during their breaks, they could catch their neighbors' acts. He and Todd had come to know the girls well enough to be admitted gratis. A bouncer let them in through a rear entrance. They watched from backstage. Sometimes they went together, sometimes separately, and they were rarely able to stay longer than fifteen or twenty minutes at a time, but those few minutes relieved the drudgery of their lives.

Their limited budgets had reduced dating to a bare minimum. Thankfully, the trio of exotic dancers had been "neighborly" to them in more ways than giving free peep shows.

One day Roark had volunteered to take Starlight's car to a garage for an oil change and tune-up. What the mechanic did for the car's engine was nothing compared to what Starlight did to Roark's. As thankyous went, Starlight beat Hallmark all to hell.

But this telephone call didn't have the tone of a come-on, and, much to his regret, Mary Catherine had never shown any romantic interest in him. She'd treated him in a brotherly fashion, while she flirted shamelessly with Todd and had graced him with several sleepovers.

"Could you, Roark? Please? I'm here by myself and, well...I need a favor."

His heart thumped with optimism. "Sure. Be right there."

"Don't mention it to Todd, okay?"

That dampened his enthusiasm somewhat, because

he would enjoy ribbing Todd about getting a middle-of-the-night call from one of his regular lays. Where women were concerned Todd was a cocksure bastard.

He pulled on a pair of shorts and a T-shirt, pushed his feet into a pair of sandals, and let himself out without waking Todd. He hurdled the foul-smelling moat surrounding the apartment building and followed the now-familiar and well-worn path to the girls' building. He took the stairs two at a time, arriving at their door slightly out of breath. Mary Catherine opened the door before he could even knock.

"I was watching for you through the window."

He stepped inside, trying not to give away how crestfallen he was by her appearance.

She didn't even resemble the stunner she was when she peeled away the vestiges of her nun's habit and stood in the spotlight gloriously naked, or even when she lay spread-eagled on the roof basting in suntan oil.

Her face was free of stage makeup. Her eyes and nose were red, as though she'd been crying. Her long, curly hair had been gathered into a scraggly ponytail. Most disappointing of all, she wasn't dressed for seduction. She was wearing an unflattering, oversized Dolphins jersey and a baggy pair of plaid boxer shorts.

"I got you up, didn't I?"

"I was writing," he lied.

"Your lights were out."

"I was plotting inside my head."

"Oh." She twisted the hem of the jersey in her fist. "I hate to ask you to do this, Roark, but..."

"Is something wrong?"

"I miscarried tonight."

He gaped stupidly and speechlessly.

"A baby." She flipped out her hand. "Well, I guess

it wasn't really a baby yet, just, you know... Anyway, I need some things, and I'm not feeling too good, so I wondered if you'd run down to the twenty-four-hour market for me."

He swallowed what felt like a bowling ball, then reflexively wet his lips. "Uh, sure. Be glad to."

"I'd really appreciate it."

"No problem, but are you okay? Should you call a doctor or something? Want me to take you to the hospital? Have, uh, things checked out?"

"No, I'm okay." Taking a deep but shaky breath, she said, "This isn't the first time."

He dragged his hand down over his mouth and chin. "You didn't do anything crazy, did you? You didn't cause it? On purpose, I mean."

She shook her head and smiled weakly. "No. Nothing that dramatic. It just happened, Roark. An accident of nature. The first time, yeah, I went to a clinic and had it sucked out. But this time it came out on its own. I started feeling bad at work. Cramps, you know."

He nodded sympathetically, although she could have been talking about ice sculpting, for all he knew about it. In fact he probably knew more about ice sculpting.

"I was invited out with the other girls to a private party. But it had all the makings of an all-nighter, so I begged off, came home, went straight to bed. Woke up about an hour ago in a... a mess." She raised her shoulders. "No more baby."

He saw tears shining in her eyes, but she quickly turned away and reached for a small slip of paper and several folded bills. "I made a detailed list. Name brands and sizes. Figured you wouldn't know what to get if I didn't."

"You're right about that," he said, trying to sound goofily cheerful and failing miserably.

"This should cover it."

He took the list and money from her. "Anything else?"

"I think it's all on there. I'll leave the door unlocked so you can just come in when you get back." He nodded and turned to go, but she touched his arm and brought him back around. "Thanks, Roark. Really. Thanks."

He patted the small hand resting on his arm. "Go lie down. I'll be back soon as I can."

* * *

When he returned, she was stretched out on the sofa, one arm across her eyes, the other hand resting on her abdomen. She lowered her arm and smiled wanly at him as he approached on tiptoe. "Find everything?"

"I think so."

"Did I send enough money?"

"Don't worry about it. Why aren't you in bed?"

"Well, as I said, it's kind of a mess."

At the end of a short hallway one of the bedroom doors was standing ajar. He set the sack of purchases on the floor beside the sofa. "Here's your stuff." Then he started down the hall toward the bedroom.

"Roark, no," she protested weakly as she sat up.

"Take care of yourself, Mary Catherine. I'll take care of this."

He did, but it wasn't pleasant.

For one thing, it was much more difficult to remain detached than he had imagined it would be. He couldn't get it out of his mind that the "mess" represented a human life, which had started out exactly as every human life did. For reasons that would never be known, it had decided to give it up, cash in early, let go. It was said that miscarriages were blessings in disguise, that it was the natural way for a uterus to discard an imperfection. Nevertheless, knowing that a life had ended tonight was depressing as hell.

Also she must have been fairly far along, because there was more bloody substance than he'd expected. As efficiently as possible, he stripped the linens, including the mattress pad, and crammed them into a plastic trash bag he found in a kitchen pantry. He sealed it tightly, then carried it out to the Dumpster behind the building.

On his way back through the apartment, he heard the shower running in the bathroom. He found fresh linens in a hall closet and remade the bed. He was finishing up when she came into the bedroom, looking scrubbed and wearing another ensemble of loose T-shirt and baggy boxers.

He swept his arm wide to indicate the bed. "Climb in." She did, sighing with relief as she lay down. "Everything all right?"

"Sure."

"Did you take some of the Tylenol?"

"Three. Figured they couldn't hurt."

"How about some tea?"

"You've done enough."

"How about some tea?"

She looked up at him. "You'd really make me tea?"

"Do you have a kettle?"

"I don't think so."

"A microwave?"

"Of course."

Five minutes later, he was back with a steaming cup of tea, packets of sweetener, and a spoon. "I didn't know if you took sugar or not."

"Two, please." As he stirred the sweetener into her tea, he glanced over at the TV. The sound was muted, but she was staring into the screen. "I love this movie," she told him. "I bought the video and must've watched it a thousand times. Audrey Hepburn and Cary Grant."

"A winning combo. Careful, it's hot," he said, passing her the mug. She made room for him beside her on the bed, and he sat down, leaning back against the wall. "What's it about?"

"She's gorgeous and in trouble. He's handsome and comes to her rescue. She's scared. He's suave. They fall in love in the end."

They watched the video in silence until it played out, then she clicked off the TV and he took the empty cup from her. "Thanks, Roark, that helped. Nobody's ever made me tea before."

"My mom always made me tea when I was sick."

"Was she nice to you?"

"Real nice. I was lucky."

"Yeah, you were. My old lady kicked me out when I was fifteen."

"How come?"

"She caught her boyfriend waving his weenie at me."

"Why didn't she kick him out?"

She laughed as though that were funny, although Roark hadn't meant it to be. "You're a nice guy, Roark." When he grimaced, she added, "I meant it as a compliment."

"Well, thanks. Must say, though, I'd rather be thought of as dashing and dangerous."

Her smile faded. Her eyes lost their sparkle and seemed to look inward into something that caused her unhappiness. "No, that's Todd."

Roark didn't know how to respond to that and reasoned that it was best to say nothing. He slapped his thighs and moved to get up. "Well, I should be—"

"Wait, Roark. You've been so sweet. I mean, really fuckin' great. I hate women who're clingy and needy, but I don't want to be alone tonight. Would you stay? Just until I fall asleep?"

"Okay. Sure."

"Lie down."

Awkwardly, Roark stretched out beside her on the bed. She snuggled against him and rested her head on his shoulder. He placed an arm around her. "Maybe tomorrow you should call a doctor," he suggested.

"Yeah. He'll likely want to do a D and C. Yuk."

Roark's thought exactly. He had a vague idea of what was involved in the procedure, and he preferred keeping the idea vague. "You weren't on the pill?"

"No. They make me fat," she explained. "And he forgot to bring condoms. At least he told me he forgot them. Guess I was stupid not to insist."

"Damn straight. Pregnancy's not the worst that can happen."

"I know, but he's the type who'd be careful about disease and stuff."

"So this guy wasn't random? I mean, he's somebody you know well?"

"Roark, don't ask, okay?"

"Okay."

"Let's talk about something else."

But they didn't talk. Not for a while. They didn't even move, except for his fingers sifting through strands of her hair, which was fanned out over the pillow, drying from her shower.

"My name's not really Mary Catherine," she confessed softly.

"No?"

"It's Sheila."

"That's pretty."

"I just use Mary Catherine for the nun bit."

"I figured."

"I thought you might. You're smart. Me, I quit school when I left home, middle of tenth grade. I'm an idiot."

"I don't think so."

"I know so. Anyway, when the customers get tired of the nun act, I'll work up something else, and I'll probably change my name to fit the new act. I'm playing with an idea. What to hear it?"

"Love to."

"I thought I could maybe be a mermaid? You know, I'd have this tail that was all pearly and shimmery. I'd wear a long, flowing wig that came down to my ass. Maybe even to my knees."

"You'd be a knockout. You could call yourself Lorelei."

"Lorelei?"

"Like the siren. In mythology." She stared back at him with misapprehension. "She had a beautiful singing voice," he explained. "She used it to lure sailors into the rocks where they would shipwreck."

"No shit? I gotta remember that."

"I can write it down for you so you won't forget."

She propped herself up on her elbow and regarded him with patent admiration. "See? You're so fuckin' smart."

He laughed, and she laughed, and then they looked at one another seriously for a long moment, and then she said, "You can play with them if you want to."

Immediately his eyes dropped to her chest. She raised the hem of her T-shirt up over her breasts. The objects of his affection and fantasies, what he had admired from afar, were inches from his eyes, his fingertips, his lips. She was giving them to him. A gift.

But when he extended his hand, it was to lower her T-shirt back into place.

"What's the matter?" she asked. "I can't screw tonight, but I could blow you."

"That's not necessary."

"You think I'd be doing it just for you? Think again." She slid her hand down to his crotch and took his penis in her hand. "I've been wondering what you packed. Starlight's a lying bitch, but I can tell she was telling the truth about you." She squeezed him, and he caught his breath. Blood rushed to the pressure point made by each of her fingers.

But he moved her hand away from him. "I'd be taking advantage of the situation."

"So?"

"I wouldn't feel right about it, Sheila."

"Jesus, most guys would kill for an offer like this. Are you for real?"

"I'm real, all right. I'll be cursing myself in the morning."

"Well, you can jerk off in the shower while you watch us sunbathe." She giggled at his astonishment. "We're not *that* ignorant, Roark. Why else would y'all take so many showers? And at the same time we're sunbathing?"

She smiled and lay back down, snuggling against

him again. "Truth is, I couldn't have given you my best tonight. I really do feel like shit, you know?"

"Go to sleep, Sheila. When you wake up, this'll seem like a bad dream."

"You're sweet."

"So are you."

He stroked her back, and caressed her hair, and continued to hold her even after she had fallen asleep. When he returned to his apartment the following morning, Todd was already up and pecking away at his keyboard. "Where've you been?"

"Walking on the beach."

Todd squinted at him suspiciously.

"Alone."

"Who is she?"

"Alone," Roark repeated testily.

"Huh." Todd went back to his typing, saying only one thing more. "Coffee's made, but I used the last of the milk."

Chapter 20

Noah decided to give Maris a week to simmer down.

He concluded that a woman who catches her husband in adultery deserves a seven-day grace period in which to lick her wounds. It was more than an adequate amount of time for an ego to be restored. If the God of Genesis could create the cosmos in that length of time, surely a wife could come to terms with her husband's infidelity.

He also set the deadline to coincide with the one that Morris Blume had imposed on him. When next they met, Noah needed to report that everything was going smoothly and proceeding according to schedule. It would be nice and tidy if he patched things up with Maris before making that claim.

He was of value to Blume only as long as he was a member of the Matherly family. His pending deal with WorldView would be jeopardized by an estrangement from Maris and Daniel. Even a minor tiff with them might cause Blume to balk. Before that important meeting, he must reconcile with Maris.

If within a week's time she hadn't approached him, he planned to go to her hat in hand and beg her forgiveness. He would rather choke than be penitent, but the ultimate reward would be well worth a few minutes of contrition. In the meantime, he had a suite at the Plaza. He would give her space, give her plenty of time to stew...and to contemplate the consequences of ordering him from her life.

Like hell, Maris, my dear. He hoped he had made himself clear on that point.

Unfortunately, he was forced to see Maris the morning following their nasty scene outside Nadia's apartment. Avoiding Howard Bancroft's funeral was not an option. When he arrived, he saw Daniel standing alone on the steps of the synagogue and knew immediately that his father-in-law was unaware of what had transpired the night before. Daniel greeted him as though nothing untoward had happened.

As they somberly shook hands, Daniel asked him where Maris was.

"On her way, I'm sure. I had to leave ahead of her so I could make a quick stop at the office." The old man bought the lie. In any case, he let Noah lead him inside to get out of the drizzle that had begun to fall.

Maris arrived a few minutes later. She looked pale and wan in an unflattering black dress. It wasn't her best color. He'd never liked her in black. She spotted him standing with Daniel in the vestibule, wearing paper yarmulkes, waiting for her.

After a slight hesitation, she moved through the crowd toward them. She was too respectful of the situation to cause a scene. He had counted on her discretion, just as he had counted on her not telling Daniel about his extramarital affair with Nadia. Besides being proud to a fault, Maris was boringly predictable.

She hugged Daniel tenderly. "How are you this morning, Dad?"

"Sad for all of us, but especially for Howard's family. Shall we go in?"

They filed down the long aisle. Maris maneuvered it so that

when they entered the pew Daniel was between them. She was the epitome of decorum, yet Noah knew she must be gnashing her teeth even to be in his presence. Imagining what an endurance test this was for her, he could barely contain his amusement.

Following the service, she consoled Daniel and, for his benefit, invented an excuse for having to take a separate taxi back to Midtown. Noah didn't see her for the remainder of the day.

Nor did he seek her out for the next several days. During scheduled business meetings, she pretended that everything was normal. They had never been overtly affectionate at work, except occasionally behind the closed door of either his or her private office. Around staff members, they had always conducted themselves in a professional manner. Consequently, no one at Matherly Press noticed the chill between them.

He went to their apartment when he knew she wouldn't be there to collect a few changes of clothing. He wasn't surprised to find that everything was exactly as he had left it. Maris had not sent for Maxine to pack up his belongings. She would never have entrusted the secret of their separation to her father's loyal housekeeper. The bad news would have gone straight from Maxine to Daniel, and Maris wanted to prevent Daniel from hearing of it. She would want to spare the old man from worrying about their marital problems and the damaging effect such problems would have on the publishing house.

Daniel, none the wiser, continued to take Noah's calls, and Noah continued to pay him brief visits in the late afternoons to discuss the events of the day. His relationship with his father-in-law remained solid. Maris was suffering in silence and alone, and she had only herself to blame. She should never have taken that haughty stance with him. She should have thought twice before issuing ultimatums that served only to make her look and sound ridiculous.

He relished the thought of her pacing, regretting her

thoughtless outburst, and having absolutely no one in whom to confide. Each time he envisioned her wallowing in her lonely, self-inflicted torment, he smiled.

After a few days, however, Noah began to tire of the situation. He considered approaching Maris and putting an end to the silliness. But he stubbornly resolved to let her brood for the full seven days before approaching her.

She would weep and call him names and beg to know how he could have hurt her so terribly when she had done absolutely nothing to deserve it. He would give her the opportunity to vent. Once she had, she would grant him forgiveness. No doubt of that.

She would forgive him for the old man's sake. Maris could always be counted on to spare Daniel any kind of unhappiness. She would forgive him also because women love to forgive and then to make the forgiven miserable every day thereafter for the rest of his postforgiven life. That wasn't going to be his future, of course, but he figured that's what Maris had planned for him. In light of his deal with WorldView, he would do nothing at this point to enlighten her. That would come later.

In the meantime, the temporary separation wasn't without its perks. While Maris wasn't speaking to him, he didn't have to listen to her harping.

Nadia was another matter entirely. She continually nagged him to divorce Maris. Her persistence had become tiresome and had created a tension between them that came to a head, ironically enough, on the final day of his self-imposed deadline.

They had scheduled a luncheon meeting in an outrageously expensive, trendy uptown restaurant. One of Matherly Press's bestselling authors was joining them to be interviewed by Nadia for "Book Chat." The writer hadn't yet arrived when they ordered prelunch cocktails.

To other diners, which included a large number of publishing industry personnel, it appeared they were having a civil conversation about current market trends or perhaps the sci-fi phenomenon that had rocked the book world by securing the top spot on every bestseller list, when, in fact, they were arguing about their immediate future.

"She knows about us, so why wait? File for divorce now and get it over with."

"I can't leave the family until the deal with WorldView is cemented," he argued.

"What does one have to do with the other?"

"That is an incredibly stupid question, Nadia."

The insulting remark froze Nadia's smile into place. Had they been anyplace else, her temper might have erupted on the scale of Vesuvius. As it was, she took a languid sip of her martini, smoothed the starched linen napkin in her lap, and adjusted the triple strand of pearls around her neck—which he noticed was suffused with angry color. "Be careful, Noah," she said quietly. "You do not want me angry at you."

Like her, he kept his smile in place, but his voice had an edge. "Are you threatening me?"

"Being the cold, heartless bastard you are, I think you recognize a threat when you hear one."

"Isn't it because I'm a cold, heartless bastard that you can't resist me?"

Seeing that the awaited writer had arrived and was being escorted to their table by the maître d', Nadia flashed him a brilliant smile and spoke for his ears alone. "Do yourself a favor, Noah, and remember that I could give you lessons on how to be heartless."

Following the tedious lunch, he escorted her out of the restaurant and onto the sidewalk. A chauffeured car was waiting for them, but Nadia politely declined his invitation of a lift back to her office.

He took her hand in what he hoped looked like a friendly

handshake between two professionals, but he addressed her with a confidential pitch he knew she would understand.

"If it seems like I'm dragging my feet on this divorce issue, it's because I don't want to make an error that could cost us this deal. I want it for us, Nadia. But in order to get it, we must be willing to make a few sacrifices. I can't dissolve my marriage to Maris now. It's out of the question. You understand that, don't you?"

To his immense relief, she smiled up at him and looked appropriately contrite. "Of course I understand. I'm just impatient to be with you."

"No more than I. In fact," he said, moving a half step nearer to her, "I want to be inside you right now."

She closed her eyes and swayed slightly toward him, then glanced around to make certain no one had noticed or could overhear. "Naughty you. You've made me wet."

"Then six o'clock can't come soon enough."

He squeezed her hand quickly, then climbed into the backseat of the waiting car, smiling to himself. The secret to keeping Nadia content was to keep her agitated between her legs. That was the mainspring of her self-worth. Her self-image revolved around it. If she was happy there, she was happy.

He disliked her constant nagging, but his argument with her had been stimulating and had geared him up for his showdown with Maris. *Call it a rehearsal*, he thought as he stepped off the elevator and pushed through the glass doors leading into the executive offices of Matherly Press.

He went into Maris's office straightaway, but she wasn't there. On his way out, he bumped into her assistant. "Can I help you, Mr. Reed?"

"I'm looking for Maris."

Her eyes were magnified by the thick lenses of her glasses as she looked at him quizzically. "She's not coming in today, Mr. Reed. Remember, she's going back to Georgia."

Going back to Georgia? Since when? *Shit!* This didn't fit into his timetable at all.

It required all his acting skills not to give his ignorance away to the secretary. "Right, right. I know she's leaving today, but she said she was stopping here briefly before going to the airport."

"She did? That's not what she told me."

"Hmm, I guess she changed her mind." He forced a smile and hoped it looked more natural than it felt. "I'll catch her on her cell phone."

He called no less than a dozen times but kept getting Maris's voice mail. It was obvious that she did not want to be reached. He cursed her throughout the remainder of the workday. If she had suddenly appeared, he could well have killed her with his bare hands.

This was the worst possible time for her to play the betrayed wife and run away. Hadn't he made it plain to her that he wasn't going to stand for any crap from her, and that if he told her to roll over and play dead that's what she was to do? Her pouting could ruin this whole thing.

On second thought, fuck her.

He had the document that Howard Bancroft had drawn up for him. Unless he was given no other choice, he would rather not use it. From a legal standpoint, that document could make things sticky, and he would rather avoid any legal stickiness. But it was there in his safe-deposit box, an insurance policy, an emergency measure to be used if it became necessary.

Feeling confident and unconquerable again, he arrived at Nadia's Chelsea apartment shortly after six o'clock. He was in the mood for a cold drink and a cool shower, topped off by hot, aggressive sex.

He was whistling as he jogged up the staircase. But when he let himself into the apartment, his whistling abruptly died.

A beefy young man dressed in a tight-fitting black T-shirt and black slacks was emerging from the bedroom, strapping on his wristwatch. He then shouldered his gym bag and casually eased past Noah on his way out the door. His only acknowledgment of Noah was a negligent nod.

For minutes after the young man left, Noah remained on the threshold in a slow burn. A burn so hot that he was a combustion chamber, well decked out in Hugo Boss. He shot his monogrammed cuffs, smoothed down his hair, wiped the perspiration from his upper lip. These were conscious gestures, activities for his hands so he wouldn't use them to rip, bash, or otherwise destroy something, animate or otherwise, he wasn't particular at the moment.

When he was finally under moderate control, he moved toward the bedroom and gave the door a gentle push. It swung back on silent hinges. Nadia was sprawled naked on the wide bed amid rumpled silk sheets. Her hair was damp and tangled. Her skin merely damp.

Seeing him, she stirred and smiled drowsily. "Noah, darling, is it six o'clock already? I lost all track of time."

The blood vessels in his temples were pounding to the point of pain, but his voice remained calm. "Who was that man?"

"Oh, you met Frankie? He's a personal trainer at my health club."

"What was he doing here?"

She levered herself up onto one elbow and looked at him with malice, mitigated only slightly by a sly smile. "That is an incredibly stupid question, Noah."

* * *

Daniel Matherly finished reading the last page of the manuscript. As he lined up the edges and stacked the pages, he said, "That's all you've got so far?"

Maris nodded. "I haven't received anything from him since I returned. I've called several times to give him a pep talk, but I've spoken only to Mike, his aide. According to him, P... the author isn't writing much these days."

"I wonder why."

"He's sulking."

"His muse has flown."

"Nothing that mystical. He's being his stubborn and mule-headed self. Like any mule, he requires prodding." She hesitated before adding, "So I'm going back."

"Really? When?"

"I'm on my way to the airport now."

"I see."

"I only stopped by to check on you, tell you good-bye, and to hear your opinion of what you've read so far."

She had postponed her departure for a week. After catching Noah in Nadia Schuller's apartment, it was a foregone conclusion that she would return to Georgia and see Parker again.

Her husband's affair had given her a green light to examine her ambiguous and conflicting feelings for Parker. But in order to be fair to him, and to herself, she had delayed going until she had thought it through from every angle. She didn't want her return to be a knee-jerk reaction to a rapid series of shocking developments in her life. She didn't want it to be the reaction of an angry and vindictive wife. Rather, she wanted it to be an action taken after days of careful consideration.

For the past seven days, she had thought of little else.

She had been terribly angry at Parker the morning she left, but the truth of the matter was she hadn't wanted to leave. She could admit that now. And every moment since her leaving, she had wanted to be with him again.

Initially, guilt had burned inside her like a live coal. She was married. She had made a commitment at the wedding altar, and she had regarded it a lifetime pledge. All her marriage vows she had taken seriously.

But apparently she had been the only one standing at the altar that day who had. Noah had broken his vows. For all she knew, Nadia wasn't the first woman with whom he had cheated. He had certainly had no shortage of girlfriends prior to his marriage. It was possible he had never changed his pattern of behavior from that of a bachelor to that of a married man. He had willfully chosen to be unfaithful to her. She would just as willfully choose to end the marriage. By taking a lover, he had squandered the right and the privilege to be her husband.

But even if she hadn't caught him with Nadia, she would be leaving him. That night on the sidewalk in Chelsea, Noah had revealed an aspect of himself that appalled, repelled, and frightened her. She would not live another day with a man who hinted at violence so effectively that she believed him capable of it. Their marriage was over. Noah Reed was her past.

What she needed to determine was if Parker Evans was her future.

She could no longer ignore or deny her attraction to him. It wasn't strictly his intellect and talent that appealed to her, as she had tried to delude herself into believing. She was attracted to him, the man. Countless times she had fantasized kissing him again, having his hands on her, having her mouth on him.

She didn't even know if he was capable of making love in the conventional sense, but it didn't matter. She wanted to touch him and to be touched. She wanted to be intimate with him on whatever level and by whatever means it could be achieved.

While married she never would have acted on that desire. During her courtship and marriage, she had never looked at another man or thought of one in a sexual context, which had made her spontaneous attraction to Parker all the more disturbing.

During her return flight to New York, she had convinced herself that the island was responsible for the romantic yearnings she had experienced there and that once she was back in familiar territory, they would stop. By the time the plane touched down at La Guardia, she had persuaded herself that the rift between her and Noah was curable, that the temporary lull in their marriage had left her open to fanciful daydreams that would vanish the moment their dozing passion was reawakened.

She had talked herself into believing that with a little ingenuity on her part she could revive their love life and feel again the exhilaration and excitement she had when she left the church on Noah's arm as his bride.

What a naive strategy that had been!

It made her angry now that she had been willing to assume all the responsibility for their marriage being out of sorts. How could she have been so gullible? Did everyone except her know about Noah's affair? The people with whom they both worked every day—had they known? Was she a comically tragic figure, the last-to-know wife? The staff must have thought, *Poor Maris,* as she toiled away at book publishing while her husband periodically slipped out for an illicit rendezvous with his mistress.

Noah had his adversaries among the staff, but he also had his allies, people he had pirated from the publisher with which he'd been formerly affiliated. Divorcing him would be easy compared to disassociating him from Matherly Press.

Which brought her to the next hurdle she must face: informing Daniel of their split.

She would postpone it for as long as possible. It would come as a double blow for him. He would be losing not only his son-in-law, but his protégé. Maris was confident that her father was strong enough to handle it, as he had handled all the other setbacks and disappointments in his life, but she saw no point in upsetting him prematurely. However, until the time came when it was necessary for him to know, it was going to be a challenge to keep up the pretense that everything was normal.

He was watching her now with his unsettling intuitiveness. It was hard not to squirm under the direct gaze. "So what do you think, Dad?"

"About the book? I think it's very good. Speaking as a publisher, I would prod the author to complete it."

"Then I guess I'm off." She stood up and began pulling on her raincoat.

"What does Noah think?"

"He hasn't read it yet."

"I wasn't referring to the manuscript, Maris. What does he think of your going away to spend more time with this writer?"

"I don't need his permission." Seeing that he was taken aback by the sharpness of her tone, she amended it. "I'm sorry, Dad. I didn't mean to snap at you."

"Apology accepted. I don't presume to interfere with your personal life. It's just that..."

"Don't stop there. You've come this far."

He reached for her hand. "It's just that I remember well when you fell in love with a book, and then with the author."

She gave him a faint smile. "Is that what you're thinking? That I've got a schoolgirl's crush on this writer?"

"It wouldn't be for the first time."

"I'm older and wiser now." She stopped herself from saying, *I've learned my lesson.* "This book, this author, have nothing to do with Noah and our marriage. Nothing whatsoever."

That was the truth. Her marriage was over whether or not she ever saw Parker Evans again. Had she never heard of Parker or *Envy,* her marriage would have ended. It would have ended because her husband was false and their marriage a sham.

"So Noah's agreeable to your going?"

Noah's feelings on the matter seemed very important to her father. But they wouldn't be if he knew the whole story. She was tempted to roll up her sleeves and show him the bruises on her arms that even a week's time hadn't faded. She could tell him how she'd spat blood for an hour after biting her tongue. What if she repeated Noah's harsh threats, using the same sinister inflection that had been almost more alarming than the words themselves? Her father would be as shocked as she had been. He would be ready to find Noah and mete out punishment with his own hand.

That's why she wouldn't expose Noah to him now. She would save it for a day when she had things more sorted out in her own mind, when she wasn't on her way out of town, when she had a workable plan for Matherly Press as well as her personal life. Until she had answers already in place in her own mind, she wouldn't detail the problems to her father.

Instead, she looked him straight in the eye and, for the first time in her life, lied to him. "Yes. He's agreeable."

He took her face between his hands and kissed her on both cheeks. "What time is your flight?"

"I've barely got time to make it." Plagued by guilt for lying to him, she embraced him tightly. She squeezed her eyes closed and wasn't surprised to feel tears in them. "You're my best friend, Dad. I love you very much."

"And I love you, Maris." He set her away from him so he could look into her face. "More than you could ever know."

Chapter 21

Parker answered the door. For several moments he looked at her blankly. Finally he said, "Did you forget something?"

"Very cute."

"Thank you."

"Are you going to ask me in?"

He hesitated as though thinking it over, then pushed his chair backward into the foyer, giving her room to step inside. "Where's Mike?"

"He went to the mainland for groceries, toilet paper, stuff like that."

"And left you here alone?"

"I'm not helpless," he said in what amounted to a snarl. "I lived by myself before Mike came onboard. Besides, I'm not alone."

He was with a woman.

Maris realized now that all the signs were there. Mike was away. Parker's shirt was unbuttoned, and his hair was more disheveled than usual. "I'm sorry. I...I should have called before I came."

"Yeah, you should have," he said crossly. "But since you've made the trip, you might just as well come on in. We're in here."

He wheeled his chair around and rolled it into the dining room. Reluctantly Maris followed, wishing there were a way she could turn and run without looking like a coward. Short of that, she wished she didn't have to meet his lady friend looking so bedraggled.

She wasn't up to an introduction to anyone, but especially not to a woman that Parker had invited over for some afternoon delight. The skirt of her linen suit was badly wrinkled. There was a run in her stocking. The raincoat, which she had needed in New York, was as out of place here as a snorkel mask in the Sahara.

She stood her suitcase in the foyer and folded her coat over it, then combed her fingers through her hair, which had been wind-damaged during the boat ride over from the mainland. There was no time for further repair. Fortifying herself with a deep breath, she stepped through the arched opening between the hallway and dining room.

Her primping had been unnecessary. Except for Parker, the room was empty. She looked at him inquisitively. "Up there," he said, motioning with his chin.

"I've noticed it swaying before," she told him, looking overhead at the chandelier. "It catches the current from the air-conditioning vent."

"Reasonable explanation. But wrong. It's the hanging ghost."

She expelled a short laugh. Finding him alone after all had left her feeling a little giddy. "Hanging ghost?"

He proceeded to tell her a tale about a planter who'd fallen on hard times. "His desperate attempts to recoup the family fortune were ill-conceived and only plunged them deeper into financial ruin. He hanged himself right here in the dining room." Upon reflection, he added, "I trust no one was having dinner at the time."

"You really believe that his ghost is . . ." She motioned toward the swaying fixture. "Up there?"

"Hell, yes."

"It doesn't bother you to have a ghost residing in your house?"

"He lived here for almost a century before Mike and I moved in." He shrugged. "He doesn't seem to mind us, so we ignore him. Ordinarily. Today, he's kept me company. Pretty damned good conversationalist."

Maris peered at Parker suspiciously, then her eyes strayed to the open decanter on the sideboard. Coming back to him, she said, "You're drunk."

"Not yet."

"But well on your way."

"Working on it." He rolled his chair over to the sideboard. "Care to join me?"

"Sure."

His head came around quickly, his surprise over her answer turning into a wicked grin of approval. "Sin suits you, Mrs. Matherly-Reed. You should engage in it more often." He took a clean glass from a silver tray and began to pour from the decanter. "Say when."

"When."

After pouring the two drinks, he wedged both glasses between his thighs and rolled his chair back to her. "Help yourself."

It was a blatant dare. Keeping her eyes locked with his, she reached between his legs for one of the glasses. "Take your time," he drawled.

She pulled the glass from between his thighs and clinked it against the one remaining. "Cheers."

He grinned again. "That might put some needed color in your cheeks, but you're gonna have to drink more than that if you want to catch up with me." After saluting her with his glass, he tossed his drink back like a shot.

She sipped the straight bourbon more cautiously. "Is this what you do now instead of write? You drink?"

"You must've been talking to Mike."

"When you refused to take my calls."

"He's a tattletale."

"Some things I can see for myself."

"You're a clever girl, all right."

"Why have you stopped working on *Envy*, and why are you getting drunk in the middle of the afternoon?"

"What better time? Besides, all the great writers were drunks. Didn't you know? I'll bet Homer went to the ancient Greeks' equivalent of AA. From Edgar Allan Poe, to Fitzgerald, to—"

"Parker, why are you doing this?"

"Why'd you come back?" he snapped in return.

"I asked you first."

"Because I don't have any of the narcotics I used to take, and I'd have a hard time hanging myself from the chandelier."

"That's not funny."

"It wasn't meant to be."

"You've mentioned suicide twice. It's offensive and tasteless. Particularly since a good friend of mine blew his brains out last week."

The exchange ended there. Parker averted his head, and for a time neither of them spoke. Maris sipped her bourbon until she'd drunk it all, then returned the empty glass to the sideboard.

Finally Parker said, "Mike finished the mantel."

"I noticed. It's beautiful." She crossed to the fireplace and ran her fingertips over the wood's satin finish. "He did an excellent job."

"Be sure and tell him."

"I will."

"Who was your friend?"

She turned back to him. "Our corporate lawyer. I'd known him all my life. He was like an uncle to me."

"I'm sorry."

"For him it was over before he felt any pain. For the people who cared about him, it wasn't that easy. They'll feel the pain of it for a long time."

"Problems?"

"Not that anyone knew of."

"Then why'd he do it?"

"That remains a mystery." Speaking to the mantel, she said almost as an afterthought, "Noah had a meeting with him that afternoon."

"He detected nothing wrong?"

"No, nothing."

"What was their meeting about?"

"Normal business. Why?"

"Just wondering."

She faced him again. "Why?"

Rather than answer, he asked if she wanted another drink.

"No, thank you. My toes are already tingling."

He glanced down at her shoes. "You're dressed for New York. Why don't you change, then you can read the segment I've been working on since you left."

She smiled in surprise. "So you have been writing?"

"Mike only *thinks* he knows everything."

* * *

"This couldn't have worked out more perfectly. We can speak freely." Noah was pretending a nonchalance he didn't feel. To further convince his visitor of his insouciance, he idly twirled the skewered olive in his martini glass. "Maris went out of town again."

"Is this typical of her?"

Morris Blume had arrived at the Reeds' West Side co-op, wearing his condescending attitude like a fashion accessory.

Noah had insisted that they meet informally and alone, without Blume's flunkies. They were like hummingbirds around a tropical blossom, hovering when they weren't actually fluttering.

Noah had given his doorman an exorbitant tip to admit Blume and to ensure his memory loss about it later. He'd been hospitably waiting for Blume when Blume stepped out of the elevator. Blume had practically marched into the apartment, surveying it as a drill sergeant would a barracks, his colorless eyes seeming to be searching for flaws. Apparently it passed inspection. "Very nice."

Noah had attributed the tasteful decor to Maris. "She has an eye for such things. Drink?"

Now they were seated on facing sofas, Tiffany martini glasses in hand, and Maris's name had entered the conversation again. "She goes away frequently, doesn't she?" Blume asked.

"Not until recently when she began working on a project with an author who lives on an island off the coast of Georgia."

"You're sure of this?"

Since Noah felt his control over his wife and his mistress had slipped lately, Blume's insinuation smarted. "Sure about what?" he asked testily. "My wife's whereabouts?"

Blume stretched his colorless lips into his distinctive facsimile of a smile. "I knew a man whose wife was allegedly interviewing interior decorators to redo their recently purchased winery in Sonoma. Turns out she was consulting with a notorious divorce lawyer in LA who did his best work in bed. The wife wound up with the lawyer, the winery, and just about everything else. Once the fleecing was over, the man considered himself lucky to come away with his dick still attached. There's a lesson to be learned there."

The implied criticism rankled, but Noah chuckled. "This writer is shriveled and disabled, wheelchair-bound. Passion hasn't drawn Maris to Georgia."

"The draw could be something more damaging than a love affair."

Noah pulled the olive off the skewer with his teeth and chewed around his lazy grin. "If you're suggesting that Maris is up to some corporate subterfuge, you truly don't know her. She doesn't think as we do, Morris. She's a bookworm. A romantic, a dreamer. Head in the clouds. Trust me, she won't be springing any nasty surprises on us."

"I assume she'll be surprised when Matherly Press becomes part of WorldView."

"We'll know soon."

"I like the confident ring of that."

Still smiling slyly, Noah set his glass on the coffee table and reached for his briefcase. With a flourish, he clicked open the latches. "Delivered on time, as promised."

He passed Blume the document prepared by Howard Bancroft. After finding Nadia naked in bed and reeking of another man's sweat, following closely Maris's inconvenient and unexpected disappearance, he had determined that his next action must be bold and definitive.

He was tired of playing cautiously, tired of other people—women, for God's sake!—dictating what he did and when he did it. He must move quickly and aggressively. It was time to take care of Noah, and only Noah, and let the rest of them go fuck themselves. Or their meatheaded personal trainers. Jesus.

Blume scanned the document, rapidly flipping through the pages. He was familiar enough with legal jargon to catch the gist of it. Noah waited to be congratulated.

But when Blume finished glancing over the last page, he returned the document to the coffee table. "Very nice. Now all that's needed is their signatures."

Noah's inflated chest emptied like a punctured balloon. "Not necessary, Morris. Didn't you read—"

"That it's valid with your signature alone?" He chuckled as

he stood up and buttoned the top button of his perfectly tailored gray suit jacket. "A problematic clause, Noah. Very. I'm already dodging antitrust laws and myriad other trade regulations." He waved his pale hand in a dismissive gesture. "They're nothing more than time-consuming nuisances. But only if everything else is in perfect order, and I mean all the *i*'s dotted and *t*'s crossed.

"I couldn't swing a deal of this magnitude with a legal trap-door like this waiting to open up beneath me. I wouldn't even want to try. This document, as it is now, would flag the feds. Even if it didn't, the Matherlys could raise a hue and cry, and then we'd all be screwed. I don't know about you, but when I get screwed, I like it to feel good."

He winked and Noah wanted to kill him.

"Now, if you'll excuse me, I have a dinner date."

He turned and headed for the door. Noah blinked the pulsing red lights out of his vision and followed. "Not to worry, Morris. I'll get the signatures."

Blume said, "I never worry."

He opened the door, then paused and turned back to Noah. "One of their signatures would probably be sufficient. Either your father-in-law's or your wife's." He mulled it over for several seconds, then nodded. "Yes. I'd feel protected with only one in addition to yours."

"You keep the antitrust thugs off our backs," Noah said stiffly. "Leave the Matherlys to me."

"Gladly. Between the two, I'd rather take on the federal gov-ernment." His grin made him look like a leering skull recently exhumed. "Call me when you have that signature. Only when you have it, all right? My time is extremely valuable, and this has taken far too long already."

Then he was gone.

* * *

An hour later, Noah entered Daniel's home study. Seared by
Blume's parting shot, he had deliberated for only a few minutes
before deciding which Matherly to approach.

He hadn't spoken to Maris in more than a week. She was still
pissed over Nadia. The power-of-attorney document was hardly
an olive branch to hold out to her. Besides, she had recently revealed a stubborn streak he hadn't known she had.

Daniel was the weaker of them. He had earned his spurs years
ago, but age had dulled them. He was no longer the formidable
force he'd been. Tired and in declining health, he wasn't as ob-
stinate as he once was. If he put up any resistance at all, Noah
was confident of his ability to wear him down.

Maxine answered the door and told him that Daniel was in
his study. "He went in there immediately after dinner. Said he
was going to read for a while before bedtime."

Sure enough, when Noah went in, an open book was resting
on Daniel's lap. But his head was bowed low over his chest, and
for a second Noah feared the old bastard had died. That's the
way his luck had been running lately. "Daniel?"

He raised his head. "Hello, Noah. I was just reading."

"Do you always snore when you read?"

"Tell me I wasn't drooling, too."

"Not that I saw."

"Good. Have a seat. Drink?"

"No, thanks."

On the way over, an unpleasant thought had crossed Noah's
mind. What if Maris had told her father about his affair with
Nadia? Maybe she had confided in Daniel before running off to
Georgia. To crown a totally shitty day, all he needed was for his
father-in-law to accuse him of adultery and order him from his
house. But the old man was behaving normally.

Noah sat down on the love seat. "I'm sorry to disturb you. But
Maris will call later, and I'll be required to give her a full report,
right down to what you ate for dinner."

"Grilled sole, brown rice, and steamed vegetables."

"A menu she'll approve. She also put me in charge of keeping you company while she's away."

Daniel snorted. "I don't need a baby-sitter."

"I agree. But please go along with me or I'll catch hell when she returns." He set his elbows on his knees and leaned forward. "What say we go to the country tomorrow for the weekend? Get in some fishing. Relaxation. I could use it, God knows."

"I rarely go up there anymore."

"Before she left, I ran the idea past Maris, and it met with wholehearted approval. I think she feels guilty for not taking you to the farm more often. If we go, it will alleviate her guilt and give her peace of mind knowing that you're enjoying yourself."

Daniel pondered it for a moment. Noah said no more. He couldn't push too hard or the old man would become suspicious. He'd made his pitch; it was time to shut up and let Daniel make his decision.

"What time tomorrow?"

Noah's tension eased and he smiled. "I have a breakfast meeting that would be difficult to reschedule. We could leave right after."

"That doesn't give Maxine much time to—"

"Actually, Daniel, I was thinking that we could go alone. Really bach it." He glanced over his shoulder as though to assure himself that the housekeeper wasn't eavesdropping. Lowering his voice, he said, "If Maxine goes, she'll fuss over you like a mother hen. You'll be accounting to her for every drink, every fat gram. Forget puffing your pipe."

"She nags worse than a wife, and everything I do will be reported straight to Maris."

"Sometimes we men must take a stand."

"Hear, hear."

"So, are we all set?"

"I am if you are."

"Great!" He stood and crossed the room to shake Daniel's hand. "I'll be over in the morning around ten. Pack light. I'll call the grocer up there and have him deliver food and drink to the house, so it'll be well stocked when we arrive." As he moved toward the door, he spoke over his shoulder. "I'll even volunteer to break the news to Maxine that she's not invited."

Chapter 22

While Maris studied his manuscript, Parker studied her.

She had taken a full hour in the guest cottage and had returned wearing a loose, casual skirt that came almost to her ankles, along with the sleeveless shirt that tied at her waist and allowed an occasional glimpse of bare midriff. She had kicked off her sandals when she settled into the easy chair and tucked her feet beneath her.

Her hair had been shampooed. A fresh application of lip gloss had left her mouth with a peachy shine. And whether it was the whisky she'd drunk or cosmetics, there was more color in her cheeks than when she arrived. She looked and smelled delectable.

He supposed he should be grateful that she found his manuscript so absorbing that she was unaware of his scrutiny. She was focused solely on the pages lying in her lap, and he was irrationally jealous of his own work for the amount of her attention it was receiving.

Before her unheralded arrival this afternoon, he'd been well on his way to getting good and trashed. He hadn't been able to write worth a crap all day, although from a meteorological stand-point it was a perfect day for it. Cloudy, gloomy, and gray, it was the kind of day when he usually immersed himself in his story and came up for air only when forced to by hunger, thirst, or needing to relieve himself.

But his mind had been a blank. Well...not a blank. He just wasn't able to write down what was on his mind, because all that was on his mind was Maris. As it had been since she left, he could think of little else today.

Maris presiding over a meeting.

Maris smiling at Noah.

Maris hailing a taxi.

Maris kissing Noah.

Maris working at her desk.

Maris sleeping beside Noah.

Maris shopping on Fifth Avenue.

Maris opening her thighs to Noah.

The revolving mental images had been enough to drive him crazy. Had been enough to drive him to drink, anyway.

He wondered now if he'd had a premonition of her arrival. Yeah, maybe he had. Because he'd been in the dining room, a room he visited only rarely. He'd been feeling sorry for himself, quaffing Wild Turkey as fast as he could pour it, and glumly star-ing out the window at nothing.

When he heard a motorized vehicle turning into the lane off the main road, he had assumed it was Mike returning. He re-membered hoping that Mike hadn't forgotten to get a bag of bite-sized Milky Way bars.

When he saw Maris behind the wheel of the approaching golf cart, his heart had sputtered and knocked like an ailing en-gine.

Subconsciously, had he been watching for her, pining like a grass widow searching the horizon for sight of her sailor's ship? He hated to think of himself as some wretched, pathetic figure waiting for Maris to grace him with her presence. God, had he sunk that low?

But he realized now that that's exactly what he'd been doing since she'd turned her back on him and stalked out of the cotton gin. Since that morning, he'd been steeping in his misery, stewing in his jealous sweat, sucking on whisky bottles, and nursing his fantasies.

Torturous fantasies of her with Noah.

Delicious ones of her with him.

At night he had erotic dreams in which she clutched him and chanted his name in breathless, urgent, orgasmic whispers. During the daylight hours, he occupied himself with visions of her caressing him, of her fingertips skimming his chest and belly, of her mouth silkily sliding—

"Was it Todd's?"

He jerked upright as though his wheelchair had goosed him. "Huh?" He cleared his throat and shook off the sexual reverie. "Pardon?"

"The baby that Mary Catherine miscarried. Was it Todd's?"

"What do you think?"

"It's suggested. Do we ever know?"

He shook his head. "I think it's better to leave it with just a suggestion. Let the reader come to his own conclusion."

"I agree." She thumbed through the pages again, stopping occasionally to reread a passage. "He's a remarkable character. Roark, I mean. He's so...well, heroic. As Mary Catherine says, he's nice."

Parker grimaced. "He's not *too* nice, is he? I don't want him coming across as a saint. Or worse, a puss."

"He doesn't." She smiled reassurance, but he continued to frown doubtfully. "Trust me, Parker. I'd tell you if he were nice to the point of being dull."

"Women readers aren't turned on by nice heroes any more than male readers lust after heroines who are too virtuous. There should be at least a hint, maybe even a promise, of corruptibility."

"You don't have to worry about Roark in that regard. Women readers will love him, for this scene alone if for no other. He's very male. His responses are instinctually masculine. He looks at everything in a sexual context first, before expanding his viewpoint to include other factors, like morality.

"At the same time, he's sensitive to Mary Catherine's needs. He declined her invitation to have sex, demonstrating that he knows where the lines of decency are drawn. Without hitting the reader over the head with his goodness, you imply that he has a strong conscience and moral fiber. He upholds a code of honor, a..." She glanced up and caught him silently laughing at her. "What?"

"You really get worked up over this stuff, don't you?"

"That's my job."

"I understand your need to get excited over it. But at the end of the day, it's still only a book, Maris."

"Not to me it isn't." She spoke softly and a bit shyly. "When I really love a book, the characters become real to me. I think it stems from losing my mother at such an early age. I needed people around me, so the princes and princesses I read about became my adopted brothers and sisters.

"I lived in palaces and on pirate ships. I climbed mountain peaks and hacked my way through dark jungles. Captain Nemo's submarine became as familiar to me as my own bedroom. The characters in my books took me along on their adventures. I laughed and cried with them. I was involved in their lives. I was privy to all their secrets. I knew their hopes and dreams as well as their fears. They became like family."

She straightened a bent corner of one of the manuscript pages and gave a small, self-conscious, self-deprecating shrug. "I suppose that passion for fiction carried over into adulthood."

For several ponderous moments, she kept her head down.

Eventually she looked across at him. He leaned toward her and spoke very softly. "If you can get that turned on by a book, I'd like to know what else you have a passion for."

She knew exactly what he was thinking. Their minds were moving along the same track. He could see it in the way her eyes turned smoky and hear it in the catch of her breath.

"The *f* word turns me on," she whispered.

"The *f* word?"

"Food."

He threw back his head and laughed. It rumbled up out of his chest and felt so good it startled him. For the first time in years, his laughter was spontaneous. It wasn't tinged with bitterness and cynicism.

She fired a fake pistol at him. "Gotcha."

"I concede. You're hungry?"

"Famished."

"Mike will never forgive me for being such a rotten host. I suppose I can put together some sort of meal, but you have to help."

"Lead on."

They moved into the kitchen and, working side by side, assembled BLTs. "Avocado?" he asked, as he set the microwave to cook the bacon strips.

"Yum."

"You have to peel it. Mike says I can't do it without bruising it."

"One thing I like about you, Parker—"

"Only one?"

"—is that you own up to your shortcomings."

"Well, there are so few of them, I can afford to be humble." She threw a Frito at him.

They ate the chips out of the bag and pickles straight from the jar. "Different from what you're used to, isn't it?" he asked around a mouthful.

"Obviously you have me confused with a pampered, spoiled brat."

"No," he replied honestly. "You work too hard to fit that description."

"Thank you."

"You're dedicated."

"Yes, I am."

"You get the job done."

"I try."

"So is that why you came back? Am I a job you left unfinished?"

"I came back to deliver the letter of agreement along with your signing check for fifteen thousand."

"You never heard of Federal Express?"

"I wasn't sure a carrier would deliver to St. Anne."

He gave her a look that said he knew better, and she got busy picking at the crust on her bread. "Okay, we're being honest. I wanted to make sure you were writing, Parker, and if you weren't, to prod you along. My dad advised it."

"Oh, so you came back because your *daddy* thought it was a good idea."

"Not exactly."

"Then why, Maris? Exactly."

She looked over at him, opened her mouth to speak, reconsidered, and began again. "We had quarreled before I left. I wanted to clear the air between us. Otherwise our working relationship would—"

He bleated a sound like the buzzer on a TV game show. "To you this might look like the backwoods, but believe it or not, we've got telephones, e-mails, faxes, various methods of communication."

"But you wouldn't take my calls or answer my e-mails and faxes."

"Eventually I would have."

"I wasn't sure."

"Yes, you were." He ended the parley there by holding up his hand and stopping her next argument. "You hopped that jet plane because you wanted to see me again. Admit it, Maris."

Her chin went up defiantly, and he thought she might deny it. But she surprised him again. "All right, yes. I did. I wanted to see you."

Folding his arms on the tabletop, he leaned toward her. "Why? Not because of my natural charm. We established early on that I have none." He stroked his chin. "So I'm wondering, did you and your hubby have a spat? Afterward, you thought, *I'll show him. I'll trot myself down to Hicksville and have a fling with a gimp.* Is that why you came back?"

He figured she would storm from the room, retrieve her things from the guest cottage, then hightail it to her golf cart and leave him in a wake of epithets. But, again, he guessed wrong. She remained where she was and addressed him in a remarkably calm voice.

"Tell me, Parker, why do you insist on being cruel? Does being mean to people make you feel stronger and more manly? Do you use meanness to cancel out the wheelchair? Or do you deliberately piss people off in order to keep them at arm's length? Do you hurt them before they have a chance to hurt you? If that's the case, then I'm truly sorry for you. Indeed, for the first time since I met you, I pity you."

When she did leave the table, her pace and posture were dignified. Her back was straight, her head high, and as Parker watched her disappear through the kitchen door, he felt like the lowest life-form on earth.

He had accused her of using him to get to Noah, when precisely the opposite was at play. He was using her to get to Noah.

Afraid she would leave before he could apologize, he backed

his chair out of the kitchen and quickly rolled it down the central hallway and through the front door. He was relieved to find her on the veranda, leaning into one of the support columns, staring out at the giant live oaks that stood sentinel on both sides of the front path.

"Maris."

"I'll leave in the morning."

"I don't want you to go."

She laughed softly but without humor. "You don't know what you want, Parker. To write. Not to write. To be famous. To be a recluse. To have me here. To send me away. You don't even know whether or not you want to go on living.

"Whatever the case, I shouldn't have come back. My reasons for returning were muddled at best, even to me. I should have stayed in New York where I belong and left you alone to luxuriate in your anger and bitterness and to keep boozy company with a ghost. You can get back to your pathetic pastimes tomorrow after I leave."

He rolled his chair directly behind her and placed his hands on either side of her waist where it flared into hips. "Don't leave."

Leaning forward, he pressed his forehead into the small of her back. He rolled it to the left and right of that shallow depression while his fingers flexed, tightening his grasp on her.

"I don't give a damn why you came back, Maris. I swear I don't. Even if you are here just to make your husband angry, I don't care. You're here, and I want you to be."

He moved his hands around to her front, where he rested them for a time on the knot of her shirt before slipping them beneath it and touching her skin. Massaging gently, he gradually drew her backward.

She spoke his name plaintively, part statement, part query, part sigh of resignation.

He continued to draw her backward until her knees bent and

he settled her onto his lap. He turned her, draping her legs over an armrest of his chair so that he was cradling her like an infant.

She looked up at him with concern. "Is this all right?"

He sifted her hair through his fingers. He stroked her cheek with his thumb, then dragged it across her lower lip. "This is perfect."

Chapter 23

It required all his willpower not to kiss her then. He knew she expected it, which was one reason he didn't. The other was because he was still feeling guilty over suggesting that her motives weren't pure. As though his were.

"Want to go for a ride?" he asked.

"A ride?"

"Down to the beach."

"I can walk."

"You can ride."

He disengaged the brake and navigated the wheelchair down the ramp off the veranda onto a paved path that led through the woods. "This is convenient," she remarked.

"I had the paths laid during the reconstruction of the house."

"Mike said you never even considered using a motorized chair, that you like doing things the hard way."

"Self-propulsion is good exercise. Mike feeds me well. I don't want to go to flab."

"What is that wonderful smell?"

"Magnolia."

"There aren't any fireflies out tonight."

"The *lightning bugs* think it's going to rain."

"Is it?"

"We'll see, won't we?"

The paved path went as far as the sand dunes, where it connected to an elevated path constructed of weathered wood planks. Sea oats brushed against Maris's legs as they went over the dunes. Beyond them, the path expanded into a platform exactly eight feet square. Parker stopped and set the brake on the wheelchair.

The deserted beach spread out before them. From this stretch of it, the mainland couldn't be seen. It looked as primordial as it had been when it was formed. The moon was obscured by the dense cloud cover, but it shed enough light to see the surf as it broke. It left a silvery residue that sparkled briefly before dissolving into the sand. The breeze was as soft as the breath of a sleeping baby, and the only sound was the redundant swish of the tide.

"This is an amazing place." Maris spoke in a reverential whisper usually reserved for church. "Dense forest growing right up to the beach."

"And no high-rise hotels to spoil the view." Rather than appreciating the view, he was rubbing a strand of Maris's hair between his fingers, studying the texture, enjoying the feel of it.

She turned her head to look at him. "What kind of narcotics?"

"Ah. I should've known you'd catch that slip of the tongue."

"I did. And it's been on my mind ever since. What kind of narcotics did you take?" Her expression wasn't censorious, simply interested. Sympathetic, maybe.

He let go of her hair and lowered his hand. "Pharmaceuticals. Painkillers. Great big quantities of them. Heaping handfuls."

"Because of your legs?"

"It was a long recovery."

"From what, Parker?"

"My own stupidity." After a short pause for emphasis, he continued. "I underwent several operations, first to reconstruct the bones and replace the missing pieces with plastic or metal. Then the muscles and tendons had to be reattached. After that, the skin...."

"Hell, Maris, you don't want to hear all that, and I really don't want to talk about it. Bottom line, I was in the hospital for over a year, then in...other facilities. I went through years of physical therapy. It was a bitch. Like hell must be, only worse. That's when I got hooked on prescription painkillers. When the doctors refused to prescribe any more, I bought the pills off the street from independent vendors."

"Drug dealers."

"With whom I became bosom buddies." She didn't appear to be shocked, but she might be if he told her the depths to which he had sunk in order to maintain his stash. So he summed it up. "I was a mess."

"But you pulled yourself out of it."

"No, I got grabbed by the balls and yanked out of it."

"Mike."

"Mike," he repeated, shaking his head over the miracle of it. "For reasons I will never understand, he befriended me. He appeared one day out of nowhere. Through the blurred vision of a drugged-out stupor, I saw him standing there amid the squalor, looking at me as though trying to decide if I was worth the effort it was going to take to save me from myself."

"Maybe he was sent to you."

"A guardian angel? Fairy godfather? At least he wasn't the Grim Reaper. Although in the weeks just following his *rescue*, I sometimes wished I was dead. Before I knew what was happening, he seized my stash and slapped me into detox."

"That couldn't have been pleasant."

"You don't want to know. Believe me. When I got out, he enrolled me in more therapy, physical *and* emotional. Cleaned me up, installed me in an apartment outfitted for the physically challenged, asked what I intended to do with the rest of my life. When I told him I had an itch to write, he set me up with a computer."

"He started you writing."

"He put it in the form of a dare."

"Which gave you a reason to go on living."

"No, by then I had decided I must go on living." *I had a damn good reason to*, he thought darkly.

"Can I ask a very personal question, Parker?"

"You can. You might regret it."

"Is Roark you?"

He'd known she would get around to it sooner or later. She was too smart not to have pieced it together. A writer writing about a writer. Naturally she would see the parallel and ask. The answer he had ready wasn't a lie, just not the whole truth. "Not entirely."

"Loosely based upon?"

"Fair to say."

She nodded solemnly but pried no further. "Did you start writing the mystery series right away?"

"No, I tried several genres. Devised and discarded a dozen plots a week for almost two years. Several thousand acres of trees went into my trash can before the Deck Cayton character clicked. He was the first thing that held my interest, that took my mind off my physical limitations.

"When I had what I thought was a publishable story, I retained an agent and told her she could submit the manuscript if she swore on her life and the lives of her children never to reveal my identity to anyone."

"And Mackensie Roone came to be." She touched his cheek. "It was a rebirth for which we can all be grateful. I'm just sorry for the suffering you had to endure to get there."

"In the long run, it's going to be worth it."

The moment the sentence was out, he realized he'd spoken it in the present tense. He feared Maris might notice and question him about his ultimate goal, but she had turned her head away from him and was gazing out across the surface of the water. The lights of a tanker winked on the horizon.

Raindrops began to fall, creating wet dimples in the sand. They fell on the wood platform in light spatters. Parker heard them even before he felt the sprinkles on his skin. They felt as warm and soft as tears.

"Parker?"

"Hmm?"

"Remember that first day I came to the cotton gin, you suggested that Noah had married the boss's daughter to further his career?"

"That yanked your chain."

"Yes. But only because you hit the nail on the head. Deep down I knew it." She turned and looked into his face. "I caught him this week with another woman." The simple statement was followed by a pause that gave him time to respond. He kept his expression neutral. "I won't bore you with the sordid details."

"How sordid?"

"Sufficiently sordid."

"Enough to send you scrambling back here? Payback time?"

"No. I swear that's not why I'm here. Noah's affair provided me with justification for coming back. But the truth is, I didn't want to leave in the first place."

"Then why did you go?"

"It was a matter of conscience."

"Over what? Nothing happened."

"Something happened to me," she exclaimed softly, pressing her fist against her chest. "I wanted to stay with you, and that was reason enough for me to leave. Being around you wasn't healthy for my marriage. What I was feeling for you frightened me. For my peace of mind, I needed to reestablish myself as a happily married woman. Ironically, I'd been back in New York only one day when I discovered that Noah had broken our marriage vows."

"He's a fool."

She gave him a smile for the indirect compliment, but it turned rueful. "So am I. I'm a fool for not acknowledging sooner that our marriage wasn't what I wanted it to be. Nor was Noah the man I wanted him to be. He wasn't the hero of his book."

"And now you think of Roark as a hero."

Shaking her head, she said, "I'm not confusing fact with fiction, Parker. I've outgrown that. You're real. I can touch you." She reached for his hand, studying it as she traced the veins on the back of it with her fingertip. "My marriage, such as it was, is over. Behind me. I don't want to talk about Noah anymore."

"Fine by me."

He gathered a handful of her hair, then wound it around his fist and drew her closer until their faces were inches apart. He hesitated for several heartbeats, then settled his lips against hers, tested the angle, readjusted. He was moderately controlled until he heard a small whimper from her. He backed off, looked down into her eyes, and recognized a desire that equaled his own.

Control was abandoned. He covered her face with wild, random, artless kisses and she was doing the same to him. Then mouths melded and tongues touched, and they kissed with carnal greed.

Eventually Parker pulled back and caught his breath, then proceeded with more temperance. His tongue stroked her lower lip; he raked it gently between his teeth. He laid light kisses at the corners of her lips before pressing his tongue into her mouth. He angled his head first to one side, then the other, but he never broke contact. Even when he withdrew, his lips remained against hers, making sipping motions as gentle as the rainfall.

Her lips barely moving against his, she whispered, "The night we met, when you kissed me . . ."

"Hmm?"

"I didn't want you to stop."

"I know."

"You *know*?"

"Don't you think I felt it, too, Maris?"

In reply, she threaded her fingers up through his hair and played sexy with her tongue. As they kissed, he unbuttoned the row of buttons, untied the knot at her waist, and pulled open her shirt.

Her breasts were proportionately small, beautifully round, and, now, sprinkled with rainwater. Heavier drops beaded on her skin. Some formed rivulets that trickled over the smooth curves, intersecting and crisscrossing in erotic patterns.

"Parker? You know it's raining."

"Yeah." He cupped her breast and reshaped it with his hand. His thumb whisked a raindrop off the tip. He leaned down and rubbed his lips across it. "As you told me once, you won't melt."

Then he took her nipple into his mouth.

"I might," she sighed.

Making his dream a reality, she folded her arms around his head and clutched him to her, repeating his name on ragged breaths.

His hand waded through what seemed like unfurled bolts of fabric until he found skin. He slid his hand between her thighs, all the way up, to her center. He touched her through her underpants. "Okay?"

She made a sound that he took for a yes. Her sex was pliant and very wet. He eased his fingers into her.

"Ohgod, Parker."

His fingers stroked her from within while his thumb drew circles on the outside. Soon she was thrusting her hips up against his hand.

"Just let it happen, Maris."

She relaxed and, although her breathing was still shallow and quick, she stopped working at trying to climax. He continued to nuzzle her breasts. Her nipples became small and hard against his flicking tongue. The stroking of his fingers intensified and the circles drawn by his thumb shrank to center on one spot.

Then he felt it, that unique tension that claimed her. Involuntary. Imperative. Impossible to bridle. Uncontainable. Her back arched. Her head fell back and she covered her eyes with her forearm. Her exposed neck begged to be kissed. He bent over it and pressed his lips against the hollow of her throat while sweet sounds vibrated from it. He remained there until the last of the aftershocks had rippled through her and she went limp.

He withdrew his hand from beneath her skirt and smoothed it back into place. He then gathered her close, securing her against his chest by resting his chin on the top of her head.

Weakly she laid her hand on his chest. "You buttoned your shirt."

"For supper. One of my mom's rules."

She undid the buttons and rubbed her cheek against his chest hair, then laid her head against his heart. "Better."

The rain continued to fall on them, soaking their hair and clothes, but neither noticed or cared. He stroked her back, his fingers stopping at each individual vertebra. "He hasn't fucked you worth a damn, has he?"

He felt her stiffen, and for a moment he feared that he'd gone too far, said too much, offended her with his blunt language. But it was an initial reaction that passed quickly. She relaxed against him again and said softly, "I thought so. Until a few minutes ago."

"You were hungry for it."

"I didn't know that until you touched me. My sex life was another self-delusion."

She must have felt his smile, because she raised her head and looked at him. "You must be feeling pretty good about yourself."

His grin was unrepentantly cocky, but it turned into a soft smile. "I feel good." He kissed her lips softly, growling against them, "But you feel better."

They kissed long and deeply. He was reluctant to end it but eventually did. "We'd better get back to the house before Mike organizes a search party."

He reached for the brake lever to release it, but she stopped him. "What about you? This?" She rocked her hips against his erection. "Don't you want me to . . . do something?"

Wincing, he clasped her firmly around the waist and gasped, "Yeah, I want you to stop moving like that."

"Oh. Sorry."

He gave her a crooked smile and curved his hand around the back of her neck. "When we make love, I want to be concentrating on the pleasure of it and not worrying about how I'm going to come without dumping us out of this chair."

"It's that earthshaking?"

"It will be, yes."

"But I had all the fun."

"Shows how little you know."

She smiled and he kissed her quickly, then turned them around and headed for home. "By the way, since I need two hands to drive this damn thing, you'd better button up your shirt or Mike'll get an eyeful."

* * *

The following morning Daniel got up early. He showered and dressed quickly, then packed a few changes of clothing to take to the country before going downstairs. Maxine had been most unhappy to hear about his planned weekend without her and had made her displeasure known. So he was very meek this morning when he asked her if it would be too much trouble for him to have his breakfast in the courtyard.

"No trouble at all, Mr. Matherly. It'll take me just a few minutes to get the tray ready."

"Perfect. I can use the time to make a couple of calls."

He went into his study and placed the first call to a number he now had memorized. He said little during the five-minute call. The majority of the time was spent listening.

Mr. William Sutherland finally said everything he had to say and asked, "Do you want me to proceed, Mr. Matherly?"

"By all means."

Daniel placed the second call of the morning to Becker-Howe. He wasn't surprised that even at this time of day, when most New Yorkers were queuing up at Starbucks and crowding subways to get to their offices at a reasonable hour, his call was answered by Mr. Oliver Howe himself.

Howe, rather pompously, had always boasted that he put in a fourteen-hour workday, except on holidays when he worked only eight. Apparently his schedule was as arduous as it had always been, despite his advanced age.

Howe's publishing career had been launched at approximately the same time as Daniel's and in a similar fashion. Howe was bequeathed his company from his grandfather within months of his graduation from his university. He and Daniel had remained friendly rivals through the years, and eventually their acquaintance had evolved into a grudging friendship. They held one another in the highest esteem.

"Ollie, it's Daniel Matherly."

As expected, his old colleague was delighted to hear from him. After exchanging pleasantries, Oliver Howe said, "I can't play golf anymore, Danny Boy. Goddamn rheumatism won't let me."

"That's not why I'm calling, Ollie. This is business-related."

"I thought you had retired."

"That's the rumor, but you of all people should know better. The fact is, I've run across an exciting proposition that I thought might interest you."

Daniel emerged from his study a few minutes later without the benefit of his cane. He felt invigorated. He was even rubbing his palms together as he approached Maxine. "Would you please go out and buy some bread at that Kosher bakery I like?"

"They don't have bread in Massachusetts? Mr. Reed said he was going to have the house stocked with food."

"I know, but I'm hungry for...you know the kind. With the seeds on it."

"I know the kind. That bakery is across town. I'll go after you've had breakfast."

"Noah will be picking me up after breakfast. Better go now. I can serve myself breakfast."

She eyed him suspiciously, and with good cause. His sudden yen for a particular bread was a ruse to get her out of the house. He had a guest coming for breakfast and he didn't want anyone to know about it.

Maxine continued to argue, but eventually she huffed out the service entrance, muttering to herself. She'd only been gone a few minutes when Daniel answered the front doorbell and invited his guest inside.

"My housekeeper is out on an errand," he explained as he led the way to the courtyard. Maxine always set the table for three on the chance that Maris or Noah or both would drop by. Even though Maris was out of town and Noah was due to arrive later, Daniel was relieved to see that she hadn't broken with habit. He indicated a chair at the round wrought-iron table. "Please sit. Coffee?"

"Yes, thank you."

Daniel poured. As he passed the cream and sugar, he said, "Thank you for coming on such short notice."

"It wasn't so much an invitation as an edict, Mr. Matherly."

"Then why did you come?"

"Curiosity."

Daniel acknowledged the candor with an appreciative nod.

"So you were surprised to hear from me?"

"Shocked, actually."

"I'm glad that we can speak frankly with one another, because I know your time is valuable and I'm on a tight schedule myself this morning. My son-in-law is picking me up at ten o'clock and driving me to our house in the country. He invited me to spend some quality time alone with him while my daughter is away." He lifted a napkin-lined silver basket toward his guest. "Muffin?"

"No, thanks."

"For bran muffins, they're not bad. My housekeeper makes them herself."

"No, thank you."

He returned the basket to the tabletop. "Where was I?"

"Mr. Matherly, I know that you're not in your dotage, so please don't insult my intelligence by pretending to be. You didn't invite me here to sample your housekeeper's bran muffins."

Daniel dropped the pose. Planting his elbows on the table, he clasped his hands together and looked at his guest from beneath his white eyebrows, now drawn into a steep V above the bridge of his nose.

"I would stake my fortune on the probability that when Noah and I arrive at our country place, he will have in his possession a document of some sort that empowers him to conduct business for my publishing house." He spoke with the brusque efficacy that had always been at his command and on which he had built his reputation for hard and sometimes ruthless dealing.

"Over the course of the weekend, I will be pressed into signing this document." He raised his hand to stop his guest from speaking. "No. Say nothing. You would do well only to listen."

Following a long, thoughtful, somewhat mistrustful hesitation, Daniel was motioned to continue.

"Envy" Ch. 20
Key West, Florida, 1988

Todd hadn't counted on it taking this long.

He was impatient to attain wealth and achieve fame—in that order.

After the mortgage on his parents' house was paid off, the profit he'd made on its sale had been a pittance. Each parent had carried a meager life insurance policy, but his mother had used his father's to bury him, and Todd had used hers to lay her to rest. Once all their affairs were settled, the leftovers that comprised his legacy were hardly worth counting. He barely had enough to finance his relocation to Florida and had arrived in Key West virtually penniless.

The cost of living was far higher than he and Roark had estimated, even though they were living in veritable squalor and eating cheaply. He earned good tips parking cars, but the cash was quickly consumed by rent, gas, food, and other necessities.

And his monthly installments on a PC. He, unlike his roommate, wasn't fortunate enough to have a great-uncle he had seen only twice in his entire life but who had felt a familial obligation to give his grandnephew an expensive college graduation gift. Roark's advantage had rankled. Todd had wasted no time in leveling the playing field and acquiring a computer on a lease-purchase plan.

He was bummed over his chronic shortage of legal tender.

He was even more bummed over his chronic shortage of creativity.

Fame, even more than wealth, seemed so elusive as to be out of the question. Writing fiction was hard work. He had dozed through countless boring lectures on the subject, but he was fairly certain that none of his creative writing instructors had emphasized how labor-intensive it was. That had never been a starred point in his classroom notes. That question had never been asked on an exam. True or false, writing is damn hard work.

At least once a week, he and Roark went to Hemingway's home. The Spanish Colonial estate was their shrine, and they went as pilgrims to pay homage. Todd had always been an admirer, of course. But he was only now beginning to appreciate Hemingway's greatness.

Talent was something you were born with. Either you had it or you didn't. But talent by itself was useless. Hours of tedious effort were required to awaken and exercise that talent, to write that riveting "one true sentence" that seemed so damn simple when read.

That simplicity was deceptive. It didn't happen by accident. Nor was it a skill easily acquired. Writing was demanding, solitary, backbreaking work. A writer mined the tunnels of his brain, using words for his pickaxe. A week's effort might yield only one nugget that was worth keeping, and you could weep with pathetic gratitude over that.

Todd admired those who wrote and wrote well. But his admiration was tinged with resentment. Hemingway and his ilk were stingy with their talent and skill. One would think that after having spent so much time studying their work, poring over every phrase, analyzing it word by goddamn word, the ability to write like that would rub off, that the brilliance would be contagious. Didn't desire count for something? But there were days when he couldn't find even a grain of genius in his own work.

Nor could anyone else, it seemed.

He balled up the written critique he had received from Professor Hadley and hurled it toward the corner of the room.

Roark walked in just as the paper ball landed on the floor several inches short of the trash can. "Hadley was a hard-ass?"

"Hadley is an ass*hole.*"

"Don't I know it. He raked me over the coals, too."

"Seriously?"

"Then left me there to smolder. So, what I thought is, tonight being our night off, we should get drunk."

"Love to," Todd said moodily. "Can't afford it."

"Neither can I. But being a bartender isn't without its perks." With that, Roark brought his hand from behind his back and waggled a bottle of cheap scotch.

"You stole it?"

"This piss won't be missed."

"You're a poet."

"And didn't know it. Let's go."

Todd rolled off his bunk. "You don't have to ask me twice."

On the beach, they passed the bottle back and forth between them, toasting the sunset, then the twilight, finally the night sky. They continued to toast the heavens until individual stars began to blur and bob and the universe became a little fuzzy around the edges.

"Starlight, star bright, first star...et cetera. Make a wish, Roark."

"I wish you'd pass me the whisky."

Todd handed him the bottle. Roark drank, handed it back, then stretched out on the sand and stacked his hands beneath his head. He began to laugh.

"What?" Todd asked as he used his butt to grind a more comfortable depression into the sand.

"Wishes," Roark replied. "Reminds me of a genie joke."

"There are hundreds. Which one?"

"This guy finds a magic lamp, rubs it, genie pops out, grants him three wishes. The guy wishes for a Ferrari, and *poof*! Next morning there's a shiny new Ferrari parked in his driveway. He rubs the lamp again, genie pops out, says he's got two more wishes. The guy wishes for ten million dollars and *poof*! Next morning ten million dollars is neatly stacked on his nightstand. He rubs the lamp again, genie pops out, says he's got one last wish. The guy wishes for a penis that would reach the ground, and *poof*! Next morning he wakes up and his legs are three inches long."

When their laughter subsided, Roark added, "Moral of the story, be careful what you wish for."

Todd grumbled, "I wish Hadley's dick would shrivel to nothing and then drop off. If he's even got one. Which I doubt."

"Which manuscript did you send him?"

"The historical."

"You've been working your ass off on that book. What'd he say?"

Todd took another swig from the bottle. "The plot stretches plausibility. My dialogue sucks."

"Hadley said 'sucks'?"

"Words to that effect."

"Hmm."

"What?"

"He said my dialogue was crisp and well paced, but my plot is predictable and needs punch." He looked over at Todd. "Maybe we should collaborate."

"Shit, no. No sharing. I've put in a two-year apprenticeship without any remuneration."

"You sold a short story," Roark reminded him.

"One lousy short story to a local magazine for twenty-five bucks. It'll be read in the crapper if at all." He pitched a seashell back into the surf. "I'm living in an apartment where the roaches are carnivorous and the tenants downstairs are armed and dangerous."

"But you can't beat the view. You can, however, beat your meat while taking in the view."

"There is that," Todd replied solemnly. "I've never jerked off so much in my life."

"The palm of your hand isn't sprouting hair, is it?"

"Here's to nude sunbathing among exotic dancers."

He raised the bottle in salute, but Roark took it from him and helped himself to another swallow.

"I'm broke all the friggin' time," Todd continued morosely. "My car's got over a hundred and sixty thousand miles on it."

"Meanwhile, you're parking Porsches and BMWs."

"A job you could train a chimpanzee to do."

"A chimp is cuter. Would probably get better tips."

Todd glared at Roark. "Are you gonna let me finish this or what?"

"Sorry. Didn't mean to interrupt your pity party." Roark passed the bottle back to him. "Have another drink."

"Thank you." Todd drank and belched a loud, gurgling burp. "When all this hardship pays off, I want the glory to go to me, myself, and I. No offense."

"None taken. I don't want to collaborate with you, either. I was joking."

"Oh." Todd flopped down onto his back in the sand. "So what did Hadley really say in his notes to you?"

"I told you."

"Was it the truth?"

"Why would I lie?"

"To make me feel better."

Roark snorted. "I'm not that charitable."

"Right, right, you're a son of a bitch. So maybe you would lie for another reason."

Roark sat up. "Something on your mind, Todd? If so, why don't you just say it?"

"You always downplay Hadley's critiques."

"I'm not gonna wear a hair shirt over one man's opinion, which is all his critiques are. I don't let myself get depressed over them the way you do."

"Maybe."

"Maybe what?"

"Maybe that explains why you downplay them. On the other hand, you might be trying to throw me off track."

Roark shook his head in bafflement. "What the fuck are you talking about?"

"Forget it."

"Like hell I will. First you accused me of lying and then you provided me with a shitty motivation for it. I take exception to both."

"And I take exception to your thinking you're a better writer than me."

"Than I," Roark corrected.

"Fuck you!" Todd surged to his feet, but the earth tilted drastically and threw him off balance. He landed back in the sand.

Roark grabbed him by the shoulders and brought him around. "Why would I deliberately mislead you about Hadley's critiques?"

Todd flung his hands up and threw Roark's off. "To get the jump on me. You can't stand the idea of me getting—of *my* getting—published before you."

"Oh, like you'd be thrilled if I sold a manuscript ahead of you."

"I'd rather have my guts ripped out up through my throat."

For several moments the narrow distance between them was volatile, teeming with molecules of hostility ready to spark. Todd made his hands into fists in anticipation of an attack.

To his surprise, Roark started to laugh. "You'd rather have your guts ripped out up through your throat?"

Todd tried not to smile, but he lost the battle and soon he was laughing, too. "In the heat of the moment, not to mention my inebriation, that's all I could think of to say."

"I don't recommend it for your book."

"Point taken."

They stared at the oceanscape for several minutes, then Roark said, "I'm done for the night. Think we can make it to the car?"

Todd took satisfaction in Roark's being the first to cave. "Fuck, man, I don't know. I'm wasted."

Roark threw his arm across Todd's shoulders and

helped him to his feet. They made it to the parking lot, although it took a while because they stumbled often and stopped frequently. Their drunken efforts made them weak-kneed with hilarity. Neither was in any condition to drive, but Roark got behind the wheel because he was slightly less drunk than Todd.

It was past noon the following day, as they medicated their hangovers with burgers and fries, that Todd resumed the conversation. "You know, a little rivalry could be good for us."

Roark groaned. "Don't start that again. I don't consider you a rival, Todd."

"Bullshit. Of course you do."

"How could rivalry possibly be good for us?"

"It makes us work harder. Admit it, when you see me writing, there's no way you can shirk off. If I'm at my keyboard, you can't sit down and watch a ball game on TV. I'm the same. If you're writing, I feel guilty if I'm not writing, too. If you put in seven hours a day, I've got to put in at least that much. That competitive edge is what drives us."

"I'm driven by nothing except a desire to write good fiction."

Todd waved his hands in the air. "Saint Roark. Glory and hallelujah."

"You're pissing me off."

"Okay, okay, I'll drop it." He took a bite of his cheeseburger. "Anyway, the point's moot. I'll be offered megabucks for *The Vanquished* before you even complete your book. Then we'll see who's green with envy."

"That is *not* going to happen."

Todd laughed. "Oh, man, I wish you could see the malicious glint in your eye. You just won my argument for me."

Chapter 24

———◆———

I s there any coffee?"

"Isn't there always?"

Parker shot Mike a dark glance as he rolled his chair across the kitchen and poured himself a fresh mug from the coffeemaker. "Usually you come and ask if I'd like a refill, check and see if I need anything."

"I didn't want to take a chance on having my head bit off. You made it plain at breakfast that Maris and I should make ourselves scarce today, and that's what we're doing."

"I'm working on a difficult passage. I didn't want any distractions or interruptions."

He was on his way back through the connecting door when he heard Mike mutter, "You could've asked us nicely."

Parker stopped and reversed direction. "Did you say something?"

Mike threw down the dish towel he'd been using and did an about face. "I said her blouse was buttoned wrong last night when you finally saw fit to bring her in out of the rain and let me know where you were."

"Wow! You covered several transgressions in one sentence, Mike. Shall we break it down and discuss it iniquity by iniquity? Or should I just acknowledge that you're riled in general and get back to my work?"

"I came home after a day on the mainland to find the house wide open, lights on, nobody home. I thought you'd been abducted."

"Did it occur to you that I could have been taken up in the Rapture and that you'd been left behind? Bet that really would've pissed you off."

"You and the Rapture are irreconcilable themes. I would never pair you with a thought about it. And I soon ruled out the possibility of kidnapping. Who'd be crazy enough to want you?"

"Man! You *are* ticked."

"I have a right to be. I wouldn't have even known Maris had come back if I hadn't noticed two sets of dishes in the sink and went out to check the guest house."

"You're a regular Sherlock Holmes."

"You could have left a note telling me you were going down to the beach."

"I could have. But I was afraid your maternal instincts would kick in and you'd follow us down there to make sure we kiddies were all right."

"And not up to any mischief."

Parker dropped all vestiges of humor, saying tightly, "That's right, Mike. I didn't want you to catch us playing naughty. I wouldn't care, but Maris might."

"Which brings me to the next point."

"I don't want to hear it."

"You've cooked up a plot of vengeance and you're going to act it out to the bitter end, aren't you?"

"We've been over this."

"Aren't you?"

"Damn right I am!" Parker shouted.

His raised voice didn't deter Mike, however. "What's the final chapter going to be?"

"What, give away the ending? Tell you and spoil the surprise? I don't think so."

Mike glared at him. "It's not going to be a happy ending."

"I'm not after rave reviews."

"Only revenge."

"Which always makes for good motivation, ergo a good plot. Now, are you finished?"

"Not quite. What about Maris?"

"She's definitely a plot device."

"You're using her, aren't you? In spite of who she is."

"*Because* of who she is."

Mike must have sensed Parker's unshakable resolve. Or maybe his imperious tone reminded the older man that he had overstepped his bounds. Or maybe he simply wore out. Whatever the cause, Mike's anger dissolved. His angry posture settled back into its elderly sag. "Parker, I implore you to give this up. Let go of it. Tell Maris everything. For your good as well as hers. Tell her."

"Tell me what?"

* * *

At the sound of her voice, the two men turned quickly. Evidently she had walked into a spirited exchange, and it felt like a quarrel. "Tell me what?" she repeated.

"I've written some new pages," Parker said. "They're printing out now."

"I'll get them." Mike gave Parker a look that was rife with meaning. But whatever the meaning was, Maris couldn't decipher it. He went into the solarium, leaving them alone.

"He just made a fresh pot of coffee," Parker remarked.

"Thanks, but I've passed my limit. If I drink any more this

morning, I'll be swinging from the chandelier along with your ghost friend."

"I'd pay to see that." His smile was forced and the attempted humor fell flat.

Maris couldn't account for the mood in the house, mainly because she couldn't define the mood. It had started last night when she and Parker returned from the beach. Mike, who had arrived in their absence, had been on the veranda watching for them, standing with his hands on his hips and looking perturbed. He'd admonished them for getting soaked to the skin. He said he expected that kind of nutty, irresponsible behavior from Parker, but Parker had no right to subject Maris to his zaniness.

He had then hustled Parker into his bedroom at the back of the house. Maris knew which room it was, but she'd never been invited to see it, not even when Mike had conducted her on a guided tour of the house, including his suite and the unfinished rooms on the second floor.

Feeling slightly downcast over the abrupt conclusion to the romantic evening, she had returned to the guest cottage. She sensed that it wasn't their getting caught in the rain or even their unexplained absence from the house that had upset Mike. He was more than slightly annoyed, more concerned than the situation had warranted.

She couldn't figure out what they had done or hadn't done to provoke him.

If it were anyone else, she would guess that the personal valet was jealous of the newcomer. It stood to reason that someone in Mike's position would resent an intruder into the comfortable life he had made for his charge. Their days had a rhythm that he wouldn't want disturbed.

Understandably the interloper would be regarded as a threat. His first instinct would be to protect his position and importance. He would also want to shield the individual he cared for against any potential harm.

But Mike hadn't behaved jealously toward her. He didn't treat her as a danger who might damage Parker. On the contrary, he seemed genuinely pleased that she had entered their lives. He'd shown her every kindness, and, in even the most insignificant disputes, he took her side over Parker's more often than not.

Nevertheless, she couldn't help but feel that Mike had a general idea of what they'd been doing down at the beach and that he disapproved. Whatever else had factored in, this was the basis of his indignation. When she returned to the guest cottage, she'd discovered that she hadn't buttoned her shirt correctly, that in her haste, she'd skipped a button. A dead giveaway to hanky-panky.

Still, she was more mystified than embarrassed. She and Parker were well beyond the age of accountability, and it should have been clear to Mike that whatever had transpired on the beach had been consensual. Could it be a moral issue with him? Not knowing the present state of her marriage, did Mike think Parker was romancing another man's wife?

In any case, their return to the house had quelled any plans either she or Parker had for continuing what had been started on the beach. She prudently remained in the guest cottage until this morning, and although she'd lain awake for a long time half expecting Parker to come to her, he hadn't. This morning at breakfast, he'd been testy and irritable. More so than usual. And he'd acted as though their time on the beach together had never happened.

All this was weighing heavily on her mind. She was trying desperately to stave off a bad case of the blues. Despite the tender lovemaking last night, her relationship with Parker was still unspecified and tenuous. At any moment, she feared a geocentric shift of emotions that would plunge her headlong into despair.

She'd been made a fool of by one man. She didn't want to repeat that particular mistake. Ever. But certainly not within the same week.

Following that first lame attempt at conversation about caffeine, neither she nor Parker had said a word. Their eye contact had been haphazard and fleeting. Parker seemed to be making a concerted effort to avoid it altogether.

Feeling awkward, she asked if he was happy with what he'd written that morning.

"It's all right, I guess," he mumbled into his coffee mug, keeping his head down.

This was silly. They were grown-ups, not adolescents. Up till now, he had seized every opportunity to slip a blatant sexual innuendo into their conversation. He certainly hadn't been shy about demonstrating his attraction to her, starting with the night they met. His sudden bashfulness made no sense.

"Did Mike lecture you?"

He looked over at her. "About the foreplay?"

"I...I was going to say about seducing a married woman."

"Is that what I did?"

"Not without a lot of encouragement."

"Then does it count as a bona fide seduction?"

"Parker, are we going to play a game of semantics, or are you going to answer my question?"

"Mike is concerned for you."

"Why?"

"He thinks I'm rotten to the core."

"He thinks the sun rises and sets in you."

"He's afraid I'll hurt you."

Looking at him intently, she asked, "Will you?"

"Yes."

Startled by his blunt reply, she sat down at the kitchen table without breaking the eye contact they had finally established. "At least you're honest."

"Brutally so. It puts most people off."

"Noted. But I'm not most people."

The hard line of his lips softened. Something sparked in his eyes, which had been so remote only seconds ago. They moved over her, alighting for a time on her mouth, her breasts, her lap. Those spots that had experienced his intimate touch began to tingle with sensual recollection.

When his gaze reconnected with hers, he said gruffly, "Noted."

They lapsed into a long stare that went unbroken until Mike reentered the kitchen, bringing with him several pages of text. "The print was getting dim, so I had to replace the cartridge." He handed the pages of manuscript to Maris.

"I need to get back to it," Parker said, wheeling his chair toward the solarium. "Don't talk about me while I'm gone."

"We've got better things to talk about," Mike retorted.

Parker slammed the door shut behind him.

Maris laughed. "You two are like quarreling siblings. Or an old married couple."

"God forbid."

"Were you ever married, Mike?"

"A confirmed bachelor. How does crab au gratin sound for dinner?"

"Delicious. Was Parker?"

"Married? No."

"Women?"

He removed a package of frozen crabmeat from the freezer and set it on the countertop before turning to her. "What do you think?"

She lowered her eyes and traced the wood grain in the tabletop with her fingertip. "Of course there have been women."

"More than a few, fewer than many. Nothing lasting. Never serious."

She nodded. He went back to assembling the ingredients for his recipe.

"Parker shared with me how you rescued him from the pit, so to speak."

When he turned back to her, she saw that this revelation had surprised him. But he recovered and said, "He gives me more credit than I deserve. All I did was tell him things he already knew."

"Like?"

"I told him that he was on a sure path of self-destruction. However, I pointed out to him what a slow path he'd taken. I asked why he was dilly-dallying. I told him that if he truly wanted to be dead, he could have found a way to take himself out."

"Good psychology."

He shrugged modestly. "The main thing is, it worked." He indicated the manuscript pages she had carried in with her from the guest house. "Do you like the latest installment?"

"I've been rereading the chapter about Mary Catherine's miscarriage. Todd is beginning to reveal himself as the villain."

"Interesting," Mike murmured. "That you think of him as the villain."

"Aren't I supposed to?"

"I believe that's Parker's intention, yes."

"Do you read everything he writes?"

"Only what he asks me to."

"Which is?"

He grinned at her as he reached into the cabinet for a casserole dish. "Everything he writes."

"I'm sure he values your opinion."

Mike scoffed at that. "He thinks the only opinion that counts is his."

"It's more the feedback than the opinion that he wants. I've learned by working with writers that they like having a sounding board. Even if the sounding board never talks back, they need someone to listen to them as they process thoughts and ideas. You perform a valuable service to Parker—beyond the obvious."

He didn't carry the conversation toward the "obvious" services he performed for Parker. Instead he asked if any of her associates at Matherly Press had read the manuscript.

"To honor Parker's request for anonymity, I'm keeping it under wraps. I did share it with my father, though. He's as positive about it as I am."

"Nobody else?"

"No."

Several times she had urged Noah to read it. Each time he had shown little interest, but in a rushed and absentminded way had promised that he would get to it as soon as his schedule permitted. Now she knew why his schedule was so tight. Much of his time had been allocated to his mistress.

Switching gears, she said, "Speaking of Dad..." It was unlikely that her cell phone had rung without her hearing it, but she took it from her skirt pocket and checked the lighted readout. No missed calls. "I should go call him again. I haven't been able to get an answer at his house this morning, and that's unusual."

She wasn't worried yet, just a little curious as to why Maxine was out so long. Ordinarily she had supplies delivered so she wouldn't have to leave the house and Daniel unattended for extended periods of time. Her errands were usually quickly dispatched.

Daniel hadn't gone to the office today; Maris had checked.

So apparently he and Maxine were out somewhere together. Maybe they'd gone for a walk in Central Park, or to a museum, or to a movie. Daniel enjoyed all those things, and Maxine sometimes accompanied him, welcoming the break from her routine.

But Maris had been trying to reach them for hours. She had left voice-mail messages for them to call her as soon as they returned. Either they hadn't checked for messages or they had been out for a very long time, and one was as uncustomary as the other.

"You're welcome to use our phone," Mike told her.

"Thanks, but I'll use my cell." Before leaving she asked Mike if there was anything she could do to help him with dinner. "I'm a working woman, but not a total stranger to the kitchen."

"I'll let you pour the wine when the time comes."

She had known he would refuse her offer, as Maxine always did, but she wanted to offer anyway. "Then will you excuse me?" Collecting the new pages of manuscript, she headed for the back door. "I'm eager to curl up with the next chapter."

Chapter 25

Noah answered his ringing cell phone. "Hello?"

"Where are you?"

"Nadia?"

"Yes, Noah, Nadia," she replied waspishly.

He took a cautionary glance over his shoulder to make certain that Daniel hadn't yet made his way downstairs. Afternoon sunlight was pouring in through the open slats of the window shutters, casting long stripes of light and shadow across the hardwood floor and lending the pale saffron walls a mellow glow.

The Matherlys' country house was a bit fussy and cluttered to suit his taste. He favored contemporary. Right angles and sleek surfaces. But for what it was, the restored Colonial had been nicely done. Several years ago it had been featured in *Architectural Digest*—the country retreat of a book-publishing icon.

Here in the living room the easy chairs were wide and deep, and each had a requisite footstool. The intricate brass fireplace screen was an original to the house. Rosemary Matherly's collection of china plates from all over the world was displayed behind the glass doors of a tall cabinet.

Scattered about on end tables and in shelves were photographs of Daniel with notable authors and luminaries from other fields of endeavor ranging from the entertainment industry, to sports, to politics, including two presidents. Pictures of Maris chronicled her childhood, adolescence, and emergence into young womanhood.

There were several photos of Noah and Maris together. One taken at their wedding reception showed the laughing bride hand-feeding him a bite of wedding cake. He took perverse pleasure in looking at it now as he talked to his most recent mistress.

"I've been calling you all day," she said.

"And I've been avoiding you. When I see one of your numbers on the caller ID, I let it ring."

"I figured that. So this time I'm calling from a friend's phone."

"Male or female?"

"That depends on whether or not you're speaking to me."

"You've got a selective memory, Nadia. Obviously you've forgotten why I'm not speaking to you."

"Of course I haven't forgotten. But I woke up this morning deciding to forgive you, so—"

"You decided to forgive *me*? I didn't boink my personal trainer."

"I've seen your personal trainer, Noah. No one would want to boink him."

She was at it again. Mocking him. Being condescending. Just as she'd been when he found her swaddled in damp sheets and postcoitus bliss. Hearing the ridicule in her voice now resurrected the rage he'd felt then. The emotion that had roiled inside him hadn't been inspired by jealousy. He couldn't care less who she fucked or how often. Being mocked by her—that's what had rankled.

Rather than reacting with embarrassment, or remorse, or shame, or fear—which was the reaction he really craved to see from her—she had smiled at him insolently. How dare the bitch.

He'd been angry enough to kill her. He'd even entertained vivid mental flashes of placing his hands around her slender neck and squeezing until her eyes bulged, squeezing until her heart stopped.

He'd had the presence of mind not to act on the murderous impulse, but it had been strong enough for him to get a glimpse of his soul's dark side. Like the dark side of the moon, it was out of sight, but always there.

Several times during his life, it had been necessary to step over the boundary between light and darkness. But those brief forays into that dark region had left him shaken, feeling that he'd been lucky to return. He didn't venture into it unless he was given no other choice.

But recently he'd taken two prolonged glimpses into its shadows. First with Maris outside Nadia's apartment following her discovery of their affair. Then again with Nadia. In both instances, he'd wanted badly to hurt the offender. Silence her. Injure her beyond recovery. Kill her.

He was intrigued now, beguiled by the extent of his dark side. He hadn't known it was so expansive and dense. The urge to explore it to its farthest reaches was almost irresistible.

Never guessing the malicious nature of his thoughts, Nadia still believed they were arguing over her fling with the weight lifter.

"The point is that you acted like a complete ass at lunch that day, Noah. I felt it appropriate to remind you that nobody calls Nadia Schuller 'incredibly stupid' and gets away with it. You got in your shot, and I got in mine. Now can we please move beyond this?"

He was tempted to call her the obscene name that so aptly applied and then hang up. That's what he wanted to do. But it wouldn't be smart to alienate her now. The deal with WorldView hung in the balance. Breaking with Nadia might jinx it. Morris Blume seemed to like her. She'd been instrumental in bringing them together. Why not continue to take advantage of her use-fulness? Ultimately she would get what she had coming, but not until the WorldView deal was secured. His reward for eating a small portion of crow now would be ten million dollars. In fact, for ten million dollars and control of Matherly Press, he was willing to do much worse.

"Noah, please. Please tell me where you are."

Her voice had turned soft and conciliatory. She was even making it easy on him. It was a win-win situation, and he couldn't ask for better.

Smiling to himself, he said, "I'm alone in the country house with my father-in-law."

"Daniel Matherly?"

He chuckled. "He's the only father-in-law I've got."

"Why would you subject yourself to that?"

"Actually I invited him. We've got business to discuss."

"Ah, WorldView. You're planning a coup de grâce."

"Precisely." He explained that Maris was out of town again and that Maxine had been left in the city. "It's just me and the old man. Fishing. Male bonding."

"Then a little arm-twisting."

"I doubt it'll come to that."

"He's not going to give in easily, Noah."

"Not easily, but he'll eventually be persuaded. I'm sure of it."

"Need a cheerleader for your side? I could drive up. You could tuck me into a corner somewhere. Is the country house roomy enough to accommodate you, me, and your father-in-law?"

"Interesting proposition. I'm tempted to sneak you in, but it wouldn't be prudent. Once the old man is into his cups, he tends to wander. What if he ventured into the wrong bedroom and saw something straight out of the *Kama Sutra*?"

"Which page?"

"You're incorrigible."

"Absolutely. I have no shame whatsoever. That's why I'm willing to risk being caught. If the old man stumbles in on us, who knows? It might do his heart good." She lowered her voice seductively. "The best sex is making-up sex, you know. I could bring along a box of chocolates. The gooey kind. The ones with the soft, creamy centers that you love to lick out."

"Good phone sex, Nadia. I'm aroused," he said truthfully.

"Give me two hours."

"I wish I could see you right now. But you know that you can't come here."

"Oh, I know it's out of the question. I have an enormous stake in this merger, too, and wouldn't do anything to jeopardize it. It's just that I miss you. Guess I'll have to be satisfied with my trusty vibrator."

"Do you have enough batteries?"

"I'm never without."

"Oops, I hear Daniel coming. Must go. I'll see you when I get back to the city."

"Later, darling."

He clicked off, then added, "Love you, too, sweetheart," to a dead phone. He turned just in time to see Daniel entering the living room. "Oh, damn! That was Maris. She wouldn't let me call you to the phone, afraid she'd be interrupting a nap. Want me to get her back? She said they were about to sit down to dinner, but I can probably catch—"

"No, no. How is she?"

"Working hard on the manuscript. Says it's awfully hot. The weather, not the manuscript," he added with a grin. "Misses us terribly, otherwise fine."

"Then don't bother her." Daniel settled into one of the easy chairs and propped his cane beside it. "I worked up quite a thirst during my nap."

Noah laughed easily as he crossed to the table that served as a bar. "Thirsty work, naps. Double scotch?"

"On the rocks, please."

"I called the deli in town. They'll soon be delivering double-thick Reuben sandwiches, potato salad made with real mayo, chocolate cake and vanilla ice cream for dessert."

"God, I love the bachelor life," Daniel said as he accepted the drink from his son-in-law. "What a good idea this was."

* * *

Maris was glad she had changed for dinner because for the first time since her arrival, it was being served in the formal dining room, the hanging ghost notwithstanding.

She was wearing a gray silk dress she had bought early in the season at Bergdorf's, thinking it would be perfect for dinner out in the country. She reasoned that the lightweight fabric, slip-style bodice, and flared skirt were also perfect for dinner at home in an antebellum plantation house. She had accessorized it with a choker of pale coral beads.

Mike had laid a beautiful table. Fragrant magnolia blossoms had been arranged in a crystal bowl in the center of the table, flanked by silver candlesticks with white tapers. He'd used china, silver, and crystal stemware that represented good taste and a sizable investment.

"This is lovely, Mike," she remarked as he held the lyre-back chair for her.

"Don't be too impressed," Parker said from his place at the head of the table. "It's all rented for the evening."

"Yes, from Terry's Bar and Grill," Mike said drolly. "Besides smoking baby back ribs, he does a huge formal party rental business."

She laughed. "Wherever it came from, I like it."

"It all belonged to Parker's mother," Mike informed her as he poured the wine, forgetting that he'd delegated that job to her.

She looked toward Parker for confirmation. "The tableware was handed down through generations of Mom's family. It was bequeathed to either the first daughter or daughter-in-law. My mother had neither, so it came to me by default. It's been in storage since she died. This is the first time it's been used." He slid a glance toward Mike. "Can't imagine what the special occasion is."

Maris raised her wineglass. "To the completion of *Envy*."

"I'll drink to that." Mike raised his glass.

"It's not finished yet," Parker reminded them, but he raised his glass all the same.

The crystal stems sounded like chimes when they clinked them together. The Pinot Grigio was cold and crisp, a perfect complement to the meal Mike had prepared.

Parker might have disavowed that this was a special occasion, but she noticed that he had changed for dinner, too. She wondered if Mike had mandated the extra grooming or if it had been voluntary. Although his only nod toward styling his hair was to rake his fingers through it, the tousled look suited him. He had recently shaved; she could smell the sandalwood soap. He was wearing his customary casual pants, but his shirt was tucked in. The sleeves were rolled back to just below his elbows, revealing his strong forearms.

The candlelight blurred the lines that years of pain had etched into his face. It softened the hardness that resentment had stamped on his features and allayed the bitterness that compromised his smiles.

He also seemed to be relaxed and enjoying himself. While they ate, he regaled them with wild stories about Terry, of Bar and Grill fame, who was reputed to be everything from a modern-day pirate to a drug runner to a white slave trader.

"I don't know or care which rumor is true or if any of them are. He grills one hell of a burger."

Maris shuddered at the memory of the tavern. "I can't recommend the place. Totally unsavory clientele."

"Hey!" Parker said, looking affronted.

She gracefully turned the conversation back to the book. "The tension mounts."

"I presume you mean between Roark and Todd."

"It's becoming palpable," she said. "What I read today leads me to believe that it's soon to come to a head."

"I'm giving nothing away."

"A hint? Please?"

He looked at Mike. "Think I should divulge a few plot twists?"

The older man considered it for several seconds. "She *is* your editor."

"That's right, I is," Maris declared. They laughed, then she leaned toward Parker to make her appeal. "What if you're about to make a fatal mistake, editorially speaking? If you talk me through the next few scenes, I could steer you clear of any potential pitfalls and save you a lot of rewrites."

Parker's eyes narrowed suspiciously. "You know what that sounds like? A veiled threat."

"Not at all." She flashed him a saccharine smile. "It's outright extortion."

He placed his palm over the mouth of his wineglass, and his strong fingers absently traced the pattern cut into the crystal. His eyes remained on her. She looked back at him with challenge.

Mike pushed back his chair and stood up. "Who's ready for strawberry sorbet? I made it myself from fresh berries."

Without disengaging her eyes from Parker's, she asked, "Need any help?"

"No, thank you." Mike went into the kitchen through the connecting door and it swung closed behind him.

Maris was slightly short of breath. Her tummy felt weightless despite the meal she'd just eaten. Two glasses of wine were hardly enough to make her feel this light-headed. So she attributed her sudden case of the flutters to the way Parker was looking at her—like she was the tastiest item at the table that evening.

"Well? What's it to be, Mr. Parker?"

"Tell you what." His eyes, which had strayed to the vicinity of her breasts, moved slowly up to her face. "We'll play a game of high-card draw."

She arched her brow inquisitively.

"Remember the scene in *Grass Widow*," he continued, "where Cayton and the reluctant witness to the murder played that game?"

"Vaguely," she lied. Actually she remembered it vividly. When the book was published, that scene had created a buzz. "Erotically charged," was how *Publishers Weekly* had described it. "The reluctant witness was a woman, right?"

"Frenchy. Fragile, fair, and flighty. So nicknamed because—"

"That part I remember."

He grinned a fox's grin. The one he grinned right after isolating the plumpest hen in the flock. Maris knew she'd been had, but she didn't care. In fact, she was struggling to contain the idiotic smile her lips were aching to smile.

Pulling a serious face, she said, "My memory is a little dim on the rules of this game."

"Easy. They used a standard deck of cards. They each draw a card. High card wins."

"Wins what?"

"If Cayton won, Frenchy had to give him a clue to the murderer's identity."

"What if she drew the high card?"

"Cayton granted her a sexual favor."

"*He* granted *her* a sexual favor."

"Right."

She tapped her pursed lips with her fingertip as though stymied by the illogic. "It seems to me that—and correct me if I'm wrong—that Cayton would win either way."

"Well, see, he made up the rules, and he's no dummy."

"But Frenchy—"

"A crotch-throb by any standards. Long red hair. Legs that go on forever. Pale freckles on her tits. An ass that...Well, you know the type. But, unfortunately, she's not the brightest bulb in the chandelier."

Maris gave the swaying chandelier overhead a glance before continuing. "So the outcome of this game was that Cayton got the information *and* the crotch-throb."

"Was that a brilliant idea or what?"

"And you expect me to be no brighter than Frenchy? You expect me to play by these rules?"

"I guess that depends."

"On how badly I want to hear those plot twists?"

"Or on how badly you want those sexual favors."

Chapter 26

Daniel was holding in his hand the final handiwork of Howard Bancroft's legal career. Noah had waited until after dinner to produce it. They were relaxing in the cozy living room, now lighted only by the soft glow of table lamps.

Daniel had just finished reading the power-of-attorney document. He peered at Noah over his reading glasses. "So, there was an ulterior motive behind this weekend of togetherness."

Noah expelled a puff of cigar smoke. "Not at all, Daniel. I could have presented this to you in the city. At any time."

"But you chose to give it to me here. Why?"

"Because here in the country your mind is uncluttered. We can talk uninterrupted, away from the distractions of the office, without Maxine fussing over you at home. We can speak frankly, one man to another, son-in-law to father-in-law."

He could see that the old man was still dubious. He had expected him to be. In fact, he had expected a fiery outburst. Daniel's reaction was much milder than Noah had been braced for.

But the old man was stubborn and unpredictable. His mood

could fluctuate drastically within seconds. There might yet be an eruption of temper, and it might come at any moment. Noah watched warily as Daniel worked his way out of his easy chair and propped himself on his cane.

Noah leaned forward solicitously. "Do you need something, Daniel? More port? Let me get it for you."

"I'll get it myself, thank you," Daniel said brusquely.

He did so, leaving Noah in a state of carefully concealed agitation. His feet were propped on the ottoman in front of his chair. His posture was a slouch. He appeared to have nothing weightier on his mind than the smoke rings he blew toward the ceiling.

Daniel returned to his chair and declined to speak until he had taken a few sips of his port. "If this is a family meeting, why have you chosen to conduct it when one family member is noticeably absent?"

Noah took his time answering. He studied the smoldering tip of his cigar as though carefully choosing, then analyzing, what he was about to say. "This is an extremely delicate matter, Daniel."

"Which is my point."

"Mine also. It's not an issue to spring on Maris over the telephone." He took a sip of his single-malt scotch. As he returned the tumbler to the end table, he noticed the wedding reception photograph of them. He touched the silver frame wistfully and smiled fondly. "Maris thinks first with her heart, then with her head." His gaze moving back to Daniel, he added, "You know that. You've lived with her longer than I have."

"She's not a child."

"True. She's a woman, and her instincts and reactions are purely feminine. They're endearing. They make her the lovely person she is. But they don't always serve her well professionally. Remember how emotionally she reacted last week when she learned of my meeting with WorldView? I predict her reaction to this document would be even more irrational."

For several moments he stared at the document that now lay

on the coffee table between them. "If I know my wife, she would panic. She would think that we're shielding her from something ugly. She would leap to an erroneous conclusion. You have terminal cancer. You need a heart transplant. You... well, you get my drift. God knows what she would imagine, and we would have a hell of a time dispelling her worst fears."

He shook his head and laughed softly. "Last week she accused us of leaving her out of the loop and needlessly protecting her from an unpleasant situation. If—"

"If I sign that document without discussing it with her first, she'll be furious with us."

"No doubt. I guess it comes down to choosing when we want to have a scene like the one we had last week. Before or after the document is in place. If it's before, her response time will be protracted. She'll put you through a battery of physical exams before she's satisfied that you're not at death's door.

"If it's after the document is signed," he continued, "her reaction time will be abbreviated. Which, personally, I think is our best option. We all have better things to do with our time and energy." He paused to take a few puffs on his cigar. "I'm thinking of Maris, too, Daniel. I'm trying to spare her from having to make a difficult decision. She cannot bring herself to accept some of life's inescapable certainties."

"Like my mortality."

Noah nodded solemnly. "Or even the possibility of reduced capacity. She is in complete denial on the subject. You've always been her hero. She would look upon this document as a betrayal of that image. She might even feel that by executing a power-of-attorney document like this, we're tempting fate. That as soon as she signs it, you'll be stricken with a debilitating malady."

He paused strategically and pretended to consider his wife's behavior. "In all honesty, I doubt Maris would sign it at all unless you had signed it first. That would ease her mind. Relieve her conscience and her sense of responsibility."

Daniel picked up the document with one hand and tugged thoughtfully on his lower lip with the other. "I'm not a moron, Noah."

Noah's breath caught in his throat.

"I see the validity of such a document."

He expelled that anxious breath slowly and tried to sound perfectly composed as he said, "Apparently so did Howard. He authored it."

"Which puzzles me. Howard knew that a similar document is already in place, along with my will and other personal documents. Mr. Stern drew them up years ago, but Howard had copies in his files."

"As Howard explained it to me, those documents were outdated."

And now came the tricky part. Up to this point, he had counted on it being an exercise in persuasion. His arguments were sound, and, as Daniel had noted, not without validity. Now, however, he must do some fancy footwork and one misstep could trip him up.

With calculated casualness, he rolled the ash off the tip of his cigar into a pewter ashtray. "I think Howard realized how obsolete that previous power-of-attorney document was. He brought it to my attention first, instead of bringing it up with Maris, for the reasons we've cited tonight. He didn't want to upset her."

"Why didn't he bring it to my attention?"

"For the same reason, Daniel." He averted his gaze as though it pained him to say what he was compelled to say. "Howard was worried what your reaction would be. He didn't want you to think that he thought you were no longer capable of making these kinds of decisions for yourself."

"We were better friends than that," Daniel snapped. "For God's sake, we'd been confiding candidly in each other for decades. I had joked with him about the foibles of growing old."

"This goes beyond complaining about a few aches and pains.

Howard was sensitive to the delicate nature of this document." Noah raised his hand when he saw that Daniel was about to interrupt. "I'm only telling you what he told me. He was afraid you would take umbrage."

"That I'd shoot the messenger?"

Noah shrugged as though to say, *Something like that.* "It's such a personal, private matter, Howard thought it might be better if someone in the family were to bring it to your attention."

Daniel harrumphed and took a sip of port. He flipped through the document again. He paused to reread a particular clause, and even before he said anything, Noah knew which clause had snagged his attention.

"Until Maris signs this—"

"I would have full power of attorney. I know. I spotted that flaw, too."

"Why would Howard construct the document this way, when he knew it would go expressly against my wishes? Not that I mistrust you, Noah, but Maris is Matherly Press, and vice versa. There will never be a decision made or acted upon without her involvement and approval."

"Of course. Howard knew that. As do I. As does everyone. When I pointed the loophole out to him, he was mortified and acknowledged that it was an oversight."

Noah chuckled. "I think his Old World heritage sneaked in while he wasn't looking. He was thinking of Maris as a daughter and wife, not as a senior executive of a multimillion-dollar company. He had enormous affection for her, as you know, and probably still regarded her as the sweet little girl in pigtails he used to bounce on his knee. Anyhow, I insisted that he add the codicil on the last page, which stipulates that the document is invalid until signed by all of us."

He hoped that Daniel wouldn't notice that the last page could be detached without it appearing that the document had been tampered with or altered. That had been a last-minute brainstorm, one he should have thought of sooner. He'd hired the unscrupulous lawyer with whom he'd threatened Bancroft to write the codicil. The legalese sounded legitimate, although it lacked the classy touch of the rest of the document. He hoped Daniel wouldn't notice that, either.

Noah took one final draw on his cigar, then ground out the lighted tip and left it lying in the ashtray. He slapped his thighs lightly as he stood up, officially closing his sales pitch. "Speaking for myself, I'm bushed. Obviously you need to sleep on this. We can talk about it later. Have you thought about what you'd like for breakfast? There's enough food—"

"I don't need to sleep on it," Daniel said abruptly. "Let me sign the damn thing and get it over with. I'm tired of talking about it."

Noah hesitated. "Don't decide anything this weekend, Daniel. Take the document back to the city. Have Mr. Stern review it."

"And by doing so question the judgment of my late friend? No. Howard's suicide has already generated nasty speculation. I won't have people saying that his competence had slipped. Where's a damn pen?"

"Signing won't make it legal. It has to be notarized." That had been another potential problem with an obvious solution— the lawyer downtown, whose breath was stronger than his principles. After this was all settled, Noah would have to deal with him or risk being blackmailed. But that was a problem for another day.

"We'll make it official once we get to the city," Daniel grumbled. "But I want this matter concluded tonight. For my own peace of mind. Otherwise I won't be able to relax, or think about breakfast, or anything else. Tomorrow, I want nothing on my mind more problematic than baiting a hook. So give me a goddamn pen."

Noah's acting performance was superb, if he did say so himself. He reluctantly produced a pen and passed it over to Daniel.

But before releasing it, he gazed deeply into Daniel's eyes. "You've had a lot to drink," he said, oozing concern. "Nothing will be lost by waiting until—"

Daniel yanked the pen from his son-in-law's hand and scrawled his signature on the appropriate line.

* * *

The dinner party on St. Anne Island was moved out onto the veranda when a yellow jacket invaded the dining room.

The buzzing menace appeared out of nowhere and alighted on the rim of Maris's as-yet-unused coffee cup. She sent up a faint squeal—ill-timed because it immediately followed Parker's statement about sexual favors.

Remembering the instruction of a summer camp counselor many years before as to what one should do when stinging insects threatened, she froze in place.

Parker, seeing the real cause of her squeal, yelled, "Mike! Bug spray! Now!"

Mike charged out of the kitchen armed with a can of Black Flag. He aimed it with deadly accuracy, and the yellow jacket died an agonizing death, witnessed by the three who fanned chemical fumes away from their faces.

Parker ventured that the pest had been hiding in the flowers in the centerpiece. Mike insisted that if the magnolia blooms had had a yellow jacket in them when he brought them inside, he would have discovered it long before now.

Before a full-blown argument could ensue, Maris tactfully submitted that the insect could have gotten into the house any number of ways, and then suggested that they take their desserts onto the veranda, which should be comfortably cool if Mike were to turn on the ceiling fans that had been thoughtfully installed during the house's refurbishing.

He served their pink sorbets in frosted compotes garnished

with sprigs of mint. Maris insisted on pouring the coffee in the gracious manner that Maxine had taught her and accomplished serving them without one rattle of cup against saucer.

Parker frowned down into the bone china cup. "This thimble doesn't hold enough coffee to taste. What's wrong with an ordinary mug?"

Neither she nor Mike paid any attention to his grumbling. She rocked contentedly in the porch swing, listening to the night sounds that had been so foreign to her when she arrived and had now become so familiar.

"Penny for them," Parker said.

"I was wondering if I'll ever become reaccustomed to the sounds of traffic on Manhattan's streets. I've gotten used to cicadas and bullfrogs."

Mike gathered their empty dessert dishes onto a tray, then carried it into the house.

As soon as Mike was out of earshot, Parker asked, "Planning on leaving us anytime soon?"

The overhead fans blew gently on his hair. The light spilling through the front windows was cast onto only one side of his face, leaving the other side in shadow. Maris couldn't make out his eyes at all, and what she could see of his expression was inscrutable.

"I'll have to leave eventually," she replied softly. "When your first draft of *Envy* is finished and you no longer need me around."

"Two different things entirely, Maris."

His stirring voice caused her tummy to go weightless again.

The front door squeaked with a homey, comforting sound as Mike rejoined them and refilled their coffee cups, giving Parker a mug this time. When he sat down in the wicker rocking chair, it creaked dangerously and they all laughed.

"Hope that relic holds up," Parker remarked.

"Are you referring to me or the chair?" Mike asked good-naturedly.

"I don't dare sit in it," Maris said, patting her stomach. "Too much dinner."

"It was a good meal, Mike," Parker said. "Thanks."

"You're welcome." He idly stirred a sugar cube into his coffee. "What we need to round out the evening is a good story."

"Hmm. If only we knew a good storyteller." Being deliberately coy, Maris looked at Parker from beneath her eyelashes.

He grimaced and groaned, but he was pleased by their curiosity. Clasping his hands, he turned them palms out and stretched them above his head until his knuckles popped. "Okay, okay, I can't fight both of you. Where'd you leave off?"

"They'd gone to the beach and killed a bottle of whisky," Maris said, the scene still fresh in her mind.

"I still don't understand why their language must be so vulgar."

Parker frowned at Mike's comment and motioned for Maris to continue.

"Todd accused Roark of being less than straightforward about the critiques he had received from the professor."

"Have you read the part where Roark got pissed?" Parker asked.

"Yes, and his anger was justified. He's never given Todd any reason to mistrust him."

"Conversely, he's been burned by Todd on numerous occasions," Mike noted.

"Most recently with Mary Catherine. I think I need to add another scene with her," Parker said, almost to himself. "Maybe she tells Roark that the child she miscarried was Todd's."

"I thought you'd decided to let the reader draw his own conclusion."

"I had. But I might change my mind. This would strengthen the animosity building between Roark and Todd. What if..." He thought it over for a moment before continuing. "What if Todd drops Mary Catherine flat? Avoids her.

Even complains to Roark that she's a pest, a clinging vine, something like that.

"Meanwhile, she pours her heart out to Roark. She admits that it was Todd's baby she lost, and that she has fallen in love with him, and so forth. Roark likes her as a friend, and he was there that night to clean up Todd's mess, literally, so he's really bothered by the way Todd treats her."

"Does Todd ever know about the baby?" Maris asked.

"No, I don't think so. Mary Catherine doesn't want him to know, and Roark won't betray her confidence by telling him."

"I told you this guy had honor."

"Not so fast," Parker said quietly. "Didn't it strike you that he protested too much when Todd accused him of being less than honest about Hadley's critiques?"

Slowly, she nodded. "Now that I think about it...Have they been more favorable than he let on?"

Parker withdrew several sheets of folded paper from the breast pocket of his shirt. "I dashed this off just before I quit for the day."

She reached for the pages, but Mike suggested that Parker read them out loud.

"Want me to?" Parker asked, addressing Maris.

"By all means. Please."

Chapter 27

Parker unfolded the sheets of manuscript and held them up to catch the light.

" 'Dear Mr. Slade,' he read, 'according to your last letter, you wish me to send future pieces of correspondence to your recently acquired post office box instead of to the street address. As it makes no difference to me, I can only assume that the request arises out of an unspecified desire to convenience yourself.' "

Parker cringed. "Good God. Verbose old bastard, isn't he?"

"Well, he does teach creative writing," Maris said. "One would expect him to be effusive."

"Effusive is one thing, but that is obnoxious."

Parker gave his outspoken valet a dirty look. "Thank you, Mike, for that unsolicited and tactless observation."

"You criticized it first."

"I'm allowed. I'm the author."

Maris smothered a laugh. "You might consider trimming some of the fat, Parker. Just a little."

"Okay. No problem. On the other hand, just for the sake of argument, Hadley's verbosity is consistent with his character. Remember that he hails from an old and distinguished southern family. They had more stiff-necked pride than money and lived well beyond their means. Confederate sabers on display in the parlor. A matriarch whose 'headache medicine' was Tennessee sour mash. A batty maiden aunt—read 'deflowered, then jilted'—who lived in the attic, smelled of gardenia, and wouldn't eat uncooked fruit."

"I remember reading those colorful details," Maris said.

"My grandparents had friends like Hadley's family is described," Parker told her. "I remember their speech being flowery and overblown."

Maris looked toward Mike for confirmation. "I rely on your superior knowledge of southern culture and heritage. Is it too much?"

"As usual, he's exaggerating," the older man replied. "But there's definitely an element of truth there. If you scratch the surface of just about every multigenerational southern family, you'll find at least one cleric, one loony, one outlaw, and enough liquor to float an armada."

Laughing, she turned back to Parker. "Go on with the letter."

He located the spot where he'd left off.

" 'Once a relationship has been built on a particular foundation, it's extremely difficult to destroy that foundation and reconstruct it with different specifications, without also destroying the original relationship.' "

"You've lost me," Mike said. "What's he talking about?"

"I agreed to trim the fat, okay?" Parker said, annoyed by the interruption. He ran his finger down several lines of text. "In summary, he's saying that they began as professor and student. He says it's hard to break the habit of assuming a professorial role with Roark, hard not to lecture or teach, and instead to address his comments to him as a peer." He looked over at Mike. "Got that?"

"Thank you."

"Okay, here... 'Not that I am your peer, Mr. Slade. Your writing has surpassed my ability to critique it. It deserves an appraisal more distinguished than mine, although you could not solicit one that would be more appreciative of your talent.'

"He goes on for several paragraphs, confessing that he had entertained writing aspirations of his own before being forced to acknowledge that he wasn't gifted with the talent. He says his role is to teach, instruct, inspire, yaddah-yaddah."

He flipped to the second page.

" 'Rarely does one with my limited ability have the opportunity to work with someone as talented as you. I consider it a privilege to witness the development of a great American novelist, for that's what I believe you will ultimately become.' "

Parker raised his index finger, letting them know that he was getting to the crux of the passage. " 'Your writing far surpasses that of any other student, past or present, including your friend Todd Grayson. He has written an engaging story with several interesting characters, specifically his protagonist. However, his writing lacks the emotional depth, the *heart,* with which yours resonates. I have no doubt that he will publish. He can produce a mechanically correct manuscript, incorporating all the textbook elements of fiction.

" 'That does not necessarily mean that he writes well.

" 'I can teach students the basics of writing, acquaint them with the rules of fiction, familiarize them with the writers who have mastered these techniques, but only God dispenses talent. That indefinable and elusive quality cannot be taught or otherwise acquired no matter how earnestly one desires and seeks it. I learned this sad truth from my own experience. Were talent attainable, I would be writing my own novels.

" 'Thank the god to whom you pray, Mr. Slade, for you were blessed with that magic. You were christened with a rare and wonderful ability. Your friend was not. I fear that eventually this lopsided appropriation of talent will cause a breach between you.

" 'During my tenure, I have observed thousands of young men and women. Because of this vast exposure to people from diverse backgrounds, I consider myself a superior judge of character. At the very least, I'm an astute observer of it.

" 'Some human characteristics are common to us all. Manifestation of these characteristics is dependent upon circumstance. Everyone has temporary displays of fear, happiness, frustration, and so on.

" 'Other traits are unique to certain individuals. They define the person and his character. Among these traits are admirable examples like humility, charity, bravery.

" 'Unfortunately these have dark counterparts like jealousy, greed, and envy. Persons governed by one of these traits typically cloak it with charm, and most are very successful at it, because along with the trait invariably comes the cunning to conceal it.

" 'Nevertheless, the trait lives and matures inside them as insidiously as an eel inside a cave, waiting, even anticipating, the times when it can strike anything or anyone that threatens.

" 'I do not wish to speak ill of your friend. I would like to think that my barometer for integrity has failed me completely, and that I am terribly wrong about the qualities that motivate him.

" 'But I remember Mr. Grayson's machinations which caused you to be late for an important meeting with me. Plainly put, it was a dirty trick with malicious overtones. Frankly, I'm surprised that the friendship survived it. It's a credit to you that it did. I don't think Mr. Grayson has it within himself to forgive to that extent, which is yet another notable disparity between your characters.

" 'I wouldn't presume to choose your friends for you. I wouldn't want the responsibility even if you were to grant it to me. But I'll conclude by using an expression I've heard around campus. It's a contemporary idiom which does the English language a grave disservice, but which, in this distance, seems appropriate: Heads-up.

" 'I look forward to reading the next draft of your manuscript. In your cover letters, you never fail to apologize for taking up my time, and to thank me for the careful consideration I give your work. Mr. Slade, be clear on this: it is a privilege, not an imposition. Sincerely yours, Professor Hadley.' "

Parker refolded the pages and returned them to his shirt pocket. No one spoke for a moment. Maris had been lulled by his words and the cadence with which he'd read them. She shook off the mild daze and gave the swing a gentle push.

"So Todd's gut instincts were right. Roark's reviews from Hadley *were* better than the ones he received."

Parker nodded. "And Roark was dishonest about it."

"I don't think that matters."

He looked across at her, and the intensity of his stare compelled her to continue the thought.

"Todd wouldn't have taken it well if Roark had said, 'You guessed right. Hadley thinks you're a hack with limited talent, while he believes I have the potential of being the next Steinbeck.' "

Mike agreed. "If Roark had told him the truth out there on the beach, Todd would have ended their relationship then and there. Your story would be over. The end."

Parker grunted a nonresponse.

Reading from the manuscript seemed to have darkened his mood, although Maris couldn't figure why. The content had obviously captivated her and Mike. The letter had been a clever way to move his story along without relying strictly on narrative. Since she and Mike had approved it, she couldn't account for his sullenness. "What's bothering you, Parker?"

"Roark's supposed to be the good guy, right? He's the lamb in the goat/lamb comparison."

"That's one way of looking at it, I suppose."

"It doesn't bother you that he deceived his friend?"

"His motivation wasn't deception. It was kindness. He was

trying to spare Todd from what Hadley referred to as the 'sad truth,' because he knew it would be devastating. Todd simply wasn't as talented as Roark. Roark might have sensed from the beginning that Todd lacked—"

She snapped her fingers. "No, he *knew* it. Didn't he? Of course he knew that he was better. He had to know it. Or else why did he get a post office box to prevent his mail from coming to their apartment? He was afraid that Todd would intercept one of his glowing critiques from Hadley."

"Nothing escapes you," he said, his mood seeming to lift. "Now forget that you know it."

"Why?"

"Because it becomes crucial in the next chapter or so."

"The mention of the post office box was a foreshadowing?"

He smiled enigmatically.

"Todd intercepts one of the letters, right?" she guessed. "Maybe even this letter, because this is the one that could be the most damaging to the friendship. It spells out the differences in their talent and their characters. Todd... uh, let's see, he borrows a pair of jeans or something, maybe without asking Roark, and he finds the letter in a pocket."

"Thanks. I hadn't figured out yet how he was going to get his hands on it. That's pretty good."

She beamed. "Todd reads this letter. He can't believe what he's reading. His secret fear is realized. Roark is superior to him. That's why he had tried to sabotage Roark with Professor Hadley. It hadn't worked. Indeed, it backfired. Hadley saw through him. Furthermore, Roark has won Hadley's praise. A double whammy for Todd. He reacts by... doing what?"

"You tell me."

She concentrated hard, unconsciously gnawing on a corner of her lip. "I was going to say that he would be crushed, but, on second thought, that would be out of character." She shook her head. "No, he's too egotistical to let a university professor destroy his ambition. I think he would be furious. Livid." She formed claws with her hands and held them at the sides of her head. "Explosively, volcanically enraged."

"How does he channel that rage, Maris?"

"He confronts Roark with the letter."

"No, he doesn't."

"Parker," Mike cut in softly.

"He's not honest enough to take that approach. He—"

"Parker," Mike repeated.

"He waits. He—"

"Parker."

"He—"

"Parker!"

"*Goddammit, Mike!* What?"

He rounded on the older man, but Mike didn't flinch from his hard look. In fact, he returned it. The air was electrically charged, as it had been in the kitchen this morning. In both instances, thoughts were telegraphed that Maris couldn't interpret.

Parker was the first to relent. He closed his eyes and massaged his forehead. "I'm sorry, Mike. Forgive me. I was following a train of thought."

"It's okay. I know you hate distractions when you're on a roll."

"Dinner was great."

"So you said."

"Oh. Yeah. Right. Well, thanks again."

"You're welcome. I'm glad you enjoyed it." Mike stood and picked up the silver serving tray that held the empty carafe and coffee cups. "Before the mosquitoes carry me off, I think I'll go in."

"Good idea. Good night."

"Good night, Mike," Maris echoed.

At the door Mike turned and addressed Parker. "Do you want me to wait up and help—"

"No, no. I'll be fine tonight. Go to bed."

The older man hesitated, glanced at Maris, then nodded and went inside.

Once they were alone, Maris raised her hands in a helpless shrug. "Explain to me what just happened."

"When?"

"Just now. Between you and Mike."

"Nothing."

"Parker," she cried softly.

He blinked innocently. "Nothing."

She stared him down, but he didn't relent. Vexed over being totally shut out, she got up from the swing. "Fine. Play word games. But play them without me. Good night."

"Don't go away mad."

"Then don't talk down to me. I hate being patronized."

He dragged his hands down his face. "And you should. I'm sorry." He sucked in a breath of the sultry air and turned his head away to stare out at the row of live oaks.

"It's this...this *thing* between Mike and me. Sometimes he sees a darkness creeping over me. A mean ugliness. Like I was when he found me. It scares him, I guess. He's afraid I'll drop back into that abyss. He yanks me out of it before I can sink too far."

Turning back, he fixed his eyes on her. "Something like that."

"Thank you."

They simply looked at one another for several moments, then he smiled crookedly. "It's been a roller-coaster evening."

"Yes, it has. But I wouldn't trade a minute of it."

He reached out, encircled her wrist with his fingers, and gave it a tug. She moved nearer, but not close enough to suit him. He curved an arm around her waist and pulled her closer. Hooking the other hand around the back of her neck, he drew her down for a kiss. She placed her hands on his hard cheeks. Their mouths melded and tongues plundered in a delirium of longing.

When at last they pulled apart, he pressed his face into the softness of her middle. "I've been craving this all day."

"There were times when I thought you'd forgotten about last night."

He gave a soft, harsh laugh. "Not fucking hardly."

His head nudged her breasts through the silk cloth of her dress. His humid breath filtered through it to her skin. He cupped her bottom in his hands, buried his face deeper into her.

Threading her fingers through his hair, she sighed, "Ah, Parker, please."

"Yes. Anything. Just ask."

"I...um..."

"What?"

"I can't do this."

"You can. You have. You did. Last night. Remember?" One hand found bare skin beneath her skirt, warmth between her thighs.

Her knees went weak, but she pushed his hand down and stepped out of his reach. "I can't. We can't."

He gulped a breath and blinked her into focus. "Why not?"

She licked her lips, tasted him. "I'm worried about my father."

"Your father?" He seemed to grope for a definition of the word. "Your father? You're afraid that he wouldn't approve? That he'd come after me with a shotgun? What?"

She smiled and shook her head. "No, nothing like that. I've been trying to reach him all day."

She gave him a quick summary of her attempts. "Finally, just before dinner, I tracked our housekeeper Maxine to her sister's house. She stays with her when she takes a day off. Which is rarely.

"Anyhow, she told me that Dad had gone to our country house in western Massachusetts for the weekend. He and Noah. They insisted she stay behind. They wanted to go by them-selves."

"So? They're big boys. What does their leaving New York for the weekend have to do with us necking here on the veranda?"

"Nothing. Directly."

"Then I don't get it."

"Maxine watches Dad like a hawk. Or a mother hen. I wouldn't be worried if she were with him. I don't like the idea of his being alone."

"He's not."

No, he was alone with Noah.

What she didn't tell Parker was that Noah had assured Maxine that Maris was aware of their weekend plans, that she had sanctioned them. The loyal employee had been distraught to learn that Maris had not been consulted. "Why did Mr. Reed mislead me?"

Why indeed?

Maxine had then told her that Daniel had entertained a guest for breakfast.

"Who?"

"I don't know." She explained about the errand he'd sent her on. "I think Mr. Matherly dreamed up a reason to get me out of the house. When I got back, he was washing dishes."

"Washing dishes?"

"He didn't want me to know that two place settings had been used. When I questioned him about it, he got defensive and said that they were his dishes and that if he wanted to use a dozen place settings at breakfast, he could. It was all nonsense, Maris. He apologized for it later. The important thing is that someone definitely came to the house while I was out, and he didn't want anyone to know about it."

"Did he seem upset?"

"No. In fact, he seemed very upbeat and eager to be off when Mr. Reed arrived to pick him up."

"Then I'm sure we're worrying over nothing."

Maris hoped her assurances sounded sincere to the anxious

housekeeper. To her own ears they rang hollow, even as she repeated them to Parker now. "I'm relieved to know where he is, and I'm sure he's all right. But I'll feel better once I talk to him."

"Did you try contacting him at the country house?"

"The line has been busy for hours. And even though I didn't want to speak to Noah, I also tried his cell phone. It was busy, too, so I left a voice-mail message and the phone number here. I hope you don't mind."

"So long as you didn't give my name."

"Of course not. But the point is moot. Nobody's called. I need to check my cell, see if there's a message on it."

"Sorta weird."

"What?"

"That your dad would agree to spending a weekend with your estranged husband."

"Dad doesn't know we're separated." He registered the expected surprise. "I guess I should have told him right away, but the time never seemed right. I wanted to choose a time when it would have the least impact."

"Do you think Noah plans to spring the unhappy news on him this weekend?"

"That was my first thought," she said tightly. "Or possibly to ask Dad to intervene on his behalf. He's got his position at Matherly Press to protect. If that's the reason he married me, that'll be his reason for wanting to prevent a divorce."

"Would your father intervene on Noah's behalf?"

"Absolutely not. He knows I've been unhappy. He just doesn't know the extent of my unhappiness." Lowering her voice, she said, "Until I came to St. Anne Island and met you, *I* didn't know how unhappy I'd been."

He groaned. "Don't look at me like that, Maris."

"Like what?"

"Misty-eyed. In fact, you'd better git before I decide not to be so gracious and understanding about this. We wasted another perfectly good hard-on. I'm oh for two."

"You're vulgar. Just as Mike said." Laughing, she smoothed her hand over his ravaged hair. "It was a lovely evening."

"It was getting lovelier," he groused.

"I'm sorry." She bent down and laid a soft kiss on his lips. "Sleep well."

"Oh, yeah, like a baby. A horny little baby."

"If it's any consolation, Parker..."

"What?"

"I can. I have. I did. Last night. And I do remember."

Chapter 28

T here were no messages on Maris's phone.

She tried Noah's cell, but a recording informed her that the number she had called was unavailable. Terribly worried now, she dialed the house telephone.

Daniel answered on the second ring.

She slumped with relief, but her greeting sounded like a reprimand. "Dad, where have you been?"

"Most recently I've been to the bathroom. Did I forget to ask permission?"

"I'm sorry. I didn't mean to jump down your throat. It's just that I've been trying to reach you all day. I didn't know you'd gone to the country until I talked to Maxine. Since then, I've called repeatedly."

"This is the first time the telephone has rung. I noticed just before coming upstairs to bed that the receiver on the telephone in the kitchen was askew. Apparently Noah didn't hang it up properly when he called in a food delivery."

More likely he had left it off the hook deliberately, knowing she would want to talk to her father. He knew she would be crazy with worry when she couldn't reach him. Was this Noah's mean form of punishment for her leaving him? It was amazing how clearly she could see his true nature now. What had kept her blind to it for so many years? *A book*, she thought, scornful of her own naïveté.

Well, she was no longer naive. She wanted him gone, expunged from their lives. She couldn't stand his being a member of their family for another day. Why wait to tell her father about the dissolution of her marriage?

Fortunately, she came to her senses before she could act on the impulse.

First of all, that would necessitate a lengthy discussion, and it was as late in Massachusetts as it was on St. Anne Island. Second, that was a conversation that should be conducted face-to-face, especially since it involved their business interests as well as their personal lives.

Setting her enmity for Noah aside for the time being, she asked Daniel if he was all right.

"Why wouldn't I be?"

"Since I hadn't talked to you, I had imagined all sorts of things."

"None of them good, I'll bet. The way I used to worry if you were ten minutes late coming home."

"Have our roles reversed, Dad?"

"Not at all. I still worry about you if you're ten minutes late. But rest assured that I've had a very pleasant day."

Starting with a mystery guest for breakfast. She wanted to ask him about that but couldn't without giving away that Maxine had tattled on him. She hoped he would volunteer the information. "What did you do that made your day so pleasant?"

"Nothing much, and that was the beauty of it."

"Was the house in order when you arrived?"

"Spic and span."

"Where did you go for dinner? Harry's or another of your favorite spots?"

"We ate in. I thought Noah would have told you."

"When?"

"When you called this afternoon. I came downstairs just as he was hanging up."

She opened her mouth but closed it without saying anything. Noah had lied to him. Apparently Daniel had caught the tail end of a telephone conversation, and Noah had pretended it was she. Damn him!

"Maybe he did mention it and I forgot."

"Not surprising," he said, seeming to have missed the anger in her voice. "You've got a lot on your mind. How's the book coming?"

"Great, actually. The story is really percolating now. It's amazing to watch how the writer's mind works. I've never been this involved with the creative process, and it's fascinating."

"I can tell that you're enjoying it."

"Immensely."

"And the author? Still the curmudgeon?"

"Either he's mellowing or I'm becoming accustomed to him. I don't know which."

"Probably a little of both."

"Probably."

Maris sensed him hesitating. Then he said, "I'm glad you heeded your instincts and went back to work with him."

"So am I, Dad. It was the right decision. I'm positive of that."

"You're happy there? With the work? With everything?"

"Yes. Very," she said quietly.

"Good. You deserve to be, Maris."

To anyone listening, the conversation sounded innocent enough. But given the one they'd had directly before her departure from New York, she knew that her father was conveying more than he was saying.

He knew she'd been unhappy with Noah and their marriage. It wouldn't surprise her if he knew about Noah's infidelity. Daniel Matherly was known for his ability to ferret out secrets. During her last visit with him, she had hardly kept secret her feelings for Parker. Without naming him, she had talked about him nonstop with the uncontainable excitement of someone falling in love.

This roundabout conversation was her dad's way of letting her know that he sanctioned it.

She swallowed a knot of emotion. "I needed to hear your voice, Dad."

"It's good to hear yours, too."

"I'm sorry I disturbed you so late."

"You could never disturb me, but in any case, I wasn't asleep."

"I'll call you again tomorrow. No, wait."

Considering the lies Noah had told today, the thought of him being with her father like the faithful son-in-law for the remainder of the weekend turned her stomach. He probably had in mind to get chummy, to get on Daniel's good side. Maybe he planned to make a tearful confession and plead his case with Daniel before Maris told him about their separation.

Not if she could help it.

"Dad, I'd like to send Maxine up there tomorrow. She's been dying to go to the country and see the summer flowers in bloom. Would you mind?"

"Flowers..." He harrumphed skeptically, letting her know the excuse was transparent. "I've had only one day's peace away from her. But," he sighed, "if it would make you feel better..."

"It would make me feel better. I'll call her first thing in the morning." It relieved her to know that Maxine would drop everything and go at a moment's notice. She could be there well before noon. "Call me when she arrives, so I'll know she made the drive safely."

"All right, sweetheart. I'll call you tomorrow. And Maris?"

"Yes."

"Make the most of your time there. Don't deny yourself the happiness being there gives you. Don't worry about anything. Are you listening to your old dad? Everything is going to work out well. Will you trust me on that, sweetheart?"

"I always have." She leaned her cheek into the small telephone, wishing it were his spotted, wrinkled hand. "Good night, Dad. I love you."

"I love you, too."

* * *

Parker's bed was a monstrosity. It was narrow by king-sized standards, but what it lacked in width, it made up for in height. The headboard was tall and carved, the wood aged to a saddlebrown patina that reflected the glow from his reading lamp on the nightstand.

The bed was standing on an area rug that looked like an authentic Aubusson. The overhead fan was like those Maris had seen before only in movies. A brass pole was suspended horizontally six feet below the tall ceiling. At each end of the pole was an axle that idly turned a set of papyrus blades.

There were no draperies on the three tall windows, only louvered shutters, which were painted white to tastefully contrast with the caramel-colored walls and dark hardwood floor. One wall accommodated a massive chifforobe that was crowned with carvings that matched those on the apex of the headboard. Apparently it held all his clothing because there was no closet built into the room.

The TV and VCR, housed in a cabinet on the wall opposite the bed, were the room's only nods toward modernity—other than the wheelchair parked in front of the nightstand. There was no other apparatus one would assume to find in the bedroom of a disabled person, but she wasn't too surprised. She'd seen him lift himself into and out of the Gator.

Parker was bare-chested, propped against the headboard reading, when Maris slipped through the door. He slowly lowered the book to his lap. "Hello. Are you lost?"

She laughed nervously, a bit breathlessly. "Nice try, but I think I was expected."

"I hoped. I even said my prayers."

"Then it's all right if I come in?"

"Are you joking?"

"I thought maybe . . . will Mike—"

"Not if you lock the door."

Since coming into the room, she'd kept her hands behind her. Feeling for the doorknob at the small of her back, she depressed the lock button to guarantee their privacy. Keeping her hands behind her back, she approached the bed.

The polished floor planks felt cool against the bare soles of her feet. Her short nightgown was no weightier than air against her skin, and judging from the intensity with which Parker was watching her as she moved toward him, he had noticed that it wasn't very substantial.

She brought her hands from behind her back. "I brought you presents. Two, to be exact."

The first was a standard drinking glass that belonged to the wet bar in the guest house. She extended it to him. He took the glass from her and held it up, looked at it for a few seconds, then laughed when he saw the winking phosphorescent lights inside. "Lightning bugs."

"I caught them myself," she said proudly. "I saw them through the guest house window while I was dressing for dinner and chased out after them."

She'd sealed them inside the glass by stretching a piece of plastic wrap over the top, then puncturing it to ensure the fireflies a longer life.

When he looked up at her, his eyes shone with feeling. "It's a great present. Thank you."

"You're welcome. Shall I?" She took them back and set them on the nightstand.

"What's the other?" He indicated the book she was now hugging to her chest. "Are you going to read me a bedtime story?"

"Sort of."

"I wondered why you were wearing your glasses."

"I took my contacts out." Nodding toward the empty side of his bed, she asked, "May I?"

"Be my guest."

She rounded the end of the bed and crawled onto it, then folded her legs beneath her and sat back on her heels, facing him. "You're already reading a bedtime story."

He closed the book lying in his lap and set it on the nightstand. "I'd rather hear yours." She turned the book toward him so he could see the title stamped in gold into the green cloth cover. *"Grass Widow,"* he read, smiling.

"A novel by my favorite author."

"What, him?"

"There's no call for false modesty."

"But you've got high standards, Ms. Matherly. You're a hard sell. What do you like about this novel?"

His use of her maiden name didn't escape her, but she didn't interrupt their game by acknowledging it. She opened the book. "Well, in particular, I like the scene where Deck Cayton, the handsome, sexy, roguish, but engaging hero, uses a card game to obtain information from the bimbo."

"Frenchy."

"Whatever. It's a provocative and involving scene."

"The fans certainly thought so. Critics, too."

She pursed her lips and frowned. "However—"

"Uh-oh. Here it comes."

"The scene has raised a few points."

"Typical editor," he said under his breath. "For every compliment there's a criticism."

"Look, Mr. Evans, if you don't value my points—"

"No, no. I do value them, those raised points of yours." His eyes dropped to her breasts. "I'll take them like a man." He placed one hand behind his head and gave her a smug grin. "That was a metaphor."

"I got it," she said dryly. "Shall I proceed?"

"Please. Give me a for-instance."

"Uh…" She dragged her eyes away from the furry hollow of his armpit. "For instance, the language is very descriptive."

"Isn't it supposed to be?"

"Yes, but in this passage it's—"

"Explicit?"

"To the extreme."

"Why's that bad?"

"I didn't say it was bad. My problem is with its accuracy."

"Accuracy."

"Right. I'm not sure that the, uh, mating positions you've described are anatomically possible. For human beings, I mean."

He snuffled a laugh, then stroked his chin somberly. "I see. Could you be more specific?"

"There are several examples. So what I thought," she said, pausing to clear her throat, as she opened to the marked page, "is that we could act it out and see if these… configurations… are doable."

"That's what you thought?" he drawled sexily.

"Yes, that's what I thought."

He remained very still for several moments, gazing at her. Then slowly he removed his hand from behind his head. "As I recall, our handsome, sexy, roguish, but engaging hero begins by placing his hand on Frenchy's thigh. It's a comforting gesture. Nothing more. He wants to reassure her that he poses no threat."

He placed his hand on her thigh just above her bent knee and squeezed it lightly. Through the baby-blue silk of her nightgown, she felt the heat and strength of all five fingers individually.

"Debatable," she murmured. "The part about him posing no threat, but we'll give him the benefit of the doubt."

"In exchange for that gesture of kindness, and despite the fact that Deck had drawn the low card, Frenchy tells him that at the time of the murder, she had heard a noise coming from the alley."

"Which caused her to look out her bedroom window. That's when she saw . . ." Needlessly Maris referred to the printed page. "The man in the red baseball cap running from the neighboring building."

"A valuable piece of information," Parker said. "Especially since Frenchy can describe the cap right down to the logo embroidered on it. Our hero thanks her with a kiss."

Parker removed her eyeglasses and framed her face between his hands. His thumbs stroked her cheekbones while his eyes touched on every feature. He followed their path with his lips. When he reached her mouth, he kissed it softly, sensually.

Maris struggled to keep her response down to a low moan of arousal.

When he pulled back, he whispered, "She tastes incredible."

"It doesn't say that."

"It doesn't? It should. He's compelled to go back for more."

"Frenchy doesn't resist."

He kept the kisses gentle. They teased and tantalized and left her wanting. It was several minutes before they separated, and by then Maris felt drugged. A delicious lassitude had afflicted her limbs. Even so, she had enough presence of mind to continue the game.

Needlessly, she reached for her glasses and fumbled trying to get them on correctly. "Never mind." She dropped them alongside the book. "I know what comes next. Frenchy, that lucky girl, draws the high card again."

"Cayton's pretty damn lucky himself. He gets to grant her a sexual favor."

"But he's uncomfortable with their position, so he pulls her astride his lap."

Parker curved his hands around her waist. She came up on her knees and straddled him. "If I'm remembering correctly, Cayton kisses her ears, her throat, her…"

But Parker was way ahead of her. He had, after all, written the scene and knew the sequence. The straps of her nightgown had been lowered before she was completely settled on him. Her breasts lay cupped in his hands, his thumbs brushing her nipples. And now he was taking one into his mouth and sucking it lustily, pressing it hard between his tongue and the roof of his mouth.

Shamelessly she folded her arms around his head, holding it fast. Whimpering wordless sounds, she kissed the crown of his head, his temple, anyplace that she could reach without dislodging him, because she didn't want him to stop.

Her sex softened and swelled, opening like a piece of fruit that had been ripened beyond its ability to contain itself. Parker reached between her thighs and when he touched her, she shuddered involuntarily. Her body closed wetly around his fingers.

"Go ahead," he urged. "You know what you want to do."

His name staggered out on an uneven breath.

"Go ahead, Maris."

She began to move, rocking her hips against his hand, forcing his fingers deeper into her, responding to his subtle stroking until she was in the throes of an orgasm.

Or so she thought.

Until he slid beneath her and simultaneously lifted her up higher, supporting her hips with his strong hands and drawing her to his mouth. She gave a harsh, dry gasp of pure shock, but it was soon expelled as a low, keening sigh of incredible pleasure.

She flattened her palms against the headboard, and when that became insufficient support, she leaned into it, resting her cheek against the cool wood while giving herself over to the mastery of his tongue.

His flexing fingers embedded themselves in her flesh. His hair was soft against her lower belly, the stubble on his cheeks pleasantly scratchy against her inner thighs.

She became lost in the sensations. Utterly lost. Her mind and body were governed by sensual impulses to the exclusion of all else. She surrendered herself to the primal rhythms pulsing through her.

Numerous times she strained toward orgasm, but he would quieten her efforts with the softest of kisses and the sweetest of words before wickedly coaxing her to the brink again. When he did let her come, it was shattering. The last tether on consciousness was clipped and she soared, lost touch, spun in delirium.

Coherence returned gradually. Languorously. A feather drifting down.

Her skin was damp, her chest flushed, her nipples taut and red. Her heart was pounding and each beat echoed inside her head. She rested against the headboard until her breathing had slowed. When she finally opened her eyes, she realized they were wet with tears.

She lowered herself to sprawl on Parker's torso like a shipwreck victim washed ashore. Her nightgown was wadded around her waist. Her hair clung to her cheeks and neck in damp strands. Parker smoothed his hands down her back, over her hips. They settled on her ass. He squeezed it gently and made her smile.

His heart was beating hard and strong directly into her ear. Each time she inhaled, her nose was tickled by chest hair. She had an up-close view of his nipple, which lay flat until she touched it, then it beaded up hard against her fingertip and she felt his quick intake of breath. Between their bellies, she could feel his erection.

"Give me a moment," she said weakly.

Laughter rumbled in his chest. "I'm not going anywhere."

Several minutes passed. She soaked up the intimacy, realizing how bloody fabulous it was to be a woman in such intimate contact with a man. No, not a man. She'd had a man. She loved being intimate with *this* man. Until now, she hadn't known there could be such a vast difference between two members of the same sex, of the same species.

"You deviated from the book," she whispered.

"Did I? My memory's a little foggy."

"There was nothing like that in the book. Nothing that even comes close. In any book."

She raised her head and looked at him, inched up and softly kissed his lips, then slipped her tongue into his mouth and rubbed the tip of his. As the kiss intensified, she seductively ground her pelvis against his erection.

He broke from their kiss and angled his head back until it was buried in his pillow. His skin appeared to be stretched tightly over the bones of his face. His hands were gripping her hips hard in an effort to keep her still.

"What?" she asked innocently.

"That's not in the book, either."

"Oh, sorry. Let's see what comes next." Without changing their position, she awkwardly reached for her glasses and slipped them on, then opened the book and pretended to read silently. "Oh, yes, I remember now. He takes her hand and guides it to..."

"His cock."

"That's what it says."

Coming off him slowly, she resumed her original place beside him. She straightened her nightgown and was about to replace the straps on her shoulders, when Parker gave his head a negative shake. Maris pulled the gown off over her head. For a few seconds she held it against her chest, then tossed it toward the foot of the bed. Parker took a deep breath, his nostrils flaring slightly.

He ran his hand over her breasts, down her rib cage and belly, and combed his fingertips through her damp pubic hair before returning to her breast. He lightly pinched the nipple between his fingers and watched it harden.

She laid her hand on his stomach. The hair grew laterally toward a silky strip that took a downward turn at his navel. Her eyes tracked it; her hand followed it beneath the sheet.

But Parker reached down and stopped it. "This is where the fantasy ends, Maris."

Her gaze swung up to his. His expression was set and hard. He wasn't kidding. In a matter of moments, he had physically withdrawn and taken a giant step backward emotionally. "I don't understand."

"This isn't fiction."

"I'm glad it's not."

"This is reality."

"I know."

"You don't have a clue," he said harshly. "You pull that sheet back and you'll get a jolt of reality you never bargained for."

She took a quick glance at his legs beneath the covering of the sheet. Smiling softly, she shook her head. "Do you think I care about your scars?"

"I think you will, yeah."

"You're wrong." She gazed into his face, and, near tears, said, "Parker, you can't possibly comprehend what you've done for me. No, listen, please," she said when he was about to interrupt. "I may only have the courage to say this once."

She removed her glasses, rubbed her eyes, moistened her lips, smiled ruefully. "I've never played sex games like this before. I've only read about this kind of play. I thought it only occurred in books. What you said the other night on the beach, while crude, was correct. With Noah, I never felt free to express myself sexually. What happened between us just now? Would have been unthinkable to me a few weeks ago.

"That was totally out of character with the woman who entered Terry's Bar and Grill looking for you. I didn't know until now what I've been missing. I've been craving that kind of passion. Sensual meltdown. Absolute and unapologetic sexual abandon. You gave me that. But it's incomplete. It won't mean anything unless we share it. Let me share it," she finished huskily. "Please."

He continued to stare at her, but his expression was no longer tense and set. In fact, he looked more vulnerable than she would have believed possible. "I'm not pretty, Maris."

"You're beautiful."

Tentatively, she leaned toward him. He didn't stop her. She began at his neck and kissed her way down. Her lips whisked across his skin, her tongue licked it softly. Her mouth wetly covered his nipple and he hissed a profanity and sank his fingers into her hair.

She pressed another openmouthed kiss just below his navel as she pushed the sheet down below his hips. He groaned her name when she encircled his penis with her hand. It throbbed with life and vitality. She stroked it slowly, varying the tension of her fingers as she worked her way up. She rubbed her thumb across the tip, smearing a pearly bead of semen that had leaked from it.

"Isn't this how Frenchy got her nickname?" she asked in a voice unintentionally smoky.

"Maris..." Her name vaporized on his lips when she bent over him.

She reveled in the musky taste and scent. She loved feeling the quickening in his belly, hearing his hoarse exclamations of arousal, experiencing the feel of him inside her mouth.

His grip on her hair tightened, not enough to hurt, only

enough to let her know it was time to switch positions. She bridged him with her thighs and remained poised above him while he took his penis in his own hand and rubbed the smooth head against her, baiting her desire until she had to have him inside her. Then she sank down, sheathing him slowly, her body stretching to take all of him.

He took several rapid breaths and as he exhaled, he whispered, "Wait."

So she remained still. He slid his hands up and down her thighs. His thumbs met in the mesh of their pubic hair and stroked her V until her head fell back against her shoulders and she moaned his name.

Only then did he angle his hips up, encouraging her to ride him. She did, changing tempos and angles, holding still when he indicated that's what he wished her to do to protract the pleasure. During those pauses, she used the walls of her body to milk him; his eyes would darken, he would swear lavishly, then he would nudge her into motion again.

Leaning down, she guided his head to her breast. He rubbed his rough cheek against it, then his closed lips, before caressing her nipple with his tongue. Lightly and rapidly. Until she called his name and pressed her hips deeply into his belly, securing him inside her.

He pulled her down onto his chest and they came together. As he pulsed inside her, he splayed one hand over her bottom, and cupped the back of her head with the other, and, holding her possessively with both, kissed her mouth. They couldn't get close enough, deep enough, into each other far enough to satisfy the passion.

When it finally waned, she stretched out on top of him. She could feel the rugged terrain of his scarred legs beneath hers. But she couldn't, wouldn't, think about that now. She had scars, too. Less visible than his, but there nonetheless. Later, there would be time and opportunity to ask questions and to listen and to sympathize, and then to return their previous unhappiness to the past where it belonged.

Right now she wanted nothing to intrude on the present. She wanted to bask in the knowledge that she had pleased Parker well. She hated Noah Reed for all the times he had rejected her overtures, making her feel awkward and undesired, and then if he did respond for making her feel somehow insufficient.

But she didn't waste this precious time thinking about him, either. The thought of him was fleeting, like a twinge in one's side, that's painful only for an instant before it disappears.

Instead she concentrated on the wonderful pressure of Parker still nestling inside her. She kept her thighs tightly closed, her belly pressed firmly against his to maximize the closeness.

Moving only her lips, she kissed his throat. "The end?"

Several moments elapsed before he replied. "Not quite, Maris."

But she had already fallen asleep.

Chapter 29

Daniel stood at the kitchen window, eating a sandwich and staring out at the rainy night. Periodically lightning illuminated the countryside, but it was a friendly storm, unthreatening and nonviolent, a summer thundershower that would dissipate quickly and leave the skies clear by dawn.

His telephone conversation with Maris had thrust his mind into overdrive. It was churning a mile a minute. He wished his body, like his brain, would experience occasional energizing jump starts like this. If it did, he'd be able to bicycle back to New York and then run a marathon. Mentally, he felt that athletic and robust.

After the call, he'd tried for an hour to fall asleep. Finally surrendering to his insomnia he had come downstairs. Midnight snacks were verboten at home, especially when they added up to more fat grams than he was allotted for a week. But Maxine wasn't guarding the refrigerator tonight, and what she didn't know wouldn't hurt her. She would be here soon enough, bossing and monitoring him as if he were a child.

Thank God, he thought with a chuckle. He didn't know what

he would have done without Maxine caring for him and Maris all these years.

He polished off the sandwich. The leftover Reuben had been satisfying—to say nothing of the warmth that two fingers of brandy had spread through him. Rather than making him feel languid and sleepy, however, the alcohol had invigorated him. He was restless and ready to act.

He'd always been a man of action, seldom placing problems on the back burner and letting them simmer. He favored confronting them immediately. Standing still wasn't his style. He preferred channeling his energy positively and productively rather than squandering it on self-doubt and hand-wringing indecision.

But this situation warranted more consideration than most. He was uncertain about the order in which to take the actions necessary to rectify it. He had his strategy in place, but it required careful orchestration and perfect timing. That's what had his mind working double-time tonight.

This situation didn't have a nucleus on which he could focus his problem-solving ability. It didn't lend itself to a swift and fatal attack. It was mercurial, constantly changing. It was a multilayered and complex conundrum involving both family and business, individuals and money, power and emotions. A complicated mix. Especially when one of the persons involved was his daughter.

He was glad Maris was in Georgia, away from New York. Things were about to get ugly. Bluntly, the shit was about to hit the fan. The more distance between it and Maris, the better. Inevitably she would catch some of the media fallout, but he hoped to buffer her as much as possible, and the geography would help. Sorting through the personal aspects of this mess was going to be painful enough for her. Doing so in the public eye would be hell.

Although, he thought, smiling, *she won't be without consolation.*

It had been evident to him for months that she was unhappy with her husband and their marriage. It had become equally evident that the book-in-progress alone hadn't drawn her back to the sea island, exotic and lush as it might be.

Her duties and responsibilities at Matherly Press were enough to keep an overachiever like her stretched thin. Normally her daily grind would prevent her from becoming personally involved with one author and one book, even if she were so inclined to invest that much of herself, which she never had been before.

It didn't take a rocket scientist to conclude that the allure wasn't strictly the book, but the author Parker Evans, a.k.a. Mackensie Roone.

Oh, yes. He had discovered the name of Maris's elusive author, as well as his successful pen name. Years earlier, when the Deck Cayton mystery series had started appearing routinely on the bestseller lists, he had tried to flatter, coax, blackmail, and threaten the author's real name out of his agent, in the hope of luring the writer to Matherly Press.

She, however, would not be intimidated, even by the venerable Daniel Matherly. "If I told you, Daniel, I'd have to kill you." She had steadfastly protected her client's identity against disclosure, and Daniel had grudgingly admired her for it.

But he knew it now.

For several weeks, he'd had a private investigator on retainer. Hoping that his misgivings about Noah were proved wrong, he had hired the investigator to probe into his son-in-law's past, including his life prior to the publication of *The Vanquished*.

The whole idea of a covert investigation had been distasteful to him. His approach had always been bold and forthright, and he despised the furtiveness associated with a private investigator. He had envisioned having to consort with a sleazy B-movie type with a stained necktie and a leering yellow grin.

But when William Sutherland arrived for their discreet appointment, he contradicted the stereotype. Sutherland was the founder of an elite and expensive agency, a retired Secret Service agent wearing a well-tailored dark suit. He had a firm hand-shake, an authoritative bearing, and a distinguished service record.

Within five minutes of that first handshake, Daniel was out-lining his requests. The last thing Daniel had expected to learn from Sutherland's initial report was novelist Mackensie Roone's true identity. That's not what he'd been looking for. Unexpect-edly, one of publishing's best-kept secrets had landed in his lap in a sealed manila folder.

But the staggering revelation was yet to come: Parker Evans and Noah Reed had a history.

They had been roommates at a university in Tennessee, and then after graduation they had lived together in Key West. There, they'd had some sort of falling out, the particulars of which were still unknown. Sutherland was presently investigating further, and Daniel was certain that soon all the facts would be disclosed.

In the meantime, he had pieced together the facts he knew, and they would have made an engrossing novel. Maris was presently residing in a plantation house on a remote island be-longing to Parker Evans, her estranged husband's former friend with whom he'd parted antagonistically. The synopsis alone brimmed with the ingredients of a juicy novel—friendship, love, hate, deception, revenge. Envy? Possibly.

The only thing lacking in this scenario was a motive for the main character, Parker Evans.

He had lured Maris with his book for a specific purpose. He hadn't selected her at random. What had motivated him to be-come involved with Maris, even professionally, when he must know that she was Noah's wife?

Daniel wondered if she was aware of their connection. Con-sidering Noah's unfaithfulness, she would feel justified to play tit for tat with his former fraternity brother. But a childish retaliation wasn't like her.

Daniel doubted she knew. If she knew, she would have been reluctant to fall in love with Parker Evans. And she was in love. That became clearer by the day.

Daniel wanted to celebrate her newfound happiness, but he would be wary of the budding romance until he knew why Parker Evans had engineered this chain of events. He had been tempted to confront the man, either in person or through Sutherland, and demand to know just what kind of story he was plotting. But he couldn't do that without tipping his hand to both Maris and Noah, and he wasn't quite prepared to do that. Close, but not quite.

So he'd been forced to bide his time while Sutherland delved deeper.

It was possible that Evans's motivation would come to light in another form—his manuscript. Having read the latest installment that Maris had shared with him, Daniel was convinced the writer was chronicling his rocky friendship with Noah. Depending on how long it took him to commit the story to paper, it might be told through the pages of his personal record before Sutherland could wade through the official one.

During the wait, Daniel's primary concern was Maris. He'd known about Parker Evans before she returned to St. Anne. He could have stopped her. He didn't. For one thing, it was clear to him that she yearned to go. He was also comforted by the fact that Parker Evans was spoken well of by the people who lived on St. Anne, who ordinarily resented the intrusion of outsiders, as Sutherland had discovered when he sent a man down there to ask questions.

Daniel had gambled that Maris, and her heart, would be safe with the writer. If his friendship with Noah had ended over a matter of honor, then Daniel must assume that Parker Evans was an honorable man.

Indisputably Noah Reed was not. Regardless of what else transpired, Noah's affiliation with the Matherlys was about to come to an end. He thought he had smiled and cajoled himself into Daniel's good graces with this male-bonding-weekend malarkey. Daniel had gone along for his own curiosity and amusement, secretly appalled by the extent of Noah's deceit.

Unbeknownst to the self-assured and insufferably smug Mr. Reed, his head was on the chopping block and the axe was about to fall.

In a symbolic gesture, Daniel dusted bread crumbs off his hands and put his plate and empty brandy snifter in the sink. Contrary to his weather predictions, the storm had intensified. Flashes of lightning were closer, the thunder louder. One clap of thunder shook the house, causing Rosemary's china plates to jingle in their cabinet.

Dear Rosemary. Twenty years she'd been gone, and he still missed her. This house made him particularly homesick for her. They'd spent such happy times here.

Switching off the kitchen light, he made his way through the dark house. As he climbed the staircase, he favored his arthritic joints by leaning heavily upon the balustrade. Damn, he hated getting old!

No sooner had the thought flashed through his mind than a voice came out of the darkness at the top of the stairs. "You forgot your cane."

"Jesus!" Daniel raised his hand to his lurching heart. In a brief glare of blue-white lightning, he saw Noah on the landing. "You startled me."

"It's careless of you not to use your cane, Daniel."

"I'm all right." He continued up the stairs, having to put both feet on each tread before progressing to the next one. "Did the storm wake you?"

"I never went to sleep."

Noah's remote tone of voice gave Daniel pause, but he smiled up at his son-in-law with affected congeniality. "I was having trouble sleeping myself, so I took advantage of being away from Sergeant Maxine to eat a snack."

By now he was only two steps below the landing, but Noah appeared to have taken root there. He made no attempt either to assist Daniel or to step aside. Indeed, he seemed to be blocking his path.

He disliked having Noah looming over him, but he tried to act casually as he indicated the sheets of paper Noah was holding at his side. "Reviewing the document I signed earlier?"

Let him, Daniel thought. *Let him memorize it, for all the good it will do him.* The document wasn't worth spit except in Noah's devious and disillusioned mind.

"No," Noah replied calmly. "This is the report on me from your private investigator, Mr. William Sutherland."

More than being shocked or alarmed, Daniel was angry that his privacy had been invaded. His lips narrowed into the firm thin line that anyone who had been subject to his stern disapproval would recognize. "That was locked in a drawer in my desk at home."

"Yes, I know. It took some rifling, but eventually I found it. Interesting reading."

"I thought so, too," Daniel said stiffly.

"Did you really think I wouldn't know I was being investigated?" Noah asked, laughing lightly. "Your bloodhound is good, Daniel. The best that money can buy, I'm sure. Secret Service training and all that. But he asked questions of one friend too many."

"According to the report, you don't have any friends."

"Call my doubles tennis partner an acquaintance, then. Smart fellow. Smart enough to see through Sutherland's lame reason for the inquiries." His smile, which had been in place up to this point, vanished. "I'm curious to know only when the surveillance began."

There was no reason now to play dumb or to equivocate. "I'd been deliberating it for months. It commenced shortly after your premature anniversary party."

"Why then?"

"Because that was the night I became convinced that you are a seasoned deceiver and liar."

Noah kept every urbane feature schooled, except one eyebrow. He raised it in query. "Really?"

"I don't know if you've been deceiving us all along or if you've been walking the straight and narrow until only the last several months when Morris Blume approached you about selling my publishing company out from under me. I prefer to think the latter, because that would make me less of a fool for being taken in by you. But I fear that one could not acquire and perfect your skills for duplicity in such a short period of time. They've been cultivated, honed—"

"You're becoming redundant, Daniel. You've already said I was a *seasoned* liar."

"Quite right. The night of the party at the Chelsea apartment, I caught you in several lies. And while some could be explained as necessary for surprising Maris, others bothered me. It was also unlike you to think so far ahead and plan a celebration, when ordinarily you rely on your secretary to buy Maris's gifts for every special occasion. So I began observing you carefully, looking beyond the obvious, beyond the man you show to the world. That's when I began seeing you for who you really are."

"How clever of you, Daniel."

"No. If I'd been clever I wouldn't have been duped at the start. You're very good at the masquerade, Noah. Exceptional. You've also proved your mettle as a businessman and publisher. I had admired your abilities long before you came to Matherly Press. Like Maris, I was impressed by *The Vanquished,* and wrongly assumed that only a person with integrity could author a book of matching integrity."

Noah folded his arms across his chest and smiled as he enunciated, "It's fiction, Daniel. It wasn't by accident that I wrote *The Vanquished* from that humble, hillbilly-righteous point of view. I created characters with high-minded ideals, not because I adhere to them, or even believe in them, but because I know that's what sells books. The average Joe and Judy want to believe that valorous people do exist, that evil can be overcome by good, that virtue is a reward unto itself. They get off on that kind of bullshit.

"*The Vanquished* was bloated with the sentimental, southern sappiness that my parents spoon-fed me. I was forced to stomach it when I was growing up. So I used it. I poured it all into that novel so I could close the cover on it and leave it there forever.

"The dewy-eyed heroine," he continued scornfully. "The flawed but valiant hero. Their blood-stirring, star-crossed love story. Every word of it was tripe disguised by pretty prose. It didn't mean shit to me, except for the royalties it earned and the reviews that brought me to the attention of publishers and ultimately paved the way into your office."

"Why ultimately to me?"

"Because, Daniel, you were the only supremely successful publisher with a marriageable daughter, who, to my good fortune, had gone on record claiming that *The Vanquished* was her favorite book."

Even knowing Noah's true nature, Daniel was stunned by this declaration. "You freely confess to being that callous? Is that how you honestly feel about your profession, about people, and life in general?"

"And then some."

Daniel shook his head sadly. "Such a sad waste of talent."

"Come on, Daniel. Let's not weep over my hypocrisy. We publish a gritty police series that's written by a flaming fag. He takes breaks from writing about his tough, heterosexual hero to get fucked up the ass by his young assistant. One of our religious book authors has been convicted of tax evasion and insurance fraud.

"Hypocrisy? On your Christmas party list are several hopeless alcoholics, a brother-and-sister writing team whose oh-so-close relationship would scandalize the mothers who read their books aloud to their children. We publish one cocaine addict for whom you've footed the bill of a rehab clinic at least twice that I know of.

"All of them write very good books, and we publish them. I don't see you getting squeamish over their addictions and aberrations when the profits come rolling in. Those profits pay for your weekly massages, and this house, and chauffeured limousines, and all the other niceties you pompously enjoy up there in your ivory tower."

"You've made your point," Daniel conceded angrily. "I've never denied keeping an eye on the bottom line. I pride myself on having been a good businessman. I've fought countless corporate battles against unscrupulous foes and outlasted economic crises that naysayers predicted could not be withstood.

"And yes, there have been times when, for the good of Matherly Press, I've had to be disingenuous. I've resorted to guile when I felt it was necessary." His eyes pierced through the darkness separating them. "That's why I was able to detect it in you, Noah. And once I got a whiff of it, it became obvious to me that you reek of it."

Noah crossed his legs at the ankles and leaned indolently against the newel post. He looked over the sheets in his hand, although he couldn't have actually been reading them. Except for flashes of lightning, it was too dark to read. "I'll admit that some of this is less than flattering."

Daniel wondered how much he knew. Was this only the initial report? He couldn't remember what had been committed to paper and what the investigator had told him over the telephone that morning, promising that he would receive a written update as soon as it was available.

Noah said, "If you believe this, I'm a wretched human being. I actually admire your ability to keep a civil tongue when speaking to me."

"It hasn't been easy."

"No, I suppose not. I assume you're most upset over my traitorous alliance with WorldView?"

Daniel chose not to disabuse him. Better to let him continue entertaining his misconceptions. "I can forgive that before I can forgive your mistreatment of Maris."

"She knows, by the way," he said placidly, dropping the sheets and letting them scatter. "About the affair with Nadia."

"I know."

He was obviously taken aback. "She told you?"

"No, but her unhappiness with you and your marriage has been apparent for some time."

"She's been happy enough," he said with a blasé flick of his hand. "She loves her work more than ever, now that she's working with this new author. He's handicapped, and that really appeals to her. It's important to her to feel needed."

So he didn't know about Parker Evans! Daniel happily clung to that secret knowledge.

"Maybe I didn't cater to the nurturing aspect of Maris's personality," Noah continued with a nonchalance that Daniel found nauseating. "I'm self-sufficient to a fault. That caused a few minor tiffs. But your precious daughter wasn't too dissatisfied with her life. Not until she caught me with Nadia."

"Her happiness came from within herself. She was happy in spite of you, Noah, not because of you. You even sabotaged her chance of being truly happy."

Noah snapped his fingers. "You're referring to the vasectomy."

"Yes," Daniel said bitterly. That had been one of the most disheartening discoveries to come from Sutherland's report. "The secret vasectomy. As I recall, you cited business obligations as your reason for not accompanying us to Greece."

"Maris had in mind for us to screw our way through the Mediterranean and return pregnant. I invented a plausible excuse for wiggling out of the trip and used the time you were away to have the procedure that ensured I wouldn't have to worry about birth control again."

"I was puzzled when I first read about the vasectomy," Daniel admitted. "Wouldn't a child have secured your ties to us and the Matherly fortune? And therein lay the answer." He looked Noah full in the face. "You didn't want a child competing with you for a share."

Noah uncrossed his ankles. "That's the first thing you've said during this conversation that's incorrect, Daniel."

"You deny it?"

"Not at all," he said blandly. "You're wrong in that I'd ever settle for a measly *share*."

Daniel snorted with contempt. "Don't count your chickens yet, Noah. That document I signed tonight is worthless."

"You think so?" he asked smoothly.

"I was only playing along, seeing how far you would go. What I really find galling is that you attached Howard Bancroft's name to that document. He would never have drawn up a—"

"Oh, but he would," Noah said, interrupting. "He did. Rather than let it be circulated that his father was a Nazi officer who was personally responsible for exterminating thousands of his kindred."

Daniel received that news like a punch to the gut. "You used that to coerce him?"

"So," Noah said with a slow smile, "you knew about his whoring mother?"

"Howard was my friend." Daniel practically strained the words through his clenched teeth. "He confided in me years ago.

I admired him for making his life into what it was instead of letting what he couldn't change defeat him."

"Well, it did, didn't it? In the long run, he couldn't live with the tragic truth."

"A truth you threatened to spread," Daniel said, seeing the clear picture now.

Noah shrugged and smiled beatifically. "See, that's the difference between you and me, Daniel. Come to think of it, between me and just about everybody. You go after what you want, but you fall short of total commitment. Your conscience has drawn an invisible line, and you never step across it. You're shackled by principles and ethics. And while that moral demarcation is admired, it's terribly restricting.

"I, on the other hand, suffer no such impediment. I am willing to do whatever it takes to get what I want. I stop at nothing, and I let nothing stand in my way. My credo is: Find a man's weakness, and you own him. To achieve the goal I've set for myself, I'll go to any lengths."

"Even to talking a man, a good man, into committing suicide."

"I didn't talk Howard into anything. He thought that up all by himself. Although I'll admit that he did me a huge favor when he stuck that pistol in his mouth. What do you suppose he was thinking about when he pulled the trigger? Heaven? Hell? His mother with her legs spread? What?"

Daniel's beloved friend Howard had suffered untold heartache over his terrible secret. All his life he had tried to atone for it with good deeds, kindness, and tolerance. At last, he had come to terms with it.

Then this travesty of a human being had tortured him with it. Worse yet, he could stand there and smile about it.

Daniel realized he was looking into the face of a pure, unrepentant depravity. Noah's indifference to the evil he had done enraged him. Tears of godly wrath blurred his vision.

Heat blasted through his veins as though the temperature of his blood had reached the boiling point in a matter of heartbeats.

"You are despicable," he growled, and charged up the last two steps.

Chapter 30

Parker was the first thing Maris saw when she opened her eyes, and nothing could have pleased her more. He was sitting in his wheelchair beside the bed watching her while she slept. Even before stirring, she smiled into her pillow and asked drowsily, "How'd you manage to get up and into your chair without waking me?"

"Practice."

She sighed and stretched luxuriously, then sat up and drew the sheet as high as her collarbone. "What time is it?"

"Time for you to clear out. Unless you want Mike to catch you flagrante delicto."

He was wearing only a pair of boxer shorts. His shoulders and arms, as she knew, were well formed, the muscles taut and defined. His belly was flat, and beneath it, his sex was appreciably full, even while relaxed.

Beyond his lap were his legs. Last night she had made a point to show no interest in them because of his self-consciousness. Apparently, their lovemaking had convinced him that his apprehension was unnecessary. He wouldn't be sitting here now with his legs exposed, making no attempt to cover them, if he didn't want her to see them.

So she looked.

And it was impossible to conceal her reaction. She stopped just short of gasping out loud, but the sudden catch in her breath couldn't have been missed, especially since he was watching her so closely.

His features were rigidly set. His eyes were shuttered. His voice sliced like a razor. "I warned you that it wasn't pretty."

"Oh, my darling, you were terribly, horribly hurt."

She slid from the bed to kneel in front of him. *Shark attack* was the first thing that came to mind. She'd seen pictures of victims who'd barely escaped with their lives, having huge chunks of their flesh mangled or ripped away. Parker's scars could be compared only to something that vicious.

The worst of them was a hollow as large as her fist where a section of his quadriceps had been gouged out. From there a scar cut a gully half an inch wide down the entire length of his right thigh and curved around toward the back of his knee. On his lower legs was a network of crisscrossing scars, some raised and bumpy, while others looked like flat, shiny ribbons of plastic that had been stretched between puckered skin. His calves were disproportionately small and flaccid. He was missing the smallest two toes on his right foot.

Overwhelmed with compassion for the agony he must have suffered, she timorously traced one of the raised scars with her fingertip. "Do they still hurt?"

"Sometimes."

She looked up at him sorrowfully, then leaned forward and kissed one of the worst of the scars that snaked up his shin. Reaching down, he stroked her cheek. She lifted his hand to her mouth and kissed the palm.

He said, "Now that your morbid curiosity has been satisfied, can we get in one fast fuck before breakfast?"

She yanked her head back. "What?"

"I think you heard me."

As shocked as if he'd struck her, she stood up, reached for her nightgown, and held it against her, a flimsy shield. "What's the matter?"

"Nothing except an early morning woodie that needs your attention."

She shook her head in befuddlement. The coarse language wasn't that startling. But he wasn't being naughty for naughtiness' sake. No flirtatious wink accompanied his words. He was being purposefully, hurtfully crude. "Why are you acting like this?"

"This is what I'm like, Maris."

"No, you're not."

He gave a dismissive shrug. "Okay, whatever." He pushed his chair backward, then turned it away from her and headed across the room toward the chifforobe. "I've got something for you."

"Parker?" she called in exasperation.

"What?"

"Why are you acting this way? I don't understand. What happened between last night and this morning?"

"You don't remember? Well, let's see. Between last night and this morning, I'd say your orgasms outnumbered mine about two to one, but after your fifth or sixth, I honestly lost count. Of course, with women it's sometimes hard to tell when one leaves off and another starts, or if they're even for real. But if you fake it, honey, you fake it convincingly."

He'd opened the door to the chifforobe and removed a box from one of the interior drawers. Now he spun around and faced her, grinning cruelly as he looked her up and down. "And I'll say this for you, Mrs. Matherly-Reed. You're tight. As a goddamn fist. And wet as a mouth. Very nice. I wonder why your husband went out for it."

Tears of mortification filled her eyes. Angrily she swiped one away as it slid down her cheek. Hastily, she pulled on her night-gown, the only article of clothing available. "I don't know what's the matter with you, but I won't continue this. I can't match you for vulgarity."

"Sure you can. You've got an expansive vocabulary. Maybe not one as colorful as mine, but if you put your mind to it, I'll bet you come up with something suitable to say. Maybe on your plane ride back to New York. I assume you're leaving."

Not even deigning to answer, she headed for the door. "Wait!" He rolled his chair over to her. "*Envy*. The final draft."

He practically thrust the box into her hands, so she had no choice but to take it. She looked at it, then at him. "It's finished?"

"Has been. All along. From the beginning. What you've been reading in installments is the polishing draft."

She gaped at him. Words failed her.

"I never submit a partial manuscript, Maris. No one sees my book until it's finished. I wouldn't have sent a prologue unless I had a book behind it."

"Why, Parker? Why?"

Deliberately mistaking her meaning, he shrugged. "Personal policy. That's just the way I work."

Maris felt as though the spot on which she stood were eroding rapidly and that at any second it would disappear out from under her altogether. But she wasn't going to sink without a fight.

"That's just the way you work?" she repeated, raising her voice to a shout. "What the hell was all this for, Parker? Or is that even your name? How many do you have? What in hell has this been about? Why the lies, the games?"

"They seemed like fun at the time. We both got laid. Several times last night you moaned, 'Yes, yes, harder, faster, Parker.' X-rated things, too. Sounded to me like you were having fun."

For several beats, she just stared at him, wondering at what point he had become this sarcastic stranger. Then she hurled the box as far as she could throw it. It upended in midair, the lid came off, and some four hundred manuscript pages scattered in that many directions across the polished hardwood floor and Aubusson rug.

Maris stalked to the door and jerked it open.

Mike was standing on the other side of it, one hand raised, about to knock. The other was holding a cordless telephone. "Maris." There was no surprise in his voice. He had expected her to be with Parker. Her emotional state, however, seemed to alarm him.

Looking beyond her shoulder, he took in the situation at a glance. The look he gave Parker went beyond reproof; it was that of a hanging judge about to hand down the sentence. Stiffly, he extended the telephone toward Maris. "For you. I hated to disturb you, but the gentleman said it was an emergency."

She took the telephone from him with a shaking hand and stepped out into the hallway. Mike went into the bedroom and closed the door behind him. Maris leaned against the wall and took several seconds to compose herself. She breathed deeply, sniffed her nose hard, blinked away tears.

Then, clearing her throat, she said, "Hello?"

"Maris?"

"Noah?" His voice was strangely muffled and subdued. She barely recognized it.

"It's imperative that you return to New York immediately. I took the liberty of making your travel arrangements. A ticket is waiting for you at the Savannah airport. Your flight departs at eleven-ten, so you haven't got much time."

Her dread was so absolute, it felt as though her heart had been replaced with an anvil. She was suddenly very cold. She closed her eyes, but tears leaked through. It would have been useless to try and hold them back. "It's Dad, isn't it?"

"I'm afraid so, yes."

"Is it bad? A stroke?"

"He . . . God, this is tough. Telling you like this. You shouldn't have to hear this news over the telephone, Maris, but...he's dead."

She cried out. Her knees buckled and she sank to the floor.

* * *

Parker was at his worktable in the solarium, but he wasn't working. Instead he was staring out at the ocean. He broke his stare only occasionally, and that was when he compressed his bowed head between his hands in abject despair and self-loathing.

He'd heard Mike when he returned from the mainland, but he didn't seek him out, and Mike didn't come to him. He'd gone straight upstairs and had been moving around in his room ever since. It sounded as though he were pacing.

Parker had been replaying in his head his last conversation with Maris. If you could call it a conversation. His stomach knotted when he recalled the horrible things he'd said to her. Her stricken expression haunted him.

She might be consoled to know that he was as miserable as she, but he doubted it. The only way she might be consoled was if he were drawn and quartered and the pieces thrown to a herd of ravenous wild pigs. Starting with his mouth. His foul, abusive, nasty mouth.

The afternoon dragged on interminably. It was hot and muggy outside and that oppression had eked into the house to contribute to his feelings of suffocation. Or was the weather to blame? Maybe he was being smothered by remorse.

"I stayed with Maris until they boarded her flight."

Parker hadn't heard Mike come into the solarium. He sat bolt upright and glanced over his shoulder toward the door. Mike was standing as stiff as a girder in his seersucker suit.

"It took off on time," he added.

As soon as Maris could pack her things, she and Mike had departed for the mainland. She left without a word to Parker, but he hadn't expected her to tell him good-bye. He didn't deserve it. He didn't deserve a *kiss my ass,* or a *go to hell,* or even a *screw you.* Her leaving without even acknowledging him had been more eloquent than any epithet. Eloquent, classy, and dignified. Typical of her.

Hiding behind the drapery, he had watched her departure through the dining room window. She had looked very small beneath her wide-brimmed straw hat. She'd also worn sunglasses to conceal her weeping eyes from prying strangers. The tan she had acquired on the beach seemed to have faded with the news of her father's death. She had looked pale and vulnerable, fragile enough to break from the air pressure alone.

Yet there was a brave dignity about her that suggested an enviable inner strength.

Mike had stowed her bags in the trailer of the Gator, then assisted her into the seat. Parker saw her lips move as she thanked him. Then he watched until the utility vehicle disappeared from sight through the tunnel of trees. He would probably never see her again. He had expected that.

What he hadn't expected was that it would hurt so goddamn much.

He had believed himself to be beyond the grasp of pain. After what he had endured, he had imagined himself immune to it. He wasn't. He had decided to anesthetize himself with several belts of bourbon, but the first one had made him so sick, he'd thrown it up. He didn't think there was an analgesic that would be effective against this particular kind of pain.

Now his back was still to Mike. He kept his stinging eyes on the surf. "Maris was worried about her father last night. Maybe she had a premonition."

"I wouldn't be surprised. They were very close."

After Noah's call, she had been in a state of complete emotional collapse, but she'd had the wherewithal to tell Mike that her father had fallen down the stairs of their country house.

She'd been told that he had died instantly of a broken neck. It had happened during the middle of the night.

The noise had awakened Noah. He had rushed to Daniel's aid, but when he couldn't get a response out of him, he called 911. The rural emergency service had reached the house in a matter of minutes, but it didn't matter—Daniel Matherly was dead.

Noah had refused to accept the paramedics' word for it. The ambulance ran hot to the small community hospital. Doctors there pronounced Daniel dead, making it official and indisputable. Noah had seen no point in calling Maris until daylight.

"She probably feels guilty for not being there," Parker said.

"She said as much on the way to the mainland."

"How was she when she left?"

"How do you think she was, Parker?"

He frowned at Mike's snide comeback, but he didn't challenge it. He had asked a stupid question with an obvious answer. "She probably felt like she'd been run through a thrasher."

"You certainly did your part."

Unlike its predecessor, that cutting remark demanded to be addressed. Parker came around. "Are you suggesting that I've been a bad boy?"

"You know it without my saying so."

"What are you going to do, Mike? Park me in the corner? Ground me for a month? Restrict my TV time? Rap my knuckles with a ruler?"

"Actually, I was thinking that you're the one who should be run through a thrasher."

Parker agreed that that was the least he deserved, but, while it was okay for him to think it, he resented hearing it from someone else. "Getting Maris into bed was part of the plot. You probably guessed that."

"I guessed it. That doesn't mean I liked it."

"Nobody asked you to like it."

"Did *you?*"

"Did I what?"

"Like it."

A scathing retort was on the tip of his tongue, but he foundered under Mike's incisive stare. Turning his head away, he mumbled, "Irrelevant."

"I don't think so. I think it's not only relevant but key to how you progress from here."

Parker went back to his keyboard. "Excuse me. I'm trying to write."

"Fine. Turn your back on me. Stare into that blank screen. Count the ticks of the cursor till hell freezes over, for all I care. Delude yourself into believing that you're writing. We both know you're not."

Parker came back around, angry now. "Obviously you've reached a conclusion that you're just dying to share. So spit it out. Get it out of your system. God knows I won't have a minute's peace until you do."

The older man refused to take umbrage. "I'm not going to fight with you, Parker," he said evenly. "But yes, I will tell you something you need to hear." Ignoring Parker's roll of the eyes, he went on. "You resurrected yourself when, for all practical purposes, your life was over. I was there to help. I needled you and badgered you along. But you did it. It was a heroic effort. You're to be commended for overcoming incredible obstacles. You beat overwhelming odds. Beyond putting your life back on track, you have thrived."

"Yay, me."

The caustic interruption went ignored and Mike doggedly continued. "Your body has healed, but not your soul. The damage done to it was a thousand times worse than the injuries to your legs. Your soul is more twisted than they ever were. Pins and plates hold your bones together, and new skin patches the places where there was no skin left, but your soul hasn't been mended.

It's still raw and bleeding, and you snarl at anyone who extends a hand to help you heal it."

"That's what I've been trying to tell you for years, Mike," he said sweetly. "I'm a lost cause."

"You're not a lost cause, you're a coward," Mike shouted angrily. "It takes far less courage to cling to the past than it does to face the future."

"Very good, Mike. I should write that down. What was it again? 'It takes far less—' "

"Sarcasm? Good. If I'm pissing you off, at least I know I have your attention." Mike's lined features softened and turned earnest. "Parker, consign Noah Reed to God. Or to the devil. Let them haggle over who's to be his judge and what his punishment is to be.

"Then go to Maris. If you can get her to talk to you, lay open your heart. Explain everything. Start at the beginning and tell her all of it. Tell her Noah's part. Confess yours. She may forgive you. She may not. But either way, you'll be rid of it. For the first time in fourteen long years, you'll be free of everything that happened in Key West. You will have saved yourself. Again. And in the only way that really matters."

Parker's heart was pounding hard and loudly against his eardrums, but he kept his expression passive. "Good sermon, Mike. Honestly. Very moving. But I'm going to stick to plan A."

"And throw away a chance to be happy with a woman you love?"

"Love?" he scoffed. "Who said that?"

"You did. Every time you looked at her."

"Have you been sneak-reading romance novels again? They're not good for your blood pressure."

"Okay, be funny. Deny you're in love with her. You're only wasting your breath. Maris hit you like those drugs you used to take. The night she came here, you got high on her, and after that you couldn't get enough. She's—"

"She's Noah's *wife*."

Parker felt his control snap like the string on a tennis racket that had been whacked one too many times.

"She is Noah's 'dearly beloved, we are gathered here' bride. That's the important thing. That's the *only* thing," he yelled, slicing the air with his hand. "Nothing else matters. Not how I feel about her, or how she feels about me, or even how they feel about each other.

"She is Noah Reed's wife, and I had her. But good. She was finger-fucked, and tongue-fucked, and mind-fucked. By *me*!" He pounded his chest with his fist, his eyes shimmering with tears spawned by the white-hot rage that consumed him whenever he thought of Noah's treachery. And now by the agony of his own guilt.

Mike's features surrendered to gravity and settled into an aged mask of profound disappointment. "Perhaps you're right, Parker. Perhaps you are a lost cause. Your cruelty to her goes beyond reprehensible. All you care about is this revenge plot of yours."

"That's right. Now you're catching on."

"What's the next chapter?"

"Well, since Maris threw the manuscript at me, I don't think I can count on her to get it to Noah. So I guess I'll have to send it to him myself, registered and receipt requested, along with a cover letter saying that *Envy* is being simultaneously submitted to every publishing house in New York. If that doesn't give his short-and-curlies a smart tug, then perhaps a postscript about his wife's talent for giving head will."

Mike shook his head with disgust. "And then what, Parker?"

"The gripping climax, of course."

Mike subjected him to a long, hard stare, then turned and picked up two suitcases, which had been left in the kitchen and up till now out of Parker's sight. "Going somewhere?"

"Away from you. I won't be a party to this."

Mike was walking out on him? That shook him up more than

he let on. "You helped get her here, don't forget. You played along."

"For which I am now very ashamed. In any case, let this serve as notice that my participation is over."

"Fine. Go. Have a nice trip."

"Will you be all right?"

"Not your problem anymore, is it?"

He spun his chair around and faced his blank computer screen. A few moments later, he heard Mike leaving through the back door. And he was truly alone.

Chapter 31

———⊸●⊷———

Afterward, Maris could barely remember her return trip to New York. She had operated in a dreamlike state, except without the subconscious surety that it was unreal and that she would wake up soon. Parker's inexplicable behavior and her father's death had been a double-barreled assault. To protect itself, her mind had put conscious thought and reasoning powers on autopilot and allowed her to function only by rote.

Discreetly Mike Strother had alerted the flight attendant to her bereavement, so she had been treated deferentially, basically left alone. She passed the flight staring vacantly out the window, unaware and uncaring of what was going on around her.

Noah was at LaGuardia to meet her. She wasn't happy to see him, but he relieved her of the arrival hassle at a major airport. Her baggage was reclaimed with dispatch. He had a car and driver waiting.

As the limo wended its way through heavy traffic into Manhattan, he somberly filled in the details that he hadn't told her over the telephone. Daniel's body was still in Massachusetts, where the autopsy would be conducted. There could have been a contributing health factor that caused him to fall, Noah explained. Pulmonary embolism. Cardiac arrest. An aneurysm that hadn't shown up during his last physical.

"Most probably," he told her, "Daniel simply lost his balance on the dark staircase."

Daniel's cane had been found in his bedroom. It was believed that he was ascending the stairs. Without his cane for additional support, he had tripped.

"He'd also had more than a few drinks," Noah added reluctantly. "You know, Maris, we had feared something like this would happen."

He informed her that following the autopsy the body would be transferred to New York. He'd made preliminary funeral arrangements but was awaiting her approval before finalizing them. Knowing she would be particular about the casket, he had held off making a selection until her return.

She commented on how expeditiously he had handled everything.

"I wanted to spare you as much unpleasantness as possible."

He was solicitous, soft-spoken, obsequious.

She couldn't bear to be near him.

She deplored even having to breathe the same air as he and instructed the chauffeur to take her to her father's house. Accepting a friend's offer to help in any way she could, Maris sent her to her apartment with a list of clothing and articles she wanted brought to her. If she could help it, she would never return to the residence she had shared with Noah.

She moved back into her old bedroom in Daniel's house. For the next three days, when she and Maxine weren't receiving people who came to pay their respects and offer condolences, they comforted one another. The housekeeper was disconsolate. She blamed herself for letting Daniel go to the country house without her, as though her presence could have prevented the accident. Maris tried to assuage her feelings of partial responsibility, all the while empathizing with them. She suffered similarly.

Her father had died while she'd been making love to Parker.

Each time her thoughts drifted in that direction, which was frequently, she halted them abruptly. She refused to wear a mantle of guilt for that. Daniel had urged her to return to Georgia. She had been there with his blessing. The last thing he had said to her was that she deserved her happiness and that he loved her. His death had nothing to do with her sharing Parker's bed.

Nevertheless, the connection between the two had been made, and she would never think of one without recalling the other.

She learned that a death in the family was a time-consuming event, especially if the deceased was a person of Daniel Matherly's standing. He was the last patriarch of the publishing dynasty; he was one of New York's own. His obituary made the front page of the *New York Times*. Local media covered his funeral.

Maris endured the day-long affair with a steely determination not to crack under pressure. Dressed head to toe in black, she was photographed entering the cathedral, exiting the cathedral, standing at the grave site with her head bowed in prayer, receiving the mayor's condolences.

The silent expressions of grief were the ones she appreciated most—a small squeeze of her hand, eye contact that conveyed sympathy and understanding. Most people said too much. Well-meaning folk told her to take comfort in the fact that Daniel had lived a long and productive life. That he hadn't suffered before he died. That we should all be so lucky to go that quickly. That at least he hadn't withered and died slowly. That a sudden death is a blessing.

Statements to that effect sorely tested her composure.

However, no one surprised or offended her more than Nadia Schuller. Noah was speaking to a group of publishing colleagues when Nadia sidled up to Maris immediately following the gravesite observance and gripped her hand. "I'm sorry, Maris. Terribly, terribly sorry."

Maris was struck not only by Nadia's audacity in attending the service, but also by her convincing portrayal of shocked bereavement. Maris pulled back her hand, thanked Nadia coldly, and tried to turn away. But Nadia wouldn't be shaken off. "We need to talk. Soon."

"If you want a quote for your column, call our publicity department."

"Please, Maris," Nadia said, leaning closer. "This is important. Call me." She pressed a business card into Maris's hand, then turned and walked quickly away. She had the decency not to lock eyes with Noah before she left.

He was the worst part of Maris's endurance test.

She tried not to visibly flinch each time he came near her. Yet he seemed determined to be near her. At the reception following the funeral, he was never far from her side, often placing his arm around her shoulders, pressing her hand, demonstrating to their friends and associates a loving affection that was grossly false. The act would have been hilarious if it weren't so obscene.

Dusk had fallen before the house cleared of guests. Maxine refused to retire to her room as Maris suggested and instead began supervising the caterers' cleanup. That's when Maris approached Noah. "I want to talk to you."

"Certainly, darling."

His ingratiating manner set her teeth on edge. He was thoroughly repugnant. It seemed that the two years she had shared a home, a bed with him had happened to another woman in another time. She couldn't fathom doing so now.

Her only saving grace, her only reasonable excuse, was that he was an excellent role player. He was an adroit liar. She and Daniel had fallen for an act he had perfected.

"You can drop the pretense, Noah. No one's around except Maxine, and she already knows that I've left you."

She led him into her father's study. The room smelled of him and of his pipe tobacco. It smelled of his brandy and the books he had loved. The room evoked such poignant memories for her, it was claustrophobic and comforting at the same time.

She sat down in the large tufted leather chair behind Daniel's desk. It was the closest she could come to being hugged by him. She had spent the past four nights curled up in this chair, weeping over her loss between brief and restless naps in which she dreamed of Parker moving ever farther away from her as she screamed his name. No matter how desperately she tried to touch him, he was always beyond her reach. She would wake herself up sobbing over the dual loss.

Noah pinched up the creases of his dark suit trousers and lowered himself into an easy chair. "I had hoped your second visit south had mellowed you, Maris. You're as prickly as you were before you left."

"Dad's death didn't change anything between us. Nor did it change your character. You're a liar and an adulterer." She paused a beat before adding, "And possibly those are the least of your sins."

His eyes sharpened. "What does that mean?"

She opened the lap drawer of Daniel's desk and took out a business card. "I came across this in Dad's day planner while I was looking up addresses for acknowledgment cards. It's an innocuous card with a scarcity of information on it. Only a name and telephone number. Curious, I called. Imagine my surprise."

He stared at her, saying nothing, then indolently raised his shoulders in silent inquiry.

"I spoke personally to the man Dad had retained to investigate you," she told him. "Mr. Sutherland conveyed his sympathy over Dad's passing. Then I asked him how his business card had found its way into Dad's day planner. He was very discreet, extremely professional, and finally apologetic.

"Ethically, he couldn't discuss another client's business, even a late client's. However, he said, if I had access to Dad's files, he was sure I'd find his report among them. If I wished to continue the investigation that wasn't yet complete, he would welcome me as a client and offered to apply the advance Dad had paid him to my account."

She spread her arms across the top of the desk. "I've searched for the mentioned report, Noah. It's not here. Not in any of Dad's files here, or at the office, not in the personal safe upstairs in his bedroom closet, or in his safe-deposit box at the bank.

"Coincidentally, you spent time in here the morning before you left for the country. While Dad was upstairs packing some last-minute items, you told Maxine that you had calls to make and came in here, ostensibly to use the telephone. You closed the door behind you. She thought it odd at the time, since you typically use your cell phone, but she thought no more about it. Not until I asked her if you'd been snooping around in Dad's personal things that day."

He shook his head and laughed softly. "Maris, I have no idea what you're talking about. I might have come in here that morning. Frankly, I don't remember if I did or not. But since when is this room off limits to me? From the time we began dating, I've been in this room hundreds of times. When I make private calls I usually close the door. Everybody does. If this is about Nadia—"

"It isn't," she said tersely. "I don't give a damn about Nadia or anyone else you sleep with."

He gave her a look that said he seriously doubted that. She wanted to strike him, to pound the conceit out of his expression. "I also spoke to the authorities in Massachusetts."

"My, my, you've been a busy girl."

"I questioned their ruling that Dad's death was accidental." She hadn't struck him physically, as she would have liked to. All the same, her statement rid him of a measure of arrogance. His smile grew a little stiff, as though it had congealed. His spine

straightened. "Honoring my request, they've agreed to reinvestigate. This time they'll be looking for evidence."

That brought him to his feet. "Evidence of what?"

"We have an appointment with Chief of Police Randall tomorrow to discuss their findings," she informed him coldly. "I
suggest you be there."

* * *

The burg's police department had a staff of six—one chief, four
patrolmen, and a clerk who also served as dispatcher and official
town gossip. The department handled minor emergencies such
as broken-down snowplows and lost pets, parking tickets when
tourists passing through stayed too long in an antique shop, and
an occasional DUI.

By big-city standards, the gossip wasn't all that scandalous. It
might revolve around who had recently gone to New York City
for a face-lift, who was selling their country house to a movie star
who futilely wished to remain anonymous, and who had checked
their daughter-gone-wild into drug rehab after a tempestuous
family intervention. Residents could safely leave their homes and
cars unlocked because thefts were rare.

The last homicide in the county had occurred during Lyndon
Johnson's administration. It had been an open-and-shut case.
The culprit had confessed to the killing when police arrived at
the scene.

The department's lack of experience as crime solvers worked
in Maris's disfavor. But it worked to her advantage in that a murder investigation stimulated more enthusiasm than tacking up
notices of a lost kitty or setting up bleachers for the Fourth of July
concert and fireworks display.

The officers had approached the investigation of Daniel's
death with a zealous desire to sniff out the ruthless killer of an
esteemed citizen, even if he was a weekender.

She and Noah drove up in separate cars. The exterior of the ivy-covered building looked more like a yarn-and-woolens boutique than a police station. Maris arrived a few minutes ahead of Noah. As soon as he got there, they were ushered into the chief's office. Both declined an offer of coffee and sweet rolls from the local bakery.

Chief Randall, a ruddy-faced man with a bad, blond combover, sensing her desire to cut to the chase, kept the pleasantries to a minimum and settled behind his desk. He seemed more disappointed than relieved to report the outcome of his department's investigation.

"I'm afraid I haven't got all that much more to tell you that wasn't in the initial report, Mrs. Matherly-Reed. My people went over the house with a fine-toothed comb. Didn't find a thing that suggested foul play."

Out of the corner of her eye, she saw Noah complacently fold his hands in his lap.

"The officers think, and I concur, that your father simply fell down the stairs. There were some bloodstains on the floor where he was found, but they're explained by the gash on his scalp. It split open when his head struck the floor."

She swallowed, then asked, "What about the autopsy report?"

He opened the case file and slipped on a pair of reading glasses that were too narrow for his wide face. The stems were stretched and caused the glasses to perch crookedly on his nose. "The contents of his stomach verify that he ate only minutes before he died, which is what Mr. Reed had assumed." He peered at Noah over the eyeglasses.

Noah gave a solemn nod. "When I went into the kitchen to call 911, there were dirty dishes in the sink. I had cleaned up after dinner, so I surmised that Daniel had gone downstairs for something to eat. On his way back up, he fell."

"Is it possible that the scene was staged, Chief Randall?"

"Staged?"

"Perhaps the dishes were placed in the sink to make everyone think Dad had used them."

"Oh, he used them," Chief Randall assured her. "His finger-prints were on them. Nobody else's."

"The dishes could have been used upstairs. He often ate off a bed tray. How do we know he was downstairs?"

"Crumbs."

"Excuse me?"

"Bread crumbs on his robe, his slippers, and on the floor near the sink. My best guess is that he stood and looked out the kitchen window while he ate his sandwich."

Patting his comb-over as though to make sure it was still in place, he referred to the file again. "His blood alcohol level was above the legal driving limit but not by much."

"Any trace of a controlled substance?"

"Only the medications he was taking. We checked out the pre-scriptions with his physician in New York. Dating from when they were last refilled, the correct amount of dosages remained. There was no sign that a struggle had taken place anywhere in the house."

"You found his cane in his bedroom?"

"Leaning against the nightstand, and yes, we checked it for prints," he said before she could ask. "His were the only ones on it. No evidence of a break-in by an intruder. Not a mark on your father's body except for the cut on his head, which the ME said was consistent with the fall. He also places the time of death within minutes of when Mr. Reed's 911 call was received. That's all documented."

He removed his glasses and rested his clasped hands on top of the binder containing the report. He cleared his throat and looked at her sympathetically. "When a tragic accident like this occurs and someone dies, their loved ones look for reasons. A scapegoat. Something or someone to blame. I know it's hard for you to accept, but it appears that your father ran into some difficulty as he was making his way upstairs. He lost his balance and suffered a fatal fall. I'm sorry, Mrs. Matherly-Reed."

Maris was neither heartened nor disappointed. The findings were exactly what she had expected them to be. She gathered her handbag and stood. Reaching across the desk, she shook hands with the police chief. "I appreciate your time and effort."

"That's what I'm here for. I've put your house on our regular drive-by route. We'll keep a check on it for you."

"That's very thoughtful of you. Thank you."

Once outside, Maris made a beeline for her car. Noah caught up with her before she could get in.

He gripped her upper arm, pulled her around, and pushed his face close to hers. "Satisfied?"

"Completely." Looking at him evenly, she said, "I'm convinced beyond a shadow of doubt that you were the 'difficulty' Dad encountered on his way up the staircase."

His narrow lips stretched into a smile that raised the hair on the back of her neck. "There's absolutely nothing to substantiate these nasty suspicions of yours."

"Let go of my arm, Noah, or I'm going to start screaming bloody murder. That nice chief of police would dearly love to rush to my rescue."

Seeing the wisdom of letting go, he did.

"Chief Randall might be interested to know that my father had retained Mr. William Sutherland to investigate you."

"Which is circumstantial. So where does that get you?"

"Nowhere. You made certain there was no evidence of wrongdoing. But you underestimate my ability to recognize a good plot."

"This isn't a novel."

"Unfortunately. But if it were, I would suspect you of being the villain. Part of my job is to isolate a character's motivation, right? His goal must be clear or the story has no legs on which to stand. Well, Noah, your goal is glaringly apparent. Why did you shuttle Dad off to the country house while I was conveniently out of town, especially since we were separated? Why, when you enjoy being waited on, did you insist that Maxine remain in the city?

"You lied about Nadia. You lied about taking up writing again. What else have you lied about? WorldView? Surely. On that I would bet everything I hold dear. When Morris Blume inadvertently mentioned that secret meeting to me, you finessed your way through an explanation. You had covered your rear by informing Dad of it, on the outside chance that one of us would get wind of it. But I wasn't convinced of your innocence then, and I'm even more certain of your guilt now.

"I think Dad was on to you. Why else would he retain Mr. Sutherland? I think he knew you were dirty-dealing. Maybe he even had proof. When he confronted you with it, you killed him.

"I hope you haven't committed murder in the hope of securing a deal with WorldView. Because if you have, you're going to be sorely disappointed. Understand this, Noah. Matherly Press will remain autonomous, just as it always has been."

"Be very careful, Maris." His voice was low, but it vibrated with menace. He reached up and took a strand of her hair, winding it tightly around his index finger. To anyone passing by who happened to glance at them, it would look like an affectionate gesture. But he pulled the strand of hair taut enough to hurt.

"It's *you* who needs to understand *this*," he said. "Nobody is going to prevent me from having everything I want."

She had been right to fear him the night before she left for Georgia. The latent violence she had sensed in him then hadn't been imagined. She had glimpsed an evil component of Noah that was no longer content to lie dormant.

But, oddly, she was no longer afraid of him. He had lost the power to intimidate or frighten her. She laughed softly. "What are you going to do, Noah? Push me down a staircase, too?"

"Daniel alone was responsible for his death. He lost his temper, reacted recklessly, temporarily forgot his physical limitations, and suffered the consequences. If you want to place blame, place it on him. But," he continued silkily, "I'll admit that his death was very convenient."

She recoiled and, because he still had hold of her hair, the sudden movement caused a painful yank on her scalp. It was sharp enough to bring tears to her eyes. But she hardly noticed. Because the yank on her memory had been even sharper.

Actually, her death was very convenient.

She'd read that line a dozen or more times. It was a key piece of dialogue, so she had dwelled on it. She had played with ideas on how the statement could be improved or enhanced, but after trying several changes she had concluded that it didn't need improving or enhancing. It was perfect as it was. Its cold candor was deliberate. It made the statement all the more shocking. Parker had used that simple sentence to provide a revealing sneak peek into the dark soul of the character. Realization slammed into her.

"You're Todd."

Noah's chin went back. "What? Who?"

Thoughts were snapping and popping in her mind like a sail in a high wind, but one thought isolated itself and became jarringly clear: This could not be a coincidence.

With more ferocity than she believed herself capable of, she said, "For the last time, Noah, let go of me."

"Of course, darling." He uncoiled her hair from around his finger. "You're free to go. Now that we understand one another."

She slid into the driver's seat and started the motor. Before pulling the door closed, she said, "You have no idea how well I understand you."

"Envy" Ch. 22
Key West, Florida, 1988

It was one of those days when the words simply would not come.

Roark pressed his skull between his hands, squeezing it like a melon, trying to force the words out through his pores. To no avail. He came up dry. So far today, he had contributed exactly two and one-half sentences to his manuscript. Nineteen words total. For the past three hours, his cursor had been stuck in the same spot, winking at him.

"Mocking little bastard," he whispered to it now. Deliberately he typed, *The grass is green. The sky is blue.* "See, you son of a bitch? I can write a sentence when I want to."

It made little difference that yesterday, his day off from the club, had been a productive one. He had put in sixteen hard hours of writing, going without food or drink and taking bathroom breaks only when absolutely forced. He had over twenty pages to show for his labors. But the euphoria had lasted only until he awakened this morning to discover that evil spirits had sneaked in during the night while he slept and robbed him of yesterday's talent. What other explanation could there be for its overnight disappearance?

His frustration was such that he considered shutting down for the day, taking in a movie, or going to the beach, or getting in some fishing. But that kind of retreat was easily habit-forming. It was too convenient to surrender to a momentary block. It might become a permanent block, and that was the dreadful possibility that kept him shackled to his chair, staring into a blank screen while being taunted by a blinking cursor that didn't go any-goddamn-where.

"Roark!"

The door slammed three floors below and Todd's running footsteps echoed in the stairwell. Lately, he had been working through the restaurant's lunch hours to earn extra money. Roark welcomed the time Todd was out, when he was left alone in the apartment to write without the distraction that even having another warm body nearby could create.

He turned around in time to see Todd barge through their door. "What's up? Is the building on fire? I wish."

"I sold it."

"Your car?" That was the first thing that popped into Roark's head. Todd was constantly bitching about his car.

"My book! I sold my book!" His cheeks were flushed, his eyes were feverishly bright, his smile was toothpaste-commercial caliber.

Roark just looked at him, dumbfounded.

"Did you hear what I said?" Todd's voice scaled upward to an abnormally shrill pitch. "I sold my manuscript."

Unsteadily Roark came to his feet. "I...th-that's great. I didn't even know you...When did you submit it?"

Todd somehow managed to look abashed while maintaining his wide grin. "I didn't tell you. I sent it on a whim about two months ago. I didn't want to make a big deal of it because I was afraid—Jesus, I was *positive*—I'd get another rejection letter. Then today, just now, less than an hour ago, I got this call at work."

"The publisher had your work number?"

"Well, yeah. In my cover letter, I listed every conceivable way they could contact me. Just in case, you know? Anyway, the manager of the club, that fag we hate, prances over and tells me someone wants me on the phone in his office. He says that personal calls aren't allowed and to please limit the conversation to three minutes. Like we were busy," he snorted.

"I hadn't parked a car in half an hour. I figured it was you or one of the babes calling." To Todd, their neighbors had collectively become "the babes." "Overflowing toilet or something, you know? But instead, *instead,* this guy identifies himself as an editor, says he's read my manuscript, says it blew him away. Those words. 'It blew me away.' Says he wants to publish it. I nearly shit right there, man.

"Then, for a heartbeat or two, I thought you or somebody, maybe the fag we hate, was jacking with me, you know, playing a trick. But no, this editor goes on and on about my story, calls the characters by name. Says he's willing to offer in the neighborhood of high five figures, but I'm sure that was only his starting point. As much as he raved over the book, there's got to be wiggle room to up the ante."

Suddenly he puffed out his cheeks, then emptied

them like a bellows. "Listen to me, will ya?" he chortled. "Holy shit! It hasn't even sunk in yet. I'm standing here talking about negotiating an advance, but I haven't even grasped it yet. I've sold a book!"

Roark, forcing himself to move, forcing elation into his expression, crossed the room and gave Todd a mighty hug, thumping him on the back, lifting him off the floor, congratulating him in the spirit of a good fraternity brother and colleague. "Congratulations, man. You've worked hard for this. You deserve it."

"Thanks, Roark."

Todd pushed him back, looked him square in the eye, and stuck out his hand. They shook hands, but the solemnity was short-lived. Within seconds Todd was whooping like an air-raid siren and bouncing around the apartment with the jerky, disjointed hyperactivity of a rhesus on speed.

"I don't know what to do first," he said, laughing.

"Call Hadley," Roark suggested.

"Hadley can go fuck himself. He didn't show any confidence in me. Why should I share my good news with him? I know," he said, vigorously rubbing his hands together. "A celebration. Blowout party. You and me. On me."

Roark, feeling less like celebrating than he ever had in his life, was already shaking his head. "You don't have to—"

"I know I don't have to. I want to. Tonight. I'll make all the arrangements."

"I've got to work."

"Screw work."

"Easy for you to say. You've sold a book. For high five figures with wiggle room."

The statements jerked a knot in the rhesus's tail.

Todd stopped bouncing and turned toward Roark. He treated him to several moments of hard scrutiny. "Oh. Now I get it. You're pissed because I sold before you did."

"No, I'm not."

"Well, that's good," Todd said sarcastically. "Because if you were pissed, you might be acting like a jackass instead of my best friend on the happiest day of my life."

True. He was acting like a jackass. Rank jealousy had turned him into a prick, and he was running headlong toward ruining the happiest day of his best friend's life.

Not that it would be any different if the situation were reversed. Todd would behave just as badly, probably worse. He would sulk and mouth about life's injustices. He would be resentful and caustic, and then he'd turn cruel.

But since when was Todd Grayson his standard for good behavior? He liked to think he was a finer person and better friend than Todd. He liked to think he had a stronger character and more integrity.

He plastered on a fake grin. "What the hell, I'll call in sick. Let that fag we hate fire me. What time's the party start?"

*　*　*

Todd said to give him time to make a few arrangements, and Roark said fine because he needed to close out his work for the day anyway. As soon as Todd flew out to run his errands, Roark surrendered to his dejection. It set in with a vengeance.

He stared into his computer screen, wondering

why he had been cursed with a burning desire to do something creative but shortchanged the ability and opportunity to do it. Why would God play a dirty trick like that? Entice you with a dream, provide you with enough talent to make it appear reachable, then keep the dream just this side of being realized?

Like a mantra, he repeated to himself how happy he was over Todd's success. And he was. He *was*. But he also resented it. He resented the sneakiness with which Todd had submitted his manuscript. They hadn't made a pact to inform each other whenever they submitted work, but it had certainly been their habit. Todd hadn't actually violated a sacred agreement, but that's what it felt like.

Uncharitably, Roark wanted to attribute Todd's success to luck, fluky timing, a slow book market, even to an editor with lousy taste, all the while acknowledging that such thoughts were unfair. Todd had worked hard. He was a talented writer. He was dedicated to the craft. He deserved to be published.

But Roark earnestly felt that he deserved it more.

* * *

Todd returned within an hour bringing a bottle of champagne for each of them and insisting that they drink them before moving to phase two of the celebration.

Phase two included Mary Catherine. One Sunday afternoon shortly after her miscarriage, Roark had taken her out for ice cream. Seeing the promenade of young couples with babies had caused her to get weepy. She confided that Todd had fathered the embryo she lost.

"Son of a bitch must've had a sixth sense about it. He's avoided me ever since."

Months went by. The two were civil to one another but cool. Eventually they reestablished themselves as friends but only friends. To Roark's knowledge they hadn't slept together again. He assumed by tacit agreement.

Today, the rift and the cause for it were distant memories. Wearing three postage-stamp-sized patches of electric-blue fabric that passed for a bikini, Mary Catherine arrived ready to party. She got there just in time to help them polish off the champagne.

"Foul!" she cried petulantly. "I only got two swallows."

"There's more where that came from, sweetheart." Todd rubbed her ass and smacked his lips, first with appreciation, then regret. He turned her around and gave her a gentle push toward Roark. "She's all yours tonight, pal. Don't say I never gave you anything."

"Consolation prize?" The good-natured question had only a trace of an edge.

"Can you imagine a better one?"

Mary Catherine looped her arms around Roark's neck, mashed her breasts against his chest, and massaged his crotch with hers. "Fine by me. I've had a lech for you for a long time." She poked her tongue into his mouth.

Courtesy of the champagne, he had a lively buzz going. She tasted good. She felt damn good. He liked her. He had sustained a blow to his ego, and Todd was trying to make it up to him. He'd be an asshole to decline his friend's gesture of condolence.

He applied himself to kissing her.

"Hey," Todd said after a few moments. "Am I gonna have to turn the water hose on you two?"

Laughing, they clomped downstairs and piled into Todd's much-maligned car. He drove them to a marina where he had chartered a boat from an old salt named Hatch Walker. They'd leased boats from him before. His rates were the cheapest in Key West, and he got only mildly abusive if you stretched your contract time and came in late.

Walker wasn't long on charm anytime, but today he was particularly querulous. He was wary of turning one of his boats over to three people who had obviously been drinking. Roark was just drunk enough on champagne—and wildly aroused because on the drive to the marina, Mary Catherine had given him a private lap dance in the passenger seat—not to care about the old man's opinion of them or the amount of their alcohol intake.

As soon as the rental agreement was signed, Todd jumped aboard and climbed the steps to the pilot's chair. Roark staggered aboard, then turned to lend a hand to Mary Catherine, who managed to stumble against him as she stepped onto the deck. "Oopsy-daisy," she giggled as she squirmed against him. She gave old Hatch a gay little wave as he untied the ropes from the cleats and tossed them onto the deck.

"Crazy kids," he muttered.

"I don't think he likes us," Mary Catherine whined.

"What I think is, you have on too many clothes."

Roark reached around to untie her top. She shrieked and slapped at his hands, but the protests were all for show. Roark came away with her bikini top and waved it like a banner above his head as Todd slowly guided the boat out of the marina. As soon as the craft cleared the channel, he gave it full throttle and it shot into the Atlantic.

Todd had proclaimed this would be a celebration none of them would ever forget and obviously he meant it. Roark was surprised by his friend's extravagance. The coolers he had brought onboard were stocked with brand-name liquors. The food came from a deli that had the self-confidence to call itself Delectables.

"This is a mean shrimp salad." Roark licked spiced mayonnaise from the corner of his lips.

"Let me do that." Mary Catherine straddled his lap and sponged away the mayo with her tongue. She had taken her role as consolation prize to heart, devoting herself entirely to entertaining him and granting his every wish. That or converting him into a hedonist. Either way, he wasn't fighting it.

The shared secret of the miscarriage had forged a special bond between them. When they were alone he called her Sheila. She'd given up on the mermaid idea as impractical because "the tail would probably be itchy." But she was considering a chambermaid routine and had asked him to come up with a catchy name for her.

Although they flirted frequently and outrageously, the friendship had remained platonic. She'd made subtle overtures, but Roark had pretended not to notice them because he hadn't wanted to mess up a good friendship.

But as she sucked at his lips, he asked himself what would be so terrible about altering their friendship to include sex. Be friends with Sheila, but don't have sex with Mary Catherine. Who wrote the rule that you couldn't be both friend and lover?

Why not make happy with the iron hard-on he was

sporting, compliments of her incredible proportions and her agile tongue and her hands, which were keeping themselves busy inside his swim trunks?

Maybe Todd had paid for her services today. So what? She was a good kid, trying to make a decent living using the assets she'd been given.

It was also possible that she was coming on to him only to make Todd jealous. He wouldn't let that bother him, either. In fact, he wasn't going to let anything bother him tonight.

Fuck writing. Fuck getting published. Fuck words that wouldn't come.

Fuck Mary Catherine. That topped his things-to-do list. Definitely. He was sick to death of being such a damn Boy Scout. Nose to the grindstone all the time. For what? For freaking *nothing,* that's what.

He was going to eat this rich food until he puked on it. He was going to get slobbery drunk. He was going to let Mary Catherine perform on him every debauched act in her extensive repertoire. He was going to have a good time tonight if it killed him.

* * *

Roark woke up with Mary Catherine draped across him. After a bout of rowdy copulation in the small berth, they had both passed out. Thirsty and needing badly to pee, he wiggled out from under her. She moaned a garbled objection and reached out to hold him back, but it was a halfhearted effort.

He successfully extricated himself and retrieved his trunks from the floor. It required some challenging concentration and a few fumbling attempts, but he finally managed to get his feet into the legs.

He was still pulling on the trunks as he stumbled up the steps to the deck. Todd had a bottle of Bacardi cradled in his arm and was staring at the constellations. Hearing Roark, he turned and smiled. "You survived?"

He stretched out the elastic waistband of his trunks and peered into them. "All parts present and accounted for, sir."

Todd chuckled. "Judging from the racket, there were times I thought I might have to come down there and rescue you."

"There were times when *I* thought you might have to." He relieved himself over the side of the craft.

Todd asked, "Did she do that thing with her thumb?"

Roark tucked himself back into his trunks, turned, smiled, but said nothing.

"Oh. I forgot. Sir Roark never shares the juicy details. A real gallant."

Roark was about to bow at the waist but figured that in his present condition that might be a tricky move, so he settled for a clumsy salute.

Todd motioned toward one of the ice chests. "Help yourself to a fresh bottle."

"Thanks, but I'm still too wasted to stand."

"And jealous."

Roark used one arm to brace himself against the exterior wall of the cabin. "Huh?"

"You're jealous."

Roark shrugged. "Maybe." He gave a weak grin. "Okay, a little."

"More than a little, Roark. More than a little." Todd raised the rum bottle to his eye like a telescope and peered down the length of it at Roark. "Admit it, you thought you'd be the first to sell."

Roark's stomach was queasy. The horizon was see-sawing. He was also uncomfortable with the direction the conversation had taken. "Todd, I couldn't be happier."

"Oh, yeah, you could. If you'd sold your book today, you'd be a hell of a lot happier. So would Hadley. I think he probably jacks off over your manuscripts. Your work makes him positively giddy, doesn't it? What was that he said about it being an honor and privilege to review your work?" He took a swig of rum. "Something like that."

"You read his letter to me?"

"Clever of you to get that post office box, but careless of you to leave his letter in the pocket of your jeans. I was short the cash to pay for a pizza delivery and saw your jeans lying on the floor where you'd stepped out of them. Raided the pockets looking for money, and . . . pulled out a plum."

"You shouldn't have read my mail."

"You shouldn't have lied to me about Hadley's enthusiasm for your work and his lack of it for mine."

"What do you care what Hadley thinks of your work?"

"I don't. Last laugh is on him and you. I've sold. You haven't."

"So fine. Let's just drop it."

"No. I don't believe I will."

Todd stood up slowly. He was steadier on his feet than he should have been, leaving Roark to question if he had drunk as much as he had pretended to. He moved along the deck with a predatory, malevolent tread.

"What's eating you, Todd? You won. Hadley was wrong."

"Maybe about my writing. Not about the other."

"Other?"

"My character. Remember how flawed I am? Driven by greed and jealousy and envy. Those undesirable character traits about which Hadley waxed poetic."

Roark's stomach heaved and he swallowed a throatful of sour bile. "That's all bullshit. I didn't pay any attention to it."

"Well, I did."

He didn't see it coming. Moving sinuously only a second before, Todd now lunged at him and took a vicious swing at his head with the liquor bottle. Roark caught it on the temple, and if it had been a sledgehammer, it couldn't have hurt any worse. He roared in pain and outrage.

But he had enough wits to see the bottle arcing once again above his head. He dodged it just in time to spare himself another concussion. Instead it shattered against the wall of the cabin, showering them with broken glass and rum.

Todd attacked with a fury then, throwing blows one right after the other aimed at Roark's face and head. Most of them connected, crunching cartilage and splitting skin. Dazed but fueled by anger, Roark struck back. He landed a fist against Todd's mouth and felt the scrape of teeth against his knuckles. It hurt, but it hurt Todd more. His mouth gushed blood.

The drawing of blood was a primal and powerful exhilaration. At any other time Roark would have been astonished over how much satisfaction he derived from making Todd bleed. Propelled by jealousy, he wanted to see more of Todd's blood on his hands. He wanted to punish him for succeeding first and making him feel like a failure.

But his hot rage was tepid compared to Todd's. Todd's bloodlust had escalated into savagery. With feral growls, he came at Roark, clawing and pounding.

Roark's temper was soon spent. He was ready to back off, cool down, and call a truce.

Todd was beyond that. He didn't let up, not even when Roark stopped being aggressive and only deflected blows in order to protect himself.

"Goddammit, enough!"

"Never enough." Todd's clenched teeth were smeared with blood. Bubbles of it foamed over his lips. "Never enough."

And he launched a fresh attack.

"Wha'sgoin'on?" Mary Catherine appeared in the open doorway of the cabin, naked except for a golden ankle bracelet. Ignored, she drunkenly staggered onto the deck and stepped on a piece of broken glass. "Ow! What the fuck is going on?"

"Shut up!"

Todd rounded on her and struck a blow that caught her at waist level. Favoring her bleeding foot, she was already off balance. His blow sent her reeling backward. The chrome side railing caught her in the back of her knees. Arms windmilling, she went overboard with a scream that died as soon as she hit the water.

Roark stared at the empty space she'd left at the boat's railing and sobered instantly. "She's too drunk to swim!"

He executed a shallow dive into the water. The salt water seared the open wounds on his face and he came up gasping. He was fighting nausea from too much liquor and what he knew must be a concussion where he'd been hit with the bottle.

But all this hardly registered. Treading water, he

blinked his eyes as clear as he could get them and frantically searched the surface of the dark water for a sign of Mary Catherine.

"Do you see her?" he yelled up at Todd, who was standing on the deck looking down at him, blood dripping from his chin onto his smooth chest. "Todd? Christ, did you hear me? Do you see her?"

"No."

"Turn on the lights."

Todd just stood there staring into the water, apparently shocked into immobility.

"Shit."

Heart pounding, head bursting, Roark jackknifed beneath the surface. Although it stung like crazy, he kept his eyes open. But it didn't matter. He might just as well have been swimming through a bottle of ink. He couldn't even see his own hands as he waved them about, searching blindly, hoping to make contact with a limb, skin, hair.

He stayed under until he couldn't stand the burning in his lungs an instant longer. Breaking the surface, he took a huge gulp of air. He was surprised to see how far he had swum away from the boat. At least Todd had shaken off his stupor and turned on the underwater lights. They cast an eerie green glow around the craft, but they didn't penetrate nearly far enough.

Although his arms and legs felt like lead and his brain seemed to have relinquished control of them, Roark began swimming toward the boat. Todd was doing something on the port side. Hope surged inside Roark's chest. He shouted, "Did you find her? Is she over there?"

Todd returned to the starboard side. "No luck?"

Luck? This wasn't a fishing trip. What was the matter with him? "Call the Coast Guard. I can't find her. Oh, Jesus." He sobbed when the full impact of the situation hit him. She might be dead already. Mary Catherine—Sheila—might have drowned because of his inability to save her.

"Call the Coast Guard," he repeated before diving beneath the surface again.

Knowing it was futile, he pushed himself through the seawater, eyes open but seeing nothing, hands groping but feeling nothing. Still, he was unwilling to give up. If there was the slimmest chance that she was hanging on, clinging to life, desperate for help...

Again and again he went down, coming up only long enough to take a breath before going down again, diving so deep it made his ears hurt.

He struggled to the surface one last time, fearing that he wouldn't make it, afraid that he had made one foray too many. At last he tasted air. Greedily he sucked it into his lungs. He couldn't survive another submersion. He was too tired even to swim the distance between him and the boat. Weakly he treaded water, barely able to keep himself afloat.

"Todd," he called hoarsely. "Todd."

Todd appeared at the rail. Roark's eyes had been scoured by the salt water. His vision was cloudy. "I can't find her. I can't look anymore. Throw me the preserver."

Todd left to get the preserver, and Roark wondered vaguely why he hadn't had it ready.

Exhausted, he longed to close his burning eyes but was afraid that if he did he would slip beneath the surface and drown before he could garner the energy to save himself. But his eyes must have closed on their own. He must have been only a heartbeat away from losing consciousness, because he was startled awake when the boat's motor roared to life.

Todd shouldn't be starting the motor. He should be throwing him a life preserver. If the Coast Guard had been given the coordinates of their location, they should stay in that spot until help arrived. It was damn stupid to start up an outboard with Mary Catherine and him in the water this close to the boat.

These thoughts flashed through his mind in a nanosecond, not in individual words, but as fully formed and intact conclusions. "Todd, what are you doing?"

He kicked his legs and feebly moved his arms in a parody of swim strokes, but it was like trying to push Jell-O through quicksand. But there was no need to try and swim after all. Look. Todd was bringing the boat to him.

Only thing, he was running it too hot and too fast for safety.

"Hey!"

It was a nightmare's yell, when you open your mouth and try to scream but you can't utter a sound and that intensifies the horror of the nightmare. He tried to wave his arms, but they weighed a thousand pounds apiece. He couldn't even lift them out of the water.

"Todd," he croaked. "Turn to port! I'm here! Can't you see me?"

He could see him. He was looking straight at him through the plastic windshield that protected the cockpit. Control panel lights were making a Halloween mask of his bruised and swelling face. His eyes glowed red. Torches of hell.

Roark screamed one last time before fear sent him plunging beneath the surface. In seconds he was engulfed in churning, strangling waters. Then the terror gripped him. Undiluted terror. The kind that few men ever have the misfortune of experiencing. Terror so absolute that death seems a blessing.

Terror championed only by pain. Excruciating and immeasurable.

Pain that splinters the body but slays the soul.

Chapter 32

Nadia arrived at the martini bar wearing a snug black dress with a deceptively demure neckline and a cocktail hat, one of those saucy numbers with a veil that covered half her face. A black feathered handbag hung from her shoulder on a slender gold chain. Very fetching. Very femme fatale.

Heads turned as she made her way through the bar. It was packed with Manhattan's in crowd and wannabes. People spoke to her as she passed by. She waved to a party of three seated at a corner table.

When she reached Noah's table, he was inflated with pride that the most exquisite woman in the room was joining him. He embraced her warmly but circumspectly. Pecking a friendly kiss on her cheek, he whispered, "I could fuck you right here."

"Ever the romantic." She slid into the banquette beside him.

"Martini?"

"By all means."

He placed their order with the waiter who had rushed to the table within seconds of Nadia's arrival, then turned to her with a smile. "You're known here."

"I'm known everywhere."

He laughed at her conceit. "I've missed your sharp comebacks. It's been far too long since I've seen you."

"That silly quarrel."

"Ancient history now." He inhaled deeply. "Ahh. Your provocative scent."

"Chanel."

He shook his head and grinned slyly. "Sex. Too bad you can't bottle it. You'd make a fortune." His adoring gaze moved over her face. "You look sensational. I like the veil."

"Thank you."

"It lends you a mysterious air that's incredibly sexy." Beneath the table, he pressed her thigh with his.

"You're coming on awfully strong tonight. You haven't been getting any, have you?"

"I've been otherwise occupied."

"Yes, you have." She seemed to become fascinated with the layered arrangement of the feathers on her handbag. She ran her finger over the smooth, iridescent plumes. "You've been busy laying your father-in-law to rest."

"What a lot of folderol."

"I thought the eulogies were rather moving."

"It was the kind of send-off Daniel Matherly merited, I suppose. I'm just glad it's over. Now the rest of us can stop applauding his life and resume living our own."

"Ordinarily you enjoy being in the limelight. I thought the role of loyal and bereaved son-in-law would have appealed to you."

He laid his hand over his heart. "I did my best." Their martinis arrived. They clinked glasses, sipped. "Actually, it wasn't all that bad, except for having to keep Maris's hysteria at bay."

"Wasn't it natural for her to be upset?"

"Her behavior went beyond normal grief." She gave up her study of the feathers and looked at him. "My wife got the harebrained notion that I was responsible for her father's fall." He peered past the veil into Nadia's eyes. "Can you imagine that?"

She raised the martini glass to her lips. "Yes. I can."

The steadiness of her gaze was a bit unnerving. He deliberately mistook her meaning. "Maris has always been excitable and reactionary, but this time she carried it to the extreme."

"At the funeral, she seemed the picture of composure."

"True. But once it was over, she lost all reason. She coerced the local police in Massachusetts to reinvestigate the fatal accident."

"And?"

"Naturally they found nothing to substantiate her suspicions."

"How lucky for you."

"Luck had nothing to do with it, Nadia."

"I'm sure that's true." She stared out over the crowd, speaking almost to herself. "If you had pushed the old gentleman down the staircase, you would be shrewd enough not to get caught."

"I didn't. But you're right. I would be shrewd enough not to get caught. And that's why you like me so well."

She turned back to him. "True. I would never become involved with a loser. I wouldn't hitch my wagon to a falling star. Only to one that's ascending."

"We're so much alike it's frightening." Leaning closer to her, he added confidentially, "At least it should be frightening to everyone else." Complacently he took another sip of his martini. "Anyhow, Daniel's dead and buried. That's the good news."

"For God's sake, Noah." She glanced around as though fearing that he'd been overheard. "What's the bad?"

"Not bad, darling. Better. His death was the final nail in the coffin of my marriage. It is now beyond repair."

She raised her glass to toast him. "Congratulations or condolences?"

"Definitely the former. Because I have even better news than that."

"I can hardly wait."

"Are you sure you want me to tell you here and now? It may bring on an orgasm."

"Have you ever known me to turn down an opportunity like that?"

His smile widened. "Before his accidental fall, I persuaded Daniel to sign an important power-of-attorney document. It enables me to sell Matherly Press to WorldView, and Maris can't do a damn thing about it."

Nadia's eyes went wide with bewilderment. "But Matherly Press isn't yours to sell."

"Nadia! There you are!" Morris Blume suddenly materialized on the other side of the table.

Noah hadn't noticed his approach, and he didn't welcome the intrusion. His plan for this evening had been to wine, dine, and romance Nadia back into his good graces. Before proceeding with WorldView, he wanted her well entrenched in his cheering section. He needed good press, and no one could provide that better than Nadia.

Of all the damn luck, running into Morris Blume. WorldView's CEO looked as colorless as ever in a gray suit, gray shirt, silver tie. To Noah, even his teeth and gums looked unhealthily gray as he smiled down at them.

"I didn't see you at first and thought there'd been a mix-up on the time," he was saying to Nadia.

"Your timing couldn't be more perfect."

She scooted from behind the table and, to Noah's dismay, walked into Blume's embrace. They locked lips. When the kiss ended, she affectionately patted his necktie back into place.

Blume appraised her from hat to heels. "You look positively gorgeous."

"I'm glad you think so. I bought the ensemble with you in mind."

"Sensational."

His compliment caused her to simper in a coquettish way that was totally unlike Nadia. Blume was stroking her waist with suggestive familiarity. Her pelvis was tilted against his, a specialty of Nadia's that made a man think of nothing except his dick and planting it inside her.

For all the attention they were paying him, Noah might just as well have been one of the pop art paintings on the wall. His whole body throbbed with anger. And something else, something rare to him—humiliation. People had noticed that Nadia was now snuggling with Blume. He'd lost the most popular girl at the party to a bloodless, bald geek.

"Ready for a drink, darling?" she asked him.

"You read my mind. You always do."

Nadia signaled the waiter, who scurried over and took Blume's order. She didn't return to sit beside Noah on the banquette, but took the chair Blume was holding for her. They now faced him across the table.

She sat as close to Blume as possible without actually sharing the same chair. Her breast was making itself cozy beneath his arm. Blume's hand was on her thigh—high on her thigh. Proprietary.

Noah was certain that these public displays of affection were for his benefit. Nadia was being deliberately seductive. She was gloating. It made him want to reach across the table and slap the shit out of her.

She had set him up. She had planned this little scenario. He had called her on his drive back from Massachusetts—following that pathetic attempt of Maris's to incriminate him—and had invited her to join him this evening. "We're free to be seen together now," he had told her.

Nadia had been her sexy self, every word suggestive, every breath an erotic promise. She had named the time and place as though she couldn't wait to see him. Instead, he'd walked into a goddamn female trap.

Okay. If she wanted to flaunt her new boyfriend in front of him, fine. It didn't change anything—except that her sex life would take a severe downward plunge. Judging by Blume's pallid coloring, getting blood to his penis would be a chore.

After thanking the waiter for his drink, Blume turned to Noah. "My secretary told me that you called today requesting a meeting."

"That's right. In light of my recent family tragedy—"

"My condolences, by the way."

"Thank you." He brushed an invisible speck off the cuff of his shirt. "Daniel's death imposed a temporary postponement of our schedule. Now we're able to pick up where we left off. You're going to be very pleased by the developments that have taken place since we last spoke. What's your schedule like tomorrow?"

"I really don't see the need for a meeting now."

"Now" was a troubling adverb. "Now" indicated that circumstances had undergone a change. Noah avoided looking at Nadia and kept his features carefully schooled. "Why is that?"

"Noah and I were getting to this when you joined us, Morris," Nadia said. "Apparently there's been some confusion." She gave Noah a pained look. "I'm terribly embarrassed."

"Well, since I seem to be the only one in the dark here, perhaps you'll enlighten me."

She glanced toward Blume as though asking his advice, but he merely shrugged. Pulling her lower lip through her teeth, she turned back to Noah. "I thought someone would have told you by now. Out of respect for Daniel, I've been sitting on this story for a week."

Noah was growing uncomfortably warm inside his clothes. One martini couldn't account for the sweat trickling down his ribs. He felt like a man about to hear the result of a biopsy on testicular tissue. "What story?"

Taking center stage, Nadia readjusted herself even closer to Blume. "Out of the blue, Daniel Matherly invited me to his house for breakfast. It was the same morning you left for the country. Who could have guessed that your retreat would end so tragically? I wish I'd had the foresight then to urge him not to go." She looked squarely at Noah and let that sink in.

"Anyhow," she said, shaking her head slightly as though to get back on track, "he gave me a scoop, but asked me to sit on it for a few days, at least until Maris returned from Georgia."

Blume was gazing at Nadia as though he might begin sucking on her neck at any moment. She was absently stroking the back of his hand still resting on her thigh. Noah forced himself to smile. "You still haven't told me the nature of this exclusive story."

"Daniel appointed Maris as chairman and CEO of Matherly Press. I thought perhaps Daniel would tell you while you were away together in the country. No? Well...he probably thought it only fair that Maris be informed first."

Eyeing him closely, she ran her fingers up and down the stem of her martini glass. "You had led me to believe that Daniel Matherly was borderline senile. Having talked with him at length, I found the opposite to be the case. He was in total command of his faculties. He knew exactly what he was doing."

Every capillary in Noah's body had expanded. Behind his eyeballs, his eardrums, behind every square inch of skin, he could feel the increased pressure of his pulse. Somehow he managed to smile. "Daniel didn't think too highly of you, Nadia. I think he played a cruel practical joke on you."

"The possibility crossed my mind. He was known to be cagey. So I had the story corroborated by a Mr. Stern, the Matherlys' attorney. He verified it. Maris's appointment is irrevocable and incontestable. Her authority can be revoked only if she chooses to resign."

Noah pried loose his tongue from the roof of his mouth where it had become stuck. "I'm curious as to why you didn't mention this to me earlier, Nadia. For instance when we spoke earlier today." *Or the night I talked to you by phone from the country,* he thought. The bitch had known then. She had been amusing herself with him.

"It wasn't my place."

"But now it is?"

"I'm sparing you having to read it in my column. The story runs tomorrow." She gave him a sympathetic smile. "Honestly, Noah, I thought that by now you would have been officially informed. I suppose that since your marriage is over, you're no longer in the inner circle. You're only hired help."

"Would you like another drink, Noah?"

"No, thank you, Morris. I'm late for another appointment." If he didn't get out of here, away from Nadia, he was either going to kill her or explode. He'd rather not do either in front of witnesses.

"Oh, please stay," Nadia said in a cajoling voice. "We've got so much to celebrate. One of Morris's fondest desires has been fulfilled. WorldView has acquired Becker-Howe. You know Oliver Howe, I'm sure, because he and Daniel were old friends. In fact, it was Daniel who put Morris in contact with him. Daniel knew that WorldView was shopping for a publishing house and that, unlike him, Ollie Howe would welcome their interest."

"I had my heart set on Matherly Press," Blume said. "But since Maris will be at the helm—"

"I felt it only fair to tell him," Nadia interjected.

"And Maris has made absolutely clear her intention never to sell it, so I decided to acquire another company."

Noah was clenching his jaw so tightly it ached. "How nice for you."

"I paid too much for it, but what the hell?" he chuckled. "It's a profitable outfit. We'll easily earn back our investment. Becker-Howe is only slightly smaller than Matherly Press. But not for long." He winked at Noah. "I'll be your competitor now. Watch out."

And the horse you rode in on, you bloodless son of a bitch, Noah thought. He made a show of checking his wristwatch. "I really hate to break up the party, but I must get on my way."

"Wait! That's not the only good news." Nadia thrust her left hand across the table. "You failed to notice—or were too polite to mention—that I'm wearing an obscenely enormous diamond ring. Morris and I are getting married next Sunday at the Plaza." She beamed at Morris, then turned back to Noah. "Three o'clock. We'll be crushed if you're not there."

Chapter 33

⸻ ◈ ⸻

*D*amn *Michael Strother.*

Cursing his friend—former friend, it appeared—was the only fresh thought in Parker's mind. Angrily he switched off his computer, concluding another unproductive session of writing. He had sat all day, hands poised above the keyboard, waiting for a burst of inspiration that never came. It was a condition that was recurring with alarming frequency.

He had been working on the next Mackensie Roone book. Deck Cayton had turned into a real dullard with nothing clever to say. He was no longer roguish or engaging. The villain wasn't innately evil; he was a caricature. And the girl...Parker didn't like the girl, either. She was shallow and stupid.

He hadn't heard from Mike since he had announced his resignation and left the house. He hadn't composed a readable sentence since then, either. The old man must have put a hex on him, something he'd learned from the Gullahs who lived on the southern tip of St. Anne. Mike had been fascinated by their language and customs, which had been passed from generation to generation dating back to their African ancestry. Parker dismissed spells and potions and such as hogwash. But maybe there was something to them after all.

When Mike was there, Parker had constantly sought solitude and silence in which to write. But it was amazing how much he missed having the old man puttering around. He found himself subconsciously listening for Mike's footsteps or the clang of pots and pans in the kitchen, the closing of a door, the whirr of the vacuum cleaner somewhere in the house. The sounds would be welcome distractions now. Comforts. Because he felt terribly alone.

Years back, while he lay in hospital wards with strangers in neighboring beds, being attended by capable but impersonal nurses, he had felt utterly friendless. Completely alone. That's when Hatred became his companion. His imaginary friend. His security blanket.

Through the years that followed, there were times when Hatred was an exhausting sidekick. Particularly after he'd succeeded with the mystery series, he grew tired of it constantly hanging around, never going home. It grew to be a nuisance. He wished to be rid of it.

Sometimes he kicked it around, hoping that it would leave of its own accord, but it never did. It stayed, and he could never bring himself to abandon it. Instead, he had fed it daily, keeping it loyal to him, until his relationship with it became codependent. It needed him to survive. He needed it for motivation.

Now Mike was gone, and he was left again with only Hatred, his trusty but parasitical ally.

He was feeling awfully sorry for himself, but the irony didn't escape him. His misery was self-imposed. "Poor you. But look at it this way, Parker," he whispered to himself. "The end is in sight."

The last die had been cast when he sent the *Envy* manuscript to Noah. It was too late now for second-guessing. One way or another it would soon be over and he'd have closure. Everything he had done, said, or written in the past fourteen years had been with this goal in mind. It all funneled down to here and now.

Whatever the outcome, whether in his favor or not, it hadn't come cheaply. He had achieved worldwide acclaim, yet no one knew his name. He had sacrificed fame in exchange for anonymity. He had money but nothing to spend it on. He owned a beautiful house, but it wasn't a home. He shared the empty rooms with only a hanging man's ghost. His need for vengeance had cost him his one true friend. Ultimately it had cost him Maris.

He missed her with a physical ache. If he were a woman or a child, he would cry himself to sleep each night. He moved through the house touching things he had seen her touch, inhaling deeply in the hope of catching a whiff of her fragrance. He was pathetic, as daffy as Professor Hadley's jilted aunt who lived in the attic with only bittersweet memories and her fear of fresh fruit.

Maris had been essential to his plot, but he hadn't expected her to become essential to him. In the brief time she had been in his life, she had become the most important element of it.

Second most important, he corrected.

If she were the most important, he would leave Noah to the devil as Mike had advised and spend the rest of his life loving her and letting himself be loved. At night when he couldn't sleep, he'd get downright sappy. He envisioned them on the beach, tossing a stick to a golden retriever and supervising a couple of sturdy, laughing kids building a sand castle. A greeting-card tableau. A Kodak commercial.

Too often for his mental health, he relived making love to her. God, it had been sweet. But perhaps the sweetest part had been holding her. Just that. Holding her close. Feeling her heartbeat beneath his hand, her breath against his skin. Allowing himself to forget for a few moments that he had only this one night with her and that, come morning, he would hurt her terribly and irreparably.

Maris was the one plot element that might have caused him to change his outline and end the thing differently.

But he couldn't have even if he'd wanted to. Because the revenge he sought wasn't only for himself. It was for Mary Catherine. He might not deserve restitution, but Sheila damn sure did. By most moral measuring sticks, she would come up short. But he knew better. That spectacular body had been home to a kind and generous spirit. In many respects, she was innocent.

And Noah had killed her.

As surely as he had killed Daniel Matherly.

Parker hoped that Maris and the authorities were thoroughly investigating Matherly's death, because Noah's account of it smelled to high heaven. It stank of Noah. It was doubtful they'd find anything that implicated him. He would make certain they didn't. He would have made the old man's death look like a tragic accident, and his explanation for how it had come about would be perfectly plausible. He was gifted that way.

Overt aggression wasn't his style. He was smarter and more subtle than that. Oh, he could hold his own in a fistfight. Parker still had the scar above his eyebrow to prove it. But Noah's real power wasn't physical. It was cerebral. His strength was his cunning. He maneuvered insidiously. You didn't see him coming until it was too late. Which made him the most dangerous kind of animal on the planet.

But he had a major flaw: his intolerance for anyone getting the best of him.

When Noah read the *Envy* manuscript, he would come south on the next flight. He'd be unable to resist. The book would be a red flag waved in his face, and it simply wasn't in Noah Reed to ignore it.

During these intervening years, if Noah thought of Parker at all, he had probably imagined him as he'd last seen him—a vanquished enemy, a threat he had eliminated.

If for no other reason, he would come to St. Anne out of curiosity. He'd come to see how old Parker had fared. He would come to see for himself what his wife had found so interesting about his former roommate.

Noah would come.

And when he got here, Parker would be waiting.

* * *

Eight o'clock classes were just about to convene when Maris parked her rental car in a lot reserved for campus visitors. It was the summer session, so there weren't as many students rushing into the classroom buildings as there would be when the fall semester began after Labor Day.

Although she had never been here before, she didn't need to be oriented or to ask for directions. The university campus wasn't similar to the one described in *Envy*. It *was* the one described in *Envy*.

And it was a long way from the police station in rural Massachusetts where she had been less than twenty-four hours ago.

With Noah's words replaying inside her head, *his death was convenient,* she'd driven back to New York with a sense of urgency. Using her cell phone, she had reserved her airline ticket to Nashville as she sped down the parkway, breaking every speed limit between Chief Randall's police department and the Matherly Press offices in Midtown Manhattan.

She had planned to be in the office only long enough to consult briefly with her assistant and check her mail, before returning to Daniel's house to pack, then to dash to the airport in time for the late evening flight.

It didn't quite go according to plan.

Her appearance in the office had galvanized her assistant.

"Thank God you're here. I've been trying to reach you on your cell."

"My battery ran out about an hour ago."

"Don't move." The secretary placed a call. "Tell Mr. Stern she just came in." She depressed the hold button. "He told me it was mandatory that he speak with you today, Maris."

"Concerning what? Did he say?"

"No, but he's been calling since early morning. He assumed you'd be coming in."

"I had an errand out of town." She hadn't had time for a lengthy conversation with the attorney and had said so.

Her assistant apologized. "He made me swear to notify him the moment I spoke to you. He'll be on line two."

Maris went into her office and sat down behind her desk. And it was fortunate that she'd been seated, because the news Stern had imparted was staggering.

"Mr. Matherly had in mind to announce his decision when you returned from Georgia. I think he wanted it to be a ceremonious occasion. Unhappily, he didn't have that opportunity, but, as it turns out, his timing for putting this into place was extraordinary." He paused, then said, "I hope you're pleased."

She was deeply touched to know that her father had placed so much confidence in her. "Enormously."

Stern had continued to go over the details with her, but the important thing she heard was that her father had entrusted her with the business that had been his life's work. She wouldn't take the responsibility lightly. But very proudly.

Stern had coughed delicately, then said, "It's at your discretion whether or not to keep Mr. Reed on staff. Mr. Matherly intimated to me that having him there even in a menial position might be awkward for you considering your pending divorce."

So he had known. Of course he had known. His timing hadn't been as extraordinary as Mr. Stern believed. Probably Daniel had been planning this for some time, realizing that upon the dissolution of her marriage, an ugly battle for control would have been waged. Daniel had seen to it that such a battle would never take place.

"Frankly, your father no longer trusted Mr. Reed to perform in the best interest of the publishing house," the lawyer had told her. "But, as I said, his continuance with the company is up to you."

They had talked a few minutes longer. Maris wrapped it up by saying, "Thank you, Mr. Stern. Thank you very much."

"No thanks necessary. I hope you'll want me to continue in my present capacity."

"That goes without saying."

"I'm honored." He paused, then asked, "Tell me, Ms. Matherly, how does it feel to be one of the most powerful women in New York?"

She laughed. "Right now? I feel very rushed to make a flight."

Following that conversation and a swift delegation of duties to her assistant, she opted to leave her car in the parking garage near the office building and take a cab to Daniel's house.

Where another shock had awaited her.

As she was jogging up the steps of the brownstone, a limousine had pulled to the curb. Nadia Schuller alighted before the chauffeur had time to come around and open the door for her.

"Hello, Maris."

She was dressed in a black dress and cocktail hat that on anyone else would have looked ridiculous. Nadia had the panache to wear it.

"I understand why you don't want to talk to me. I know you think of me as something to be scraped off the sole of your shoe. But I need one minute of your time."

"I don't have one minute. I'm in a hurry."

"Please. I fortified myself with two martinis before I came."

Maris debated it for several seconds, then reluctantly agreed to hear her out.

She had listened with dismay as Nadia told her about her breakfast meeting with Daniel. "I was told he'd had a mystery guest. You would have been the last person I would have guessed."

"Me, too. I was floored when he called and extended the invitation. I got the feeling that he was sneaking me in while his housekeeper was out. But the real shocker came when he told me about this bogus document Noah was going to press him to sign. He then offered me an exclusive on your promotion. Congratulations."

"Thank you."

"The story about the transfer of power will run in my column tomorrow. Mr. Matherly asked me to hold it for a week. I agreed. Of course, when I did, I had no idea that...that he wouldn't be here to read it."

Maris had been further surprised to see tears in Nadia's eyes that even her veil couldn't conceal. "Your father was a gentleman, Maris. Even toward me." She covered her mouth with her hand for several seconds before continuing. "I wish I had warned him not to go."

"With Noah?"

She nodded. "Maybe even more than you, I know how treacherous Noah can be. I never thought he would go so far as to commit murder. But when I heard the circumstances of Mr. Matherly's death, I wondered."

"So did I."

"Noah said as much."

Maris then told her about hers and Noah's meeting with the Massachusetts police. "If he did push Dad down those stairs, he got away with it."

"That morning, as I told your father good-bye, I should have said something. Should have warned him." Her eyes pleaded with Maris for absolution.

"I had a chance to warn him, too, Nadia. I didn't, either."

"I guess all of us underestimated Noah."

"I guess."

"By the way, he and I are history."

"I don't care."

Nadia nodded, one woman understanding another's scorn because it was deserved. "Just before coming here, I had the pleasure of telling him about the shift of power from your father to you. I don't think he took it well. Be careful, Maris."

"I'm not afraid of him."

Nadia looked at her closely and with admiration. "No. I don't believe you are." She ducked her head for a second, then looked bravely into Maris's face again. "I never feel guilty over anything. This was a rare exception. Thank you for listening."

Maris nodded and had turned toward the steps. But before reaching the stoop, she turned back. Morris Blume had stepped out of the limo and was holding the door for Nadia. He nodded politely to Maris, but it was Nadia whom she addressed.

"Why do you suppose Dad invited you to breakfast and gave you this story?"

"I asked myself that a thousand times. I finally reached a conclusion. Speculation, of course."

"I'd like to hear it."

"He knew Noah had cheated on you, but Mr. Matherly was too old to defend your honor by beating him up. So he wanted to use my column to kick him in the teeth. He knew Noah would be publicly humiliated when the article appeared and it was there in black and white for all the world to see that publishing's boy wonder had been stripped of his stripes." Smiling over the irony, she added, "And no doubt your father saw the poetic justice in baiting Noah's illicit lover with a story she couldn't resist."

"No doubt," Maris said with a fond smile. It was her aged father they'd all underestimated.

"Maris, if it means anything to you..."

"Yes?"

"I think he had fun doing it. He was in great spirits that morning."

"Thank you for telling me that. It means a great deal."

She was in the townhouse less than half an hour and had arrived at the departure gate as they were boarding the flight to Nashville. She had checked into an inexpensive chain motel near the airport and collapsed into bed without even undressing. This morning she had eaten a lumberjack's breakfast, then driven two hours to reach the university.

Now, as she strolled along the paved paths of the campus reviewing yesterday's startling events, she could hardly believe she was here. She had strong feelings of déjà vu, which wasn't surprising. She had been here before, through the pages of Parker's book. Although he had assigned a fictitious name to the university, his descriptions had been dead-on.

She walked straight to the fraternity house, knowing precisely where it was located. It was exactly as Parker had described. The three-story brick building with the gabled windows and the Bradford pear trees lining the front walkway had been abandoned for the summer, but she could imagine how lively it would be when it reopened for occupation in the fall.

From the fraternity house, she followed the path that Roark had taken that blustery November morning two days before Thanksgiving holiday. Parker's vivid narrative led her to the classroom building where Professor Hadley had his office. She ascended the stairs where Roark had been greeted by a classmate and invited to join a study group.

The second-floor corridor stretched out in front of her—long, dim, deserted, and silent. She passed only one office with an open door. A woman was working at a computer terminal, but she didn't notice as Maris walked past.

She continued all the way down the hallway to the office numbered 207. The door was standing slightly ajar, as it had been that morning Roark approached it with his capstone manuscript inside his backpack. Her heart was thumping as hard as his as she gave the door a gentle push and it swung open.

A man was seated at a desk, his back to her. "Professor Hadley?"

He turned around. "Hello, Maris."

She sagged against the doorjamb and snuffled a laugh of self-deprecation. "Mike."

"Have a seat."

He picked up a stack of books and magazines off the only other available chair and set it on the floor, alongside several other similar towers of reading material. Maris lowered herself into the chair, but her eyes never left him.

He smiled at her. "I knew you'd eventually figure it out. What was the breakthrough?"

"I guessed days ago that Roark was Parker. At least aspects of him. Yesterday Noah said something that was almost a direct quote from the book. About how convenient my father's death was to him."

"As his mother's death was. It enabled him to move to Florida without further delay."

"I should have realized sooner that you were Hadley."

"Frankly, I'm glad you didn't. Parker's descriptions weren't always flattering. I'd have been insulted if you'd seen me in them."

Her eyes roved the cluttered office. "Parker described your office to a tee. What's your position here at the university?"

"Professor emeritus."

"That's an honor."

He harrumphed. "It's an empty title that doesn't mean a thing except that you're too damn old to do what you used to do. I get to keep the office till I die. In exchange, once each semester I give a lecture on Faulkner to a couple hundred bored young people who attend only because they're required to. I'm flattered if one of them stays awake for the duration of my lecture. Beyond that, I have no responsibilities whatsoever."

Quietly she said, "I'll bet Parker stayed awake for all your lectures."

"He was exceptional. In his book, he hasn't exaggerated how I felt about 'Roark' and his budding talent. If anything, he's minimized it."

"Is it true that you rescued him from drug addiction?"

"As I've said many times, he rescued himself. He'd become reliant on painkillers. Considering what he suffered, I can't say I blamed him. But it had reached a point where he was taking the pills more to dull his emotional pain than anything else.

"All I did was sound the alarm inside his head. He's the one who went through the hell of withdrawal and then whipped himself back into shape." He smiled. "I guess it's fair to say that I handed him the whip."

"Still, he's indebted to you."

"As I am to him. I've been privileged to work with an amazingly talented writer."

"Too bad he's not as fine a human being as he is a writer."

Mike studied her for a moment, then reached across his desk and pulled forward a manuscript that was bound with a wide rubber band. He passed it to her. She looked down at the cover sheet and her lips curled with bitterness. "I've read it."

"Most of it," he corrected. "Not all. There's some you haven't read. Read it before you judge Parker too harshly." He stood up and made his way to the door. "I'm going for coffee. Can I bring you back something?"

Chapter 34

One of Noah's strongest personality traits was his ability to deny that anything was wrong. Refusing to acknowledge a setback was the same as there being no setback to acknowledge.

The morning following his disastrous martini date with Nadia, he took a taxi to Matherly Press, pretending, indeed believing, that he would manipulate his way through this problem and actually come out better in the long run. On the Richter scale of complications, this was a blip.

He was glad that Matherly Press would remain autonomous. WorldView had bought itself a white elephant. Becker-Howe had been hanging on by its fingernails for years, and everybody in the industry knew it. Ollie Howe was more stiff-necked than Daniel. He was unyielding to the rapid changes taking place and baffled by the concept of electronic publishing.

Noah would personally see to it that the merger was an abysmal failure and that Morris Blume became an industry laughingstock, first for fancying himself a publisher, and second for marrying a whore. Every man he shook hands with was likely to have had a piece of his wife.

As for Nadia's exclusive story, he would deny it.

Daniel wasn't around to corroborate it. Nadia was probably lying about Stern's corroboration. Noah would claim she had written it out of spite. He would admit that he and Nadia had engaged in a temporary and ill-advised affair, one he now deeply regretted. The sudden death of his father-in-law had made him see the error of his ways and returned him to his wife and the sanctity of their marriage. When he broke off with Nadia, she retaliated by fabricating this story about him and his family.

By the time all the hubbub died down, no one would remember the details of the original story. The facts would have been confused in the multiple retells. No one would know what or whom to believe. He could walk away from the whole mess virtually unscathed and looking valorous for owning up to an extramarital affair for which he would publicly ask his wife's forgiveness.

His wife. Maris was the hitch in this plan.

He was counting on her to ignore Nadia's story. She wouldn't give Nadia the satisfaction of denying or confirming it. But it went beyond that. What was he to do if in fact Daniel had given Maris control of Matherly Press? Say the attorney, Stern, had knowledge of a transference of power and the documentation to prove it. What then?

All right. He would go along. He would say that Daniel had informed him of it while they were in the country. Yes! They'd discussed it at length, and Noah had agreed that Maris should have the title and the authority that it conveyed. But Daniel had asked him to be her helpmate. To serve as her advisor. To guard her back against marauders and steer her around pitfalls.

Yes, that was very good. And who could contradict him?

Perhaps he should confess that he had flirted with the idea of merging Matherly Press with a media giant and had met with Blume to discuss it. But now that Daniel was gone, he looked forward to working side by side with Maris to preserve and even strengthen Matherly Press.

Excellent.

Now, what to do about their personal relationship? Tricky to resolve, but not impossible. She was so easily pacified. Maybe he would take a special interest in this book she was so excited about. He would offer to become personally involved in its publication and devote himself to making it a huge success. She'd like that.

Or maybe he'd suggest that they try harder to produce an heir to continue the dynasty. Physically impossible, of course, but she could be happy in her ignorance until he devised something else to keep her preoccupied and malleable.

There were several options from which to choose. He was confident one would be a workable solution for their present rift.

Finally, there was the problem of the private investigator. He might dig deep enough to uncover that nasty business in Florida. But what if he did? It was an unhappy story, nothing more. He had never been incriminated. Resurrecting the incident might generate some unfavorable speculation about him, but he would dismiss any rumors as vicious gossip.

Having worked out these solutions, it was with a jaunty and optimistic air that he stepped off the elevator and walked briskly down the hallway toward his office. Even his assistant was standing at attention at her desk, wringing her hands as though anxious to please him. "Coffee, please, Cindy."

"Mr. Reed, he—"

He sailed past her and entered his office, where he came to a standstill so abruptly he might as well have walked into a glass wall. "Stern?"

Appearancewise, this attorney and Howard Bancroft were practically interchangeable. The same bald, pointed head bobbed as the man said curtly, "Mr. Reed."

"What the fuck are you doing in my office, behind my desk?"

Overlooking the obscenity, Stern gestured toward the two men with him. "These gentlemen work as paralegals for my law firm. They have agreed to help you box up your personal items. A project I will closely monitor. You have one hour to complete the task, at which time I will relieve you of your keys to this office and your security pass into the building. I will then escort you out through the Fifty-first Street exit.

"When stipulating to me the terms of your immediate dismissal, Ms. Matherly was very specific about that. She did not want to cause you any embarrassment by conducting you outside through the main entrance. In my opinion, that was most gracious of her and more consideration than you deserve." With a quick motion of his hand, he activated the paralegals. He checked his wristwatch. "The clock is ticking. I think we should begin."

Cindy squeezed in through the door behind him. "Excuse me, Mr. Reed? The deliveryman won't release this package until you personally sign the return receipt."

She was the most convenient outlet for his rage. He rounded on her, eyes blazing.

She recoiled but thrust the package at him and managed to say, "It's from a Mr. Parker Evans."

* * *

Maris had just completed her read-through when Mike returned. She was sitting motionless, the manuscript pages lying in her lap. She had stared at the last line until the letters blurred.

Pain that splinters the body but slays the soul.

Because she was dazed by that line and those that had come before it, Mike's return didn't register until he nudged her shoulder. "I remembered that you enjoy tea sometimes. I hope that's all right."

Nodding dumbly, she took the warm Styrofoam cup from him. He sat down in his desk chair. When he ripped open a packet of artificial sweetener, the sound seemed abnormally loud in the small room. "One or two?" he asked.

"One's fine."

She removed the tight plastic lid from her cup. Mike dumped the contents of the packet into the fragrant, steaming tea, then passed her a plastic stir stick. She stirred much longer than required to dissolve the sweetener. When she tasted the tea, it burned her tongue.

"This isn't the ending, is it?" she asked.

Mike frowned into his coffee. "He hasn't shown the last chapter even to me. I'm not sure he's written it. It may be too painful for him to write."

"More painful than this? God," she cried softly. "It's incredible. I can't believe it happened."

Mike looked at her meaningfully. What she'd said was rhetoric, because actually she believed every word of Parker's account. Noah had done this to his friends. She knew he had. She knew he was capable of it.

"What happened afterward, Mike?"

"Todd—"

"Noah. This isn't fiction."

"Noah returned to the marina."

"As related in the prologue. He faked hysteria. Claimed that Parker had gone crazy onboard the boat. Abused the girl. Attacked him. They fought. The girl went overboard and so did Parker. Noah tried to save them."

"He must've gone into the water so his clothes would be wet and it would appear he'd searched for them."

"He blamed Parker's violent outburst on envy."

"A lie, of course. But a damn good one. Believable. The Coast Guard organized a search-and-rescue effort."

"Mary Catherine?"

"Her body was never recovered. It was officially ruled death by drowning."

"What about Parker?"

Mike sipped his coffee before answering, a delay tactic she saw through.

"Parker was found that night by sheer accident. A fisherman spotted him. The coordinates Todd had given the Coast Guard were 'approximate.' "

"Meaning off by miles."

"Miles. After being in the water for hours, it was a miracle that Parker was still alive. Shock probably saved his life. He had kept his arms moving so he wouldn't sink and drown, but God knows how he was able to move at all. His legs had been chewed to pieces by the blades of the outboard motor. When the fishermen first saw him, they mistook him for an animal carcass that had been used for chum. There was so much blood around him, you see."

With a shaky hand, Maris set aside her tea, untasted after that first sip.

"For over a week, his condition was listed as critical," Mike continued. "Somehow, he lived. Eventually his legs were pieced back together bit by bit."

"He told me he underwent several operations. What was Noah doing all this time? Surely he was afraid that Parker would give his version of the story and convince the authorities of the truth."

"I've given you a much-abbreviated summary," Mike explained. "The reconstruction of Parker's legs took years. In those first few days, the trauma doctors worked frantically just to keep him alive. Eventually he was taken off the critical list, but he spent weeks in an ICU fighting off infection. There weren't drugs strong enough to keep him unconscious except for brief periods. The rest of the time he spent screaming, begging them to kill him. He's admitted that much to me."

Maris covered her trembling lips with her hand, which was cold and clammy. Tears stung her eyes.

"He'd suffered tremendous blood loss. Perhaps that's why they didn't amputate his legs immediately. They were afraid he'd bleed out on the operating table. Or they wanted his condition to stabilize before they attempted a surgery that traumatic. I'm surmising. I don't know. I learned all this long after the fact. No one notified me of the incident. I found out later, by happenstance.

"When he was strong enough to begin the reconstructive process, he fought like hell if any of the consulting physicians so much as mentioned amputation. Even partial. Honestly, I don't know why they heeded his wishes. Maybe because he was a young man. Maybe...I don't know," he repeated with a shrug. "Divine intervention? Providence? Maybe the doctors simply admired the power of his will and decided to honor it. Anyway, they didn't take his legs. They elected to rebuild them the best they could."

"I've seen his scars."

"The visible ones. The ones you can't see are even deeper."

"Caused by Noah's betrayal."

"During those weeks that Parker was fighting for his life, Noah was putting on quite a dog-and-pony show for the authorities. Mary Catherine wasn't there to dispute his version of what had happened. It came down to his word against Parker's. He painted Parker as a jealous, envious hothead who had gotten drunk and snapped, turned violent. He attacked Noah. When Mary Catherine tried to break them apart, Parker lashed out and knocked her over the railing. His momentum caused him to fall overboard, too.

"By the time the doctors granted the investigators permission to question him, Parker had already been cast in the defensive role. Confronted with these false accusations, Parker, by his own account, played right into Noah's hands. He reacted like a jealous, envious hothead with violent tendencies. His ranted denials made him appear guilty rather than innocent. From his hospital bed, he threatened to kill his lying friend."

Mike smiled. "I imagine that he put his command of the English language, as well as his gutter vernacular, to good use. I can imagine him pulling against arm restraints and practically foaming at the mouth."

"That probably isn't exaggerating by much."

"In any case he came across as a raving maniac, dangerous to himself and others. Noah was believed. Parker wasn't. He was charged with involuntary manslaughter for Mary Catherine's drowning. When he was well enough to leave the hospital, he was taken to court for his arraignment. He pled no contest."

"Why?" Maris exclaimed. "He wasn't guilty."

"But he felt responsible."

She shook her head. "Noah was."

"I agree with you. But Parker blamed himself for being unable to save her. Noah didn't attend Parker's sentencing, but he sent a videotaped deposition. He was humble, sorrowful, soft-spoken when he wasn't openly weeping. He said he regretted having to tell the horrible truth about that day. A dual tragedy had occurred, he said. Mary Catherine's drowning. And the death of his friendship with Parker Evans. He thought he knew him, but in a matter of hours his best friend had become his enemy.

"He said that he and Parker had been closer than any two brothers. But when Noah succeeded ahead of him, it did something to Parker. Twisted him. Noah looked earnestly into the camera and sobbed. 'I don't understand what happened to Parker that day. He turned devious, lecherous, and murderous.' I think I'm quoting correctly."

Maris took a deep breath and expelled it slowly. "So Noah went to New York in a blaze of glory because of *The Vanquished*."

"And Parker went to prison."

"*Prison?* Prison." She lowered her head and ground her palm against her forehead. "He told me once that he had spent years in rehab hospitals and 'other facilities.' I would never have imagined he was referring to prison."

"Because of the mitigating circumstances of his case and his physical condition, he was sent to a minimum-security prison and allowed to continue with his treatment program and physical therapy. He was released after serving twenty-two months of an eight-year sentence.

"He might have been better off if the state had kept him longer. On his own, he didn't fare very well." He looked at her from beneath his eyebrows. "I believe you know that he'd sunk pretty low by the time I heard what had happened to my star pupil and went looking for him."

She picked up the manuscript pages in her lap and straightened them. "I regret that I ever met Noah Reed. I loved him, Mike. Or thought I did. I was married to him. Wanted to have his children. How could I not have seen what he is?"

"You weren't looking. You didn't know to look."

"But I should have read the signs. I knew this is where he'd attended university, but he never talked about his life before coming to New York. Not even a casual reference. He didn't have any keepsakes or photographs, except one of his mother and father with him as a boy. He was never in touch with old friends. He never reminisced. He said he preferred living the present to visiting the past, and I stupidly accepted that explanation without question. Why did it never occur to me that he was hiding something?"

"Don't be too hard on yourself, Maris. Noah is like two different men occupying one body. You weren't the only one he hoodwinked."

"Was it a plot device for *Envy,* or did you actually write Parker a letter, cautioning him not to turn his back on Noah?"

"I wrote a letter very similar to the one Parker read aloud to us. Almost word for word, in fact."

"So *you* saw through Noah, and he was only your student. I

was his wife. Not a strong recommendation for my perception skills."

"Parker lived with him, too, remember. For nearly six years. Here at the university, then in Florida. Occasionally he saw traces of selfishness and self-absorption, but not until he was in the water that night did he realize that Noah is evil."

"I believe that. Recently I've had glimpses of that evil alter ego." Looking down at the pages still lying in her lap, she ran her fingers across the top sheet in something like a caress. "Parker's not evil like Noah. But he's cruel." Raising her head and looking across at Mike, she said, "Why did he do this, Mike?"

"Revenge."

"Why did he involve me?"

"I apologize for my part, Maris. I was uncomfortable with it from the start. I certainly didn't like it once I came to know you." He eased back in his chair and focused on a corner of the ceiling as he arranged his thoughts. "You see, in that damning video deposition, Noah accused Parker of lechery with Mary Catherine."

"So he made the accusation a reality. With me."

"Something like that. Parker's success with the Mackensie Roone books should have been enough for him. But it wasn't. The best revenge he could devise was to write his and Noah's story and write it well enough to captivate you, a respected editor."

"Who also happened to be Noah's wife."

"I think the idea sparked when he read that Noah had married you."

"I was the element that made the plot work."

Mike nodded somberly. "Every good plot has one component that links all the others. The common thread that seams the pieces together."

"What's the ending to be?"

"He wouldn't tell me."

"Maybe he doesn't have an ending. Maybe deceiving me, bedding me, and being able to laugh up his sleeve at Noah over it is vengeance enough for him."

Mike responded to the bitterness she couldn't conceal. "I'm not justifying what he's done, Maris. But I can understand it. Parker feels everything passionately or not at all. It's the only level of experience that makes sense to him. Otherwise, why bother? How could he be less passionate about vengeance?

"He wanted Noah to experience at least twinges of the pain he had suffered because of him. He wanted Noah to know what it felt like to be deceived and betrayed to the nth degree. So Parker tricked you into coming to him. You both betrayed Noah by sleeping—"

"Oh, my God!" She reached out and gripped Mike's sleeve. "I've just figured out his plot."

"His—"

"*Plot*. His ending." She wet her lips, spoke hurriedly. "Earlier, you quoted Noah from his videotaped deposition. He claimed that Parker had turned devious, lecherous, and…"

"Murderous," Mike finished, slapping his forehead. "Goddamn me for being so old and stupid. As many plots as I've analyzed, I should have realized where he was going. That's why he hasn't shared the last chapter with me."

Maris rattled off her racing thoughts. "Parker's done everything Noah accused him of. Except—" She looked at Mike with alarm. "He couldn't," she said huskily. "He wouldn't. I know he wouldn't."

"I don't believe so, either."

But neither sounded convinced. "He's not capable of it," she stressed. "I wouldn't have been attracted to him, wouldn't have—"

"Loved him?"

"For God's sake, Mike, I fell in love with the main character of *The Vanquished*. And transferred that love to the author. Look where that got me. I no longer trust my emotions. I believed that

Parker at least cared for me. If I hadn't believed that, I wouldn't have slept with him. But maybe I'm wrong again. Maybe..."

She pressed her fist against her heart, recalling how cruel Parker had been that awful morning. Considering all the pain and resentment, bitterness and anger that had been simmering inside him for the past fourteen years, perhaps he was capable of murder.

To his mind, Noah had stolen the life he'd had planned for himself. Tit for tat. An eye for an eye. Noah's life for the one Noah had taken from him. Noah's life in exchange for Mary Catherine's.

Now, *that* she could easily believe. Parker might not kill for revenge, but he might for justice. He had liked that girl. He had regarded her as his friend and felt compassion for her. He would feel justified seeking vengeance for her death.

She surged to her feet. "We've got to stop him."

But at the door, she drew herself up short. She had panicked unnecessarily. Clasping her hands, she bowed her head over them as though in prayer. "Thank God." Turning back around, she said to Mike, "We're not too late. Noah doesn't know that the writer I've been working with is Parker. He hasn't read *Envy.*"

Mike dragged his hands down his face, groaning, "Oh, no."

Chapter 35

Noah, fresh off a chartered boat from the mainland, entered Terry's Bar and Grill with a condescending attitude that immediately catapulted him to the top of the endangered species list.

The locals disliked nonislanders in general, but they particularly disliked any who looked down their noses at them. They despised Noah Reed on sight. In fact, he might not have been allowed to tie up his boat at the dock if Parker hadn't spread word around that he was expecting a citified visitor from up north. If anybody spotted such a person, he was to be directed to Terry's, where Parker would be waiting.

Noah approached the bar and addressed Terry with a rude, "Hey!"

Terry, who happened to be uncapping a longneck at the time, sent the bottle of beer sliding down the bar toward one of his regulars, ignoring Noah.

"Didn't you hear me?"

Terry shifted a gnawed matchstick from one corner of his mouth to the other. "I heard ya. People wanna talk to me, they talk to me proper, else they're likely to disappear. Now get the fuck outta my place."

"I think you've already worn out your welcome, Noah." At the sound of his voice, Noah spun around. Parker grinned up at him. "Record time, too."

Noah gave Parker and his wheelchair a long, slow once-over. "She told me you were a cripple."

Terry produced a baseball bat from beneath the bar. One of the regulars reached for the sheathed knife attached to his belt. Others merely glowered.

"She told me you were a prick," Parker returned, keeping his smile in place. "But then I already knew that."

Noah laughed. "Right back to our usual banter, aren't we? I didn't realize how much I'd missed it."

"Funny. I haven't missed it at all. Want a beer?"

Noah glanced at Terry. "I think I'll pass."

Parker motioned with his head for Noah to follow him outside. "I'll settle up with you later, Terry."

"No problem."

Every eye in the bar was on them as they left through the screen door and went out into the sweltering heat.

"You've got nerve, Noah. I'll give you that."

Noah scoffed. "Coming to see you?"

"No. Going into Terry's bar wearing those loafers." He looked down at Noah's Gucci shoes with the gold trademark on the vamp. "Very fancy."

Noah ignored the dig and slipped off his jacket. "Lovely climate," he said sarcastically.

"Sorta reminiscent of Key West."

Noah never faltered, but he didn't take the bait, either. Parker led him to the Gator. "Climb in."

"How quaint." He settled into the bright yellow seat. "You don't see many of these on Park Avenue."

Using his arms, Parker raised himself into the driver's seat, then reached down for his wheelchair, folded it, and placed it in the trailer. As he clicked on the ignition, he said, "Noah, you've grown into a regular Yankee snob."

"You've just grown old."

"Pain and suffering will do that to you."

For the next five minutes, they rode in silence. Noah showed a marked lack of interest in the island. He kept his eyes on the narrow road ahead, never once commenting on the scenery or even looking at it. Parker, on the other hand, returned the waves of people they happened to pass along the way.

After one lady called out a greeting from her front porch, Noah turned to him. "What are you, the local celebrity?"

"Only cripple on the island."

"I see."

"And the only professional writer they know."

"You haven't sold this book of yours yet."

"No, but the Mackensie Roone books sell like rubbers in a whorehouse."

Finally. He'd finally gotten an honest reaction out of Noah. He laughed at his stunned expression. "You didn't know? Well...surprise!"

With an aplomb that Parker remembered, Noah recovered quickly. "So that's how you afford the lovely home and loyal valet that my wife mentioned."

Parker was quick to catch Noah's possessive reference to Maris, but he didn't address it. "I'm trying to make the house a home. It still needs a lot of work. And my loyal valet up and quit on me this week."

"How come?"

"He thinks I'm a rotten person and said he wanted no part of me."

"You call that loyal?"

"Oh, he'll be back."

"You're sure of this?"

"Fairly sure, yes."

The sun had sunk below the tree line by the time they reached the derelict cotton gin. The gathering dusk made it appear even more forlorn than it did in full daylight. Its enshrouding vines seemed to be hugging it tighter, as though to protect it from the onset of darkness.

Noah assessed the dilapidated building. "I can see what you mean by the place still needing a lot of work."

Parker reached into the trailer for his wheelchair and swung it to the ground. "It's not the homestead, but it's an interesting building. As long as you're here, you might just as well get a taste of local history."

He wheeled his chair into the gin, leaving Noah no choice except to follow. Inside, waning sunlight squeezed through the cracks in the walls. The holes in the ceiling projected miniature disks of light onto the floor. They looked like scattered coins. Otherwise, the interior was gloomy with deep shadows. The air was so heavy and still it almost required conscious thought to inhale it.

Like a tour guide with a rehearsed spiel, Parker pointed out certain aspects of the gin and related some of its history and fact-based legends, as he had related them to Maris, including the failed plan to convert to steam power.

Noah tired of the monologue and interrupted Parker in mid-sentence. "I read your book."

Parker slowly brought his wheelchair around to face him. "Of course you did, Noah. You wouldn't be here if you hadn't. When did you receive it?"

"This morning."

"Quick response. Every anxious writer's dream."

"I only had to read the first few pages to realize where the plot was going. It's very good writing, by the way."

"Thanks."

"I chartered a private jet to ensure the shortest trip pos-

sible. On the flight, I scanned the remainder of the manuscript."

"But you already know the story."

"I know it'll never see print."

Parker shrugged goofily. "Just goes to show how wrong a person can be. Here I was thinking that maybe, after all these years,
you'd be ready to relieve your conscience."

"Cut the bullshit, Parker." Noah's voice cracked across the
stillness like a whip. "I assume this *Envy* is the manuscript that
Maris has been raving about?"

"The very one. She's read every word. Several times. Likes the
story. Loves the concept, the dynamic of the competitive friends.
Says the characters are vividly drawn. Thinks Roark is a prince
and Todd is... well, not a prince."

"She's easily impressed by melodrama."

"Wrong. She's a good editor."

"A schoolgirl playing dress-up."

"She's a classy lady."

"Jesus." Noah snickered. "You've fucked her, haven't you?"

Parker clenched his jaw and refused to answer, which caused
Noah to laugh.

"Ah, Parker, Parker. Your hair is graying and your face has
more lines than a road map. But some things haven't changed.
You're still the chivalrous lover who never kisses and tells."

He shook his head with amusement. "You always did have a
soft spot for the ladies. Of course, I know why you had a burning
desire to get Maris in bed. You wanted to cuckold me. You went
to a hell of a lot of trouble to do it, so I hope you weren't too disappointed. She's not exactly a firecracker in the sack, is she?"

He looked pointedly at Parker's lap. "Or maybe you're piti-
fully grateful for any kind of sexual activity. Even Maris's stilted
efforts." Thoughtfully, he scratched the side of his nose. "She
does have that luxuriant bush, though. If you left the lights on,
I'm sure you noticed."

Parker wished very badly to kill him then. He wanted to watch
him die, slowly and in agony and feeling the flames of hell licking at his ankles.

Seemingly oblivious to the murderous impulses he was foster-
ing, Noah continued nonchalantly. "Not that I'm complaining
about Maris, you understand. She's certainly proved herself useful."

"In the furtherance of your career."

"That's right." He took a step closer. "And you must know,
Parker, that I won't let anything or anyone rob me of all that I've
achieved. This book of yours will never be published."

"Actually, Noah, I didn't write it for publication. I wrote it for
myself."

"As a cathartic autobiography?"

"No."

"As a ticket to fuck my wife?"

"No."

"You're stretching my patience, Parker."

"I wrote it to get you here, on my turf, so that I could be
watching your face when you die, just like you were watching me
from the pilot's wheel of the boat that night."

Noah snorted. "What? You're going to run me down with
your wheelchair?"

Parker merely smiled and withdrew a small transistor from his
shirt pocket.

"Oh, I see, you're going to beat me to death with a remote
control."

"I own this building," Parker said conversationally. "I like it.
Good atmosphere. But some folks think it's a hazard to kids
who might wander in here. That abandoned well and all." He
hitched his thumb in that direction. "So I've decided to do my
fellow islanders a favor and destroy it."

He depressed one of the rubberized buttons on the transistor.
Out of the shadows in a far corner came a loud pop followed

by a spark. Startled, Noah spun around and watched as a flame leaped up against the weathered wood.

Parker gave his chair a hard push toward him. Noah, sensing the motion, turned and lunged at him. Noah's daily workouts in the gym had kept him trim. His reflexes were good. He landed a couple of good punches.

But Parker's arm and chest muscles were exceptionally well developed from years of having to rely on them. He staved off many of Noah's slugs and had enough upper body strength to keep himself in his chair. His real advantage, however, was in knowing how Noah fought. Noah fought dirty. Noah fought to win. And he didn't care how he won.

When Noah began pushing him backward toward the open well, Parker wasn't surprised. His efforts became defensive. He took reckless swings that Noah easily dodged. Sensing that Parker was weakening, Noah fought even harder. Parker's frantic struggling only increased Noah's determination to defeat him. He came on more ferociously, blindly, the predator moving in for the kill.

Then, at precisely the right instant, Parker jammed down the brake lever of his wheelchair. It bit into the rubber wheel and brought the chair to a jarring stop. Noah hadn't expected it. Inertia propelled him forward. His Gucci shoes caught the low rim of the well, tripping him. He groped at air. Then he stepped into nothingness.

His startled cry was a hellish echo of Mary Catherine's scream as she fell backward over the railing of the boat.

Parker's breathing was harsh and loud. He wiped his bloody nose on his shirtsleeve.

"You son of a bitch!" Noah shouted up at him.

"So the fall didn't kill you?"

"Motherfucker!"

"You're a sore loser, Noah. The cripple outsmarted you. Isn't that what you had in mind for me? To push me down that well?

Why do you think I kept referring to it? Foreshadowing, Noah. Any writer worth a damn should have recognized it for what it was."

"Get me out of here."

"Ah, don't be such a crybaby, Noah. It's not nearly as deep as the Atlantic. To the best of my knowledge there are no salt-water carnivores in there. Don't know about snakes, though," he added in an intentional afterthought.

"What are you going to do, flood it with water and let me drown?"

"Give me some credit. All you'd have to do is keep treading water till it got to the top."

"Then what's the point?"

Parker set off another of the charges. "There are twelve more like that, Noah. But long before I've set all of them off, you'll already be choking. Smoke inhalation doesn't have quite the drama of ocean water flooding your lungs, or being eaten by a shark, but it's pretty damn effective, wouldn't you say?"

"Ooh, you're scaring me, Parker. You expect me to believe that you would let me die down here?"

"Why wouldn't you believe it? I'm a killer. You said so your-self. Remember? Come on, flex the old memory muscles. I'm sure you'll remember. After all, you must've rehearsed that blub-bering speech a thousand times. The tears were a convincing touch, I must say. Even I came close to believing you. We were David and Jonathan until that day on the boat. Then I turned devious, lecherous, and murderous. Does that jiggle your mem-ory?"

"I was...I was..."

"You were sentencing me to prison. Since I did the time, I think it's only fair that I commit the crime."

Noah was silent for a moment, then said, "I think my ankle's broken."

"You're breaking my heart."

"Listen, Parker, I'm in pain down here."

"Don't even go there, Noah."

"Okay, what I did...it was wrong. I got scared. Froze up. Ran away. Once I realized what I'd done, there was no way out for me but to do what I did. I can understand your carrying a grudge. But you've made your point."

"Like you could have made yours by leaving me in the ocean to die. Wasn't that enough? Did you have to let Mary Catherine die, too?"

"You won't get away with this," Noah said in a new tone of voice.

"Oh, I think I will. You did."

"People will see the smoke, call the fire department."

"It's on the other side of the island. You'll suffocate before they get here."

"And you'll be blamed."

"I don't think so. Everyone inside Terry's heard your cruel remark. They know your wife's been living under my roof for a couple weeks. They'll figure you came down here from Yankeeland to bust my ass. But to them I'm the poor crippled man who lives down the lane. Now, who do you think they're going to believe? Who do you think they'll *choose* to believe?

"All I have to do is tell them the truth. We had words. You attacked me, and I've got the bloody nose to prove it. You lost your balance and fell into the well. Unfortunately, I had already set off the charges and couldn't stop the inevitable. I tried to save you, but it was no use. I'm a cripple, remember?"

He peered over the rim and smiled down at Noah, whose face was a pale oval looking up at him from the bottom of the dry well. "It's as plausible as the story you told the Coast Guard, don't you think?"

"Parker. Parker. Listen to me."

"Excuse me just a moment." He depressed a button and another charge sparked. By now flames were eating the wood on the outside walls in two places, working their way up toward the loft.

"Stop this, Parker," Noah cried.

"No."

"For God's sake!"

"For God's sake? Don't you mean for your sake, Noah? I think even God would understand and forgive anything I did to you. I thought of shooting you and getting it over with. I'd've pled self-defense and would have gotten away with it.

"But then I thought about the hours I flailed about in that fucking ocean before I was rescued. I thought about the hours I spent in excruciating pain in rehab hospitals. Somehow shooting seemed much too good for you. I had to wait fourteen years for this. If you met death quickly, it wouldn't be nearly as gratifying. I considered cutting off your balls and letting you bleed out, like I nearly did. But that would have been messy and I couldn't think of a reasonable defense.

"Then one day I was in here plotting a Deck Cayton novel, and I happened to catch myself staring at this well, and just like that," he said, snapping his fingers, "the idea came to me. I got a mental image of you struggling for air, your eyes streaming tears, your nose running snot. I got so aroused, I nearly came inside my shorts.

"By the way, the equipment works just fine, thank you. And Maris might have been married to you, but she was never your *wife*. You don't know her. You never even came close to knowing her.

"Now, where was I? Oh, yeah, I got an ol' boy who lives on the island to set these charges for me. Simple. Like automatic fireplace starters. I sent out notices that I was going to burn the place down. A controlled fire, you see. Like they once used to burn the sugarcane fields right here on the island. Not much flame. Lots of smoke."

By now the smell of it was strong.

"Parker, you've got to get us out of here."

Parker laughed. "I won't have trouble getting out. I've got wheels. You, by contrast, are screwed."

Noah tried another tack. "Okay, you want me to beg. I'm begging. Get me out of here."

Parker coughed on smoke. "Sorry, Noah. Even if I wanted to, it's too late. I've got to save myself. I'll be depriving myself the pleasure of watching you die, but—"

"Parker! Don't do this." Noah sobbed. "Please. Don't let me die. What can I say?"

Parker stared down at him, his features turning hard, all traces of humor vanishing. "Say you're sorry."

Noah stopped sobbing but remained stubbornly silent.

"Did you even know Mary Catherine's real name?"

"What difference does it make?"

"It was Sheila. You should've at least known the name of the girl who miscarried your baby."

"It wasn't a baby. It was a female trick. A trap."

"So you did know," Parker murmured. "I wondered."

"Ancient history, Parker."

"Wrong. It's very timely. If you want to get out of here alive, Noah, admit that you knocked Mary Catherine overboard and did nothing, fucking *nothing*, to try and save her."

Noah hesitated. Parker placed his hand on the wheels of his chair and started to turn it around. "See ya."

"Wait! All right! What happened to Mary Catherine—"

"Sheila."

"Sheila. What happened to Sheila was my fault."

"And me. You deliberately ran that boat over me."

"Yes."

"Say it."

"I deliberately ran that boat over you."

"Why?"

"I...I was trying to kill you and make it look like an accident. I wanted you out of the way."

"Of your career."

"That's right."

"Was that also why you killed Daniel Matherly?"

"Damn you!"

"You did kill him, didn't you?" Parker shouted down at him. "Admit it or you suffocate, you son of a bitch. If you don't drown in your own nervous piss first."

"I . . . I . . ."

"How'd you arrange that fall, Noah?"

"I provoked him. About this old friend of his. He got angry, came at me. I deflected—"

"You pushed him."

"All right."

"Say it!"

Desperate now, Noah relented. "I pushed him. I didn't have to, but I did. Just to make sure."

Parker coughed on smoke. It was stinging his eyes. "You are an abomination, Noah. A miserable human being. A murderer." He shook his head regretfully. "But you're not worth killing."

Parker wheeled his chair backward. Panicked, Noah shouted his name from the bottom of the well. He was out of sight only for the amount of time it took him to retrieve the rope he had stashed earlier in preparation for this moment. He dangled it above the well where Noah could see it. "Are you sure you want me to save you? You'll go to prison, you know."

"Throw it down." He was reaching up in an imploring gesture.

"I know exactly how you feel," Parker told him. "I knew my legs were shot to hell. I'd have done anything to stop the pain. Anything except die. I thought I wanted to. But when those fishermen reached for me, I grabbed hold for all I was worth."

He threaded the rope down to Noah, who grasped it frantically. "Make a few loops around your chest and tie it tightly," Parker instructed.

"Okay," Noah called when he was done. "Pull me up."

Parker backed away, pulling the rope taut. "Ready? If you can get some footholds, walk the wall."

"I can't. My ankle."

"Okay, but easy does it. Don't—"

He was about to say "yank." But it was too late.

Chapter 36

I n his panic to be rescued, Noah had pulled sharply on the rope. Parker wasn't braced for it. He was jerked forward out of the wheelchair, landing on the packed dirt floor. "Goddammit!"

"What? What's happening? Parker?"

For several seconds, Parker lay there with his forehead resting on the floor. He took several deep breaths. Then, using his forearms to pull him along, he inched his way over to the rim of the well and peered down into it.

"You pulled me out of my chair."

"Well, get back in it."

"I'm open to suggestions on how I should go about it."

"Well, do something."

Noah's voice was now ragged with desperation. Even at the bottom of the well, he must have been able to hear the crackle of old wood burning. The smoke grew thicker by the second.

"Parker, you've got to get me out of here!"

"Can't help you, buddy. I'm a cripple, remember?" He shook his head ruefully. "I'll admit this isn't the way I had the ending plotted. I never intended for you to die. I wanted to give you a taste of what it's like to face your mortality. To experience that all-encompassing terror. I wanted to scare you into confessing your sins. I wanted you to grovel and beg me for your life. And you did. It was supposed to end there."

He laughed. "I realize that you're panicked, Noah, and that your mind is preoccupied with surviving. But I hope you're thinking clearly enough to grasp the irony of this situation.

"Think about it. I'm your only hope of salvation. But I'm powerless to save you because of the injuries you inflicted on me. That's rich, isn't it? It's a shame that neither of us will have the opportunity to use it in a book. It's the kind of built-in irony that Professor Mike Strother loved."

At the mention of their mentor's name, the distance between them seemed to shrink. Their eyes made a connection that was almost audible. Parker spoke softly. "You have one more sin to confess, don't you, Noah?"

"I had to be first, Parker. I had to be."

"Professor Strother hadn't heard from either of us for more than a year. All his correspondence had been returned un-opened, addressees unknown, no forwarding addresses. He was puzzled and slightly offended by our sudden and inexplicable disappearance.

"He didn't realize you'd sold *The Vanquished* until he saw it in his local bookstore. He recognized the title and your name im-mediately, of course. He purchased a copy. He was curious to read how you had finalized your manuscript. He wanted to see if you had incorporated any of his suggestions. Naturally, he was proud that one of his students had written the novel that was all the rage, the topic of conversation at cocktail parties and beauty shops and office commissaries, the book that was on every best-seller list."

"Parker—"

"Now imagine Professor Strother's surprise when he settled into his reading chair, adjusted his lamp, opened his copy of *The*

Vanquished by Noah Reed. And read the first page of my book. *My* book, Noah!"

"It was that letter," Noah shouted back at him. "Strother always favoring you. Always thinking you were the one with the most talent. He thought your manuscript was so fucking fine. I thought I'd test it, get a second opinion. One day while you were out, I went into your computer and printed out a copy. I put my title on it and submitted it under my name."

"And when it sold, you had to get rid of me. Immediately. That day."

"That was the plan."

"Bet you shit when I turned up alive."

"It gave me pause, but I didn't panic. I hurriedly put your book into my computer, and mine into yours. You couldn't have proven your claims to the authorities because by then I had painted you as unstable and violent."

"Strother always gave you credit for clever plotting."

"Our dear professor was another concern, but I figured that if he ever came forward and tried to expose me, I'd..."

"You'd think of a way to worm your way out."

"I always have."

"Until now."

"At least I'll die knowing that you're right behind me. You might even beat me into hell."

"You think so?"

"You can't crawl along on your belly fast enough to get out of here now, Parker."

"No, but I can walk fast enough." Then, as Noah watched with mounting disbelief, Parker struggled to his knees and then stood up.

"You cocksucking son of a—"

"It's a Mackensie Roone trademark, Noah," Parker said, smiling down at him. "Save one final plot twist for the very, very end."

"I'll kill you, Parker. I'll see you in hell! I'll—"

"You all right, Mr. Evans?" Deputy Sheriff Dwight Harris rushed through the door, accompanied by two other deputies.

"Exhausted," Parker told him. "Otherwise okay." He depressed a button on the remote control and the flames immediately died.

"Fire truck's outside. We were getting worried." Just then the spray from the fire hose struck the exterior wall with a hard *whomp.*

"I was getting a little worried myself," Parker said. "Those smoke machines are killers."

Deputy Harris glanced at the scorched walls. "Those smudge pots did some damage to your building."

"It's survived worse. Besides, it was worth it."

"So you got it?"

"Every incriminating word." Parker pulled out his shirttail and removed a cassette tape recorder clipped to the waistband of his pants. He disconnected it from the microphone wire and passed it to the sheriff. He winced only slightly when he ripped off the tiny microphone taped to his chest. "Thanks for setting this up, Deputy Harris."

"No thanks necessary. I appreciate your calling me. It'll probably be the only elaborate sting of my career." The two shook hands.

Noah had continued to shout obscenities, but the deputy hadn't acknowledged him until now. "I'm anxious to meet your guest here, Mr. Evans. Let's haul him up outta there," Harris said, motioning to the other two deputies, who were standing by with ropes.

"How you doin' down there, Mr. Reed? The police chief up in Mass'chusitts sure is anxious to hear what you had to say about your daddy-in-law's fall. My department's talking to the folks down in Florida, too."

Parker turned away, symbolically leaving Noah to the devil as Mike had urged him to.

He was taken aback, but not really shocked, to see his old friend standing just beyond the gin's wide door. Mike always seemed to be there when he'd most needed him.

Maris was standing with him.

Deputy Harris noticed his hesitation and sidled up behind him. "They were tearing up the road in a golf cart. Intercepted them before they could barge in here and ruin the whole thing. Had a hell of a time keeping them out. They were worried about you."

"Afraid Noah would kill me?"

"No, sir. Afraid *you* would kill *him*."

Parker smiled. "Wonder where they got that idea."

"The old man said something about your plot. Said Ms. Matherly pieced it together, figured it out."

"That doesn't surprise me."

Shuffling across the dirt floor in a stiff-legged, awkward gait, his legacy of Noah's treachery, he slowly made his way outside. Mike seemed to know he needed to make this walk alone and didn't rush to assist him. He was within touching distance before Mike asked if he wanted his wheelchair.

"Thanks, Mike."

Mike went to fetch his chair. Maris continued to stand stone still, staring at him.

"You thought I was paralyzed?"

She nodded.

"I figured. Thought it best to let you go on thinking that. For this to work, I needed Noah to think that, too." He decided he might just as well tell her the worst of it flat out. "I ride whenever I can. This is about the best I can do. Will ever do."

A tear rolled down her cheek. "It doesn't matter. It never did."

* * *

"The sweetest gift I ever received in my life was that glass of fireflies." Parker was stroking her back in the aftermath of love-making.

"Lightning bugs."

He chuckled. "You're learning. With help you might become a bona fide belle."

"That was a sweet night all-'round. The sweetest. Until tonight."

"Maris, that next morning—"

"Shh. I understand now why you had to be so wretched."

"You do?"

"You had to get rid of me before you could bring Noah here."

He tipped her chin up so he could see her face. "But you know I used you to get to him."

"Your original plan was probably to have him catch us like this."

He glanced down the length of their entwined bodies. "Yeah."

"But that changed when you fell in love with me. You couldn't bring yourself to subject me to an ugly scene like that. So you hurt me in order to protect me. You made certain I would leave."

He stroked her cheek. "You're so smart you amaze me."

"So I'm right?"

"As rain. Especially about me falling in love with you."

"You did?"

"I am. Present tense." He lifted her face toward his and kissed her in a way that left no room for doubt.

"There is one thing I can't figure out," she said when the kiss finally ended. "I know we promised not to talk about this tonight, but I'd like to have one point clarified."

They had agreed that they wouldn't rehash everything tonight. They faced months, possibly years, of legal entanglements before Parker was exonerated and Noah was tried and punished for his crimes. She had a publishing house to run, and he had books to write. They didn't yet know how they were going to divide their time between New York and St. Anne Island. She would grieve her father's death for a long while yet, and Parker was deliberating whether or not to reveal Mackensie Roone to his legion of fans. They had much to work out but were committed to making it work.

However, they had agreed that tomorrow didn't start until sunrise and that they deserved tonight to strictly enjoy one another.

"I don't want to invite Noah into bed with us," he said.

"I understand. And agree. But this isn't really about him."

"Okay. One point and then I want to do some more of what we were doing."

"I promise," she said, smiling. "Mike discovered that *The Vanquished* was actually your book with Noah's title on it."

"Right."

"And he tried to contact you for an explanation."

"It took him almost a year to track me down. By then the paperback edition had already come out."

"Why didn't Mike expose Noah then?"

"Because I threatened his life if he did."

"Why?"

"I was in piss-poor condition, Maris. An ex-con who looked like a beggar and was living like one. I was wheelchair-bound. Only after years of physical therapy am I able to walk at all. If you can even call that walking. When Mike found me, I was weak, wasted. Addicted to pills." He shook his head stubbornly. "I refused to confront Noah in such a reduced state when he was the book world's crowned prince."

"Enjoying the success that rightfully belonged to you."

"I chose to wait until I was strong and confident."

"And successful."

"That, too. I wanted to challenge him as an equal, when I had the credentials to back up my claim that he'd stolen my book. I knew it might take years, but I was willing to wait."

"I'm surprised you got Mike to agree."

"He didn't agree. He just gave in."

"Or?"

"Or I swore that I would never write another word as long as I lived."

"Ahh. That would have cinched it."

Now that he had answered her question, she eased herself on top of him and opened her thighs. With a grunt of satisfaction, he pressed himself inside her, began to stroke with the barest upward motion of his hips.

"Hmm. You are incredibly talented, Mr. Evans."

"Yeah, and I can write a fairly decent book, too."

Sitting up, she reached behind her, between his legs, and stroked the underside of his penis at its base. He strained a curse between his teeth. "You've got talents of your own, Ms. Matherly. Where'd you learn that trick?"

"I read it in one of your books."

"Damn, I'm good."

She continued to caress him until he pulled her down onto his chest and hugged her tightly around the waist while he pushed into her as high as possible. His raw, choppy breaths were muffled against her breasts.

Finally he relaxed, his head falling back onto the pillow. She smoothed his hair back from his damp forehead. "Felt good?"

"It still does." Cradling her face between his hands, he kissed her, whispering into her mouth, "We're being awfully messy here."

"I don't mind it. I'd like a baby."

"I can live with that."

"Or two."

"Even better."

"Parker?"

"Hmm?"

"Make me come."

She was ready. It took only a few strokes of his fingertip.

Later, they lay facing each other, their heads sharing the pillow. He was tracing her fragile collarbone when she said, "I recognized you the first time you kissed me. The night we met."

His finger fell still in the hollow just beneath her shoulder. He raised his eyes to hers. "What?"

"That's why that kiss alarmed me. Because I knew you. And not just knew you, but knew you well. Intimately. I had spent so many nights with you, poring over every word. Your book was like a personal love letter. Like you wrote it to me. Just for me.

"When you kissed me, it was so familiar, it was as though you had kissed me like that a thousand times." Adoringly, she touched every feature of his face. "I have loved you for so long, Parker. For years. From the day I first read *The Vanquished*."

He swallowed hard. "When you talked about it with such passion... You got it, Maris," he said with glad emphasis. "You got exactly what I had wanted to get across with those characters and that story. God, listening to you talk about it, my heart nearly burst. Can you imagine how hard it was for me not to tell you that I was the author? That it was me, not Noah, you'd fallen in love with?"

"Why didn't you tell me?"

"I couldn't. Not then. Not yet. Besides, I was afraid I wouldn't live up to your expectations."

She ran her fingers through his hair. "You surpassed them, Parker. You created my fantasies. Now you're fulfilling them."

They kissed long and deeply and when they finally pulled apart, she asked him what his original title had been.

And he told her.

And she told him that she liked it much better.

About the Author

SANDRA BROWN is the author of seventy *New York Times* bestsellers. There are more than eighty million copies of her books in print worldwide, and her work has been translated into thirty-four languages. In 2008, the International Thriller Writers named Brown its Thriller Master, the organization's highest honor. She has served as president of Mystery Writers of America and holds an honorary doctorate of humane letters from Texas Christian University. She lives in Texas.

Prologue

A cheerless drizzle blurred any view of the body on the beach.

Mist formed halos around the lampposts along the pier, but didn't diffuse the glaring portable lights that had been put in place by first responders. In a grotesque parody of catching someone in the spotlight on center stage, they shone a harsh light on the covered form.

A police helicopter swept in low. Its searchlight was unforgivingly bright as it tracked the length of the pier. Its beam skittered over the marina where boats rocked in a lulling current that was out of keeping with the surrounding chaos.

Before shifting out onto the surf, the searchlight cut a swath across the corpse. The chopper's downwash flipped back a corner of the garish yellow plastic sheet to expose a hand, inert and bone-white on the packed sand.

Since the discovery of the body, officers representing several law enforcement agencies had converged on the scene. The colored lights of a search-and-rescue helicopter blinked against the underbelly of low clouds hugging the harbor. Beyond Fort

Sumter, a US Coast Guard cruiser plowed through the waters of the Atlantic, its searchlight sweeping across the swells.

TV satellite vans had arrived, disgorging eager reporters and camera crews.

On the pier, the inevitable onlookers had congregated. They vied for the best vantage points from which to gawk at the body, monitor the police and media activity, and take selfies with the draped corpse in the background. They swapped information and speculation.

It was said that the deceased had washed ashore with the evening tide and had been discovered by a man and his young son while they were exercising their chocolate Lab on this stretch of beach.

It was said that drowning was the obvious cause of death.

It was said that it was the result of a boating mishap.

None of these conjectures was correct.

The unleashed Labrador had run ahead of his owner, and it was the dog, splashing in the surf, that had made the gruesome discovery.

One of the spectators on the pier, overhearing the exchanges of facts, fictions, and laments, smiled in self-satisfied silence.

Chapter 1

———◦◦◦———

Three weeks earlier

The automatic doors whooshed open. In one surveying glance, Drex Easton took in the hotel lobby. It was empty except for the pretty young woman behind the reception desk. She had a porcelain-doll complexion, a glossy black ponytail, and an uncertain smile as she greeted him.

"Good morning, sir. Can I help you?"

Drex set his briefcase at his feet. "I don't have a reservation, but I need a room."

"Check-in isn't until two o'clock."

"Hmm."

"Because... because for the convenience of our guests, check-out isn't until noon."

"Hmm."

"Housekeeping needs time to—"

"I realize all that, Ms. Li." He'd read the name badge pinned to her maroon blazer. He smiled. "I was hoping you could make an exception for me."

He reached behind his back to remove a wallet from his pants pocket and, in doing so, spread open his suit jacket wide enough to reveal the shoulder holster beneath his left arm. Upon seeing it, the young woman blinked several times before rapidly shifting her gaze back up to his, which he held steady on her.

"No cause for alarm," he said quietly. He flipped open the wallet that contained a badge and photo ID that classified him as a special agent of the Federal Bureau of Investigation.

The kids were tan and lean, attractive and self-assured to the point of cockiness. Hatch figured that between the three of them they probably hadn't done an honest day's work in their lives. They were locals, or at least permanent transplants. He'd seen them around.

"Let me see what I can do."

"I would consider it a big favor."

Graceful fingers pecked across her keyboard. "Single or double?"

"I'm not picky."

Her eyes scanned the computer monitor. She scrolled down, then back up. "I can have housekeeping service a nice double room for you right away, but the turnaround could take up to half an hour. Or, there's a less nice single available now."

"I'll take the less nice single available now." He slid a credit card across the granite counter.

"How long will you be staying with us, Mr. Easton?"

She was no slouch. She'd noted his name. "I'm not sure. Two other...Two associates of mine will be arriving shortly. I won't know how long I'll be staying until after our meeting. I'll have to let you know then."

"No problem. You may keep the room until you notify me of your departure."

"Great. Thanks."

She ran his credit card and proceeded to check him in. She had him initial the room rate on the form and sign his name at the bottom; then she returned his credit card along with the room key card. "That key also unlocks the door to the fitness center on the second floor."

"Thanks, but I won't be using it."

"The restaurant is just down the corridor behind you. Breakfast is served—"

"No breakfast, either." He bent down and picked up his briefcase.

Taking the subtle hint, she pointed him toward the elevators. "As you step off onto your floor, your room will be to your left."

"Thank you, Ms. Li. You've been a huge help."

"When your associates arrive, am I at liberty to give them your room number?"

"No need, I'll text it to them. They can come straight up."

"I hope your meeting goes well."

He gave her a wry grin. "So do I." Then he leaned forward and said in an undertone, "Relax, Ms. Li. You're doing a fine job."

She looked chagrined. "This is only my second day. Were my nerves that obvious?"

"Probably not to anyone else, but sizing people up quickly is a large part of what I do. And if this is only your second day, I'm even more impressed with how you handled a troublesome guest."

Hatch recognized the same level of wild panic in this young man's eyes. This was no prank, no showing off, no drunken escapade, as he'd originally thought. The kid—the one who'd smartly saluted him earlier—was in distress to the point of hysteria.

He gave her a lazy smile. "You caught me on a good day."

The less nice single wasn't a room the hotel chain would feature in an ad, but it would do. Drex opened his briefcase on the desk and booted up his laptop. He texted Mike the room number, then went over to the window. It afforded a fourth floor view of a freeway interchange and not much else.

He returned to the desk and checked his email inbox. Nothing of importance. He went into the compact bathroom and used the toilet. As he came out, the hotel telephone was ringing. He picked up the extension on the desk. "Yes?"

"Mr. Easton?"

"Ms. Li."

"Your associates are here."

"Good." Sooner than he'd expected.

"Would you like for me to send something from the kitchen up to your room? Perhaps a fruit platter? A selection of pastries?"

"Thank you, but no."

"If you change your mind, don't hesitate to call down."

"I'll do that, Ms. Li. Thanks again for accommodating me."

"You're welcome."

Although the open drapes let in plenty of daylight, he switched on the desk lamp. He adjusted the thermostat down a few degrees. He glanced at his reflection in the mirror above the dresser and thought he looked presentable, but hardly spiffy. He'd showered and dressed in a rush.

At the soft knock, he went to the door and looked through the peephole before opening it. He stood aside and motioned the two men to come in.

As they filed past him, Gifford Lewis said, "The girl at the desk stopped us to ask if we were Mr. Easton's associates. She's moony for you."

"Anything Mr. Easton wants," Mike Mallory grumbled. "As long as she was offering, I could have done with the fruit platter and pastry selection. You could still call down."

Out of habit, Drex checked the hallway—which was empty—then shut the door and flipped the bolt. "You wake me up at dawn, say, 'Find a place where the walls don't have ears.' And don't waste any time doing it, you said. I don't waste any time, I find a place, and here we are. Never mind the fruit platter and pastries. What's up?"

The other two looked at each other, but neither replied.

But, in all fairness, Hatch had to hand it to the Coast Guard officials and local policemen who'd questioned the young man and organized a search-and-rescue party: They hadn't been assholes about it.

Gif stationed himself against the wall, a shoulder propping him there. Mike rolled the chair from beneath the desk and wedged his three hundred forty pounds between the protesting armrests.

Drex placed his hands on his hips, his expression demanding. "For crissake, will one of you speak?"

Mike glanced over at Gif, who made a gesture that yielded the floor to Mike. He looked up at Drex and said, "I've found him."

Mike's tone conveyed all the gaiety of a death knell. The *him* didn't need specification.

For years Drex had been waiting to hear those words. He'd imagined this moment ten thousand times. He'd envisioned himself experiencing one or more physical reactions. His ears would ring, his mouth go dry, his knees buckle, his breath catch, his heart burst.

Instead, after his hands dropped from his hips, he went numb to a supernatural extent.

Gif and Mike must have expected an eruption of some sort, too, because they looked mystified over his sudden and absolute immobility and silence, which were downright eerie, even to himself.

A full minute later, when the paralyzing shock began to wear off, he walked over to the window again. Since last he'd looked out, nothing cataclysmic had occurred. Traffic hadn't stilled on the crisscrossing freeways. No jagged cracks had opened up in the earth's surface. The sky hadn't fallen. The sun hadn't burned out.

He pressed his forehead against the window and was surprised by how cold the glass felt. "You're sure?"

"Sure? As in positive? No," Mike replied. "But this guy looks real good on paper."

"Age?"

"Sixty-two. So says his current driver's license."

Drex turned his head and raised his eyebrows in a silent question.

"South Carolina," Mike said. "Mount Pleasant. Suburb of—"

"Charleston. I know. What name is he going by?"

"Un-huh."

That brought Drex all the way around. "Excuse me? What does that mean?"

Gif said, "Means that you're not getting a name until we know what you plan to do with the information."

"What the hell do you think I plan to do with it? First thing is to haul ass to Charleston."

Gif exchanged a look with Mike, then pushed himself away from the wall and squared off against Drex. He didn't take a combative stance, which would have been laughable because Drex was physically imposing and Gif was nowhere near. But he set his feet apart and braced himself as though Drex's self-restraint was iffy and reasonableness was way too much to hope for.

He said, "Hear me out, Drex. Mike and I talked about it on our way over here. We think you should consider...That is, it would be advisable to...The smart course of action would be to—"

"*What?*"

"Notify Rudkowski."

"Not a fucking chance in hell."

"Drex—"

Louder and with more emphasis, Drex repeated his statement.

Mike shot Gif a droll glance. "Told ya."

Drex's ears had begun to clamor after all. Now that the reality was setting in, his blood pressure had spiked. The window glass had felt cold against his forehead because his face was feverish. The blood vessels in his temples were throbbing. His scalp was sweaty beneath his hair. His torso had gone clammy.

He pulled off his suit jacket and tossed it onto the bed, wrestled off the shoulder holster and dropped it on top of his jacket, loosened the knot of his necktie, and unbuttoned his collar, all as though he were preparing for a sparring match, which, if necessary, this argument might result in.

Willing himself to at least *sound* composed, he asked again, "What name is he using?"

"Assuming it's him," Mike said.

"You assume it's him, or you wouldn't have suggested this secret meeting. Tell me what you have on him, starting with his name."

"No name."

Mike Mallory was an all-star when it came to excavating information from a computer, but a people person he wasn't. He harbored a general contempt for his fellow man, considering most to be complete morons, Drex and Gif being the only possible exceptions.

He was so good at what he did that Drex put up with his truculent attitude and lack of social graces, but right now he muttered an epithet that encompassed both Mike and Gif, who, on this point, had taken Mike's side.

"Fine," Mike said, "call us nasty names. We're thinking in your best interest."

"I'll think for myself, thank you."

"After you hear everything, you may decide against taking matters into your own hands."

"I won't."

Mike shrugged. "Then it'll be your funeral. But I'm not digging your grave, and I'm sure as hell not climbing in with you. Fair warning."

"Fair enough. I'll find out his frigging name myself. Just put me on the right track."

Mike nodded. "That I'll do. Because I don't want him to get away, either. If it's him."

Drex backed down a bit and rolled his shoulders, forcing them to relax. "Does the mystery man hold a job?"

"Nothing I could find," Mike said, "but he lives well."

"I'll bet," Drex said under his breath. "How long has he been in Mount Pleasant?"

"I don't have that yet. He's lived at his current residence for ten months."

"What kind of residence?"

"House."

"Leased?"

"Purchased."

"Mortgaged?"

"If so, I couldn't find it."

"Cash purchase, then."

Mike raised his beefy shoulders in an unspoken *I guess.*

Gif speculated that maybe the property had been inherited, but none of them really thought that, so no one pursued it.

Drex asked, "What's the place like?"

"Based on the real estate listing, it was pre-owned, not new," Mike said. "But an established neighborhood. Upscale."

"Price?"

"Million and a half and change. Looks spacious and well kept on Google Earth. It's all on here." Mike groped beneath his overlap for his pants pocket and produced a thumb drive.

Drex took it from him.

"Won't do you any good without the password, and you're not getting it till we've talked this out."

Drex scoffed. "I can get the password cracked. When applied to you, the word *geek* sounds ludicrous, but you're not the only computer geek around, you know."

Mike raised his hands. "Be my guest. Get a geek to go digging. But if you're found out, how are you going to explain your interest in this seemingly law-abiding citizen?"

"A bribed hacker won't care what my interest is."

"A bribed hacker won't blink over taking your money, then—"

"Stabbing you in the back with it," Gif chimed in.

"Your hacker would get the man in South Carolina on the phone and tell him there's a guy in far-off Lexington, Kentucky, who's spying on him."

Gif picked up. "For more coin than you're paying him, the hacker would sell you out."

"Then it would be *you*, Special Agent Easton," Mike continued, jabbing a stubby index finger at him, "who would be spied on, caught committing God knows how many violations and crimes, civil and criminal, and that would squash this and any future chance you might have to finally nail this son of a bitch, which has been your main mission in life." He wheezed a deep breath. "Tell us we're wrong."

Drex sat down on the end of the bed, propped his forearms on his thighs, and dropped his head forward. After a moment, he looked up. "Okay. No hacker. I'll moderate my approach. Satisfied?"

The other two exchanged a look. Gif said, "Exercise a little caution, some discretion."

"Don't go off half-cocked," Mike said.

Gif added, "That's all we're saying."

Drex placed his hand over his heart. "I'll be cautious, discreet, and fully cocked. Okay?"

Neither approved of that last bit, and they didn't look wholly convinced of his sincerity, but Mike said, "Okay. Next question?"

"Do you have a picture of him?"

"Only the one on his driver's license."

"And?"

"Looks nothing like he did the last time he surfaced."

"Key West," Gif reminded them, although they didn't need reminding.

"You'd never know it's the same man," Mike said. "Which means I could be dead wrong about this fella."

"If he is," Gif said, "but you rush in hell-bent and create havoc in this guy's life, you'll land yourself in a world of hurt. Especially if Rudkowski were to get wind of it."

"Rudkowski can go fuck himself."

"Rumor is, he's tried, but can't quite figure out how to go about it."

Gif's quip got a rare snort of humor out of Mike and a reluctant grin from Drex. Gif was good at defusing a tense situation. Of average height and weight, with thinning brown hair, and not a single feature that was distinguishing, Gif's averageness was his camouflage. He could observe others unnoticed and unremembered, which made him a valuable asset to the team. He was also a reliable predictor of human behavior, as he'd just demonstrated.

Drex's impulse had been to rush in hell-bent and create havoc.

Needing a moment to collect his thoughts, he motioned toward the minibar. "Help yourselves." He stood up and began pacing in the limited space between the bed and the window.

Mike and Gif made their selections and popped the tops off soda cans. Mike complained that he needed a crowbar to get the lid off the jar of mixed nuts. Gif offered to give it a try. Mike scoffed at that and called him a weakling.

Drex tuned out their bickering and focused his thoughts on his quarry, a man he first knew as Weston Graham, although that could be just another of his many aliases. Having eluded the authorities for decades, he could have turned up enjoying a Frosty at the Wendy's across the freeway or burning incense in a monastery in the Himalayas, and neither would have surprised Drex.

He was a chameleon, exceptionally good at altering his appearance and adapting to his environment. Among the ones in which he'd lived comfortably and without arousing suspicion were a penthouse on Chicago's Gold Coast, a horse ranch outside of Santa Barbara, and a yacht moored in Key West. Other locales that he had oozed his way through—those that Drex knew of—weren't that ritzy. They hadn't had to be. All had been extremely profitable for him.

When his cohorts had resettled, Drex asked, "What put you onto the guy in South Carolina?"

"I run my trot lines continually, but what finally tipped me?" Mike said around a burp. "An online dating service. Figuring he vets his victims somehow, I troll those services periodically just to see if something clicks. Day before yesterday, I came across a profile that did. The wording of it jostled my memory. Felt like I'd read it before.

"Took me a while to find it, but there it was. Except for the physical description of himself, it was word for word, comma for comma, identical to this most recent one. Likes, dislikes, five-year goals, philosophy of life and love. All that bullcrap. But the kicker? It was posted six months before Pixie went missing."

Patricia Montgomery, known as Pixie to her friends, had vanished from her Tulsa mansion, never to be seen again.

"Coincidence, Mike," Drex said. "Acquaintances of Pixie's who were interviewed swore that she never would have used a dating service to meet men."

"The acquaintances of all the missing ladies have sworn that. They've also sworn their friend was too savvy to be taken in by a con man. But Pixie disappeared within days of selling her stocks and emptying her bank accounts of her oil fortune."

Gif said, "The only thing missing from her home was her PC. Her seducer left behind tens of thousands of dollars in jewelry and furs but took an outdated computer."

"So there wouldn't be evidence of an online flirtation," Mike said. The leather seat beneath him groaned as he leaned forward to take the near-empty jar of nuts from Gif. "You're frowning," he said to Drex.

"I want to be excited, but this is awfully thin."

"You're right. Thin as onionskin. So I went back to his victim after Pixie. At least the one we *suspect* to have been his victim."

"Marian Harris. Key West."

"Eight months before her disappearance, the same damn profile was posted. Different dating service, but one that also caters to 'mature' clients with 'discriminating tastes.'"

"Word for word?" Drex asked.

"Like a fingerprint."

"Bad joke," Gif said.

The man they sought had never left a fingerprint. Or if he had, no one had found it. Freakin' Ted Bundy.

Mike shook the last of the nuts straight from the jar into his mouth. "Pittsburgh didn't take him as long," he said as he noshed. "He solicited 'companionship' with 'a refined lady' only three months before Loretta Doan's disappearance, more than six years ago."

"Are all the services you scanned nationwide?"

"Yes. Relocation isn't a deterrent to him. I think the asshole likes the changes of scenery."

"When was this most recent profile put out there?"

"Couple of months back."

Drex grimaced. "He's looking for his next lady."

"That's what I deduced. So I gave it a test run. I replied, using buzzwords I figured would make me sound like a prime target. I described myself as a childless, fifty-something widow who's financially secure and independent. I enjoy fine cuisine, good wine, and foreign films. Most men find me attractive."

"Not me," Gif said.

"Me neither," Drex said.

Mike gave them the finger. "He must not have, either. He hasn't taken the bait."

Gif thoughtfully scratched his forehead. "Maybe you oversold yourself. You sounded too self-assured, sophisticated, and smart. He looks for women with a dash of naïveté. Vulnerability. You scared him off."

"Or," Drex said, "he picked up on the buzzwords, smelled a rat, figured that this dream lady was actually a fed on a fishing expedition."

"Maybe," Mike said. "But another, more likely possibility—the one I fear—is that he jumped the gun. Solicited too soon. He hasn't responded because he hasn't ditched his current victim yet."

It was a reasonable theory to which Drex gave credence because it caused his gut to clench. "Meaning that she's in mortal danger as we speak."

"Worse than that."

"What's worse than mortal danger?"

Mike hesitated.

"Give," Drex said.

The heavy man sighed. "I repeat, Drex, I may be wrong."

"But you don't think so."

He raised his catcher's mitt–sized hands at his sides.

"Why do you think it's him?" Drex asked.

"Just promise me—"

"No promises. What makes you think this guy is our guy? *My* guy?"

"Drex, you can't go—"

Gif said, "Rudkowski will—"

"Tell me, goddamn it!" Drex said, shouting above their warnings.

After another pause, Mike mumbled, "He's married."

Drex hadn't seen that coming. "*Married?*"

"Married. Do you take? With this ring. I now pronounce you."

Gif confirmed it with a solemn nod.

Drex divided a perplexed look between them, then shook his

head and huffed a laugh of bitter disappointment. "Well, that shoots everything to hell, and you've wasted my morning. If we hurry down, the restaurant will still be serving breakfast." He pushed his fingers through his hair.

"*Shit*! Here I was getting all excited, when what it looks like is that our lonely heart has struck out again and is still seeking his soul mate. But he's not our man. Because a wife doesn't jibe."

"It did once," Gif reminded him.

"Once. Not since. Matrimony, do you take, with this ring, hasn't fit his profile or MO in years. Not in any way, shape, or form."

"Actually, Drex, it does," Mike said solemnly.

"How so?"

Gif cleared his throat. "The wife is loaded."

Drex looked at each of them independently. The two men couldn't be more dissimilar, but they wore identical expressions of fear and dread.

He turned away from them, and where his gaze happened to land was on his reflection in the dresser mirror. Even he recognized that, since he'd last looked, his countenance had altered, hardened, become taut with resolve. There was a ferocity in his eyes that hadn't been there only minutes ago, before he had learned that a woman's life hung in the balance. Delicately. And dependent on him to save it.

He kept his voice soft but put steel behind it. "Tell me his name."

Chapter 2

———◆———

"Need help?"

Drex set the empty cardboard box on the curb, turned, and had his first face-to-face with his nemesis.

If this was indeed Weston Graham, he was around five feet eight inches tall and, for a man of sixty-two, extraordinarily fit. His golf shirt hugged firm biceps and a trim waistline. He had a receding hairline, but his graying hair was long enough in back to be pulled into a blunt ponytail. His smile was very white and straight, friendly, and wreathed by a salt-and-pepper door knocker.

Drex swiped his dripping forehead with the ripped sleeve of his baggy t-shirt. "Thanks, but that's the last of them."

"I was hoping you'd say that. I only offered to be nice."

The two of them laughed.

"I'll take one of those beers, though," Drex said. "If you're offering."

His neighbor had crossed the connecting lawns with a cold bottle in each hand. He handed one to Drex. "Welcome to the neighborhood."

"Thanks."

They clinked bottles, and each took a drink. "Jasper Ford." He stuck out his right hand and they shook.

"Jasper," Drex said, as though hearing the name for the first time and committing it to memory, as though he hadn't had to wring it out of Gif and Mike, as though he hadn't spent the past week gleaning as much information on the man as he possibly could.

"I'm Drex Easton." He watched the man's eyes for a reaction to his name, but detected none.

Jasper indicated the pile of empty boxes Drex had stacked at the curb. "You've been hard at it for two days."

"It's been a chore to lug everything up those stairs. They're killers."

He chinned toward a steep exterior staircase that led up to an apartment above a garage that was large enough to house an eighteen-foot inboard. The structure was a good thirty yards behind the main house. Drex figured it had been positioned there to take advantage of the concealment provided by a massive live oak tree.

He squinted up through the branches and pretended to assess the apartment from a fresh perspective. "Moving in was worth the backache, though. It's like living in a tree house."

"I've never seen inside," Jasper said. "Nice?"

"Nice enough."

"How many rooms?"

"Only three, but all I need."

"You're by yourself, then?"

"Not even a goldfish." He grinned. "But, despite the ban on pets, I may get a cat. I spotted some mouse droppings in the kitchen area."

"I can see how a mouse could sneak in. The owners are snow-birds, down here only during the winter months."

"So Mr. Arnott told me. They come down the day after Thanksgiving, stay until the first of June."

"Frankly, when I learned the apartment had been rented out, I was concerned."

"How'd you hear about it?"

"I didn't. You showed up and started carting boxes upstairs."

Drex laughed. "And going through your mind was 'WTF?'"

By way of admission, the man smiled and gave a small shrug. "I have Arnott's number in case of an emergency, so I called him."

"I was an emergency?" Drex glanced down at his ragged shirt, dirty cargo shorts, and well-worn sneakers. "I can see where you might think so. You got one look at me and thought 'there goes the neighborhood.'" He flashed a grin. "I clean up okay, I promise."

Jasper Ford laughed with good nature. "Can't be too careful."

"That's my motto."

"Good fences make for good neighbors."

"Except that there's no fence." Drex looked across the uninterrupted expanse of grass between the two properties. Coming back to Jasper Ford's dark gaze, he said, "I'll confine my rude behavior to this side of the property line. You'll never know I'm here."

Jasper smiled, but before he could comment, his cell phone signaled a text. "Excuse me." He took the phone from his shirt pocket.

While he was reading the text, Drex arched his back in an overextended stretch that caused him to wince, and took another swallow of beer.

"My wife," Jasper said as he thumbed off his phone. "Her flight has been weather delayed. She's stuck at O'Hare."

"That's too bad."

"Happens a lot," he said somewhat absently as he glanced over his shoulder toward his house, then came back around to Drex. "How about some surf and turf?"

"Pardon?"

"I've got crab cakes ready for the pan. Steaks marinating. No sense in half of it going to waste."

"I couldn't impose."

"If it was going to be an imposition, I wouldn't have invited you."

"Well..." Scratching his unshaven cheek, Drex pretended to ponder it. "I haven't stocked the pantry or fridge yet. I've been subsisting on fast food."

Jasper chuckled. "I can do better than that. See you at sunset. We'll have drinks on the porch." He reached out and took Drex's beer bottle. "I'll toss this for you."

Drex stepped out of the shower and reached for his ringing cell phone, which he'd balanced on the rim of the sink. He looked to see who was calling, then clicked on. "Hey."

"How are you faring?" Mike asked.

"Right now, good. I'm standing naked and wet under a ceiling fan."

"Spare me."

"The fan squeaks, but this is the coolest I've been since I got here. Why didn't you tell me this apartment wasn't air-conditioned?"

"You didn't ask."

Once it had been decided among the three of them that Jasper Ford warranted further investigation, Drex flew to Charleston. He wasted no time in driving to Mount Pleasant and locating the Fords' home.

Google Earth hadn't done it justice. The two-story house was built of brick, painted white. Classically southern in design, a deep front porch ran the width of the façade, twin columns framing a glossy black front door with a brass knocker in the shape of a pineapple. The house was surrounded by a sprawling lawn and shaded by decades-old trees.

The residence looked lived in. Blooming flowers in all the

beds. Thriving ferns on the porches. An American flag hanging from the eaves. Newspaper and mail delivery.

By contrast, the house next door looked less tended, and for the three nights Drex surveilled it, lights came on at the same time, went off at the same time. Timed to do so. No flowers, ferns, or mail.

He returned to Lexington, briefed Mike and Gif, and instructed Mike to find out who owned the property neighboring the Fords', which appeared to be a second home or otherwise infrequently occupied.

Mike did his due diligence, got a name and contact info off tax records.

Then Drex did his thing. He made a cold call to Mr. Arnott, who, with his wife, resided most of the year in Pennsylvania, but, upon retirement, had purchased the place in South Carolina to escape the cold and snow.

Drex, laying it on thick, told him of his situation, which was a complete fabrication. Then he got down to the heart of the matter. He was seeking temporary lodging in or near Charleston. During a scouting expedition to see what might be available, he'd crossed the Cooper River into Mount Pleasant, and as he was driving around getting the lay of the land, so to speak, he'd spotted the garage apartment. It was ideal: Secluded. Quiet. A "cabin in the woods," within the confines of a scenic and safe neighborhood.

The apartment would provide all the space he required. He would live there alone, no pets. He was a nonsmoker. And, in the bargain, he would keep an eye on the main house.

"Honestly, Mr. Arnott, if I'd been a burglar, I'd have chosen your house to break into. It's obvious that you're an absentee owner."

When Arnott hedged, Drex was tempted to play his FBI card. He didn't, fearing it would be tipped to Jasper Ford that he had a fed moving in next door to him. Instead he provided Arnott several fictitious references, all written by Gif, whom Arnott actually called to confirm his high recommendation. Mike also got a call to verify the reference letter signed by him. Between them, they convinced Mr. Arnott that Drex Easton was a man of sound mind, good character, and everything he claimed to be.

Arnott agreed to lease him the apartment for the requested three months, although Drex would be there for only two weeks—his allotted vacation time. Only Mike and Gif would know how his time away was being utilized. Until he had a major breakthrough, he was keeping everyone else in the dark.

Besides, asking Arnott for a three-month lease lent credibility to his story and made him seem like a stabler, more responsible tenant. He paid the full amount of rent up front.

"Besides no AC, how is it?" Mike asked now. "Are you moved in?"

From the open bathroom door, Drex could see practically the entire apartment, and virtually every square inch of it was empty, as had been most of the boxes he'd carted up the stairs for the benefit of his audience next door. The apartment had come furnished, though sparsely. He'd brought only the essentials needed to keep himself clothed and groomed. He'd brought a coffeemaker, but he hadn't lied about a steady diet of fast food.

"All settled in," he told Mike. "My laptop is on the kitchen table. My pistol is between the mattress and box spring."

"In other words, it's the same as your place here," Mike said. "And you've lived here for how long?"

"Is there a reason for this call? If so, get to it. Because I don't want to be late for my date."

"In two days' time you've already lined up a *girl*?" Mike said. "When you said 'fully cocked,' you really meant it? I'll have to check my charts, but I think this might be a record."

"There's no girl, and cut the bullshit. Is Gif with you? Put me on speaker." When Drex could tell that Mike had switched over, he said, "Jasper Ford invited me over for dinner tonight."

After a second or two of stunned silence, Mike and Gif exclaimed their surprise.

"Here I have my high-powered binocs focused, all set up to spy on him, and he comes over today with a cold beer and a handshake, welcoming me to the neighborhood. I'm glad he made the first move. That saved me from having to devise a way to put me in his path and make his acquaintance."

He gave them a run-down of their conversation. "It was casual, friendly, but definitely an appraisal. When he saw me moving in, he called Arnott to check me out."

"Paranoid, you think?" Gif asked.

"Or just a watchful property owner, cautious of strangers," Mike said. "Anybody in that kind of neighborhood would be."

"It could be either," Drex said. "I should have a better feel for him after our dinner."

"What about the missus?" Mike asked.

It had been a worry to them that, although Drex had spotted Jasper coming and going over the past two days, he hadn't seen any sign of his wife. "He told me that she's been out of town, which I hope is the truth and that she's still alive. While we were talking, he did receive a text ostensibly from her." He told them about the delayed flight.

"Why Chicago?" Gif asked.

"He didn't say. But he did say that her being delayed happens a lot, indicating that she flies often."

"Makes sense," Mike said. "She was in the travel business."

"Yes, *was*," Drex said. Mike had discovered that the sale of Shafer Travel, Inc., had been the source of Mrs. Ford's mega bucks. "Question is, why is she still frequently on the go?"

When no answer was forthcoming, Drex said, "I'll feel better when I can confirm she's still with us. Maybe I'll get a lot of questions answered tonight. Speaking of..." He glanced out the window. The sun was sinking. "I've got to go now, get dressed, make a run to the liquor store."

"What for?"

"It wouldn't be neighborly to show up for dinner empty-handed."

As he signed off, he was thinking how neighborly it had been of Jasper to bring him a beer and then offer to toss the bottle for him.

However, wouldn't it have been more neighborly to let Drex finish drinking the beer? But no, Jasper Ford had wanted that bottle back.

"White for the crab cakes. Red for the steaks." Drex held up the bottles of wine in turn as he approached the screened porch where Jasper was sitting in a rocking chair beneath a twirling ceiling fan.

He got up and held open the screen door. "You didn't have to do that, but thank you." He took the bottles from Drex. "How about a drink first?"

"What are you having?" Drex motioned toward the highball glass on the wicker table next to the rocking chair.

"Bourbon on the rocks."

"Water?"

"No."

Drex grinned. "Perfect."

"Have a seat." Jasper put the white wine in the mini fridge beneath the built-in bar and poured Drex's drink. As he handed it to him, he said, "You do clean up okay."

Drex raised his glass in a quasi toast. "I try." He'd shaved, but had left a scruff. He'd worn casual slacks and a button-up shirt, the shirttail out. Docksiders, no socks.

Jasper resumed his seat in the rocker and sipped from his drink. "So, you're a writer."

Drex pretended to strangle on his sip of whiskey and looked at his host with surprise.

"Your literary agent was one of the references you gave Arnott."

"Oh! For a second there, I thought you were a mind reader."
Looking abashed, he said, "I'm trying to be a writer. Can't claim
the title yet. I haven't published."

"Your agent told Arnott that you have real potential."

He waved that off. "All agents say that about their clients."

"She must believe it or she wouldn't be representing you."

"He."

"Sorry?"

"My agent is a he."

"Oh. My mistake."

My ass, Drex thought. That had been a test.

"Are you writing full-time?"

"Lately I have been."

"How do you support yourself?"

"Frugally." Jasper gave the expected laugh. Drex said, "My
dad died a couple of years ago and left me a small inheritance.
Nothing to boast about, but it's keeping a roof over my head
while I work on the book."

"Fiction or non?"

"Fiction. Civil War novel."

Jasper raised his eyebrows, encouraging him to continue.

"I don't want to bore you," Drex said.

"I'm not bored."

"Well," Drex said, taking a deep breath, "the protagonist
takes a sort of Forrest Gump journey through the conflict, from
Bull Run to Appomattox. He grapples with divided loyalties, his
moral compass, mortal fear during battle. That kind of thing."

"Sounds interesting."

Drex smiled as though he realized that was a platitude, but
appreciated it all the same. "My agent likes the story, and said
my research was factually sound. But he felt the narrative lacked
color. It needed more heart, he said. Soul."

"So you came down here to get color, heart, and soul."

"I hope to soak up some while working on the second draft.

And," he said, stretching out both his legs and the word, "I needed to get away from the distractions of the everyday grind."

"Like a wife?"

"Not anymore."

"Divorced?"

"Thank God."

"You sound bitter. What happened?"

"She accused me of cheating."

"Did you?"

Drex looked at him and cocked an eyebrow, but didn't answer. Instead he sipped his bourbon. It was a smooth, expensive one. "The divorce cost me dear and taught me a hard lesson."

"You'll never cheat again."

"I'll never marry again."

"Ah, never say never," Jasper said, shaking his index finger at him. "After the loss of my first wife, I grieved for her and stayed single for a long time. Thirty years, in fact."

"Man, that's loyalty. How'd she die?"

Looking Drex straight in the eye, he said, "In pain." He held the stare for a beat, then finished his bourbon in one shot, stood, and headed for the kitchen. "How do you like your steak?"

The medium rare rib eye had been seasoned and grilled to perfection. Jasper apologized for serving the meal in the casual dining room, rather than the more formal one, but the table was set a lot fancier than Drex was used to, and he confessed as much.

While they ate, Drex probed his host for more personal information, but in a manner he hoped would seem natural. "This house is really something."

"Thank you."

"You hire a professional decorator?"

"Only to consult. Talia knew what she wanted."

"Talia? That's your wife's name? Pretty." He glanced around. "She has good taste."

"She has great taste."

"Expensive taste?"

Jasper only smiled at that, but didn't respond.

Drex took a sip of the Cabernet he'd brought, blotted his mouth, and then picked up his utensils and cut into his steak again. "You seem to do all right," he said, applying his knife to the meat. "What's your line of work?"

"I work at enjoying the fruits of my labors."

Drex stopped chewing and looked across at Jasper to gauge whether or not he was joking. Jasper's expression didn't change. He didn't even blink. Drex swallowed and laughed out loud. "Lucky you. You retired early?"

"Several years ago."

"From what? Must've been a healthy business."

"I created some software that proved to be lucrative."

Or did you accumulate a fortune by rooking women out of theirs?

That's what Drex was thinking when Jasper smiled at him congenially and said, "I have lemon sorbet for dessert."

Drex declined the sorbet. And since it was obvious that Jasper didn't want to elaborate on his former field of endeavor, Drex let the subject drop. He also declined to have coffee, not wanting to outstay his welcome.

Although he offered to help with the cleanup, Jasper refused.

As Drex was about to leave, he mentioned that the apartment didn't have air-conditioning. Jasper insisted on lending him a box fan. He fetched it from his garage and told Drex to keep it for as long as he needed it.

"Thanks. Thanks for everything." Drex extended his hand.

As they shook, Jasper said, "Talia texted that she should be home by midnight. We're taking a boat out tomorrow afternoon. Not too far offshore. Just puttering around. Why don't you join us?"

Drex was anxious to meet his wife, gauge her, but didn't want to appear too eager. "Nice of you to offer, but it's been days since

I looked at my manuscript. The move-in and all. I really should work tomorrow."

"You can't take off a Sunday? I'm sure the Lord would understand."

Drex pretended to have been persuaded. Jasper gave him the name of the marina and the number of the slip. "Meet us there around noon. We'll go ahead and get things ready. Come hungry. We'll have a picnic lunch on board."

"Sounds great." Drex thanked him again for the evening and carried the box fan across the lawn and up the stairs.

He began undressing by reaching under his loose shirttail and removing the holster from his waistband at the small of his back. Call him a cynic, but surf and turf had seemed a little over the top for a first visit even if the meal hadn't originally been prepared with him in mind.

Fifteen minutes later, he was stripped down to his underwear, the fan was on high, all the lights were off, and he was at the window watching through binoculars as Jasper went about cleaning up. When he was done, he locked the doors and turned out the lights. A few moments later an upstairs light came on. Minutes after, that light was also extinguished.

He hadn't waited up for his wife. Talia.

Drex repositioned the fan so it would be blowing across the bed. He lay down on his back and stacked his hands on his chest. But, tired as he was, he was still awake when he heard a car. He returned to the window that offered the most advantageous view of the Fords' house.

Turning into the driveway was a late-model BMW sedan. Drex checked his wristwatch. Mrs. Ford had overshot her ETA by twenty-seven minutes. She must have opened the garage door with a remote. She drove in, and the door went down.

Drex never distinguished more of her than a shadowy form, but by the lights being turned on, then off, he tracked her progress through the house. The last light to go out was behind a shade in a small upstairs window. He presumed it was a bathroom. Drex stayed at the window for several minutes more, but the house remained dark.

He returned to bed but lay awake, his mind troubled with thoughts of Talia Ford, lying beside her husband. When she got into bed with him, had she whispered good night, kissed his cheek, snuggled against him, reached for him, and initiated lovemaking? The thought of it made Drex ill.

At least she was alive. But for how long? Because if Jasper was the man Drex suspected him of being, his wife's days were numbered. If Jasper Ford was the man Drex had first come to know by the name of Weston Graham, then this woman would be the next of many whom Jasper had befriended, wooed, and robbed of millions before they disappeared without a trace. Drex was convinced that he had disposed of those women.

How'd she die?

In pain.

The words, Jasper's implacable doll-like stare when he spoke them, had made the hair on the back of Drex's neck stand on end. In that moment, it had felt as though Jasper was baiting him.

Drex hadn't taken the bait, but he'd wanted to.

He had wanted to lunge across the short distance separating them, grab the man—the good cook, the perfect host, the friendly neighbor—by the throat, and demand to know if he was the psychopathic son of a bitch who had killed his mother.

Chapter 3

The vessel moored in the designated slip wasn't just a boat, but a yacht. It wasn't the largest in the marina, but it held its own among them, being impressively sleek and shiny. Drex felt like he should be wearing white pants and a blue blazer, maybe with a jaunty pocket handkerchief, and have a hat with gold braid and a shiny black brim.

Instead, he was in khaki shorts, a chambray shirt, and base-ball cap.

Jasper waved to him from the aft deck. The woman beside him called down, "Ahoy, Drex. You're just in time for Champagne." She hefted a magnum by the neck.

He gave her his best smile and started up the ramp. "I'd settle for a beer."

"We have that, too."

A decade younger than her husband, she was very pretty in the soft and—what was the word Gif had used? Naïve? She had that dash of girlish naïveté that a con man would target. Her hair was blond, short, and artfully tousled. She was dressed in white capri pants and a bright pink sleeveless top with a scooped neck-line that showed off a deep cleavage. The best that money could buy, Drex guessed.

As he joined them on deck, he and Jasper shook hands. "Have trouble finding us?"

"None at all." He took in the yacht, then divided a look be-tween Jasper and his wife, landing on Jasper. "You're a lucky bastard. This is some beauty you have here." Then he leaned in, adding, "The boat's not bad looking, either."

All three of them laughed. Mrs. Ford flattened a hand against the swell of her breasts, the diamonds on her fingers flashing rainbows in the sunlight. "Why, thank you. Jasper warned me that you were a charmer. I'm so glad you joined us today, even though I understand we're dragging you away from your work."

"Thank you for the invitation, and it didn't take much arm-twisting to get me here. A writer looks for any excuse not to write."

"I would be completely daunted by the prospect of writing a book," she said.

"I'm completely daunted by it, too, Talia. I'm sorry, is it okay if I call you Talia?"

She and Jasper looked surprised, then both began laughing. She said, "You could call me Talia if that was my name. I'm Elaine. Elaine Conner."

Taken aback, Drex was about to stammer an apology when Jasper looked beyond him and smiled. "*Here's* Talia."

Drex did an about-face.

A woman dressed all in white was coming up the steps that led from the galley, a tray of canapés balanced on her right palm. Hearing her name, she tilted her head back and looked up through the hatch, straight at Drex.

His stomach dropped like an anchor, because, in that instant, he knew: *I'm so screwed.*